CITY OF DAWN

KAT ROSS

ACORN PUBLISHING

For the beautiful and brave Blessed of this world and others.

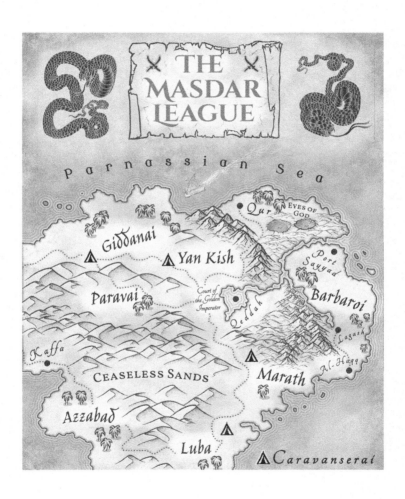

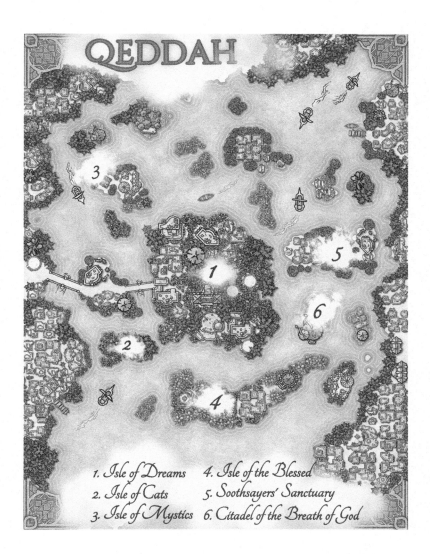

QEDDAH

1. Isle of Dreams
2. Isle of Cats
3. Isle of Mystics
4. Isle of the Blessed
5. Soothsayers' Sanctuary
6. Citadel of the Breath of God

Chapter One

The young buzzard caught an updraft, black wings extended as it circled the dunes. The scent of death drifted on the wind. An enticing hint only.

Something fresh.

The air was cool, the sky strewn with chains of bright stars. The Ladder and the Throne. The Seventh Gate. Amira's Hourglass. The Broken Feather. Many others, each with a tale to make the listener laugh and weep.

Local clans had shared these stories around their camp-fires once, but that time was long past. The Ceaseless Sands were an empty wasteland now. Caravans wound along its fringes on their way to the capital, though none stopped for long—and those that wandered too deep never came out again.

The buzzard, which had not eaten in eleven days, cared nothing for stars or stories. She widened her search, clever brown eyes scanning the sands.

There.

In the velvety shadow of some hills, a dead fox.

The bird looked for others swooping down to the carcass but saw none. Lucky to be the first to arrive and enjoy an uninterrupted meal. With an ungainly flap, she alit next to the carcass. Soon the sands would boil and the fierce winds blow, but dawn was still a whisper to the east.

The buzzard pecked out the eyes first. Then she started on the rest of the *fenak*, which was one of the desert varieties with enormous ears and a small, lean body. It had died sometime the day before, which she preferred to riper carrion. Her bloody beak was deep in its belly when a scraping sound made her head tilt.

The noise came from a cleft in the rock. The vulture took a curious, shuffling step forward and stopped. She was barely a year old, but she knew that whatever moved in there smelled wrong. Not living *or* dead. With a regretful look at her half-eaten breakfast, the bird took to the air.

A minute later, something emerged from the crevice, sinuous body gleaming in the starlight. It had slept for a long time. *How* long exactly it did not know. Only that it had dreamt and now it was awake again.

The journey to the surface had taken the better part of a week, though the creature had little concept of either time or distance. It had crawled and slithered and wormed its way through crevices in the rock, driven by some long-buried instinct. Having achieved its goal at last, it was content to coil itself in the sand and rest.

The constellations wheeled across the sky. The Ladder and the Throne sank behind the hills. In no time at all, the sun broke the horizon, dazzling the creature's slow-blinking eyes, which were the clouded blue of chalcedony. With some effort, it remembered its own name.

Borosus.

Like a master key, this unlocked room upon room of other memories. War and rebellion. Blood and fire. The Mother gone, her children scattered, and her servants, of which Borosus was one, spelled into slumber.

One name burned brighter than all the rest. Borosus had

loved him once. Now he nursed an implacable hatred. The mist left his eyes. They caught the sun like slivers of volcanic glass.

"Morning Star," he whispered. "O, Empyreal Prince. *Deceiver*. Will you face me now?"

Borosus regarded what was left of the fox. Talons flexed as he launched into the air, following the southeasterly path of the buzzard.

He, too, hunted.

Chapter Two

"Speak, woman," Paarjini snapped.

Jamila al-Jabban stared at the pattern of interlocking ovals on the carpet, black eyes glittering with fury. Bound hands gripped her skirts. She sat in a chair next to a square porthole. White-peaked waves rolled and crested beyond the glass, the salt spray mixing with flurries of rain.

"I ought to throw ye overboard and be done with it," Paarjini muttered with a scowl.

She stood next to the prisoner, one hand braced on the bulkhead of the tilting ship. Each finger held stacks of rings. Milky moonstone, fiery ruby, speckled sandstone. Bracelets of tin, gold, silver and bronze circled her wrists. Her chestnut hair was braided and caught up in a jeweled net.

Kasia shot Nikola Thorn a quick look. It was an empty threat and they all knew it. Jamila might be an enemy, but none of the three women would murder a prisoner in cold blood.

Besides which, she was far more useful alive.

"We could dangle her over the side again." Nikola's silver tooth glinted in a wolfish smile. "Let her think on it some more."

Jamila swallowed hard. When she'd first refused to answer questions, the witches had dangled her upside down beyond the stern rail, a hand's breadth above the foaming wake of the ship. Jamila's olive skin had a greenish cast when they finally hauled her aboard, but she'd remained stubbornly silent.

Nine days since the *Wayfarer* had sailed from Nantwich. Now they were almost at the Masdar League, where the body-snatching alchemist Balaur awaited them, along with an unknown number of witches and the khedive of Luba.

The last thread of Kasia's patience snapped. She would *not* fail again.

She strode up to the prisoner, looming over her. "We already know about the City of Dawn. Tell us the rest and it'll go easier for you. What are Balaur's plans? He seeks an elixir of immortality, but how does he mean to find it?"

The Masdari woman clamped her lips tighter as if to keep the words from spilling out. Her gaze swung to the two pretty raven-haired children in the corner. Tristhus was drawing a hunting knife along a leather strop while his older sister scratched Alice's pointy ears. Sydonie caught Jamila's eye and smiled. On another child, the missing front teeth would be endearing, but Sydonie was a mage from Bal Kirith. The Saints only knew how many people she'd killed in her short life.

"I bet Mirabelle could make her talk!" Sydonie raised her sleeve, exposing the Mark of a sinister doll on her forearm— one eye half closed, the other staring with malicious glee.

Tristhus shook a lock of black hair from his eyes. It flopped down again and he tucked it behind an ear. "She could, miss. Mirabelle's a *bitch*."

The Markhound lay at the children's feet. She lifted her massive head and growled at the prisoner, a vicious rumble that was audible above the creaking timbers and surging seas. Jamila tore her gaze away. Lightning forked beyond the port-hole, followed by a drumroll of thunder that made her flinch.

"What is it yer so afraid of?" Paarjini asked in a gentler tone. "If ye cooperate, we promise to protect ye. They abandoned ye, Jamila! Left ye behind to rot in the Curia's cells. What more do ye have to lose?"

The Masdari woman stared at her feet, chin trembling. After a minute, she gave a bitter laugh. "You know what I fear. The ley has been too deep beneath the waves for Balaur's hand to touch my dreams during the journey, but we will make land soon."

She spoke Osterlish with a soft, slurring accent. "There will be no escape from him then. Not for any of us!" Jamila raised her bound wrists, covering her face and weeping.

Kasia shook her head in disgust. In Nantwich, the woman had sat at Balaur's right hand. Now she pretended to be an innocent victim who was only following her mistress's orders. Jamila claimed she was the khedive's servant, and perhaps that much was true, but Kasia couldn't summon pity for her. She could have run away. She'd had a hundred chances.

Jamila was also tied to the Danzigers. Kasia had first seen her in Kvengard, the night of Jann and Hanne's party to honor the Masdari trade delegation. Kasia despised the whole family, but she reserved a special hatred for the nephew, Jule. She fervently hoped he was with Balaur, so she could finish them both for good.

She turned her back and followed Paarjini across the pitching deck, using the bolted-down furnishings to steady herself. A large globe in a stand spun lazily as the ship wallowed one way, then the other. The cabin stretched the entire width of the stern. The rear bulkhead had another much larger porthole with a dozen square panes that looked out over the heaving sea. Nikola waited with palms braced on the captain's desk. Rolled sea charts bound in ribbon covered the wooden surface.

"Do you think she's acting?" Nikola asked in a low voice.

"Definitely," Kasia said. "But it makes little difference. We need information and the woman knows more than she's telling."

"Can't ye force her to speak?" Paarjini asked. "Yer an aingeal yerself—"

"I'm *not*." Kasia reined in a surge of irritation. "I was born to mages, but I was raised to despise them and everything they stand for."

Tessaria Foy had plucked her from the streets of Novostopol and helped Kasia discover her gift for cartomancy. More than that, she'd taught her how to reason out the correct thing to do. Kasia knew Tess would not approve of her attempting compulsion—not even to stop Balaur.

"Why can't *you* do it?" she asked the witch.

"It might be possible, but I don't know the spell for such a thing," Paarjini replied. "'Tis not a part of the magic we learn."

"Well, Jamila's right about one thing," Nikola said. "The seas are shallow enough that I can sense the ley again." She eyed them both in turn, her face serious. "If you prefer not to do it, Kasia, I understand. But I think we must ask the mages to question her."

"Will it do permanent harm?" Paarjini asked with a slight frown.

Despite her frustration, Kasia nearly argued against it. There was something singularly vile about compulsion. But many lives depended on the outcome of their mission. And it was better than physical coercion, which was the last option left.

"Malach used compulsion on me once," she admitted. "The first time we met. He was looking for a letter and he thought I had it."

Nikola nodded with an air of embarrassment. She knew the story.

"It can't imagine it was pleasant," Kasia continued, "but I

remember almost nothing of what happened and I didn't suffer any ill effects afterwards."

Paarjini gave a short nod. "Sydonie," she called. "Go fetch your cousins."

The girl jumped to her feet, pulling her brother along, and darted out the cabin door. Jamila watched them go with wide eyes and a frozen expression. "Wait," she stammered. "What are you doing?"

"Takin' drastic measures," Paarjini replied coldly.

The Masdari licked her lips. "What is it you want to know?"

Nikola strode over to her. "Only what we've asked you a thousand times!" she said in exasperation. "How do we find the City of Dawn?"

"It is the abode of the Alsakhan," Jamila said quickly. "The Great Dragon. He breathes out the ley—"

"We already know that nonsense," Paarjini snapped. "And we know that Balaur seeks an elixir of immortality."

Jamila nodded, eager to please. "The Aab-i-Hayat. It is mentioned in an ancient fragment of text. Told to a wise *sahir* by a witch named Cathrynne Rowan." She swallowed. "It says that whomever drinks the elixir cannot be killed by Marked or Unmarked, man or woman, during the night or day, awake or asleep, inside or outside, with a weapon nor by bare hands."

"Sounds like a nursery tale," Nikola said with a frown.

"Believe what you will, mistress," Jamila replied. "But Balaur and the khedive of Luba say it is prophecy."

"Is that the exact wording?" Kasia asked.

Jamila nodded again. "I heard them speak of it many times. It struck me as unusual. Very . . . *specific*."

"And the city itself?" Nikola prompted. "Where exactly is it?"

Jamila shrank beneath her stare. "That is the problem, mistress. As I told you before, no one knows, except that it lies within the region known as the Ceaseless Sands. If you give me paper, I will draw a map."

Kasia rummaged through the captain's desk and found a scrap of blank parchment and chewed nub of pencil. She brought Jamila over and sat her down in the swivel chair. Jamila held up her bound hands with a hopeful look. "Do you think—"

"Not a chance," Paarjini interrupted. "Just do the best ye can."

Jamila lowered her face. A curtain of dark hair hid her expression, but not before Kasia saw her mouth twist in annoyance. The scratch of the pen was the only sound as she began to awkwardly sketch with her wrists tied together.

"I don't believe Balaur intends to wander around the desert until he stumbles over this city," Nikola said. "There must be a way to find it."

Pain lanced through Kasia's forehead. She pressed fingertips to her temple, gripping a railed shelf of navigational instruments with her other hand.

"Are you well?" Nikola asked with concern.

"It'll pass," Kasia said tightly.

"One of the buried memories?" Paarjini eyed her with a mixture of wariness and sympathy.

Kasia gave a brief nod, eyes watering from the pain. The two witches helped her to an armchair as a wave of dizziness crashed down. She closed her eyes, seeing Balaur as he had looked before he stole Rachel's body. A man of middle years with cropped blond hair and blue eyes, wearing a priest's black robe.

He'd known how to sneak into Kasia's dreams—and erase her memory of their encounters. For months when she was at Nantwich, Balaur had spied on her innermost thoughts. Planted lies and suspicions and the ley only knew what else.

Meeting him face-to-face had brought much of it back, though not all. Sometimes the buried memories broke loose fast and hard, like boulders rolling down a mountainside. Nikola's words—*There must be a way to find it*—had triggered this one.

Balaur had come into her Garden, the place her mind went when she dreamt. He'd pretended to be a weary pilgrim, just passing by, and engaged her in conversation before she realized who he was. Then he had told her things. Shown her things . . .

Help me, Kasia. There is another way. Balaur waved his mutilated left hand. *Look at these and tell me what they mean.*

Seven keys hovered in the air above his head. Each had a unique shape and was forged from one of the alchemical metals. Silver and gold, bronze and tin, mercury, iron and copper. A dense mist obscured the willow trees and the pond with its emerald lily-pads. In their place stood a series of gates and a city of golden minarets.

What do you see? Balaur demanded in harsh, commanding tones. *Where can I find them?*

She hadn't known and wouldn't have told him if she did, but the force of his will gripped her like a set of iron tongs. Kasia pushed the memory away, fleeing his cold blue eyes . . .

A wet tongue licked her palm. A warm body nudged her leg. The image faded. Alice's warm brown eyes peered up at her. Kasia gave the Markhound a pat.

"I'll only be a moment," she said, rising and hurrying to the hatch.

"Where are ye goin'?" Paarjini demanded.

"To my cabin," Kasia replied over her shoulder. "There's something I've been meaning to show you."

She darted into the passageway—and drew up short. Sydonie and Tristhus were approaching, followed by Valdrian and Caralexa. Valdrian had a close-cut beard and unruly blond hair that always looked as if he'd just woken up. Caralexa's scalp was shaved on the sides, leaving a strip down the center that she'd dyed bright purple. All four mages wore the green cloaks of Bal Kirith.

They were kin to her brother Malach, which made them kin to her, too, but the only thing she felt towards them was mistrust. Until a week ago, the nihilim were the sworn enemies of the Via Sancta. Kasia would never consider herself one of them.

Kasia didn't mind the children as much, but the adults made her uneasy. Valdrian and Caralexa seemed to feel the same way about her. They nodded coolly and swept into the captain's cabin. Kasia hurried to the berth she shared with Natalya Anderle, her dearest friend in the world.

Despite the queasy rocking of the ship, Natalya sat against her pillows, lips moving silently as she read one of Aemlyn's books in Masdari. With Tashtemir's help, she'd set herself to mastering the language of the League. She had the prodigious visual memory of an artist and her progress had been swift.

Now her curly hair was braided for bed, her face clean of makeup. It made her look very young, though she and Kasia were the same age—twenty-eight.

"How's it going?" she asked, closing the book and holding the place with one finger.

"Jamila is playing her usual games," Kasia said. "Refusing to speak until she's threatened, then dropping cryptic hints. But the ley is back. Paarjini is asking the mages to compel her."

Natalya rubbed her bare arms. A vividly colored dragon Mark wrapped around one bicep. "I feel it, too," she said softly, peering out the porthole at the inky night. "The deep ocean is behind us. I suppose we'll be making port soon?"

"Another day or so. Which makes it critical to know what we face." Kasia tugged a suitcase from under her bunk. She unbuckled the fastenings and took out a large book bound in dark red leather. "Jamila claims that Balaur doesn't know exactly where to find this elixir of life, either. I hope it's true."

"What's that?" Natalya eyed the book with curiosity. "Looks old."

"*Der Cherubinischer Wandersmann* by Angelus Silesius," she replied. "One of the Kven mystics. It means *The Wandering Cherubs*. And it is old. Very." Her chest tightened. "Alexei thought it might have some of the answers we need."

"We'll find him." Natalya grasped her free hand and gave it a reassuring squeeze. "Don't you doubt that for a second."

"If my brother hasn't murdered him yet," she muttered. "Or vice versa."

Natalya chuckled. "Let's hope they aren't that stupid. Or at least that they're willing to wait to settle their grudge until Balaur is dealt with."

"Well, the witches should be able to track Malach with the kaldurite stone. That's another thing we can try now." She glanced at the door. "I'd best get back. I want to keep an eye on things."

Natalya nodded. She felt the same about the mages. "Hurry, then."

When Kasia arrived at Captain Aemlyn's cabin, she found Valdrian and Caralexa leaning casually against one wall. The other witches aboard, Cairness and Ashvi, had also been summoned. The four of them eyed each other with hostility.

Ignoring the tension, Kasia walked up to Jamila and set the book in front of her. She turned the fragile, yellowing pages with care, leaving it open at the last page.

An illustration depicted the same city of golden minarets that Balaur had shown her. It was framed by an intricate border of the sun and moon and seven keys. The Kven legend identified it as *Die Stadt der Morgenröte*. The City of Dawn.

Jamila stared at the image, transfixed.

"This is the place Balaur seeks," Kasia said. "But what is the meaning of the keys? Are they required in a literal sense? Or do they represent something else?"

"I do not know, mistress," Jamila whispered. "Truly!"

Paarjini stepped forward. "I'd like to trust ye, Jamila. Really, I would. But I have the unfortunate feelin' that yer lyin' to us again."

She nodded at Valdrian, who pushed off the wall and came forward. With his firm jaw, straight dark brows, and finely chiseled features, the mage would have been handsome if his expression wasn't so hardened. In that respect, Kasia felt sympathy. Knights had severed Valdrian's right hand years before; he covered the stump with a leather cap. The left gripped Jamila's bound wrist.

"I know nothing more!" she shrieked, trying to jerk away.

A current of abyssal ley flowed upward. It infused the wooden hull of the ship and surged into Valdrian's palm, which flared a bloody red. Everyone in the cabin had the ability to sense what was happening. Nikola crossed her arms. Tristhus muttered something that sounded like "*Vicious!*" The two witches, Cairness and Ashvi, whispered heatedly to each other until Paarjini shot them an irritated look.

Caralexa just smirked as Jamila's protests cut off. Her jaw slackened. Dark eyes stared unblinking. In the corner, Alice gave a nervous whine.

"Take the hound to your cabin," Kasia told the children.

Sydonie frowned. "But we want to watch."

"*Now*," she said firmly.

The siblings viewed her as an oddity—but a dangerous one. The girl scrambled to her feet and jerked her chin at the boy. Scowls conveyed their disappointment at missing the interrogation, but another sharp gesture sent them scurrying for the door.

"Come *on*," Sydonie muttered, pushing at the dog's hindquarters.

Alice pretended to snap but allowed herself to be herded away. Kasia still couldn't believe that Alexei's Markhound, bred to hunt nihilim in the Void, had let the children adopt her as their mascot. But the dog was complicated and full of surprises—just like her master.

A sideways swell buffeted the ship like an angry toddler kicking a toy. Kasia grabbed the back of Jamila's chair. Paarjini caught the book as it slid across the desk. There were a few muttered oaths as her companions steadied themselves. Jamila herself gazed vacantly through the porthole.

"Can ye make her speak true?" Paarjini asked Valdrian once the ship leveled out again.

The mage nodded. "Her will is mine, Paarjini an dàrna," he replied formally.

Nikola had explained that the term meant "second." With the witch-queen dead, Paarjini was in charge until a full coven gathered to choose the next Mahadeva Sahevis. Kasia was glad. Unlike Cairness and Ashvi, Paarjini had a level head and didn't seem to bear a grudge against anyone. Not even the mages, who were the witches' sworn enemies.

Nikola had the same live-and-let-live attitude, which made sense since she had loved Malach once—and, Kasia strongly suspected, still did, though she never talked about him. Now she stood with purple-haired Caralexa, the two of them entirely at ease with each other.

"Ask her again what Balaur intends," Paarjini said. "It wouldn't hurt to confirm what she's already claimed."

Valdrian repeated the question.

"To find the elixir and become immortal," Jamila said in a monotone. "He promised his followers the same."

"Are *you* his follower?" Valdrian asked.

"No."

Kasia arched a brow. *That* was unexpected.

"Explain," the mage pressed.

"He will help Luba to seize the imperial throne." Jamila's chin lifted. "But he does not stand above us."

The woman is stronger than she makes out to be, Kasia thought. *And more dangerous.*

"So you are allies with different interests," Valdrian said thoughtfully. His gaze settled on the book in Paarjini's arms. *Der Cherubinscher Wandersmann.* "What about those keys? Are they hidden somewhere?"

Jamila's eyes rolled up, showing only the whites. She made a high, keening noise that stirred the hair on Kasia's nape. Valdrian tightened his grip on her wrist. "Tell me!"

Jamila shook her head, long hair whipping back and forth.

"The answer is buried deep," he said. "But she knows it."

Red light poured from his sleeve. Jamila gasped and writhed. Kasia gripped the deck of cards in her pocket with a sweaty palm as Valdrian dug deeper, methodically crushing all resistance. At last the prisoner went still, head low. Lank hair shadowed her face.

"The blade of Gavriel was the first sign." Her voice was a raven's croak. An airless vault sifted with the dust of ages. "Seven locks and seven keys, forged by the seventh son." Slowly, Jamila's face lifted to the light. "That which has slept awakens."

Her pupils were huge. *Like two black suns*, Kasia thought uneasily.

"You're doing very well, Jamila. Where are the keys?" Now that she'd broken, Valdrian's voice was softer. Coaxing.

"Each of the seven khedives holds one," she answered, her voice again without inflection. "Seven locks and seven keys, forged by the seventh son." Fingers twitched in her lap. "*Seven.*"

Kasia wondered if she'd looked the same when Malach compelled her on the rooftop in Novostopol. Like a puppet jerking on his strings.

"Who is the seventh son?" Valdrian asked.

"Gavriel."

"Where are the keys now?"

"Luba has one." *Twitch.* "The others will be taken to Qeddah for the ascension of the new Imperator."

"So Balaur does not have them all?"

Kasia held her breath. If he'd already found the city and taken the elixir . . .

"Not yet," Jamila said. "He must wait for the ascension."

A collective exhalation of relief went around the cabin. Kasia glanced at the map Jamila had drawn. It was crude but resembled those she'd seen of the Masdar League. Qeddah, the capital, sat in the middle. Jamila had planted an X to the southwest. The Ceaseless Sands.

"Why is he waiting?" Valdrian asked.

"They are only in the same place once every seven years." Jamila gave another twitch at the word *seven*. "The rest of the time, they are guarded by the Nazaré Maz."

"What is that?"

"The priests."

"So Balaur has gone to Qeddah?"

"Yes."

"Then it is there we will find him," Valdrian said to the others, satisfaction in his voice. He turned back to Jamila. "Does the Imperator know of these plans?"

"No."

"So she is not involved in this scheme?"

Jamila's fingers spasmed. "Not directly."

"How then?"

"She must be made to choose Luba."

"When does the succession take place?"

Jamila answered instantly. She'd clearly been tracking the passage of time since her capture. "In five days."

Paarjini muttered an oath. Caralexa stalked over. "We'll be cutting it fine," she said.

"I spoke to one of the crew," Nikola said. "She expects we'll make port tomorrow. From there, we can sail downriver to the capital. Another two days or so. We'll make it in time. But we need to know exactly how this works."

Valdrian nodded. "You said the keys would all be brought to the same place," he told Jamila. "Where is that?"

"Inside the Imperial Palace."

"Be more specific."

"I cannot." Her jaw clenched. "I have not been told where they are kept. It is why we must wait for the succession. Then they will be given to us."

The mage considered for a moment, dragging his left hand through his short flaxen hair. It stood on end like a brush. "How many witches are with Balaur?"

"I do not know."

"What do they want?"

Jamila's shoulders hunched. "I do not know. I have never met them."

"Why is he using them? How are they of value to him?"

"I do not know." A tear leaked from one eye. "I want to please you. Ask me something else. Anything!"

Nikola touched the hilt of Caralexa's blade. Valdrian grasped her meaning.

"You said Gavriel's sword was the first sign. Tell me more," he commanded.

Jamila nodded with relief. "It was found in the desert two years ago by one of the trade caravans."

"You already gave us that," Valdrian said sternly. "I want something new. You said it has runes. That the man who carried it sickened and died. But does it have any other special—"

A hard thump sounded on the deck above. All heads tilted to the ceiling. All except Jamila, who gazed at Valdrian like an adoring hound.

"What was that?" he asked softly.

"I'll go take a look," Kasia offered.

In truth, she was dying to escape that cabin. Seeing Jamila turned into the mage's slave turned her stomach. Worse—it perversely made her want to feel the red ley herself.

But the abyss was a dangerous place. The first time she'd seized it was by accident. Dr. Ferran Massot had touched her with his gloves off and she'd blindly lashed out. Without even realizing it, Kasia had inverted his Nightmark and pushed the doctor over the edge into madness. Since then, she had used it only a handful of times. Each time, it had been harder to let go.

But the red ley carried a price. Use it too often and she could lose the humanity Tessaria Foy had worked so hard to instill.

"Want company?" Caralexa asked, hand dropping to the blade at her hip.

Kasia forced a smile. "It was probably nothing. I'll call if I need you."

The mage shrugged. "Suit yourself."

Kasia hurried down the companionway. A warm, salt-laden wind flapped her cloak as she climbed out of the hatch. Lamplight spilled from the pilothouse, but both sea and sky were black as pitch. The ship rode up another swell. Kasia lurched to the quarterdeck and knotted her fingers in the ratlines. The *Wayfarer* had four masts. If one of the smaller ones had snapped off . . .

She peered through gouts of spray and rain but saw no obvious damage. The mainsails were furled, leaving only a storm jib to keep the carrack pointed into the wind. Everything else was lashed down tight. Occasional glimmers of lightning illuminated raging seas all around and, far in the distance, a black coastline.

Kasia picked her way across the slippery deck to the pilot house. Captain Aemlyn was inside with her first mate Fritha, a tall redhead with a ribald sense of humor and a ready smile. They looked over as she entered in a swirl of rain.

"Did you hear that?" Kasia pushed strands of wet hair from her eyes. "It sounded like something hit the ship."

The two women shared a quick glance. "Danna has the watch," the captain said. "Did you see her?"

Kasia shook her head. "You posted a watch in this weather?"

"She was tied into a safety harness. But this part of the Parnassian Sea has dangerous shallows. I need eyes on deck."

The captain of the *Wayfarer* wore snug trousers and a white shirt that set off her deeply tanned face. A blue jacket with silver bars on the shoulder hung across the back of a chair. Like the rest of her crew, she often went barefoot at sea.

"What could it have been?" Kasia wondered.

"No idea. But if we're taking on water, I need to know about it." Aemlyn grabbed a slicker from a hook and put it on, cinching down the hood. "You have the bridge," she told her first mate.

"Yes, captain."

Six sailors had died when a group of witches who followed Balaur had tried to seize control of the ship back in Nantwich. Cairness and Ashvi fought them off, but the *Wayfarer* was running with a skeleton crew. After working double shifts, the sailors—all women—generally stumbled to their bunks and passed out. Kasia didn't know *when* Aemlyn slept. She always seemed to be around, looking alert and competent.

"Stay close," the captain shouted over the wind as they stepped out to the deck. "Tie this around your waist."

She handed Kasia a tether, knotting another around herself. Together, they moved across the pitching deck. Even with most of the sails down, the ship was being pushed at a ferocious pace by the wind. Kasia made it to the stern rail. She was peering over the side when a shout made her turn. Aemlyn held a flapping object in her hand. It took a moment to realize it was a torn harness.

Her gut tightened. She scanned the turbulent sea, searching for any sign of life. It seemed futile. If Danna had gone over the side, she would be far behind them by now.

Kasia was turning away when something erupted from the water about ten meters off the starboard bow. Long and gleaming fiery copper in the stormlight. She ducked as it flew overhead. A gout of flame licked the mainmast.

The ship rolled hard to port. She clung to the rail, heart hammering against her ribs. Lightning stabbed the dark bellies of the clouds above. If the sails had been raised, the whole ship might be burning. But the masts were wet and nothing had caught fire—yet.

Saints! Her hands shook as she checked the rope around her waist. Captain Aemlyn had vanished. She searched the skies and saw a shadowy silhouette arrowing downward in perfect silence.

It was coming around for another pass.

The creature's skin was the pulsing red-black of banked coals. A jet of flame roared from its jaws. The sea below sizzled and hissed.

Quelling a flood of panic, Kasia plucked a random card from her deck. As it swept down, she raised the card high like a shield and tried to pull ley from the seabed.

Valdrian made it look easy. Perhaps it was for him.

But the power rested beneath fathoms of water. Kasia pulled harder. She could almost taste it. A boiling cauldron of ley. Shivers wracked her as she caught the edge of it, and then it was stirring, flowing upwards from the black depths.

Blue ley burst forth from the card. The color of the Curia's Wards. The color of rational thought and Sanctified Marks. It bathed the ship, reflecting back from the frothy waves and the creature's deep-set eyes.

For an instant, she saw it clearly. A flaming mane licked the ridges of its back. It had six powerful legs tipped with silver claws, and a barbed tail covered with overlapping metallic plates. The immensity of it, the sheer *strangeness*, erased any thought save for one.

"Go away!" she screamed.

Glowing eyes fixed on her. This was no dumb beast. She sensed intelligence. And malevolence. Kasia got the distinct impression that she had just been marked somehow.

Then it banked and wheeled upwards. In a moment, the clouds swallowed it up.

She waited for a long minute, but it did not return.

Kasia released the ley. She sagged against the rail, hardly daring to believe she'd driven it off. A tug on the rope around her waist made her twist in alarm, but it was only Aemlyn. The captain hauled herself across the bucking deck. Her face looked ashen.

"What in the seven watery hells was *that*?" she gasped.

Kasia stared into the windswept darkness. The card was crushed in one fist. She slowly unfurled her cramped fingers. It showed a woman taming a lion. She gripped it by the mouth, fingers a hair's breadth from its sharp teeth.

Fortitude. The eighth trump of the Major Arcana.

"I think . . ." Kasia turned to the captain, fear mingling with wonder. "I think it was a *dragon*."

Chapter Three

"Father Bryce?"

Alexei opened his eyes. A face swam into focus, pale with light eyes and short, fluffy blond hair.

"I bring soup. Do you sit?" A crooked grin. "Or do I feed you again?"

It was the boy. His name was . . .

Alexei knuckled his forehead. *Karl.* That was it. Karl from Kvengard.

He pushed himself up to sit. A lamp had been lit, though daylight filtered through the curtains of the wagon.

"Your fever, it breaks," Karl informed him in halting Osterlish. "You sleep for a long time."

"How long?" Alexei managed.

"Six days. You remember?"

He scrubbed a hand across his jaw. It was furred with beard.

"Some. I remember *you.*"

Karl looked pleased. "You wake up sometimes." He mimed eating. "Take water and a little food."

"How did you find me?"

"Your friend. Malach."

Alexei frowned. "He's not my friend."

Karl looked puzzled. "He saves your life."

"Did he?" Alexei asked in surprise.

The boy nodded. "What else you remember?"

"We're in the Masdar League."

He did recall the last few days in flashes of wakefulness. The swaying of the cart. Karl giving him water. Voices speaking in a foreign tongue.

"Bad witches send you here," Karl said in a sympathetic tone. "Eat now."

Alexei accepted the bowl. Fragrant spices met his nose and he realized he was starving. He spooned some into his mouth and swallowed.

"Thank you," he said.

Karl waved a hand. "Any person do the same." He glanced out the window and stood. "Your . . . er, *soutane*. Sorry, I don't know the word."

"Cassock?" Alexei supplied.

"Yes! Cassock. It is there if you like to dress. But no hurry." A brief smile and he ducked out the door.

Alexei finished the soup and threw the sheet aside. He could feel his thoughts starting to wind up and drew a slow, deep breath. The situation was so bizarre, so utterly surreal, he didn't know where to begin. Kasia had told him what Nikola Thorn did back in Nantwich—vanishing into thin air after Malach killed the Pontifex Luk—but he hadn't really believed it.

The ley just didn't work that way.

Questions crowded his mind. Why had the witches done this? What had happened to Kasia? To his brother, Misha? Were they in danger? And, most important of all, how was he going to get back?

He pulled the cassock over his head and checked his reflection in a vanity mirror. His blue eyes were puffy and bloodshot, with shadows the color of a fresh bruise lurking beneath. The skin of his face looked stretched too tight over the blade-sharp bones.

Not much different from the usual.

But the Masdaris had treated him well, for he felt stronger than he expected to. Alexei opened the door and climbed down two steps to the sand. Four brightly painted wagons were drawn up in a circle. There was a queer orange light in the sky.

People moved about, rolling up tents and lashing the poles together. One of them was Malach. The mage wore a long white robe like the others. He glanced at Alexei without expression, then returned to his task.

Alexei walked over. The mage ignored him, so he turned to his companion, a handsome, slender man who gave Alexei a friendly smile.

"Please accept my gratitude for the generous hospitality you have shown me," Alexei said in Masdari.

The look on Malach's face was priceless. Shock and irritation, quickly smoothed over.

"You speak our language!" the young man exclaimed.

"I know some phrases," Alexei replied modestly, though he knew far more than that.

The man bowed. "I am Hassan. And it has been my honor to welcome you to our caravan."

Alexei bowed in return. The wind was picking up, sending swirls of sand dancing around their feet. "A storm is coming," he said, squinting at the horizon.

Hassan nodded. "A bad one, I think. That is why we are breaking camp."

"Is there shelter nearby?"

Hassan glanced at the western horizon. His face was calm, but worry tinged his dark eyes. "We are not too far from Luba. I think we can reach the walls in time if we make haste."

"How can I help?"

Hassan nodded. "You can work with Malach to roll that

rug."

He pointed to a large carpet that must have been inside one of tents before it was dismantled. Malach looked up at his name. Alexei explained in Osterlish. Malach stalked over to the rug. They each took a side, shaking out the sand and rolling it lengthwise.

"Who are they?" Alexei asked in a low voice.

"Performers."

"Like actors?"

"Singers. Dancers." Malach looked at a brown-skinned woman in a satiny emerald turban who was folding camp chairs. "Koko recites poetry."

They lifted the rolled rug and started for a supply wagon.

"Just tell me one thing," Alexei said, staggering along sideways. "What happened in that room back at the Arx?"

"What happened?" Malach repeated. There was a flat edge to his voice.

"Yes." Alexei's Marks flared, trying to suppress sudden anger. "I deserve to know that much."

Malach dropped the rug. "*You* got in my way, that's what happened. I almost had her!"

"Had *who*?"

His jaw clenched. "Rachel."

"The only reason I was there is because *you* Marked my brother," Alexei reminded him. "I wanted to make sure you kept your promise to ask the witches to remove it."

Malach's hazel irises darkened. In that moment, he looked uncannily like Kasia. "Fuck your brother!"

Alexei mastered himself with an effort. "Just tell me what happened. I only came through the door because I heard a voice." The memory of it raised gooseflesh on his arms. "It sounded like a little girl, but—"

Malach's fist balled. Alexei ducked, but the blow landed like a battering ram, clipping his ear. Alexei bulled into him and they tumbled to the sand, trading punches and kicks.

It only lasted a few seconds. Someone grabbed the hood of his cassock, dragging him back. Another man—heavily muscled, clad in a leather jerkin—wrestled a panting Malach into submission.

Hassan jogged over, lips tight. "You behave like rowdy children," he admonished. "What is this?"

They both muttered apologies. Just the minor fracas left Alexei gasping and weak-kneed.

"Release them," Hassan told the two guards. He pointed at Malach, then at one of the wagons. "Go!"

To Alexei's surprise, Malach meekly obeyed. The dark-skinned woman, Koko, stood on the steps, hands propped on her hips. She shook her head and led him inside.

"What do you fight about?" Hassan asked.

"What has he told you?" Alexei asked warily, wiping blood from his mouth.

"That the witches took his child and banished him here."

"Do you know what he is?"

"He is Malach."

Alexei frowned. "I don't mean his name. I mean that he is nihilim."

Hassan nodded with a touch of impatience. "Yes, *malak*. We know this already."

It was the Masdari word for *angel*, Alexei remembered. What they called the mages.

"And . . . you don't mind?" he ventured.

"We do not revile them as the Via Sancta does," Hassan replied. "He is as welcome to our fires as you are, priest." His voice hardened. "But I cannot tolerate violence. Give me your word this will not happen again."

"He started it," Alexei retorted, and immediately felt foolish.

"I will speak to Malach, as well. But we have no time for feuds. Do you see?" Hassan pointed to the horizon.

A yellow wall was bearing down on them. It had already erased the sun, casting the land in eerie twilight.

"Yes," Alexei said quickly. "I promise to stay away from him."

"Good." A quick, humorless smile. "Then let us pray to the Alsakhan that we outrun this storm."

The rest of the camp was already broken, the camels waiting in their harnesses. Alexei ran to Karl's wagon. The boy was lounging on silken cushions, smoking a water pipe. The moment the door was sealed, cries of *Hoi!* went up outside and the big wooden wheels rolled forward.

"Will the camels be all right?" Alexei asked, switching back to Osterlish.

"They own three of this," Karl replied, touching an eyelid. "And they can close their noses." He smiled. "Do not worry, they travel this way many times."

Alexei pushed the curtain aside. The wind moaned, low and menacing, whisking the loose sand like a giant broom.

"How far to Luba?"

Karl shrugged. "Not so far."

"What if we don't make it?"

He laughed. "Then we make a circle and hope we don't blow away."

Alexei wondered if he was joking. He looked around the wagon, truly seeing it for the first time. Costumes hung on racks, mostly spangled bodysuits, along with a variety of high-heeled shoes and boots. Stands held wigs of every length and color. The vanity was covered with cosmetics.

"How did you come here, Karl?" he asked.

A shadow crossed the young man's face. "It is not easy for me in Kvengard. They are conservative there. My mother did not like it when I dress up in her clothes. My father like it even less."

Alexei nodded. "I lived there for a little while. It is very . . . traditional."

"But you are from Novostopol." He blew a series of smoke rings. "I know by your accent."

"Yes. It's different there. We have clubs where men dress as women, and the reverse. No one cares."

"And you?"

Alexei frowned. "Why would I judge another for who they wish to be?"

"You are a priest."

"There is nothing in church doctrine that forbids it. The opposite, in fact. Free self-expression is a human right, as long as you do not harm anyone else."

Karl looked relieved. "I am glad to hear that, Father."

"Are you Marked?"

He shook his head. "My parents send me here just before the test. They expect me to fail." He eyed Alexei curiously. "You have many."

"Sometimes I think I have *too* many," Alexei admitted.

"Why?"

"I can't sleep more than a few hours. I have this problem for years now."

A puzzled look. "You just sleep for six days."

"And that'll last me for a while." He smiled. "What's your stage name?"

The boy smiled back. "Katy Wulf."

"So the Masdaris embrace you?"

"We are . . ." He thought for a moment. "Popped?"

Alexei frowned. Karl mimed cradling a baby, cooing and making eyes at it.

Alexei laughed. "Pampered?"

"Yes! That one. I am lucky to be part of Hassan's company." His chest swelled with pride. "We are the best."

"So Hassan is in charge?"

"He is both father and mother to us."

"He seems young for such responsibility."

"Hassan is young in years, but we have trust for him. If it

is something important, we all talk together."

The wind rose to a howl. Sand hissed against the outside walls.

"*Aqaf!* We must close the windows," Karl said, jumping to his feet.

They went around the wagon, hooking the latches on the shutters. Alexei's last glimpse of the world beyond was dire. Reddish gloom cloaked the land like an antechamber to Hell.

"Why do you not like Malach?" Karl asked, once they had settled on the cushions again. "Because he is nihilim? No offense for the question."

Alexei no longer hated all mages. How could he when he was in love with one? But Malach . . .

"He struck a bargain with my brother. And my brother got the worse end of the deal."

Karl cocked a brow.

"We were both knights," Alexei admitted. "We fought in the war together. When I first met Malach, we were on opposite sides."

"And now?"

"I don't know." That was the truth. "But I promised Hassan I'd behave myself."

And let's hope Malach does the same, he added to himself.

"What will you do now?" Karl asked.

"Try to return home. I didn't mean to come here."

"The witches do it."

"That's right. I suppose there might be a ship sailing for Kvengard, though I haven't any coin for passage."

"I help you," Karl said immediately. "I save money." He ran to the vanity and took out a small box. "Not much, but perhaps enough."

Alexei pushed it away. "No, I couldn't—"

"Yes, yes, you take it." His face was earnest. "Your need is bigger than mine, Father." A quick smile. "I want new stockings, but Koko will give me."

Alexei was quiet for a minute, deeply touched by the boy's kindness. After seeing the depths of human depravity in both Kvengard and Nantwich, he'd wondered if the Via Sancta's teachings were just a pipe dream. But there were kind people in the world still.

"Thank you," he said. "I will pay you back as soon as I can. Did Malach say anything else? He refuses to speak to me."

"Only that he has a friend in Luba."

Alexei kept his expression neutral. "Do you know the name?"

"Jamila al-Jabban."

He'd heard about her. A Masdari who came to Nantwich with Balaur and had been caught trying to flee after he was killed. Why would Malach be looking for the woman *here* when she was in a prison cell back at the Arx?

"Please, Karl. Anything you know would be a huge help."

The boy looked uncomfortable. "I do not want to get in the middle of this."

"I won't breathe a word to Malach, I swear it. But I'm desperate."

"I wish I could help, but truth, he says little to me. All I know is he asks about her."

Alexei waited.

"He describes her clothes. I say she is a servant of the khedive," Karl added with some reluctance. "That is the only thing I can tell him."

"Will we be seeing the khedive?"

"I do not know. We pass the night in a caravanserai. But this is my first time in Luba." He struggled to explain. "When I come, I have thirteen years. There is a new Imperator. Now I have twenty years. So the Imperator changes, ja?"

Alexei nodded. He understood the seven-year system.

"We only make, ah, big trip when there comes a new

Imperator." Karl swept his hand in a wide circle. "Go every-where, understand?"

Alexei was familiar with maps of the Masdar League. Qeddah lay in roughly the center, with the seven emiratis forming a circle around the capital.

"Where are you based?"

"Qeddah. It the most grand city your eyes will ever enjoy." Karl nodded encouragingly. "You find a ship there."

Alexei nodded, feeling better. "One other question. Do you have my gloves? The leather ones I was wearing?"

He remembered pulling one off just before he entered the chamber in the Arx. By some miracle, he'd kept hold of it in the madness that followed. Alexei felt sure he'd been wearing them both during the arduous trek across the desert.

Karl looked around with a frown, then snapped his fingers. "Yes, I keep them." He rummaged through a pile of clothes and found one, then the other.

Alexei exhaled a slow breath. He tugged them on.

"The ley is weak, but it still takes an effort to hold it at bay without my gloves," he explained. "You are Kven, you understand."

"*Ja*," Karl said. "I do. But . . . Father, you must never use ley where someone sees. It is *verboten* here. Ah, forbidden."

"Yes, I've heard that." He held his hands up. "That's what these are for."

The wind continued to rise, rocking the wagon on its wheels. Alexei was just thinking they would have to stop when Karl cracked the shutters.

"We arrive," he said, flashing a quick smile of relief.

Through the driving sand, Alexei could make out high walls the same color as the desert. The first wagon drew up and a figure emerged, bent against the storm. The face was swathed in a white scarf, leaving only a slit for the eyes, but something in the graceful gait made Alexei think it was Hassan.

He banged on a small door set next to the gates. A minute passed. A narrow slot opened. After a brief exchange, the gates swung open just enough for the wagons to pass through. Once they entered the city, the wind died a little. Buildings of sun-baked mud slipped by, all sealed tight. Date palms lined the larger avenues, their fronds swaying. The streets were utterly deserted.

At a walled compound, the three guards hopped out and pushed open a pair of wooden doors. The caravan rolled into a dusty yard.

"Take this," Karl said, handing him a length of cloth. He showed Alexei how to wind it around his head, leaving a space to see and breathe. Karl threw a rucksack over one shoulder and they exited the wagon, joining the rest of the troupe. A long, low white building stood in front of them.

One of the guards gave a loud whistle. Three scrawny boys in knee-length tunics emerged. They began to unhitch the camels from their traces, leading them toward an enclosure to the left.

Even inside the compound, visibility was barely a few meters. Karl tugged him toward a portico and then into a courtyard filled with drifts of sand. Alexei tucked his chin, eyes fixed on the ground ahead, as they trudged through another door. It shut behind them. The relentless wind finally ceased. He unwrapped his face and drew a breath of clean air.

He'd expected simple accommodations from the drab exterior, but the chamber had brightly colored silk screens and thick, lustrous carpets. A stone trough held clear water. Alexei followed the company's lead, rinsing his hands and face and drying off with one of the towels stacked on an elegant *bokang* table. Shoes were removed and lined up on a small rug next to the door.

A woman bustled up with a smile. She had a round, plump face framed by a scarf patterned in gold and green. Layers of embroidered robes were belted with a wide sash, also in gold and green. She wore silver-threaded slippers with bells that tinkled softly as she walked.

"Welcome, sister-brothers," she said with a broad smile, taking Hassan's hands in her own. "We were expecting you, though I prayed to the Alsakhan you would not be caught up in the storm."

"It was a near thing, Ama," he said, kissing each of her rosy cheeks. "But He saw fit to bring us through safely."

She greeted each of the others in turn with a nod and smile, though her gaze caught on Malach for a moment. The mage was staring too hard at Alexei to notice.

"I held your usual rooms," she said, turning back to Hassan, "though you could have your pick. Most of the traders are already in Qeddah."

"Is is too late for supper?"

"Never," she replied. "I will see that a feast is laid out in the private dining room. It is not often we are honored to serve the Blessed." She touched his cheek fondly. "Seven years and you only grow more beautiful, daughter-son."

Hassan smiled. "And you have not aged a day, Ama."

The innkeeper laughed. "I would rather be fat than wrinkled. At my age, a woman needs a little padding."

The trio of boys returned from tending to the camels, each now carrying baggage from the wagons. In short order, they were escorted to their rooms. The caravanserai was larger than it had looked from the outside. A boy led Alexei through a warren of corridors with ornate scrollwork that gave glimpses into adjacent rooms with tinkling fountains and indoor gardens whose blossoms scented the air with a musky fragrance.

Alexei was glad to find his own chamber *did* have solid walls. There were no chairs, just a low table with cushions and a mattress that rested directly on the floor, but everything was clean and comfortable.

With nothing to unpack, he stayed just long enough to brush

the sand from the various crevices it had burrowed into. Then he followed his nose back to the dining room. It had a table similar to the one in his room but much longer and laid with an orange cloth. Each setting held three spoons of various sizes, but no forks or knives. Little bowls of water sat next to each place. The array of food made his mouth water, but Malach was the only one there and it seemed rude to start eating.

Alexei sat on a tasseled pillow as far from the mage as he could get. Malach opened his mouth as if he were about to speak, then scowled and closed it again. Alexei stared at the hangings on the walls, though he barely saw them. It took every ounce of will to keep his promise to Hassan and not leap over the table and throttle answers from the mage.

They waited in brittle silence until Koko appeared. She made a tsking noise and sat down between them, adjusting her skirts. She'd taken the time to change and freshen her makeup and looked immaculate—unlike the scruffy men on either side.

"I hear you recite poetry," Alexei remarked in Masdari, delighting in Malach's grim expression.

Let him wonder what they were talking about.

"I do," she replied. "Would you like to hear some?"

"I would be honored."

She thought for a moment. Her brown eyes turned inward.

In Barbaroi
Cold wind before dawn
When the dark is a roof
Or a drape never drawn.

When shadows dance on the edge of a blade
And the night seethes with rain
The wet silence drums like a fierce hurricane.

As she spoke, her hands moving in gentle sweeps, Alexei both heard the words and *saw* their meaning, vivid and present. The hissing downpour. The black sky and roiling clouds. More than that, a terrible loneliness as if no one else existed in all the world.

The lament of the wind fills empty streets
The arcades groan in pain
And the lamps softly weep.

A guard passes with halting steps,
Lightning paints his thin frame.

Koko's voice lowered to a bare whisper.

But shadows intercept.

Alexei blinked as she fell silent. He had the curious sensation of awakening from a dream—though the Sanctified Marks kept his unconscious on such a tight leash that he never dreamt at all. Even Malach had shed his usual scorn. The mage sat still, his face solemn. He couldn't have understood, yet it seemed to have moved him anyway.

"An old poem," Koko said. "It is about a poor girl sleeping in the streets. Sad, but I have always liked it."

"That was . . . extraordinary," Alexei said. "I have never heard words spoken so. It was like I stood beside her watching it unfold."

He wondered if Koko had used the ley somehow. The poem reminded him of a sweven—a direct transference of memory from one person to another. Yet she had no Marks. No cards or gemstones. And the currents of ley swirling at her feet hadn't changed.

Koko made a self-deprecating gesture, but he could see she

was pleased. "I studied with a master storyteller. She taught me my tricks."

"They are not tricks," Hassan said, dropping down gracefully at her side. "You have the gift."

The rest of the company trickled in, taking their places. Some, like Hassan, wore simple tunics, while others, like Koko, dressed always as women. Alexei learned their names. Sister Najlah. Kareem, the Mermaid Queen. Maazin, who went by Nizaam when she performed. Ameer, still in training. And Farasha, which meant *butterfly*.

The three guards were brothers who had served the Blessed for six years now. Each wore a curved dagger in his sash, but they were clearly viewed more like family than armed protection from the bandits who haunted the fringes of the Ceaseless Sands.

Hassan spoke a brief prayer of thanks to the Alsakhan. Everyone dipped their fingers in the water bowls, discreetly shook off the droplets, and dug in.

Malach ate like the animal he was, shoveling food into his mouth with mechanical efficiency. But despite the empty ache in his belly, Alexei watched the Masdaris for a minute, learning the etiquette. The little spoons seemed to be for sauces, the round, deep ones for rice and meat, and the third kind, which was made of wood, for stirring a sweetened milky drink in vase-shaped glasses.

Karl sat next to Alexei, explaining which dishes were hot and which sauces were cooling. When he accidentally bit into a fiery pepper and gasped for air, Malach burst out laughing until Koko smacked his wrist with her heaviest spoon.

"Rude!" she said, holding up a finger with a long, lacquered red nail.

Malach rubbed his wrist and gave her a mock frown, then shrugged eloquently. They seemed fond of each other and had a system of communicating with exaggerated gestures that would have been amusing if the mage weren't such a prick.

Alexei doused the inferno on his tongue with a spoonful of minty yoghurt sauce. He stuck with plain rice and slivered almonds as the innkeeper appeared to pour tiny glasses of a clear liquid and pass them around. One sniff of the eye-watering anise-flavored liquor and he set the glass back down.

No way was he was drinking with Malach sleeping nearby.

Conversation turned to the khedive of Luba, who hadn't been seen publicly in weeks, and speculation about who the Golden Imperator would name as her successor, but Alexei listened with only half an ear, his thoughts fixed on Malach.

Karl claimed that he'd directed them to the place where Alexei had fallen in the desert.

Why? He could have just left me there and no one would have been the wiser. He had nothing to gain from it. He despises me as much as I despise him.

It was puzzling. Malach obviously blamed him for whatever had happened to his daughter, though Alexei didn't even know what that was. Maybe Nikola Thorn had brought the witches to take their child back and the claim of removing Marks was a pretense. But then there was that horrible voice. Not exactly like a child being taken by her own mother—

"Fra Bryce?"

Alexei looked over. Karl was staring at him. They were the only two people left at the table.

"I'm sorry," he said ruefully. "I wasn't paying attention."

Karl laid a hand on his forehead. "No fever, but I think you are still . . . not normal, *ja*?"

Alexei doubted he'd ever been normal. "Yes," he agreed. "I think rest would serve me well."

They said goodnight and found their rooms, but now that Alexei had hold of the lion's tail, he couldn't let it go. He lay back on the mattress, thoughts churning.

What was the mage up to?

Chapter Four

Six rooms away, Malach paced his chamber, waiting for the sounds of the caravanserai to subside.

He had learned much at dinner. Two months before, the khedive of Luba had locked herself away from all but her closest advisors. No one had seen or heard from her, though there were whispers that one of her trade caravans had found something in the desert. An ancient relic buried in the sands.

Several members of her household had died suddenly, the bodies swiftly burned and the deaths blamed on bad water from one of the wells. People began to wonder if she, too, had succumbed to the mysterious illness.

But then, at dusk a week before, the gates to the palace had opened. A wagon train set forth heading for the capital of Qeddah. The khedive would be expected to attend the succession, of course, though no one believed she would be chosen. Luba was a backwater. The poorest and weakest of the seven emiratis. It had not ruled from Qeddah in ten generations.

Malach still didn't understand exactly how the succession worked. It had seemed more prudent to keep his mouth shut and ears open.

He'd learned that the khedive's palace was not far.

And so, when all grew still, Malach slipped from his chamber and made his way to the outer doors. A boy slept on a pallet nearby, presumably to alert his mistress in the event of late arrivals. Malach retrieved his boots and tugged them on. Wind gusted through the crack when he eased the door open. His heart pounded as the boy stirred. He had nothing to buy his silence.

But the boy must have been worked hard that day, for he flung a slender brown arm across his face and went back to sleep.

Malach slipped into the outer courtyard and silently closed the door behind him. The sandstorm was still raging. He wrapped his face in the *kufya* and set out, leaning into the wind. There was no danger of being seen. No one else was foolish enough to be outside.

Driving sand scoured every bit of exposed flesh, but Malach plowed forward, taking streets that led toward a higher vantage point. Of course, the higher he climbed, the fiercer the wind became. At last, he huddled in the doorway of a shuttered shop perched atop a hill. The curtains of sand parted just long enough to reveal a walled enclosure overlooking the city. Square and topped with a dome.

Malach marked its location and continued on, his body bent nearly double. It seemed he walked for hours, stumbling into blind alleys and backtracking until he found another way around. None of the streets ran in straight lines. If not for the innate sense of direction he'd acquired rambling through the Morho Sarpanitum as a boy, he would have been hopelessly lost.

Despite the protection of the *kufya*, sand crunched between his teeth and stung his eyes. He'd endured storms before—of the watery variety. This was something else.

At last, when he'd nearly given up hope, a wall appeared directly in front of him. He leaned into its meager shelter for a moment, catching his breath. Then he followed the stone, more by touch than sight, to a pair of high wooden gates. They were locked.

He thought for a moment, then groped along the wall again. *There.* A tiny crevice. He jammed his fingers into the crack, found another above it, and began to scale the wall. Halfway up, a gust of wind slammed into him like a fist.

Malach's tenuous hold slipped. He plummeted back to earth.

"Ow," he muttered, curling into a ball.

A few minutes passed. The pain grew bearable. Nothing broken. If it had been, the pain would only get worse.

Malach found the first handhold and began to climb again. This time he gained the top, slithered over, dangled for a moment, then let go. The impact lanced through his bruised hip, but at least he landed on his feet.

He groped his way back toward the gates. There were no guards in sight. Because of the storm, or another reason?

Malach staggered along a pathway toward the hulking mass of the khedive's compound. Palace, he decided, was too grand a title. Like the city, it was made of mud-brick in desperate need of repair. The walls were cracked and flaking, the tiles beneath his feet dirty and broken. Not a gleam of light penetrated the swirling gloom of the outer courtyard.

He slipped through a forest of sagging stone columns, gaze sweeping the shadows. If they'd ever held up a roof, it was long gone. Sand skirled through the gaps, giving the illusion of furtive movement at the edges of vision. It was impossible to tell if he was being watched.

The itch between his shoulder blades sharpened as he approached the main building.

There might be witches inside, but he still had a lump of kaldurite in his belly. Their power couldn't touch him.

Other than that, Malach had no plan. The only certain thing was that the khedive of Luba was Balaur's creature. Someone had to know something.

If his daughter *were* there, he would take her away. Or—if he could manage to capture a witch, she might be able to use lithomancy to eject Balaur from Rachel's body.

Malach was able to think these words without losing his mind. But when he pictured Rachel now, his beautiful little girl, he saw a faceless, misshapen parasite clinging to her back, moving her limbs like a puppet—

He forced the image away and drew the dagger he'd lifted from one of the caravan guards at dinner. He avoided the main entrance, skirting the building until he found a smaller door. A quick twist of the blade and the latch gave. It was surprisingly flimsy. Either the khedive was overconfident or she really had departed for Qeddah.

Some of the household must have remained behind. At the least, Malach intended to pry information from one of her servants.

He found himself in a large, dark room empty of furnishings save for some dusty carpets. Malach loosened the *kufya*. A gleam of light drew him onward, into a corridor with an arched ceiling. Torches sputtered in brackets along the walls.

Someone *was* at home.

He moved on the balls of his feet, alert to any sound. Once he thought he heard a quiet footfall behind. Malach froze for several long minutes, but it didn't come again. He held the knife lightly in his left hand, gripped with the point facing backward. If anyone appeared, they wouldn't even see it coming.

Yet he met not another soul as he moved deeper into the citadel. The hour was late. Could they all be abed?

Then he saw the first scorch marks. Black smears on the stone, stinking of sulphur. He touched one with a finger. The stone beneath was cracked and still faintly warm.

His pulse beat swiftly. One of the witches must have forced in this spot. So they *had* come here.

Malach found more of the charred patches as he

continued onward, some quite large. It made him uneasy. Then he reached an octagonal inner courtyard. The heart of the citadel. It was capped with the great dome he had spotted from the city. Corridors led outward like spokes from a wheel.

And in the center, sprawled around an empty pedestal, five bodies.

He kept to the shadows, watching. They were clad in trousers and belted knee-length coats with overlapping plates that shimmered like the scales of a serpent. The sashes were blue and white—the colors of Luba. Curved swords lay next to their hands. The quantity of blood confirmed that they were all dead.

The only question was whether the killers were still here.

Malach hesitated, then crept forward to examine the bodies. Long wounds rent them from throat to crotch. At least one had lost control of his bowels. The smell choked Malach's throat.

He forced himself to bend down and unwrap a sand-colored veil. The face beneath was sallow, pitted with old scars. Not the kind you got from fighting. These looked like the ravages of some terrible disease. The man's eyes were open. The whites had a greenish tint.

Fingers shaking slightly, Malach unwrapped the others. All were the same.

He swore softly and let the veil fall.

Then he saw something else, buried deep in one of the gashes. Swallowing revulsion, Malach dug his fingers into the wound.

It was a claw.

Smooth and yellow like the old ivory game pieces he'd played with as a child. They were one of the few items to survive the looting of Bal Kirith and had been his aunt Beleth's prized possession.

Malach was studying this disturbing item when he sensed

a flicker of movement. It came from the mouth of an unlit corridor to the right.

He stood, the claw digging into his palm.

A *thing* stalked slowly into the light.

It walked on all fours. It had a tail. And a head, of sorts.

But there were no discernible features. It appeared to be made of liquid silver.

Malach stared, both mesmerized and appalled. Its skin flowed in currents of blazing metal, throwing back the torches like a mirror. Where it stepped, the rock fizzed and bubbled.

He finally summoned the will to turn around—only to find three more emerging from corridors behind him.

A quick glance at the poor bastards on the ground and Malach knew he'd be joining them in seconds. Still, he raised the knife.

The one closest to him began to change form, rising on hind legs. The silver melted away, leaving a pale man-shaped figure with slits for nostrils and onyx eyes. A forked tongue flickered from its mouth.

Syllables spilled forth. Not Osterlish, but perhaps a language similar to Masdari. The sibilant hiss blurring the words made it hard to tell.

But the rising inflection at the end definitely sounded like a question.

Sweat trickled down Malach's spine.

How he wished he knew the correct answer.

Chapter Five

It wasn't easy tracking Malach through the storm.

Alexei had to hang back far enough that he wouldn't be seen, and nearly lost him twice when Malach took unexpected turns and was swallowed up by the sweeping curtains of sand.

Both times, Alexei was forced to pull off a glove and use liminal ley to find the trail again. The violet layer governed chance, bending the odds in his favor when he made a random choice. It had led him to the khedive's compound, where he spotted Malach at the top of the wall an instant before he disappeared. Alexei had taken the same route.

From there, it was simple enough to follow the mage's faint footsteps.

Now, pressed into the darkness of a dim corridor, Alexei questioned his judgment in coming. He'd been unsure what to expect—but it wasn't this.

They must be creatures of the ley, though unlike any he'd ever heard of. Markhounds and Marksteeds looked the same as their run-of-the-mill counterparts, aside from their ability to blend with shadows and seem to vanish.

But the four things surrounding Malach bore no resemblance to any living animal that walked the earth.

One had just stood up and begun to speak. He grasped the dialect, in bits and pieces. An ancient form of Masdari. But the words made no sense to him.

Nor to Malach, it seemed.

"I don't understand," the mage said, taking a step back.

The thing tilted its head. The face was not built to convey emotion—it was too reptilian, too *alien*—yet Alexei sensed its displeasure at this response.

Slitted nostrils sniffed the air. It stared hard at Malach and spoke again. There was no mistaking the anger in its tone.

Alexei felt sure the creatures didn't know he was there—so far. Every instinct screamed at him to quietly retreat and return the way he'd come before that situation changed.

Three things stopped him.

First, his brother. Misha was still tied to Malach by the Nightmark. If the mage died, he would, too.

Second, Kasia. For good or ill, Malach was her brother.

Third, the mage had saved his life. He wouldn't shrug off that debt.

Alexei vented a silent breath. Attacking the creatures would be foolhardy. He wasn't sure they *could* be killed and he carried no weapon anyway.

All he had was the ley.

He expected Malach to use it himself, but the mage just stood there, brandishing his dagger, eyes flicking from one to the next.

"Anut najmati kalsabah," the thing spat. "Anut alkhayin!"

Malach shook his head in confusion. "I have no quarrel with you."

A jet of white flame spewed from one of the creatures on all fours. Malach dove aside an instant before it incinerated him. He rolled away from another set of snapping jaws. Moving with the grace of large cats, the creatures closed a circle around him.

Alexei dropped to a crouch. He tore a glove off and

slapped his hand to the stone floor. Twenty Marks flared with liminal ley.

That got their attention.

They spun toward him, tails lashing. The one that stood erect—their leader?—narrowed its eyes. The intelligence that regarded him was ancient and cunning.

Also . . . surprised.

Alexei pulled deeper, sinking into the abyssal ley. His sanctified Marks fought the forbidden layer of power. His stomach twisted, but he held on, riding the torrent.

Subtle, unpredictable power flowed through his palm. It poured out again from his Marks, changed now by the intention of his conscious will.

The leader hissed a command. With serpentine grace, they flowed toward him, wisps of smoke rising from the ground where their feet tread.

"Saints, help me," Alexei cried through gritted teeth.

A trickle of dust sifted down from the dome above. It was followed by a tremendous crack. The leader looked up just as chunks of stone started to rain down on the circular courtyard.

"Here!" Alexei shouted.

Malach leapt over one of the molten bodies. He skidded into Alexei's corridor as the dome gave way in a shower of dust and sand. Wind howled through the gap. The torches died. Blackness descended, broken only by the silvery glow of the creatures as they milled around in the rubble.

Alexei doubted it would slow them for long.

He couldn't see Malach's face, just the dim outline of the scarf around his head. Shoulder to shoulder, they sprinted down the corridor.

Alexei feared he might have drawn too much ley. Enough to bring the whole place down. But the ceiling above their heads held firm as they fled through a maze of chambers, through a vast, dark kitchen reeking of sour milk, and into what looked like a dining hall.

A dozen more bodies lay clustered in a far corner, men and women both, dressed in the plain white tunics of servants. None wore veils or the scaled coats of the five in the innermost courtyard.

"They were slaughtered where they stood," Alexei muttered.

The group must have huddled together for safety behind one of the overturned tables. It had done them no good.

Malach stared at the maimed corpses, his face pale. "We must search the keep. There could be some still alive."

Alexei eyed him dubiously. "I don't think—"

Somewhere behind, an inhuman scream of rage echoed through the citadel.

Malach threw open the shutters on an arched window. Alexei smashed the glass with a gloved fist.

Another roar, closer this time, sent them vaulting through the broken window. From there, it was a quick dash to the wall. Malach wordlessly cupped his hands, giving Alexei a leg up. He found a crack and started to climb.

The wall was the worst part. It left him vulnerable and utterly exposed. The storm had started to subside, though sand still scoured his eyes. He gained the top, fingers bleeding, and looked back to make sure the mage was coming. Malach clung to the wall below, already halfway up. He briefly met Alexei's gaze, mouth tight, then ducked his head and kept going.

A minute after Alexei dropped down, Malach landed beside him.

They took off sprinting again for the city below. Alexei had a moment to be grateful for the fact that at least it was all downhill. When they were well into the twisting alleys of Luba, he grabbed Malach's arm and drew him to a stop.

Then he sagged against a building and took a minute to catch his breath.

The mage was panting, too. The scarf had slipped from his head and hung in folds across his broad shoulders.

"Thank you," Malach said grimly. "Though you shouldn't have followed me."

Alexei sucked air into his burning lungs. His pulse was still galloping. "Why . . . did you go there?"

Malach turned away, staring into the windswept darkness "Looking for Rachel."

"Well, you found something else." Alexei straightened. "What were they?"

"Not a clue."

He stared hard at the mage, but Malach looked as bewildered as he was.

"Well, they seemed to know *you*," Alexei said.

Malach gave him a dark look. "What does that mean?"

"I understood what that thing was saying," Alexei replied. "It's an archaic dialect of Masdari."

The mage pulled him deeper into the sheltered gap between the buildings. "What did it say?"

"After *you* tell *me* what happened back in Nantwich."

Malach's gaze settled on the Raven on Alexei's neck, then slid away. A muscle feathered in his jaw. "All right, priest. I suppose I owe you the truth."

Alexei listened in mounting horror to the mage's tale. "Balaur isn't dead," he said tonelessly.

It flipped everything upside down. The threat wasn't over. In fact, it was a thousand times worse. If Balaur had the child's power to rain destruction from the heavens . . .

"Not in the sense you mean it." Malach gripped his hair. "We burned the body to ash. I don't know *what* he is now. Will? Spirit? All I know is that he's taken my fucking daughter!"

It seemed insane, but Alexei had been there. Heard that

terrible voice, both a little girl's and something deeper and burning with fury.

Everything made sense now—including Malach's reaction when he'd broached the topic.

"And the witches?" he asked.

"Paarjini and Nikola are the only ones I trust. They both fought back. But the rest . . ." He trailed off. "Balaur knows the khedive. She sent one of her servants to attend him in Bal Agnar."

"Jamila al-Jabban."

"That's right. I hoped I might find them here." Malach briefly closed his eyes. "I don't know what to do . . . I . . ." He seemed unable to finish the sentence.

"I'm truly sorry," Alexei said. "But listen, maybe you can use the ley to catch their trail? I don't understand how the red works very well."

He'd meant to be helpful, but the words had the opposite effect. Malach looked more enraged than ever.

"I can't touch it, priest," he said coldly. "The witches hobbled me."

Alexei frowned. "What? How?"

"Never mind *how*." A baleful look. "I spent most of my life in the Void so it's not exactly a novelty to lose the ley. But it's still a massive pain in the ass!"

Alexei was silent for a moment. "Those things will be looking for us. We should get back to the—"

Malach's hand shot out, gripping his cassock. "Not until you tell me what it said," he snarled.

Alexei held his palms up. Malach let go, fists balled at his sides.

"Sure," Alexei said. "Though I can't say I understood it all." He translated the phrases as best he could. "First it called you *najmati kalsabah*. I think that means Morning Star."

Malach frowned.

"Then it called you the betrayer. *Anut alkhayin*. Does that mean anything to you?"

"It does if they're in league with Balaur. Obviously, he would consider me a traitor. What else?"

"Something about a sword." Alexei thought of the empty pedestal at the center of the chamber. "I think they were looking for it."

Malach shrugged. "I know nothing about that. But here's what I don't understand. If they were waiting for me at the khedive's orders, why did they kill those men? They wore the colors of Luba."

"And the servants," Alexei said. "I agree, it doesn't make sense. But it seems the khedive and most of her household have gone on to the capital. I suggest we leave at first light."

If they don't hunt us down first, he added silently.

Malach nodded. They slipped out to the street and began the trek back to the caravanserai. The wind had eased, making their progress swifter, though Alexei half-wished for the cover of the storm. He looked up at the racing clouds, hoping the things couldn't fly.

"What could make something like that?" he wondered. "Do you think they could be servants of the Imperator?"

"Or the witches. They can do things I never imagined." Malach cast him a sideways glance. "How is it you speak Masdari?"

"It's the oldest language in the world. Far older than Osterlish or Kven. All the foundational legal texts are written in it."

"So?"

"I used to be a lawyer," Alexei admitted.

Malach grunted. "A prosecutor, I suppose."

"Defense attorney, actually. I minored in Masdari in college before I went to law school. It was useful when I researched precedents."

Malach looked surprised but said nothing more until they

reached the gates of the caravanserai. He stopped at the front doors.

"I'm going to tell Hassan that I must leave the troupe," he said. "Tonight. And all the rest of it. He deserves to know the danger."

It was Alexei's turn to be surprised. He'd expected Malach to use them until he got where he needed to go.

"I agree," he said. "You trust him?"

"Yes."

Alexei nodded. "Good. So do I."

A SHORT TIME LATER, the three of them sat together in Hassan's suite, which had a real bed on a raised platform and a sunken marble pool for bathing. Fresh rose petals were scattered across the tiled floor. A priceless-looking urn occupied a niche in one wall. Another was hung with a rug depicting an eight-legged dragon with a golden mane, each stitch lovingly rendered.

The boy at the door had been roused to fetch strong black tea. Alexei cupped a steaming glass in his hands, serving as translator while Malach told the full story of how they had come to the Masdar League.

He'd insisted that he be the one to relate it. Alexei thought the mage would try to cast himself in a better light, but he told it plainly, including the fact that he had served Balaur himself until learning about the Kven children and his alchemical experiments.

Hassan reclined on a cushion in a silken robe, his expression hard to read, but he sat bolt upright when he heard the truth about Malach's child.

"By the Root," he exclaimed, taking Malach's hands. "You have my greatest sympathy, brother!"

"Thank you," Malach replied. "But now you must know

the rest. I went to the khedive's palace seeking answers. The priest followed. At first, it seemed empty. But then I found five bodies. They looked like men, but their eyes were strange. Greenish. And the skin was scarred."

Hassan nodded as Alexei translated. "The Breath of God," he said softly.

His eyes unfocused for a moment; they seemed to hold an old, buried pain.

"What is that?" Alexei asked.

Hassan let out a long sigh. He rose and dumped his cup of tea in a chamber pot, then filled it with wine instead and took a bracing sip.

"Warrior-priests dedicated to the Alsakhan. A bit like you, Father Bryce. Each emirati has its own order. They are supposed to serve God first, the khedive second, but it is not always so." He glanced at the door and lowered his voice to a whisper. "There is an order within the order. Assassins. They take poisons from childhood. In very small amounts—not enough to kill, but to inoculate themselves against the effects. Over time, their breath becomes lethal. Sometimes their skin, as well."

"Saints," Alexei muttered, quickly translating for Malach.

"They volunteer for it," Hassan said with a twisted smile. "Or their families simply send them. If there are too many sons, the youngest are given to the Nazaré Maz."

Malach studied his hand with a worried expression. Then he slipped it into a pocket and withdrew a yellow claw. "I pulled this from a wound."

Hassan drew back, pressing two fingers to his throat and then spreading his hand in a starburst. The gesture looked like a ward against evil.

"It is from the creatures who killed the priests," Alexei explained. "There were four. They had silver bodies, like molten metal."

Hassan's features froze. Then he withdrew a chain from inside his robe. An identical claw hung from it.

Malach leaned forward. "What were they, Hassan?"

The Masdari seemed to grasp the question with no need for a translation.

"The Sinn é Maz," he replied slowly. "The Teeth of God. But they have not been seen since the Dark Age." He slipped the claw back inside his robe. "This was handed down through my family for generations. You say . . . you *saw* them?"

"They attacked Malach at the khedive's palace," Alexei said. "We managed to escape, but—"

"We must leave now," Hassan said, leaping to his feet. "There is no time!"

"It's me they're hunting," Malach said, rising to join him. "I will go alone." He gestured impatiently at Alexei to translate.

"No, no," Hassan muttered, stuffing his belongings into a rucksack. "We all go together."

"But—"

"You will never make it to Qeddah without wagons and supplies. It is a journey of several days," Hassan replied with equal impatience. He pointed imperiously at the door. "Go! Meet us at the wagons. I will rouse the others."

Malach must have picked up enough to grasp the import of his words. He gave a grateful nod and followed Alexei into the hall. Neither had anything to pack so they made straight for the outer courtyard.

"Harness the camels," Alexei told the boy sitting against the door.

He'd drifted off again, chin propped on one fist. Alexei gently shook his shoulder and repeated the command. The boy gave a jaw-cracking yawn.

"Now!"

He blinked and darted outside, bare feet slapping against

the sandy courtyard. A moment later, his mistress appeared. She was fully dressed despite the late hour. Alexei remembered the way her gaze had fixed on Malach when they first arrived.

"What has happened?" she asked, wringing her hands. "Did something displease you?"

"All is well, Ama," Hassan called out. He strode down the corridor with a hearty smile on his face, rucksack over one shoulder. "The fare and accommodations were first-rate, as always. Did I forget to mention that we intended an early start? The sandstorm left us behind schedule. You know what a catastrophe it would be if we were late to the festivities."

"But it's still dark out!" she protested. "Surely you can stay for breakfast—"

"I'm afraid not," he said firmly as the rest of the company appeared behind him, red-eyed and tousled. Koko, in particular, looked put out. She scrubbed a hand through short, kinky hair.

"I must look a horror," she declared with an accusing glance at Hassan. "Why must we—"

"Later, my darling one," he said in a placating tone. "And you're as beautiful as the sunrise."

"Only after it actually *rises*," she protested, but allowed herself to be led to the wagons.

The innkeeper trailed them the whole way, complaining that it would ruin her reputation if anyone found out that the Bride of Azzabad and her illustrious troupe had skipped out after only half a night beneath her roof, but Hassan turned a deaf ear to the tirade, lavishly praising her hospitality while refusing to budge.

Once the camels stood in their traces and the luggage was stowed, the innkeeper finally gave up. She allowed him to kiss her cheeks with a sour expression.

"So Luba no longer even gets a performance," she

muttered. "That is how low we have fallen in the eyes of the League!"

"I'll make it up to you," Hassan promised. He hung out the open doorway of his wagon as it started off in the lead, blowing a flurry of kisses. "I promise!"

Alexei watched her through the rear window as they rolled through the gates of the caravanserai. She stood with hands on hips for a minute, then marched back inside, shouting at the boys to seal the gates behind them.

He let the curtain fall and turned to Hassan. The false smile had faded. The Masdari looked grim.

"If they are watching the road, we are done for," he said. "The stories say the Sinn é Maz see in darkness even better than in daylight. You were lucky to escape them."

His tone suggested that he knew how they had managed it, but didn't care to ask. Alexei resolved to be careful about using the ley. They had enough problems as it was.

"How far to the capital?" he asked.

"Three days. I had planned a more circuitous route, but it's better if we go directly. Our chapter house is in Qeddah. We will be safe there. But we must stop at another caravanserai in Marath. It's on the way."

The sky began to lighten. A few people were in the streets, sweeping in front of shops and houses, shaking out rugs and surveying the damage. A mottled dog barked at their passage and was chastised by its owner, who gave a respectful bow to the wagons.

A red dawn broke over the city as they left through the northern gates. Malach stood watch on one side of the wagon, Alexei on the other. Featureless desert stretched to either side again, looking exactly as it had before the storm.

"It is like one of my grandmother's tales," Hassan said ruefully, sinking to the cushions. "Two strangers appearing from nowhere. The Sinn é Maz walking abroad again." He scowled. "And the khedive of Luba conspiring with this devil Balaur you speak of."

"The Sinn é Maz," Alexei ventured. "Whom do *they* serve?"

Hassan hesitated. "The Teeth of God served the Alsakhan. Not like the priests, who play the games of power my compatriots are so fond of. I mean *directly*. They were the flesh and blood of the great dragon himself. In the olden days, they were seen often. But the dragon sleeps and so do his children."

"Is this true or just stories?" Alexei asked.

Hassan laughed. "All stories are true, if one chooses to believe."

"Do you?"

He withdrew the claw on its chain and gave Alexei a level look. "I think I would be a fool not to."

"They were looking for something. A sword."

Hassan seemed puzzled. "Any one in particular?"

"I don't know. How about the Morning Star?"

Something flickered in his eyes. "Ah, yes. Lord Gavriel. It was one of his titles."

Malach was staring out the window. He turned at the name. Alexei quickly recounted the conversation.

"And the Betrayer?" he asked.

"He was called that, too," Hassan replied. "In the witches' lore. An angel who maimed their goddess Valmitra."

Alexei frowned. Why did the Teeth of God seem to believe Malach was someone who had lived more than a thousand years ago? Either he was the spitting image of this Gavriel, or . . . did the creatures even realize that so much time had passed? It was an intriguing question.

"Ask him something for me," Malach said, staring at his hand. "I touched one of those priests. Will it poison me? I can't stop worrying about it."

Alexei repeated the question.

Hassan spoke at length in rapid Masdari. It was a convoluted explanation of the poisons ingested by the Nazaré Maz, the potency of each, and what they did to various organs. A good many recruits never made it to adulthood. Those who survived had different levels of toxicity in their blood.

"Well?" Malach demanded, foot tapping against the floor.

Alexei gave him a thin smile. "He said not to worry. You'd be dead already."

Chapter Six

"A dragon?" Paarjini said in disbelief. "As in big wings and breathin' fire?"

"Yes," Kasia replied, meeting her gaze. "Exactly."

The witch turned to the captain. Aemlyn had recovered her usual poise, but her expression was grim as she held up the snapped harness.

"I've never laid eyes on anything remotely like it," she said. "Whatever it was, the thing took Danna."

Nikola fingered the shredded harness, her brow furrowed. "And you got rid of it with ley?"

"I had no choice," Kasia replied. "I'm sure it would have sunk the ship. But I don't think I hurt it." She gave a hollow laugh. "I'm not sure what *would*."

They were silent. The two other witches had left to watch the skies. Caralexa was with the children. Only Valdrian remained, keeping a close eye on Jamila al-Jabban.

Paarjini shook her head. "The Mahadeva said the Great Serpent was stirrin' at last. It could be a sign."

"Of what?" Aemlyn asked uneasily.

Paarjini chewed her lip. "Let's ask Jamila."

The prisoner watched them approach with a defeated

expression. She seemed to realize that she'd spilled her secrets. When Kasia described the creature, Valdrian's brows shot up.

"Are you serious?" he asked in a low voice.

Kasia nodded. He rubbed his beard, light eyes roving around the cabin as he absorbed this bit of unpleasant news.

"Do such things exist in your land?" he finally demanded, looking down at Jamila.

"No. I . . . that is to say, not for a thousand years," she stammered.

"But they are part of your lore?" Kasia pressed.

A frightened nod. "The Sinn é Maz. The children of the Alsakhan."

Kasia briefly closed her eyes. There were no gods in the Via Sancta. Hers was a secular faith. Yet she had just seen something that wasn't supposed to exist—except as a fanciful Mark on Natalya's arm.

The witches worshipped a three-headed snake. The Masdaris claimed the ley came from some kind of dragon. If they were, in fact, real entities . . . how many angry gods was she dealing with?

"Are these creatures part of Balaur's plan?" Valdrian demanded. "Do they serve him now?"

"I have never seen one," Jamila insisted. "Neither he nor my mistress ever spoke of them, I swear it!" The skirts bunched in her fists. "This is . . . an unexpected development."

"Should I compel her again?" Valdrian wondered, turning to Paarjini.

The witch shook her head. "No. I think we'd better lie low for now. It could have been abyssal ley tha' attracted it."

"I'll rouse two of my crew," Captain Aemlyn said. "We'll drop anchor and keep a watch from inside the bridge."

They dispersed to their respective cabins. After telling Natalya the story, Kasia fell into a fretful sleep. She woke at every creak and bump, but whatever had attacked the ship did not return.

Dawn broke overcast and windy. By late morning, a bright sun was peeking through the clouds. The black, mountainous seas of the night before turned to placid aquamarine.

The rigging on the mainmast was swiftly replaced. Happily, the spar itself was intact. But the loss of Danna weighed heavily on everyone. Kasia hadn't spoken to her more than once or twice, but she remembered a petite, agile woman with braided hair who seemed to get on well with the others.

None of the crew looked Kasia in the eye when she came out on deck. They seemed sullen and angry, gathered together in small, whispering groups. She wondered if they were close to mutiny. But the appearance of the captain got everyone moving. The *Wayfarer*'s sails were hoisted. In moments, they swelled with a light breeze. The dark blur of land she'd glimpsed the night before transformed into a rugged coastline of barren red hills.

An hour later, she saw Port Sayyad, a settlement on the northeastern tip of the Masdar League. Now, everyone save the captain and crew were crowded into the secret smuggler's hold. It was a dismally small space, the ceiling just high enough to sit with legs crossed.

The four green-cloaked mages occupied one corner. Sydonie and Tristhus leaned together with dark heads bowed, playing some game that involved spinning the boy's knife. Valdrian and Caralexa stared at the six knights on the opposite side.

The knights stared back, but they sat in pairs as far apart as they could manage. Kasia knew they trusted each other almost as little as they trusted the mages. It didn't seem to matter that the Kvens aboard weren't the same ones who had invaded Nantwich. The two Nantian knights saw only the Wolf Marks on their necks.

The ones from Jalghuth disliked both the Kvens and the Nants because their respective pontifices had betrayed Lezarius—Luk by allying himself with Balaur and Clavis by sending Alexei north on an assassination mission which, of course, he'd refused to carry out. That Luk was dead and Clavis taken hostage didn't seem to matter.

Bad blood still simmered.

Then there were the four witches, who flanked the shrouded bodies of their dead queen. Paarjini and Nikola were engaged in quiet conversation, but Cairness and Ashvi eyed everyone else with thinly veiled contempt.

Kasia sat with her own clique—the Markhound, Natalya, and Patryk, who was forced to lean forward with his balding head practically between his knees.

"Bloody martyrs," Natalya muttered, glancing around. "It's like my old high school lunchroom."

Spassov gave a mirthless chuckle. "Worse, since they're armed to the teeth."

The only person no one actively despised was Tashtemir Kelevan. Nikola said he was a friend of Malach's. Through a series of misadventures, he had ended up on board the *Wayfarer*. After Balaur fled to the League, Tashtemir had offered his services as a local guide. The Masdari sat midway between the mages and witches, looking morose. Jamila al-Jabban lay trussed and gagged next to him. Her black eyes glittered in the darkness.

"Did you really tame a dragon last night?" Patryk asked. His voice was teasing, but his eyes looked deadly serious.

Kasia glanced at the prisoner. "Jamila called it Sinn é Maz. A servant of the Alsakhan. She said they disappeared a thousand years ago."

Natalya rubbed the dragon Mark on her arm. "I wish I'd seen it. Was it beautiful?"

"Yes." She laughed softly. "I was scared spitless. I just hope the encounter was random. That it wasn't hunting *us*, you know?"

"Why would it be?" Patryk said. "If anything, it should go after Balaur. We're the good guys."

"True, but we know nothing about this Alsakhan," Natalya pointed out. "What it is, what it wants. Maybe we pissed it off."

"That's a reassuring thought," Spassov said dryly.

"We have to consider it," Natalya said. "It might not be an actual god—whatever that means. Maybe it's just a big-ass dragon that lives in the desert. Which is pretty amazing, except if we're on its bad side, then we're totally—"

The hatch opened. "We're in port," Captain Aemlyn whispered through the gap. "Sit tight. It might be a while."

The hatch closed. A moment later, the ship bumped gently against the pier. Feet drummed on deck.

"All of ye, shut up," Paarjini said. She shot a hard look at Jamila. "If ye so much as squeak, I'll turn ye into a worm."

The dim space fell silent. Small holes had been drilled to allow fresh air and a few rays of light. Now, voices drifted through. Captain Aemlyn and a deeper baritone that must be the customs official, who was examining the cargo in the official hold one level above.

There was a long exchange in Masdari that Kasia would have given much to understand. She caught Tashtemir's eye and cocked a brow. He smiled and gave an encouraging nod.

The festivities surrounding the transfer of power gave Captain Aemlyn the perfect excuse to be sailing downriver toward Qeddah. Like other mercenary freebooters, she'd be bearing gifts for the new Imperator to secure his or her good-will for the coming seven years. The hold was full of gems and minerals. It would all work out as long as the officials didn't discover Aemlyn's passengers.

A long interval passed in which the requisite bribes and customs duties were settled, and supplies of food and water brought aboard. Natalya fell asleep with her head on Spassov's shoulder. An unlit cigarette rested between his lips. He held a box of matches that he kept sliding open and shut.

The others were equally restless. Only Nikola Thorn looked serene, staring into space with a meditative expression as if she had experience waiting in claustrophobic spaces.

Kasia toyed with Alice's ears, bending them and watching them snap back into sharp points, until the dog fanged her hand. It wasn't a bite, just a quick slide of one tooth against her palm.

"Okay, okay," she whispered, wiping the saliva on her dress. "I'll stop."

Hours passed. The scant daylight faded. Kasia's legs were numb by the time the ship cast off again. It left the chop of the harbor and smoothed out until she could scarcely tell if they were moving at all.

The hatch opened. "We're through," Aemlyn called down.

Everyone groaned with relief. They could only get out single file, but a reasonable degree of decorum prevailed, even among the mages.

"Kids first," Paarjini said, waving them up one at a time. She seemed careful not to show any favoritism and was the last to leave.

Kasia made her way up to the deck, eager both for air and the sight of land after so many days at sea. Port Sayyad already lay behind them, a cluster of low white buildings surrounded by date palms. Fertile fields dotted with homesteads stretched out on either side of the river, though beyond those lay a red desert.

"Barbaroi," Tashtemir said, joining her at the stern rail. "One of the richest emiratis. The khedive here commands the busiest port leading to the capital. His palace almost rivals that of the Imperator—though he is not foolish enough to make it grander."

He glanced up as a hawk circled above the ship, then

wheeled away toward the city. Its white breast caught the setting sun for an instant. Then it vanished entirely.

"A Markhawk," Kasia exclaimed in alarm. "It must have seen us!"

"Do not fear," Tashtemir replied. "They are trained for one thing only—to watch for unusual currents in the ley." He smiled. "It will not count our numbers and compare them to the customs manifest. The Markhawks are clever, but not *that* clever."

Patryk Spassov ambled over, the cigarette still dangling from his mouth. He'd caught the last part of the conversation. "So they can see if someone is working ley?" he asked, cupping his hand around a lit match.

"They can infer it. Then the trouble begins. The hawk will report to the priests, and the priests will investigate."

"Why?" Spassov touched the cigarette to the flame. He drew in smoke and exhaled. The breeze carried it over the river.

"The ley is forbidden to all but a few." Tashtemir frowned. "I assumed you knew that."

"*I* did," Kasia said. "Paarjini told us." She nudged Patryk with her toe. "You just weren't listening." She turned back to Tashtemir. "Is there any way I can do a reading? Can the hawks be evaded?"

"Wait until we are farther from Port Sayyad," he advised. "They cannot cover all of the land—it is too vast. So the priests keep their eyes focused on the larger towns and cities."

She nodded. "Thank you. I am grateful you came, Domine Kelevan."

"Well, your brother always looked out for me. Malach was the first mage I ever met. He did not turn out to be as I expected. In some ways, yes. But not in others."

"He is The Fool," Kasia said. "Full of surprises."

She took out the card, careful to handle it with gloves so she didn't accidentally draw on the ley. It showed a man walking with a carefree stride, face tilted to the heavens, as he approached the edge of a cliff.

Tashtemir laughed. "Yes, that is Malach."

"You know him well?"

At first, Kasia had rejected her brother outright. But he'd proven himself capable of good deeds as well as bad. She'd always felt that Tessaria and Natalya were her true family, and they still were. But as Malach said to her once, blood was blood. She'd barely begun to know him before he was snatched away.

"Fairly well," Tashtemir said. "I lived at Bal Kirith for four years. I know his aunt Beleth, too." He gave a little shudder. "Truly, I do not envy the party that has gone north to meet her."

"Much is at stake," Kasia agreed. "Let us hope we all succeed." She laid a hand on his arm. "But our chances are far better with you among our number."

A shadow crossed his face. "I hope so. I . . . will you excuse me, Domina Novak?"

"Of course." She watched him hurry to the ladder leading down to the cabins, brushing past Natalya, who was on her way up.

"What's his story?" Natalya asked, frowning over one shoulder.

"I don't know." Kasia chewed her lip. "But we don't need any more secrets that might bite us later."

Natalya held up one of her sketchpads. "I thought I'd do a little work. Maybe a landscape. It's been ages since the deck was steady enough that my lines didn't go all over the place."

"Sure," Kasia muttered.

I hope so. What did *that* mean?

"Or maybe I'll paint a nude of Patryk. Right here on deck. Just socks and a smoke. We can send it to his mother for Caristia. What do you think?"

"Fantastic idea," Kasia said, still staring after Tashtemir.

"See?" Natalya shook her head. "She's not even listening."

"I would have done it," Spassov said. "We still could."

"What?" Kasia forced a chuckle. "Oh. Right, no I did hear you."

Natalya clucked her tongue. "First you tell me we're going on a beach holiday. Sure, I was a little drunk, but I was celebrating. Then you forget to pack my bathing suit—"

"I'm sorry." This time, Kasia's laugh was genuine. "It was a wicked impulse."

Natalya slung an arm around her shoulders. "I'd only be angry if you'd left me behind. Go ask Nikola Thorn about Tashtemir, if it's troubling you. She knows him."

"Good idea." Kasia frowned at Spassov. "And please keep your pants on."

"That's what all the women say to him," Nashka remarked sadly. "If he were the *Meliora*, that would be the first sutra. The foundational doctrine." She lowered her voice to a stage whisper. "*Please keep your pants on.*"

He snorted. "Are you forgetting your grandmother? Babushka Galya told me—"

Kasia, accustomed to their endless banter, gave a wave and strode off. Maybe it was her years as a cartomancer listening to clients' confessions. Or maybe it was her own natural skill for deception. But Kasia had a sixth sense for liars and, as much as she liked Tashtemir Kelevan, she knew one when she saw one.

Given the contentious atmosphere aboard the Wayfarer, she'd stuck to her cabin during the journey. But now they were in enemy territory. It would be wise, she thought, to know exactly *what* he was covering up.

Nikola was not in her cabin, nor was she in the mess where they gathered for meals. The knights there hadn't seen her. Nor had the mages, when Kasia overcame her distaste and knocked on their doors. The witches were huddled with

Captain Aemlyn in the pilot house—but their number did not include Nikola.

Finally, on a hunch, she stuck her head into the smugglers' hold. The glow of a lantern told her she'd found her quarry.

"May I come down?" she called softly.

There was a pause. "Kasia? Sure, okay."

She crawled into the low space. Nikola sat next to the three bodies of the Mahadeva Sahevis. Mother, Maid and Crone. They were wrapped in white linen to the shoulders, leaving their faces bare. Gemstones and crystals wound through their hair. The Crone's was snow white, the Mother's threaded with gray, and the Maid's a rich, curling chestnut. Spells preserved them against any hint of decay. Their expressions looked peaceful.

Nikola was holding the Crone's hand. She disengaged her fingers as Kasia neared. "You must think I'm weird," she said.

"No, I don't," Kasia replied honestly. "If I had the body of the woman I considered a mother with me now, I would sit with her, too. Do you talk to them?"

"Sometimes," Nikola admitted. "It gives me comfort."

Kasia joined her, sitting cross-legged next to the Maid. Even in death, her elfin features held a hint of mischief. "I wish I'd known them for more than a few moments," she said.

"I hated them at first," Nikola admitted. "Hated all the witches. I only allowed them to train me so I could get revenge." A rueful laugh. "They probably knew that all along."

"But you had the inborn talent for lithomancy," Kasia said. "And that grew on you until you made it your own. It is part of you now. Something no one can ever take away."

Nikola eyed her. "Exactly so."

"That's how I feel about the cards." She tilted her head. "Do you remember when we first met?"

A tiny smile. "I knew Malach was looking for you. I made

him promise not to harm you. But I was trying to find out what you knew so I could spare him entering the Arx."

Kasia laughed. "And here I pitied you. An Unmarked char."

"You asked me what it was like."

"I felt guilty for passing as Marked." The women shared an amused look. "I think the Curia underestimated us both rather seriously, don't you?"

Nikola touched the corner of her eye. It shone like a mirror in the light of the lantern. "You should have seen Falke's face when he saw me in his bedchamber," she said.

"Falke." Kasia shook her head. "I cannot defend his actions. I'm not sure he would try to himself. Not anymore. Yet there is decency in him, too."

"I know," Nikola conceded. "He allowed me to leave the Arx."

Kasia frowned. "But he did steal your child."

"That, too." Nikola shied away from the topic of Rachel. "Who did *you* lose?" she asked. "The woman you said was like a mother."

"Tessaria Foy. Without her, I never would have discovered my own talent. But she was much more than that. Tess was a spy and saboteur for the resistance in Bal Agnar during the war. She was the bravest and wisest person I've ever known."

"She was killed?"

"By one of Balaur's followers. A man named Jule Danziger. He was at Nantwich." Kasia managed to keep her voice calm, though hatred boiled up inside her. "He escaped me then, but he will not do so again."

"You think he's come here?"

"I'm sure of it."

Nikola nodded grimly. "So the cards are your Marks?"

"That's right. In some ways, it makes me stronger. I have seventy-two to draw on and each governs a specific quality." She sighed. "But without them, I cannot touch the ley at all."

"The gems and stones are the same." Nikola thought for a minute. "Which hand do you use to choose the cards for a reading?"

"The left," Kasia answered immediately.

"Why?"

"It's my non-dominant hand. Also . . . well, it might sound silly, but in school I learned that each of the brain's hemispheres controls the opposite side of the body. The right brain is more intuitive, so I use my left hand to choose."

"What about when you actively use the ley to make something happen?"

Kasia frowned. "I never really thought about it before. But . . . my right hand."

"Always?"

Kasia closed her eyes. She flipped through her memories as one might turn the pages of a book. The doctors called it hyperthymesia. Perfect recall of every single day of her adult life—not just the big events but the mundane details. What she wore. What music was playing on the radio. Each word she spoke or heard.

The condition was extraordinarily rare. Kasia suspected it had to do with her nihilim ancestry—perhaps even the fact that she had not been Marked at birth like every other mage.

"Yes," she said after a moment. "I am certain."

Nikola looked excited. "That's just like lithomancy. Receptive and projective magic. Your readings are passive, merely interpreting a message from the ley. But when you wield it, you must use your dominant hand."

Kasia grinned. "This is fascinating. I wonder what else we have in common."

"Could you make yourself invisible?"

Her brows rose. "I wish. But no, I doubt it."

"Could you force? Violate the laws of nature in any way you chose?"

Kasia laughed. "Like fly? Definitely not. The red compels.

The violet twists chance. But it must be something possible—if unlikely."

"Why?" Nikola wondered. "The underlying power is the same."

"Not even the Pontifex of Novostopol could explain to me what the ley actually is," Kasia said. "I asked him."

"What did Falke say?"

She recalled the words verbatim. "He said the ley is not always linear." She imitated the gesture he had made, looping a finger in the air. "Sometimes it works in spirals. Just when you think you are farthest from your goal, it leads you around a bend and what seemed impossible is waiting right in front of you."

"Huh," Nikola said. "That's pretty meaningless."

"Yes, but it's also true. Do you believe in destiny?"

"Not anymore. I used to accept what they taught me. That I was born broken, somehow less than human, and nothing I did could ever fix it." Her dark eyes flashed. "It was through my own will that I managed to break free."

"Fair enough. But the cards show me things that have not yet come to pass. That is a fact. I'm certain there is a greater design."

"Whose design?" Nikola demanded.

Kasia gazed at the serene faces of the Mahadeva. "I would very much like to know," she replied quietly. "The witches use divination, too, don't they?"

"The Mahadeva was strong in it," Nikola admitted. "Although her attempts to manipulate Malach proved fruitless."

"Because his destiny was too strong."

A sour smile. "That's what *she* said."

They both turned at a scraping sound by the hatch. Paarjini stuck her head down. The rest of her followed a moment later.

"Ah," she said, crawling over. "Keeping 'em company, are ye?"

Paarjini leaned over and kissed each of the Mahadeva's cheeks. Her eyes swam with tears when she turned back. Kasia looked away as Paarjini used a sleeve to wipe her cheeks.

"I have a question for you," Nikola said. "You dragged me back against my will. Why can't we do the same to Heshima?"

Paarjini's face darkened at the name of the witch who had betrayed them and helped Balaur escape.

"Because *ye* were an inexperienced novice and *she* is the toughest, most seasoned sister we've got. After me, o' course."

"Could she break the Mahadeva's spell containing Balaur inside Rachel's body?"

"Aye. With ease, I think."

Kasia considered this. "I would be glad if he released the child, of course. But then he might take any body at all?"

She still had no idea how to kill a creature that seemed to be pure spirit—and suspected the witches didn't either. If Balaur could jump from person to person, they might never catch him.

"It's a possibility," Paarjini said. "I still canna fathom *why*. Heshima was always a devout sister! What does she have to gain from this alliance?"

"Immortal life?" Nikola ventured. "That's what he offered the others."

"I suppose." Paarjini shook her head. "But she is *laoch*. A guardian witch, bound to serve Valmitra. And she hates the aingeals. I've known her for twenty years and of that I am certain."

"It is a mystery we will only solve once we find them," Kasia said.

"Or sooner. I came to tell ye that Tashtemir thinks it's safe to work the ley. We're far enough downriver. Cairness is casting the stones in her cabin."

Kasia felt a surge of excitement. "Then I can do a reading!" She dug out her deck and fanned the cards in a semicircle, adjusting them just so.

"May I watch?" Paarjini asked. "I'm curious to see how ye manage it."

Something in her voice made Kasia look up. "What do you think the ley is, Paarjini?"

The witch eyed her. "It's the dream o' the Mother, o' course."

"Valmitra?" Kasia had heard enough aboard the ship to know that this was the witches' god.

A nod. "Your kind lost the ability to use it fully when Gavriel cut her head off. The third one that birthed the aingeals, I mean. But we are still her children in good standing. So are the Masdaris. I can't speak to how they handle their own gift, but ours is pure."

"Which is why witches can use the ley in ways that the mages cannot," Nikola said slowly.

Paarjini frowned at her. "Did ye not pay attention during yer lessons? I canna believe Heshima failed to mention that."

"I don't recall it if she did," Nikola replied, a touch defensively.

"Well, somewhere in yer family tree, ye'll find a witch," Paarjini said. "And her blood runs in yer veins, Nikola Thorn."

Paarjini glanced at Kasia. There was no hostility, but Kasia knew what she was thinking. *Aingeal blood.* The witch cleared her throat.

"To finish the tale," she said, "the Mother retreated deep into the earth to nurse her wounds—and her broken heart. Gavriel was a clever one. He figured out how to make Marks. It restored some of their power, but his kind used to be ageless. That much they never got back."

Kasia detected a hint of satisfaction in her words.

"He grew old and died," the witch continued, "and when

he did, the empire he left behind fell to pieces. Factions o' aingeals fighting other factions for a hundred years. What ye call the Second Dark Age."

This was history Kasia had never known about. The Via Sancta claimed the records of everything prior to the building of the Arxes was irrevocably lost. She leaned forward. "So what was the first Dark Age?"

"The rebellion." Paarjini's face was solemn. She folded her arms around her bent knees, the gems on her bracelets gleaming softly in the yellow lantern light. "Gavriel waged war on heaven itself."

"But why?" Nikola wondered.

"Now that is a matter of dispute. Some say for love. Others for love of power." She sighed. "'Tis a very long time ago we speak of now. Dur-Athaara kept well out of it all." She gestured at the cards. "But we've wandered afield. Will ye try a foretelling while we have the chance?"

Kasia nodded and formed a question in her mind, wording it carefully. She didn't only want to stop Balaur but to reclaim her niece, as well.

How can Rachel be saved?

She let her fingertips wander across the cards. Instinct guided her, a tiny tug telling her to choose *this* one and *that* one. She set four aside, exhaled a nervous breath, then turned them over.

The Twins, The High Priestess, Fortitude, and The Wheel.

"What do they mean?" Paarjini asked. "'Tis different from the casting of the stones."

"I am the High Priestess," Kasia replied. "Balaur and Rachel are the Twins. The Wheel is destiny." She eyed the small, flailing figures bound to its spokes. "Also an allegory for a fall from grace. One must pass through the depths in order to ascend once more to enlightenment.

"Now Fortitude . . . It marks the end of the worldly sequence and the start of the inward-turning series that culminates in the Wheel." She tapped the card. "You see how the woman tames a lion? It represents the energy of the unconscious mind. All the fears and desires we repress. Fortitude tells us that to conquer our demons, we must venture beyond the ego. Sometimes into dangerous waters."

Paarjini nodded, a bit impatiently. "Tha's very interestin', but how does it help us?"

"There will be something I must do." Kasia studied the cards. "Something I will not like."

The Twins were a mirror image. No matter which way you held the card, one was upright, the other inverted. Each stood before a tower—one black, one white. The faces were similar though not identical, the features androgynous. The most remarkable aspect was the mismatched eyes. One blue, one hazel.

Balaur and Rachel.

"Did Natalya do that on purpose?" Nikola asked in a funny voice.

She reached for the card, then jerked her hand back as if it might bite her.

"I asked that," Kasia replied. "She said that when she sits down to paint a deck, the images come to her whole. She said she doesn't pretend to understand them. That interpreting the cards is my job."

"Well, it's uncanny," Nikola muttered.

"Natalya's images often are."

Kasia moved on to The Wheel. The great circle in the middle dominated the picture. Its rim was emblazoned with arcane symbols that signified the ever-shifting winds of fortune. But now her eye caught on the background. Flowerbeds and winding paths. A pond with a gazebo. In the distance, a dark wood. A jolt of recognition swept through her.

The Garden.

"I must think on this more," she said, sweeping up the cards.

"And I'm gettin' a cramp in my hip," Paarjini said. "Let's go back up and see what Cairness learned."

They paid respects to the Mahadeva. Kasia touched the hand of the Crone, who reminded her most of Tessaria. It was cool and soft, as if the witch-queen merely slept.

She thought she knew what the message from the ley was, but she would not tell the others. Not just yet.

If she did, Kasia knew they would try to stop her.

Chapter Seven

"Do you miss Rachel?"

Nikola looked down at Sydonie. They sat in the bow watching the muddy riverbanks slide by. The child had voiced the question no one else dared to.

"Of course," she replied automatically, though she barely knew her own daughter. "Do you?"

Sydonie nodded. "Yeah."

Nikola had met Rachel three times. The day she was born. The day they'd saved her from Balaur. And the day Nikola had returned to the Arx with the Mahadeva to remove the child's Raven Mark and discovered that Rachel had not, in fact, been saved at all.

The image that stuck in her mind wasn't the squalling, red-faced infant or the terrified child Malach had carried from Balaur's bedchamber. It was the Rachel who'd plunged a knife into the Maid. She knew it wasn't her daughter, yet the horror remained as fresh as if it had just happened.

"What's she like?" Nikola asked.

Syd shrugged. "Just a kid."

"Come on. Tell me something you did together."

The children exchanged a smirk.

"We tried to teach her stuff," Tristhus said.

"Such as?" Nikola pressed.

"I don't know," Syd replied casually. "Like, gravity."

Nikola arched a brow. "Let me guess. You told her to drop things."

"Off a roof," Syd admitted. "But we didn't hit nobody!"

Nikola laughed. "What did Malach do?"

"Nothing," the girl replied with a note of wonderment. "Beleth would have beaten us stupid, but he just made us stop and sent us to our room." She frowned. "The Cardinal's changed."

He's not the only one, Nikola thought. The Markhound dozed with her head on Syd's knee, snoring softly.

"Alice has taken a liking to you," Nikola said, patting the broad head.

"'Cause we give her food," Trist said. "That's what you have to do."

"Did you ever have a pet before?"

"No," Trist answered, at the same time Syd said, "I tried to tame a crocodilian once."

"What happened?"

"Didn't work," the girl said.

"She gave it scraps for a month," Trist said, laughing, "but when she went to pet it, it still tried to eat her."

"Shut up," Syd growled.

"It *did*."

She scowled. "Yeah, but I was too fast."

Nikola shook her head. "How old are you, Syd?"

Mage children grew so oddly, in sudden spurts, she had no real idea.

"Twelve," she replied with a worldly air.

"I'm nine and a half," Tristhus put in.

Nikola smiled. "When's your birthday?"

"He doesn't know," Syd said.

"I do, too!"

"So when is it?"

"In a few months," he mumbled.

She gave Nikola a look that said, *see?*

"You don't know yours, neither," Trist pointed out.

Sydonie was quiet for a minute. "I always give you a present, don't I?"

He nodded.

"So be nice or you won't get another one." She turned to Nikola. Her gaze was guileless, but Nikola sensed an undercurrent of hurt. "How come you left?"

"Bal Kirith?"

A nod.

She sighed. "I didn't know the knights were coming, I swear to you. They ending up catching me anyway."

"Yeah, but why did you leave the Cardinal behind?"

"I was scared," Nikola admitted. "Of Dantarion."

It was a half-truth. Mainly, she didn't want to fall under Malach's spell. When he set his mind to something, he was relentless. And she'd felt herself weakening.

Nikola wondered what would have happened if she had stayed. Would they both be dead? Or—and this twisted the knife even deeper—would they be with Rachel somewhere far away, living happily together?

But that was a stupid fantasy. She'd seen the poor women in her Unmarked housing project. A gaggle of offspring by different fathers, the mothers themselves barely out of their teens and unable to cope. Not all of them were like that, but enough.

There was one boy, the son of a next-door neighbor, who she used to feed when his mother hit the bars and forgot about him. Maksim. Nikola wondered what had happened to him. If it got bad enough, the Curia would send priests to take the kids away. She didn't know where they went.

Part of her understood that none of them had a chance. The mothers, sometimes the fathers, too, believed what the

Curia said about Unmarked and stopped caring. But another part—bigger than she liked to admit—feared that she even lacked the capacity to be a decent parent.

I can barely keep a plant alive, she thought. *Let alone a human being.*

Now she wondered how Malach's cousin Dantarion was faring. She tried to picture the mage changing a dirty diaper and couldn't manage it.

The children swapped a considering look. "The bishop ain't so bad," Syd said. "There's worse."

Having spent time at the ruins of Bal Kirith, Nikola didn't dispute this. It made her rundown apartment complex look like heaven.

"I'm sure there is," she agreed.

"Dantarion had a baby, too. I hope I get to play with it someday." Syd looked wistful.

"Do you know if it's a boy or a girl?"

"Don't know. I guess they're with Beleth."

Another boat passed in the channel. It looked like a merchant vessel with black fan-shaped sails, each emblazoned with a serpentine figure in red and gold. The Alsakhan.

"Did a dragon really eat Danna?" Trist asked.

Nikola nodded.

He gave a low whistle. "That's vicious."

Syd tossed her black hair back and smiled. Both front teeth were gone now, the sharp edge of a new one poking through on the right. "Could you teach me lithomancy, Nikola?"

The thought was unnerving. Yet she wondered if she might test Paarjini's claim that only someone with witch blood could do it.

"Close your eyes," she said.

Syd obediently squeezed them shut. Nikola chose a stone from her pouch. "Now calm your mind."

The child's skinny chest swelled with a huge breath. Her

lips clamped shut. Then she released it with a whoosh of air. Alice's ear twitched.

Sydonie squared her shoulders. "I'm ready."

Nikola pressed the stone into the child's grubby palm. "What can you tell me about this? Anything that comes to mind. Pictures, sensations."

Syd's face scrunched up in concentration. One eyelid cracked. "Uh, it's green."

"What else?"

"It has lots of power to blast people!"

In fact, she'd given the girl a mostly depleted olivine stone with just enough ley that she could have recognized its qualities, if she had the talent. Olivine was receptive, not projective, and associated with protection, love, and luck. When Nikola was a novice, the first task Heshima gave her was to sort through a pile of stones and describe her impressions. She'd known nothing about lithomancy, but she'd instinctively felt the different resonances.

"I don't think I can teach you," Nikola said.

Syd's delicate brows furrowed with disappointment. "Why not?"

"It's something you have to be born with."

"Then how come *you* can? You aren't even from Dur-Athaara!"

"I'm not sure," Nikola conceded.

"Let me try!" Tristhus thrust out his hand.

Nikola gave him another mostly depleted stone, with similar results.

"Can we keep them?" Syd wheedled. "*Pleeeease?* We could practice."

Even if she was wrong, both the stones were receptive. Harmless.

"Sure," Nikola said.

Syd turned to her brother. "Bam!" she cried, shoving her hand in his face.

Trist fell back with a choking sound. The Markhound snorted and sat up, looking around blearily.

"Nikola!"

She turned. Kasia stood on the quarterdeck, dark hair flying in the breeze, head tilted in a question. Nikola left the children springing their fingers open and pretending to wreak destruction on each other.

"Can we speak for a moment?" Kasia asked.

"Sure." Nikola knuckled her back. She'd been sitting on a coil of rope and her rear was numb. They found a quiet space some distance away where she could keep an eye on the two young mages.

"I meant to ask you about Tashtemir Kelevan earlier, but then I clean forgot." Kasia's gaze was level. "It's obvious he's hiding something. I don't mean to pry, but if it poses a danger to us all, I'd like to know about it."

Nikola nodded. "He told me the story the first time we met, so it's not a big secret. Tashtemir had an affair with the Imperator's wife. It led to several years of exile with the mages. That's where I met him. In Bal Kirith."

"Ah. I knew he was friends with Malach, but I didn't know how."

"Malach saved him from a pack of mercenaries. They were hunting Tash on the continent."

Kasia looked uneasy. "Did Malach Mark him?"

"No." Nikola smiled. "He's a veterinarian. Malach offered him protection if he'd serve as their medic. That's all."

"But Tashtemir is a wanted man?"

"Yes," Nikola admitted. "Not for much longer though. Once the Imperator steps down, all her decrees become null and void. The moment her successor takes the reins of power, Tashtemir's death sentence will be vacated."

Kasia didn't look thrilled at the words *death sentence*.

"He served at the court in Qeddah caring for the Imperator's bestiary," Nikola added quickly. "Tashtemir's knowledge of the capital will be invaluable when we arrive."

"Assuming he manages to avoid arrest."

"Yes. But the city will be packed. If he stays out of sight, just for a few days, he'll be in the clear. We *need* him, Kasia."

She gave a reluctant nod. "His crime could have been worse, I suppose. But why would the Imperator's wife bed a man?"

Nikola shrugged. "I guess she likes both sexes."

"Do you know what happened to her?"

"I get the impression that Tashtemir took the brunt of the Imperator's anger. If you love someone with all your heart, you forgive them when they make a mistake, even a painful one."

As soon as the words were out, Nikola's cheeks heated. A blush wouldn't give her away, she was too dark-complected for that, but Kasia seemed to sense her regret.

"I won't butt in," she said quietly. "But I'll tell you what I told Malach."

Nikola's heart beat swiftly. "What was that?"

"That you value love over power. That you might act impulsively sometimes, but there is no cruelty in you."

She arched a brow. "Me or him?"

"Both." Kasia smiled. "I suggested that you not judge each other so harshly. Malach cannot help his nature. He's the wild card, you see. The Fool."

Nikola frowned. "He is many things, but I never thought him a fool."

Kasia laughed. "Not that kind. He stands at zero in the Major Arcana. The Fool is an enigma. He can be exuberant, joyful, something of a mad genius. He can also be prone to folly. The potential is limitless."

"So what determines his choices?" Nikola frowned. "Don't say the ley."

"No," Kasia agreed. "He made his choice back in

Nantwich with no ability to touch the ley at all. It came from his heart. And the cards that surround him. Me, you, Rachel. Even Falke."

"Which am I?" Nikola wondered.

"The Empress. Would you like to see?"

Nikola nodded. Kasia took out her deck and chose a card from near the top. The Empress held a scepter in one hand, a falcon in the other. Flowers bloomed at her feet and a river flowed behind her. Her form was voluptuous and sensual, her half-smile revealing a silver tooth.

"That really is me." Nikola stared in amazement. "What do the other things mean?"

"The scepter stands for your natural authority, but it tilts away, you see?" Kasia looked amused. "In another moment, you might carelessly drop it!" A shrug. "That kind of worldly power is not of much interest to you. Yet you clutch the falcon tight. You value living things much more." A fingertip traced the white blossoms at her feet. "The Empress is also a symbol of fertility. The river behind her symbolizes the primal waters of life."

Nikola tore her gaze from the card. It was the strangest conversation she'd ever had.

"I cannot bear children myself," Kasia admitted. "I am barren."

Nikola met her calm, unreadable eyes. "I'm sorry."

"Don't be. I do not wish for them." The woman's gaze was too penetrating, as if she saw straight into Nikola's own conflicted heart. "But I vow to see yours returned safe and sound. And what you decide then is entirely up to you."

People said that sort of thing all the time. Few actually meant it. But Nikola got the feeling that Kasia Novak didn't judge her in any way. She might have passed as Marked in polite society, but she bore the scars of an outcast nonetheless. The kinship left Nikola feeling lighter than she had in months. She impulsively seized Kasia's free hand.

"I . . . I would like us to be friends."

Kasia smiled, suddenly warm and human again. "So would I."

———————

KASIA POINTED to a pair of shimmering blue circles off the starboard side of the ship. Each was perfectly round and at least a kilometer across. "What is that?"

"We call them the Eyes of God," Tashtemir replied. "Twin craters from an ancient starfall. They are shallow lakes now. But the water has a strange taste, no good for drinking."

She had decided to seek him out after speaking with Nikola. Not to confirm his story—she believed it—just to get to know him a little better. He spoke Osterlish fluently and seemed like a learned man. Somewhere in his thirties, she guessed, with a long, melancholy face set off by thick, wavy black hair.

"How much farther to Qeddah?" she asked.

"No more than a day or so."

She eyed him. "Are you glad to be home, Tashtemir?"

A hand rose to stroke the long mustache he'd shaved off days ago. The bare skin was a lighter hue than the rest of him. "Yes," he said quietly, letting his hand fall. "I have missed it very much."

"It can't have been pleasant to live at Bal Kirith," Kasia remarked.

"Pleasant? No, but I felt safe there." He smiled. "You find that odd, but Beleth's court was much like any other. Once you learn the different factions, know who holds the reins of power and what they want, it is not so hard to—"

A shriek of outrage cut through the words. Nikola was combing knots from Sydonie's hair. The girl squirmed and yelped melodramatically, though Kasia could see Nikola was being careful.

"They've been feral for a long time," Kasia said with a frown. "I wonder if they can ever be tamed at this point."

The children hoarded food in their cabin and stole anything that wasn't nailed down. Valdrian and Caralexa left them to fend for themselves, so Kasia hardly blamed them. But they made her nervous.

First, because she didn't want them to come to harm. Second, because they were nihilim—and who knew where the mages' loyalty lay?

Alice liked them, which counted for something, but they were always stuffing her with treats. The Markhound had grown a little potbelly.

"Syd and Trist?" Tashtemir sighed. "They are a handful, certainly. I saw them torment the Perditae sometimes, but they were only copying their elders."

"Who were their parents?"

"I've no idea. Malach never spoke of them. I'm not sure he knows."

The crater lakes gave way to rolling, empty hills. The ship was beyond the river's floodplain now. The last village and cultivated fields had dwindled hours ago, the terrain gradually rising up to meet the mountains. A native of rainy, flat Novostopol, Kasia had never seen peaks so high and sheer, though they were not covered in snow, as she imagined Jalghuth to be.

"Why are you risking so much?" she asked frankly. "You could have waited to return until after the new Imperator comes in."

"I could have," he agreed. "And perhaps you would have made your way to Qeddah without trouble. With some effort, I could have convinced myself to believe this."

"But you chose not to."

He let out a soft breath. "I believe in both good and evil. Of the latter, there seems no doubt. I used to wonder why the Alsakhan allows it."

"I have asked myself the same question about the ley."

"This is no answer, but here is what I decided. Evil exists so that good may fight it." He glanced at Nikola, who was hugging a tearful Sydonie and whispering in her ear. "Every time we do something kind or generous, it pushes the darkness back a little bit. Like many small lights in a great void."

For a moment, Kasia saw a raven's wing sweeping across the land. And beneath, in its lengthening shadow, a thousand sparks, each guttering in the cold wind but still twinkling boldly.

Tessaria Foy had been among them, once.

"That is . . . " Kasia swallowed, her throat tight. "I like that."

"It is just one way of looking at it." He smiled and gave her a formal bow. "But I would add my light to yours, Domina Novak."

"Kasia," she amended. "And I welcome it."

Tashtemir patted her shoulder and drifted away.

So far, the trip downriver had been uneventful, yet she had the sinking feeling events were outpacing them. The one bit of good news was that Nikola had taken a fix on the kaldurite. Malach was indeed in the League, somewhere to the south.

The last spell she'd cast, that very morning, had detected the stone more strongly than before, indicating that he was traveling towards them. Kasia fervently hoped that Alexei was still with him.

Yet it all smacked of pieces on a playing board being moved about by some invisible hand. Kasia preferred Nikola's worldview. It was disturbing to think free will was an illusion.

Jamila al-Jabban had sunk into sullen silence. Paarjini believed she'd already told them all she knew. Kasia wasn't so sure, but she lacked the stomach to ask Valdrian to compel her again.

Of course, there was another way. And if she had read the cards correctly, the ley seemed to agree.

"No point in waiting any longer," she muttered, heading belowdecks.

She was almost at her cabin when raised voices in the mess made her pause.

"For fuck's sake, I wasn't staring at you, witch!"

This was greeted with a stream of angry Athaaran. It sounded like Cairness.

Kasia stuck her head into the dining cabin. Caralexa perched on the edge of a table. Cairness faced her with hands on hips, while Ashvi eyed them both with a wary expression.

"What's going on?" Kasia asked.

"This bitch is crazy, that's what," Caralexa replied, pushing off the table and squaring her shoulders.

"The aingeal has a bad attitude," Ashvi said flatly.

Caralexa laughed in disbelief. "I'm not the one with the attitude."

Kasia stepped between them before someone reached for a gem or blade.

"Why don't you both go cool off?" she suggested.

Cairness muttered something.

Caralexa lifted her chin. "She's the one—"

"Who started it?" Paarjini finished, striding through the hatch. She glanced at Cairness, who had gone bright pink. "That could be true. A word, sisters?"

Cairness opened her mouth, then snapped it shut again. She swept out of the mess, Ashvi at her heels. Paarjini gave Kasia a long-suffering look and followed.

"Why," Caralexa wondered, "did I ever think this was a good idea? Those women could teach a thousand-year-old regnum tree to hold a fucking grudge!"

Paarjini treated Kasia as a friend, but she knew the other two witches lumped her in with the mages. Aashi was barely civil. Cairness had never even spoken to her. It was infuriating.

"Well, you don't have to rise to the bait, do you?" Kasia snapped.

Caralexa's lips thinned. "You'd take their side? After what they did to your brother?" She shook her head and stalked away.

Kasia sank into a chair. Two knights from Nantwich sat in the corner. They'd buried their faces in their plates during the altercation. Now they looked over cautiously, as if unsure whether she was safe.

"What?" Kasia demanded.

A grizzled, middle-aged knight whose Crossed Keys tabard stretched tight across heavily muscled shoulders held his hands up. "Easy, cartomancer. Just trying to finish our bloody meal without getting killed, if that's all right with you."

She rubbed her forehead, thinking of Tashtemir's little lights. "Sorry."

They exchanged a look and returned to the meal without further comment.

Was this the heroic band Cardinal Gerrault had envisioned when she gave her speech about Marked and Unmarked, witches, mages and knights? Probably not, Kasia reflected, getting wearily to her feet. Little more than a week and they were halfway to doing Balaur's job for him.

The confinement wasn't helping. She knew they were all anxious to reach Qeddah. To finally take action. The problem was that no one seemed to agree on what it should be. Balaur had used alchemy to abandon his failing body. It was an arcane, hideously complex branch of pseudo-science they had no hope of unraveling in such a short time, even if they had the books and materials, which they didn't.

Paarjini thought lithomancy might be able to manage it— in theory. But there was no spell for ejecting the spirit of a dead man from a living child. Not without killing her, too.

Kasia had pondered this problem for the last week. She'd come to several conclusions, which she had not yet shared with the others. One was that Balaur existed in a liminal space now. It was only logical. He'd become a pathetic shadow, an in-between thing, which is why he was so desperate to find this elixir.

It seemed likely that his ability to walk in dreams stemmed from a natural strength in the liminal ley. It governed chance, but it was also a real place. She had seen evidence of that in Nantwich.

If she could catch him there, where his spirit dwelt . . .

Natalya wasn't in their cabin. Off somewhere with Spassov, no doubt. Kasia shook her head. Besides the fact that they were both from Novostopol, the two had little in common. He was twenty years older, an ordained priest who'd spent the bulk of his career wrestling mentally ill people into the back of his car. She was a professional nightclubber who barely even pretended to be an upstanding citizen of the Via Sancta.

Yet the pair of them got on like a dacha on fire.

Had Natalya been inclined to tumble him into bed, she would have done so without a second thought and bragged about it to Kasia the next day. And if Patryk harbored some secret longing, he kept it well-hidden. Setting aside her occasional bouts of mild jealousy, Kasia found the relationship refreshing. Men and women could just be friends.

She sank down on the bunk and wiped damp palms on her skirt. Well, it suited her to have the cabin to herself.

As always, when she thought of her Garden now, Kasia felt angry and ashamed—and more than a little afraid. Balaur had violated her innermost sanctum. But that wasn't what sickened her the most.

No, it was the fact that she was, quite possibly, to blame for everything.

Malach had never uttered a word of reproach. She wondered if he even remembered what Balaur said, moments after they burst into the Pontifex's bedchamber and found him with Rachel in his lap.

I pried the truth from your own mind! You betrayed them both!

She'd called him a liar, but how else could he have learned of their plan? He'd even known where to find Rachel, in Kasia's old rooms at the Villa of Saint Margrit.

What if you forget it all again? a voice whispered. *What if he uses you, as he did before?*

"He will *not*," she said aloud. "And if there is a chance I can save the child and prison him in my Garden . . . Well, then I must try."

Kasia removed the shard of amethyst from beneath her pillow and stowed it in her suitcase. Everyone on the ship slept with one. A charm against nightmares.

Kasia closed her eyes. She folded her hands across her belly and let the *Wayfarer* rock her into sleep.

Chapter Eight

Kasia's Garden was a mix of untamed wilderness and groomed flowerbeds with gravel pathways, all surrounded by a high brick wall. She wore a pair of old sweatpants and a purple tee-shirt that said *Ask Me* on the front and *About Your Future* on the back. It had been washed so many times, the airbrushed script was barely legible.

Kasia knotted her hair into a bun and pulled on a pair of thick cotton gloves. Then she waded into the brambles with a pair of shears.

She liked to keep a berry patch for snacking but left untended, the thorny plants took over *everything*. Sun warmed the back of her neck as she knelt down and clipped the new growth at the base, just above the root. It was the only place she could touch the plant without getting pricked through her gloves.

The thorns were long and wicked sharp. They snagged her pants, but she kept at it until she had a large pile of cuttings. She used the shears to grip one of the plants. The rest stuck to it, spines tangled together, as she dragged the mess over to the compost heap by the well.

"Can I help?"

Kasia turned. A girl stood at the grassy edge of the pond. She had black hair, shaved into a strip like Caralexa, and skin like maple sugar. She was barefoot and wore a yellow sundress. Hazel eyes identical to Kasia's gazed at her innocently.

"Of course," Kasia said with a smile, though a warning buzzed. "We can put down some mulch together." She beckoned the child forward and gave her a shovel. "Fill that wheelbarrow."

Kasia watched her closely as she started on the task. She had a glassy, vacant expression Kasia didn't care for.

Worse was her shadow. Long and misshapen and dark as spilled ink.

"Do you know where we are?" Kasia asked.

"The Garden," Rachel replied absently, hurling a shovelful of wood chips in the direction of the wheelbarrow. Most of them missed, but she didn't seem to notice.

"Did someone bring you here?"

Her face tightened for an instant, then smoothed out again. "Grandpapa."

The word hit Kasia like a bucket of ice water. *He is the master of lies*, she reminded herself.

"I like it here better than . . ." Rachel's brows drew together. She trailed off.

"Better than what?"

"Than the other place." She stopped shoveling. "It's lonely there."

"Well, you can stay with me as long as you like." Kasia approached, bending down to look her in the eye. "You may called me Auntie. And *your* name is Rachel."

"I know." There was a terrible emptiness in her voice, as if she didn't care what her name was. Didn't care about anything at all.

Kasia took the shovel from the child's hands. They were cold so she cupped them between her own. One of the few happy memories of her adopted family was after their cat had run away. She'd loved that cat and was overjoyed when it finally returned, two months later, in the midst of a torrential rainstorm. Even her mother, normally a cold woman, had softened at the surprise gift that arrived the next day.

"Do you like kittens, Rachel?"

"What is kittens?"

Mage offspring grew so fast, it was easy to forget how young she was. Kasia released her and walked to the wheelbarrow. She picked up a wicker basket. Mewing sounds came from within.

"This," she said with a smile, "is kittens."

Rachel peered into the basket. Some of the vagueness left her face. She clasped her hands to her thin chest.

"You can play with them, if you like. Just be gentle."

The child cast her an anxious look.

"It's all right. Go ahead."

It was a mixed litter of five. They'd just gained their legs and were eager to explore the soft blanket lining the basket. Kasia set it on the ground. Rachel sat down and tentatively picked up the orange one. They all had the pewter eyes of newborns. Little witch cats.

Rachel pressed the kitten to her cheek and closed her eyes. When it mewed a complaint, she put it back with its siblings and lay down on her side, head propped on one hand. Her laughter warmed Kasia's heart.

"They're so wobbly," Rachel said.

"Soon they will be leaping around and fighting like demons," Kasia promised. "For now, you can watch them and make sure they don't wander off. And they need names. Why don't you think of some?"

Rachel nodded, eyes bright.

Kasia moved a short distance away. "Show yourself," she said in a low voice.

The child's monstrous shadow detached. It seemed to sink

into the earth like sewage down a storm drain. A moment later, a man came around the bend in the path. He leaned on a stick, though she knew he was not so infirm as he pretended.

"Kasia!" he said with a smile, blue eyes twinkling within the black priest's hood. "We've been waiting for an invitation."

The rage she'd kept so tightly in check erupted in a volcanic wave. She raised her hand, willing him to burst into flame. To die a thousand deaths, each worse than the last. Her whole body trembled with effort, bending every iota of will to unmooring his soul and destroying him utterly.

A deck of cards took shape. It wavered in the air, transparent but gaining solidity. She felt an instant of triumph as The Twins floated from the deck. Kasia reached for it—and the cards dissolved like so many soap bubbles.

Balaur chuckled. "This is my realm, daughter. You caught me off guard once, but it will not happen again."

She sagged against the wheelbarrow, panting.

"Not even the Wards at Jalghuth could stop my dreamwalking," he said, settling on the stone bench that faced the pond. "It is my power alone, so do not fault yourself."

Kasia stalked over. "I am not your daughter!"

His head tilted. "Malach didn't tell you? I'm afraid it's true. Your real mother was not faithful. Both of you are mine. Ah, do not frown so. Marriages among our kind are for convenience only. Affairs are common enough. If you doubt me, I will say this. I could not have . . . *borrowed* . . . young Rachel if she were not my own blood. Even the most potent alchemy has its constraints."

Kasia turned away, fury replaced by a sickening weightless sensation. Mage blood she could stand. She might not like it, but it was tolerable.

But not this. Not him.

Balaur smirked, delighting in her turmoil. She wanted to scream. To set the whole Garden ablaze and kill them both. Heat built in her veins—

And then her eye fell on Rachel. The child seemed oblivious. She chattered at the kittens, petting and kissing them. Her spirit was still intact. The Mahadeva's protective spell was holding. For whatever reason, Heshima had not broken it yet.

Kasia found a steely calm. He would say anything to provoke her. To sow doubts. But Balaur was right about one thing. She had hoped he would come. And if she couldn't best him, perhaps she could learn something useful.

"Give her back," she growled.

"I haven't harmed her," Balaur protested.

Kasia stared at him for a long moment. "That's a ludicrous statement," she said at last. "Even for you."

His gaze turned cold. "You know nothing, Kasia."

"I know enough."

Balaur's wide mouth curled in a smile. "You mean Jamila al-Jabban? She knows nothing, either. Only her own small part."

"You seek the Aab-i-Hayat."

"Which I already told you myself. It is no secret."

She wanted to punch the amused look right off his smug face.

"So now you gather the keys to the City of Dawn. But what would happen, I wonder, if you failed to find them?"

"I am destined to have the keys," Balaur responded. "You cannot prevent it. Nor should you want to. That elixir is the only thing that might restore my own flesh. If you truly want the child back, you will not hinder me."

"Why," she asked, "do you even *want* to live forever?"

He shook his head sadly. "You have been deceived. We are not nihilim or mages." A note of contempt. "Nor are we the revered Praefators who founded the Via Sancta. Those are words invented by the clergy to explain something they cannot comprehend. But the witches remember. We are *angels*. A divine race that once had the gift of immortality. Gavriel, in his foolishness, caused our downfall. I merely want my birthright back."

So that was the heart of it. She imagined living on while Alexei grew old and died. Natalya and Patryk. Everyone she knew and loved. The long centuries passing as she stood aloof and distant from the natural cycles of life.

"It sounds like a nightmare to me," she said.

"Says a healthy young woman who has never known sickness save for the common cold," he spat. "Never seen her own body decay and weaken. But one day you will understand. And the suffering will be that much more acute for knowing that you were meant to be more!"

Balaur touched his sagging jowls with disgust. "I used to be a handsome man. Strong and hale. And I will be so again." He studied her. "Once I offered you a chance to join me, but that time has passed."

"What a disappointment," she said acidly.

He laughed with a touch of bitterness. "Yes, you are. You and your brother both. The nihilim have fallen far, but I will restore us to our rightful place."

"What, lording it over everybody? Saints, but you're boring."

He watched warily as she came forward, halting on the bottom step of the gazebo.

"I, on the other hand, am unpredictable," Kasia continued. "You already made one mistake in telling me your plans. I remember everything now. So I am not so weak as you believe." She smiled. "Half-blood."

He winced at the word. "It is unseemly to bandy insults, Kasia."

"I didn't mean it as such. But I know you better than you think."

They stared at each other for a minute. Balaur did not seem uneasy. If anything, she suspected he enjoyed the challenge.

"It's a shame your thinking was warped by the Via Sancta," he said at last. "I have spied upon the dreams of thousands of people in my time. Millions, even. Most were useless but a small number . . . ah, they each knew a fragment of the truth."

"What truth?"

He chuckled. "You would not believe me even if I told you, Kasia. It is . . . weirder . . . than I ever imagined."

She gazed into his inscrutable blue eyes. "You know what the ley is."

Or you think you do, she added silently.

A slow nod. "What it is, where it comes from, and how to seize the source for myself."

Her gut dropped a notch. "That isn't possible."

"No?" he inquired mildly. "We shall see." He stroked the maimed stumps on his left hand. "But you understand now. It is not merely *boring* immortality I seek."

Why was he telling her this? A taunt? Or some darker design?

"I understand that your own arrogance blinds you," she replied. "I do believe in fate, but yours is not so grand, I think. The ley will not allow it."

This seemed to amuse him even more. "The ley is a dream," he said. "And soon it will be *my* dream. I will remake this world, Kasia. Into a beautiful jungle, red of tooth and claw."

A breeze swept the Garden. It held a hint of smoke. Like burning leaves—

Balaur rose, leaning on his staff. "If you prefer it, I will leave Rachel's spirit with you. A gift to convince you of my good intentions." He cast a fond look at the child. "She seems to like it here."

Kasia frowned. Something was wrong—more than his unwelcome presence. She heard distant sounds off in the woods.

"Are you listening, Kasia?"

Suddenly, Balaur stood next to her, gripping her wrist.

"Let me go!" She tried to yank her arm away. He held fast.

Rachel was still playing with the kittens. She had liberated them from the basket and spread the blanket across the grass. The pair of calicos inched forward on their bellies, stubby tails waving. The orange, black, and tiger-striped ones balanced on her stomach, which quivered with laughter.

"But we are still conversing," Balaur said, baring his teeth. Perhaps it was meant to be a reassuring smile, but they were yellow and stinking and Kasia reared back so hard she managed to break free of his grip.

"Stay with me!" he barked in a commanding tone.

But the Garden was breaking apart, fading to mist. Claw-like fingers dug deeper into her flesh—

KASIA'S EYES OPENED. Natalya stood over her, shaking her hard.

"We're under attack," she hissed. "I thought you'd never wake!"

"What?" Kasia rolled to her feet, looking around wildly. "The dragon? Balaur?"

"Men," Natalya replied grimly, knives appearing in both hands.

Darkness pressed against the porthole. Kasia palmed her deck, shaking off the remnants of the dream. She would consider it later. But the faint sounds she'd heard in the woods roared all around. Shouts and screams. The clash of steel.

She realized why Balaur had tried to keep her in the Garden. Maybe he hoped her throat would be slit while she slept. But she had escaped—and she recalled every detail of the encounter. A small victory, yet it gave her hope.

"I was asleep, too," Natalya whispered as they crept down the companionway. "Then I heard a ruckus. I can't believe you slept through it."

They reached the captain's cabin just as Patryk Spassov emerged with a sword in his hand. He was barefoot and wearing only a pair of boxer shorts decorated with little red hearts. Normally, Natalya would have been all over *that*. But her face was grim as they looked past one broad, hairy shoulder and saw the knights who had been guarding Jamila al-Jabban sprawled on the carpet.

One from Nantwich, one from Jalghuth. It had been Paarjini's idea to make them serve guard duty together in hopes of fostering friendship—or at least something more than open mistrust. The knights' bodies showed no injury, but the tongues lolled from their mouths, black and swollen.

"Death ley?" Kasia murmured, transfixed by the gruesome sight.

"I don't know," Patryk replied, jaw tight. "I was asleep. But they took Jamila."

Ley roiled above their heads. It was all muddled and told her nothing except for the fact that the witches and mages were fighting back. Together, they ran for the ladder leading up to the deck.

Kasia burst into the humid night air just behind Patryk and Natalya. The Wayfarer had anchored for the night in a narrow part of the river. Rugged foothills rose to either side. A single lantern gleamed atop the mainmast, but no other light broke the solid darkness along the shore.

Knots of people did battle in the shifting moon shadows. Sydonie stood in the bow, her face pale and intent. She drew fletching to ear and released an arrow. It took an attacker in the throat. She'd nocked another before the body hit the deck.

A streak of fire set two of the figures alight. They dove into the water. The flare revealed more swarming over the rails. Captain Aemlyn was backed against the pilothouse, facing a tall silhouette in a long coat. Natalya's arm blurred. Her knife bounced off the attacker's back. The coat had some kind of armor. He spun around, a curved blade in one hand. A veil covered his face, leaving a slit for the eyes. Spassov bellowed and strode to meet him.

Ley popped in bright bursts as the witches drew on their gems. Tiny Ashvi, who barely reached Kasia's shoulder, unleashed a gout of power that tumbled three attackers over the side. A second later, another materialized at Ashvi's side.

It leaned in and lowered its veil as though meaning to kiss her. The features were a pale blur. Suddenly, the witch screamed, dropping to her knees. She clawed at her throat. Made terrible gasping sounds. Valdrian stepped up. A blade sprang from the leather-capped stump of his left arm. He swept it across the attacker's throat.

Kasia whipped a card from her deck. The Four of Storms. Violet ley traced the lines of a lightning-struck tree. She was searching for a target when Alice barreled past, barking madly. She lunged at one of the veiled figures.

"No!" A small, green-cloaked person tackled the Mark-hound, hugging her around the shoulders. It was Tristhus. They were nearly the same size. Alice bucked and fought, but he held her fast.

The pair were lost in the shadow of the wheelhouse. Then Kasia saw the glint of a curved blade. She drew deeper on the liminal ley, gaze fixed on the boom above them. It slipped loose and swung into the veiled form that loomed over boy and dog. Bone cracked. The man flew clean over the rail.

A faint voice cut through the chaos, issuing orders in Masdari. Kasia ran to the bow, passing more dead and wounded. A small boat bobbed in the current upstream. Five of the veiled figures were aboard, Jamila al-Jabban in their midst. She looked up and met Kasia's eye.

Gone was the weeping, terrified prisoner. This woman stood

straight-backed and confident. She barked another command. The attackers still aboard the *Wayfarer* dove over the side and began stroking for shore. Jamila ducked as one of Natalya's knives whizzed past Jamila's ear. It caught the man behind her. He clutched his throat, eyes wide through the gap in his veil.

Jamila crouched at the bottom of the boat, hidden now by a press of bodies. An outboard motor sputtered to life. The boat shot forward. In seconds, it was rounding the bend into the mountains ahead.

Kasia quickly moved aside as Nikola stepped up to the bow. Her fingers sprang open. The reddish gem cradled in her palm flared with light. The blast sent a line of waves arrowing after the boat. It rocked hard but didn't capsize. She muttered an oath and tossed the stone aside.

The ones who were swimming made shore and took off into the darkness. Kasia looked around. She'd drawn another card, but there was little she could do with it now. With an effort, she let go of the ley.

The *Wayfarer* had gone quiet except for the moans of the injured. A quick survey confirmed that the attackers were either dead or fled.

Kasia strode to one of the veiled bodies and tore away the face covering. The man's skin was scarred and pallid, the whites of the eyes oddly discolored. She crouched down for a better look.

"Don't touch!" Tashtemir hurried over. A trickle of blood ran from one temple. He gripped an iron bar, also wet with blood.

Kasia drew her hand back.

"They are the Breath of God," he explained, still panting. "Priests from Luba. They feed on poisons until they develop an immunity. But their flesh is tainted. That is why they wear the veils."

A hand shot out, gripping her cloak. The assassin smiled

through a mouthful of gray teeth. His eyes held the light of a fanatic.

"The god . . . *will* be freed," he croaked.

Kasia jerked away. The cloth was smoking where the man had touched it. She quickly shrugged the cloak off. Tashtemir grabbed the hem and flung it overboard. By the time they looked back, the priest's head lolled to the side. He gave a last rattling breath and went still.

"Saints," Nikola breathed, staring at the ravaged face. "I've never—"

"Help!"

The childish voice sent them all running. Sydonie knelt over her brother. Alice sat next to them, nosing at the boy's face and whining through her nose. Nikola sank down. "Trist?"

"He was stabbed," Sydonie said, lip trembling. "Do something. *Please.*"

The boy's hand curled into Alice's fur. The deck was slippery with blood.

"She . . . tried to bite them," he whispered. "But I . . ." He closed his eyes. "I saw what happened to the . . . the knights."

"And you saved her," Nikola said, briefly cupping his pale cheek. "Let me see."

She drew his cloak open. When she quickly closed it again, Kasia's heart sank.

"You'll be just fine," Nikola said cheerfully, though she could hear the lie. "Let's get you below."

A shadow loomed over them.

"I'll carry him," Patryk said.

Sydonie watched anxiously as he lifted the child in strong arms. Kasia's gaze swept the ship as they walked to the hatch, taking a tally of the missing.

Paarjini still stood. So did the captain and most of her crew. But only one knight from Nantwich and one from Kvengard were visible. Ashvi was gone. Cairness wept quietly over her body, which had suffered the same terrible end as the knights guarding Jamila.

Kasia walked over to Paarjini. Her hair had tumbled loose from its jeweled net. She glared at the assassins' bodies as if she wished she could kill them all over again.

"The knights on watch were taken by stealth," she said, glancing at a pair of bodies. "I did'na even realize we'd been boarded until I went to use the head and found Jamila gone. We caught them on deck, but by then it was too late." Her sharp gaze found Kasia. "Will the boy make it?"

"I hope so. He's with Nikola. Can lithomancy heal?"

She shook her head. "His life is in Valmitra's coils now." Her mouth twisted. "They went to a lot o'trouble to get Jamila back. I should have expected this, but they'd left her behind before. I thought . . ." Paarjini swayed. Kasia caught her arm and steadied her.

"Are you hurt?"

"Just banged up. I got hit by the backwash of Ashvi's projective spell." She squared her shoulders. "Let's deal with the dead and see what we can do for the living."

Caralexa limped over. "I almost grabbed one of those fuckers." She sounded shaken. "Thought I'd turn him against the rest. Trist warned me not to." She looked around. "Where is that kid?"

When the mage heard what happened, she hurried below. Kasia and Paarjini joined the crew in searching the ship. A Kven was found dead, bringing the toll to three knights, one from each city. The second knight from Jalghuth had been knocked unconscious, but he seemed to have only minor injuries. The sole survivor from Nantwich was the older man who had spoken to Kasia in the mess earlier. He helped the other Kven carry the man to his bunk.

Kasia ducked her head into the cabin Sydonie shared with her brother, but it was already crowded. Natalya sat in the corner, knees drawn up. Her face was blank, which Kasia knew signaled some intense emotion. When she got like that, the best thing was to leave her alone for a while.

Patryk stood at the foot of the bunk. Nikola and Caralexa were dressing the child's wound, while his sister patted Alice with a mechanical, distracted air. The only bit of the boy Kasia could make out was a thatch of black hair.

She caught Patryk's eye. He did not smile or nod. He just gazed back with weariness in his eyes.

Kasia knew then that the child was dying.

She turned away, pressing against the wall to make way for Valdrian. He cradled Ashvi in his arms. Cairness walked behind him. She seemed too stunned to object to one of the despised *aingeals* carrying the body. Kasia laid a hand on her shoulder. Cairness looked up with red eyes.

"Can I help?" she asked gently.

The witch shook her head. "We'll put her with the Mahadeva."

Kasia nodded and waited for them to pass. Part of her wanted to go straight to the Garden, to scream Balaur's name until he appeared and tear him limb from limb. But she was too wound up to sleep again this night.

He would only laugh in my face, she thought darkly. No, I must find him in *this* world. But then . . . how to kill him without killing Rachel?

When she returned to the deck, the two knights, both wearing thick leather gloves, were dragging the veiled corpses to the rail and heaving them overboard. Kasia watched the current take the bodies. Only true zealots would maim themselves like that. She had known fanatics in the Via Sancta. Maria Karolo sprang to mind, and the Pontifex Luk. Even Dmitry Falke, in his way.

But even they had their limits. The sacrifice suggested an intense spiritual devotion, which did not fit with the khedive's hunger for power and riches. Yet these men followed her. Gave their lives at her command.

"One of them spoke to me," Kasia said to Paarjini, who stood in the bow, staring at the mountain pass where Jamila's boat had vanished. "He said, 'The god will be freed.'"

Paarjini frowned. "Freed?"

"Tashtemir says they're priests." She gathered her courage. "I was sleeping when they came, but I deliberately set the stone you gave me aside."

The witch's features went still.

"Balaur came to my dream," Kasia said. "With the child."

"Are ye mad?" she demanded flatly. "Ye should have told me first! At least set someone to watch over ye!"

"I was afraid you'd refuse me," Kasia admitted. "But we needed information! I didn't trust Jamila and I turned out to be right."

Paarjini blew out a breath. "Well, I . . . you . . . ah, what happened?"

"I remember it all, so that's one good thing. He tried to hold me there, he must have known we were under attack, but Natalya dragged me out."

Kasia described the encounter, reciting it nearly word for word.

"I just hope he kept his promise and left Rachel there," she said. "It is her spirit only, but the poor child . . ." Fury tightened her voice. "It is no kindness on his part. I think he just wishes to be rid of her."

"Ye must return then," Paarjini said. "Keep an eye on her."

"I plan to. I think she would help us if she could, but she seemed unaware of anything."

"I don't envy ye telling her the truth." Paarjini sighed. "Can ye defend yourself in the dream?"

"The Garden is *my* place. It grants me some protection. But Balaur is much stronger than I am," she admitted. "I wish I knew his tricks."

Paarjini listened in silence as Kasia related his claims about seizing the source of the ley.

"That canna be good," she said dryly.

"If it's true," Kasia agreed. "He lies with nearly every breath. But if we put it together with what the priest said . . . Tell me something. This Alsakhan the Masdaris worship. Does he have some connection to your own goddess?"

"Not to us," Paarjini replied slowly. "But to them, yes. They say the Alsakhan is Valmitra's brother." She shrugged. "I do not ken why they believe this. The Mahadeva often said that Valmitra and the Alsakhan were one and the same, called by different names."

"Did the Mahadeva commune with her directly?"

"No. She left this world when Gavriel did what he did. Her gifts remain—the gems, the ley." She looked sad. "But she is gone."

"What if . . ." Kasia chewed her lip. "What if she isn't?"

"I don't ken ye."

"What if she's . . . I don't know, trapped somehow? In this City of Dawn?"

The witched looked startled. "How do ye trap a god?"

"I haven't the foggiest. But her seventh son might have found a way."

"Gavriel?"

"He hurt her, didn't he? But you told me that the Second Dark Age came about when he died, years later, and his empire fell apart. Why didn't Valmitra take vengeance on him?"

Paarjini frowned. "He was still her son. She showed mercy—"

"Did she really? What would *you* have done? Just let him walk away after he cut one of your heads off?"

The witch's silver eyes narrowed.

"I'm not trying to be cavalier," Kasia said, more softly. "Or to give offense. If I did, I apologize. But this story does not ring true to me. Valmitra is a god! Would she suffer such an act to go entirely unpunished?"

Paarjini stared into space for a long minute. "It canna be," she muttered. "It just . . ."

Kasia waited for her to work through it. She saw the exact moment that Paarjini arrived at the same conclusion Kasia had already reached.

"Heshima," she exclaimed. "*Tha* is why she aids Balaur!"

"It is not immortal life your sister seeks," Kasia agreed. "It's Valmitra. Heshima learned the truth and she's using him, just as he is using her."

Dawning horror stole across Paarjini's face. "But . . . are they mad? Balaur . . ."

"Has Gavriel's sword," Kasia finished. "I think he means to slay a god."

Chapter Nine

"Malach is coming, sister."

Heshima kept her expression serene. It would not do to let the others see her fury. She prided herself on keeping a cool head, unlike many of her fellow witches.

"How soon will he get here?" she asked.

"That I cannot say. Only that the *aingeal dian* is alive and headed in our direction. The priests in Luba must have failed to kill him." Darya dropped the depleted tracking stone into her lap and blotted the sweat from her brow. Brown eyes flashed. "A needless complication. If Nikola Thorn had not interfered, he would already be dead."

It was the hundredth time she had expressed this complaint.

"That tide has already gone out," Hashima said crisply. "We will still prevail."

"Will we?" Darya demanded. "This has been a disaster from the start. The Mahadeva—"

"Is with Valmitra," Heshima interrupted. "A terrible sacrifice, but we had no choice. We cannot turn back now. It is the goddess we must focus on, sister. We are so close." She put a touch of steel in her voice. "Calm yourself."

The novice Bethen watched them both in wide-eyed silence. Darya gathered her poise, though her hand shook as she poured a carafe of iced wine into a silver-chased cup. Red droplets sloshed over the edge, pooling on the table. Like everything else in the Luban embassy at Qeddah, it was exquisitely crafted and inlaid with rare woods.

"Fetch a rag and clean that up," Darya snapped at Bethen.

The young witch leapt to her feet and ran from the chamber. Her spun-gold hair had been lopped off at the chin, making her even more childlike. Heshima regretted bringing her along, but at least Bethen did as she was told. With Torvelle dead, it was down to the three of them. She hoped it would be enough.

As always when she thought of Torvelle, Heshima saw the witch's terrible end. Her body sliced in twain when the lithomantic box shattered. Heshima had been standing right next to her. Another few inches and she would have shared the same fate. She'd tumbled from the box in Luba soaked in Torvelle's blood.

It was a miracle any of them had survived the forcing. But now they had to stick together—whether or not they liked each other.

"Abusing Bethen will only gain the girl's ill will," Heshima pointed out. "There are a thousand servants here to do our bidding."

"I'm weary of sitting in this place doing nothing!" Darya exclaimed. "And I trust Balaur not a whit."

"Nor do I," Heshima agreed. "Yet we cannot do it without him."

Their eyes turned, unwillingly, to the sword propped in the corner. It was sheathed in a jewel-encrusted scabbard and cloaked with powerful spells of protection—not to safeguard the blade but to keep its taint from killing them all. Most of the time, Heshima avoided looking at it. Gavriel's sword inspired a loathing so intense it made her physically ill.

Appropriate, since Balaur claimed the blade's name was *Anathema*.

She had glimpsed the naked steel only once. Aingeal runes covered it from tip to hilt, glowing like fire in the dim chamber at Luba. But that wasn't what had shocked Heshima to her marrow when she first saw it atop its pedestal. The sword was also ensorcelled with lithomancy.

A witch had been part of its making.

She sensed multiple layers of magic. Illusion and conjuration in dizzyingly complex patterns, but also abjuration. The branch of lithomancy that defended against magical attacks and, in extreme cases, threw up a lethal barrier around an especially dangerous object.

Six servants who'd handled the blade were dead by the time Heshima, Darya and Bethen joined hands to lay their own containment spells. Then they had tried to destroy it, but the ancient witch who aided Gavriel had knowledge far beyond their own skill. All attempts were repulsed. When Bethen's hair burst into flame, Heshima gave up.

Balaur had watched them from the shadows. He did not seem surprised that the attempt had failed. No doubt he'd expected them to try.

"The Mother will unmake the sword," Heshima said. She tried to swallow and found the spit had dried in her mouth. "Until then, we will ensure it does not fall into the wrong hands."

Darya nodded and buried her face in the wine cup.

A minute later, Bethen returned with one of the white-clad servants. Heshima gave the girl a nod of approval. At least she'd shown a bit of spine in refusing to clean it up herself. The servant quickly blotted the spilled wine. It had stained the pale wood crimson.

"Shall I replace the table, mistress?" he asked with downcast eyes.

"No." Heshima waved a hand and he scurried off.

She stared out the window at the brightly blooming shrubs and hint of azure water beyond. The heat was even worse than Dur-Athaara at midsummer. How she wished Torvelle were still alive. She was strong in foretelling and could have guided them. But Heshima was hopeless at it, and so were Darya and Bethen.

They were so close, yet all could still be lost.

"Malach," she said at last, each syllable a poison in her mouth. "Will you manage him, sister?"

Darya rose to her feet, smoothing her dress. "I came to know him during his time at the Pit. Only an aingeal could pretend humility with such arrogance."

"You should have let him die on that surgeon's table," Heshima said sourly.

"Yes, but I was with other sisters who would not have permitted it." Darya tilted her head. "I think that next time he will not be so lucky."

She strode from the room. Heshima didn't care how she handled the matter, only that she did.

"When will we leave for the desert?" Bethen asked. She had a sweet voice that matched her smile, though Heshima suspected there was more to her than met the eye. It was why she had chosen Bethen for this mission. Nikola would have been even better, but there was no chance she'd have gone along with it. She was too mature, too confident, to blindly take orders. And she was in love with the aingeal.

When Nikola broke the lithomantic box, Heshima had been caught by surprise—a stupid mistake. She might be a novice, but she was also the strongest witch Heshima had ever trained. The strongest she'd ever *met*.

Given time, Nikola might have been able to decipher the spells on the sword and untangle them.

"Another tide that's already ebbed," she muttered.

"What?" Beleth's wide blue eyes stared at her.

Heshima patted her hand. "Nothing, child. We are all

eager to find the City of Dawn. You may attend me while I consult our allies."

She left spells at door and window that would alert her if any but a witch tried to enter the chamber. Then the two of them walked through graceful marble halls to a large inner courtyard with six archways. The Nazaré Maz, the Breath of God, stood guard at each entrance.

Thank the Mother they cover their faces, Heshima thought as she approached the guards, Bethen a half step behind. It irritated her that they refused to let her pass until Balaur, who sat with the *sahir* next to a cooling fountain, gave a nod.

Heshima had grown accustomed to seeing his cunning intelligence staring out from the girl's innocent features, but it still left her uneasy. Of all the forms he could have taken, it had to be a child! Perhaps Balaur imagined that this would lull her into complacence. If anything, the masquerade made it worse. Rachel resembled her mother and Heshima had spent weeks training Nikola—time during which the woman had earned her grudging respect.

We have no choice but to deal with this demon, she thought, making herself believe it. *No choice.*

Jule and Hanne Danziger stood nearby, whispering together. He was big and fair, his aunt small and birdlike with shrewd blue eyes. The Kvens fell silent when they saw Heshima and Bethen. Jule gave a slow smile that Heshima did not return.

"I would speak with you," she said to Balaur in a cool tone.

"Of course." He flicked a finger. The musicians playing a soft melody in the corner immediately rose and departed with their instruments. Heshima waited for the footfalls to subside.

"First, to reiterate the terms of this alliance," she said. "We retain custody of the sword. It will stay here, with two of my sisters, when we all set out for the City of Dawn."

Balaur dabbled his toes in the fountain and gave a childish

giggle that set her hair on end. "I already promised you that, Heshima. I have no interest in the blade."

"So you say."

"And it is the truth! I let you keep it, didn't I?" A small pout.

"Very well. Second, and equally important, I want to know your plans. My sisters and I grow weary of waiting. What if the Imperator does not name Luba as her successor? Do you have another plan to secure the keys?"

Balaur glanced at the *sahir*. He was a shriveled old creature with a white beard and thick black brows. That a man should fill the role of the khedive's most trusted advisor, and that Heshima was expected to defer to him, was another indignity. But Valmitra had chosen her to lead this crusade because unlike her hotblooded sisters, Heshima knew how to keep a level head. Once the god returned, she would restore the natural order of things. The loyal would be rewarded and the disloyal punished—as they should have been in the first place.

"We must wait until the festivities conclude," the sahir said with a shrug. "Otherwise, impossible."

"Are all seven keys in Qeddah *now*?" Heshima demanded.

"Patience. The succession, that is important to the khedive." He made a placating gesture with his palms. "Everything in its proper order."

"And where is she? I have not even met the woman."

"Gathering information," Balaur said. "I already told you that. Never fear, she will not miss her own coronation."

Heshima gave an irritated nod. Each faction had its own interests to protect. Balaur wanted some elixir he claimed would restore his own youthful body. The khedive wanted to be named Imperator, along with whatever plunder she could seize. Heshima wanted to free the Mother.

She was well aware that these interests were at odds with each other. Betrayal was inevitable. But she would deal with that when the moment came.

A soft rustle made her turn. Jule was scratching at his wrist like a flea-ridden dog. As Heshima watched, a piece of skin peeled off in a long, ragged strip. He stared at it for a moment, expressionless. Then he tossed it into the fountain.

Bethen looked horrified, though no one else in the chamber seemed bothered. "What is wrong with him?" Heshima asked, swallowing revulsion.

"The flesh fails," Balaur said, kicking the pale strip away as it floated past. "It always does, but in Herr Danziger's case the process is accelerated. I'm afraid the man who restored his body is no more."

"Fucking Luk," Jule put in with a savage grin. "He lost his head!"

Madness flickered in the Kven's bright blue gaze.

"You refer to the Pontifex of Kvengard?" Heshima asked.

"The same," Balaur said. "Luk had the power to shape the ley into living things. Hawks, hounds, horses." A glance at Jule. "Even people."

"*Ja*," Hanne said, cocking her little sparrow's head. "But one must also have flesh to mold and Luk used poor materials." She gave a trilling laugh. "I think I could do a better job myself."

Darya said the Danzigers dabbled in alchemy. That Hanne, in particular, seemed obsessed with the poison culture of the priests. She wore a long-sleeved, high-necked gown despite the heat. Sweat matted her dark hair. What was she covering up?

Heshima's nerve nearly failed, but the Kvens had influence over the Imperator. They were very wealthy and had traded with the Masdar League for years. She had to tolerate them, just for a little bit longer. The Mother had shown her what needed to be done. And Heshima would obey.

"So you see," Balaur continued smoothly, "we are as anxious as you are to depart and claim our prizes."

No blood ran from the flayed wound along Jule's arm. The

flesh was the color of soot. He tugged the sleeve down and lit a cigarette with the flick of a gold lighter, exhaling a series of smoke rings.

The Kven was blandly attractive, with a square jaw, defined lips and high cheekbones. As he drew on the cigarette, the planes of his face twitched like grease on a hot griddle. A moment later, they snapped back into place, but the overall impression was slightly askew.

"And when will that be?" Heshima asked.

Her voice was amazingly calm considering that she wanted to scream and run from the courtyard.

"As soon as—" Balaur cut off.

Swift, decisive footsteps approached down one of the corridors. The priests at the doors turned, making obeisances.

"We have prayed for your return," the *sahir* cried, rising from the bench. "All blessings to the Alsakhan!"

A young woman strode into the chamber. She wore a plain, rather dirty dress with white and blue beads sewn into the hem. Her dark hair hung unkempt around her face. But she held her chin high as she regarded Balaur.

"Never," she snapped, "will I endure captivity again."

He leaned forward. "But you learned their plans?"

"I learned enough."

The *sahir* hobbled forward. He whispered in her ear. She nodded, kissing his sunken cheeks. "You did well." Her gaze swept the assembled company. "They are coming to Qeddah. But that is not my most important tidings."

Heshima stared. Could the khedive really be this disheveled woman? And what did she mean, *captivity*?

Obviously, she and Balaur had been scheming together behind the witches' backs. The anger Heshima kept carefully banked flared to life. She found herself reaching for her pouch and stilled her hand. *Not yet.*

"I am a witch of Dur-Athaara," she said, stepping forward. "What news do you bring?"

"This," the khedive said curtly. "The Teeth of God are awake."

Heshima's knees weakened with relief. She clasped Bethen's hand. It was a sign. If her draconic children had returned, Valmitra herself must finally be stirring.

The *sahir* whispered a prayer—or an oath. A ripple went through the veiled priests at the doors. Balaur looked thoughtful, Bethen confused.

Only Jule Danziger kept smirking, unaware of the cigarette burning to ash in his long, elegant fingers.

Chapter Ten

"Do you think I'd make a pretty woman?" Malach asked in Masdari.

Koko sat at her dressing table, painting one eyelid with sparkly gold powder. "You're learning fast," she said, meeting his gaze in the mirror.

He winked and gave her a saucy grin. Karl burst into laughter.

"What?" Malach asked, switching to Osterlish.

"You say pretty prostitute," Karl replied, "when I think you mean to say lady."

"How do you say it right?"

"Al*ka*na is a lady. Alkan*ah* is a whore. A special kind that does things with her feet."

He wiggled his bare toes. The nails were painted bright coral, making it somehow even more suggestive. Malach made a half-hearted grab for one foot. Karl scooted away, laughing harder.

The priest had offered to give Malach language lessons during the long, empty hours of the trek north from Luba to Marath. He'd failed to explain this rather crucial difference.

Koko's lips pursed as she flicked the tiny brush across the lid.

"Do not blame Father Bryce," she said. "The words are, unfortunately, very close." She picked up another pot of powder, this one a shade darker, and carefully lined the crease. "Yes, with a fair amount of work, I think you would make a pretty prostitute, Malach."

She managed to keep a straight face, though he heard the laughter in her voice.

Malach reached for one of her wigs, a long blonde one. Koko snatched it away.

"These are not toys," she admonished. "*If* I decide to let you try, it will be the proper way."

"I already picked a name," Malach said, settling back on the cushions.

Koko started on her other eye. "What is it?"

"Lucy Fur."

It took Karl about thirty seconds. Then he slapped his knee and fell over.

"I do not understand the joke," Koko complained.

Karl caught his breath and explained. A pun on the Old Tongue word for light-bringer.

Her full lips curled in a reluctant grin.

"When can I try?" Malach wheedled.

Koko set the brush down and turned to face him. "Why do you want to?"

The answer was clearly important. "Because I am . . . Karl, what is the word for curious?"

"Batak."

He repeated it. "I am curious how it feels to be someone totally different. Even for a little while."

Koko glanced at him sideways. "We shall see."

Malach knew her well enough by now not to pester. She had an easygoing nature, but the Blessed were different from the drag queens he had seen in the clubs of Novostopol. Their dual nature was revered with religious awe here.

It was a serious thing he was asking permission for, but Malach meant every word. He was curious not simply about how he might appear, but how it would *feel* to embrace a female persona entirely.

"What does Lucy look like?" Karl asked, getting into the spirit.

"Ice blonde," Malach said. "Spiked heels. Short leather skirt and stockings with sexy seams up the back."

"What about her Marks? Does she show them off or hide them?"

He gave Karl an *are you serious* look. "Lucy shows them off. Lucy don't care."

"Hmmm." Karl scrutinized him, chin on fist. "You have big shoulders. Maybe something gauzy like a wrap to play it down—"

Koko dabbed powder on her nose and snapped her compact shut. "Lipstick," she said, holding out a hand.

Malach plucked a tube of bloody crimson from the vanity. "See, that's *exactly* the color Lucy would wear."

She cast him an amused glance. "This Lucy sounds like trouble."

"No, no. She's a nice girl," he protested. "Just . . . Karl, how do you say misunderstood?"

"Sat khalem."

"I don't want red." Koko studied herself critically. "I want Plum Paradise."

He rummaged through the makeup bag. "I can't find it. How about Naked Berry? It's pretty close."

She sighed and held out a hand. Koko carefully tinted her lips, then blotted them and lined the sharp ridges with a pencil. She always looked good, but the makeup made her eyes even bigger, her dark skin flawless. A chin-length chestnut bob completed the look.

She rose from the padded bench with a rustle of glossy, semi-sheer fabric. Malach followed Karl down the steps—Katy Wulf, actually, since she was in costume now. The proper genders muddled in his head sometimes, but the Masdari language itself was neutral, with a single pronoun that could denote male, female, neither or both depending on the context of the sentence, which made it all very easy—and impossible to accidentally give offense.

They were camped in a mountain pass, still too far from Marath to make it before dark. Hassan had decided to stage a full dress rehearsal in honor of their guests—and also to assess the newest acts one last time ahead of their arrival in Qeddah.

Canvas chairs were pulled up around a roaring blaze. The priest sprawled in one, chatting with Kareem, who wore a tight, shimmering gown that mimicked a mermaid's scales. The others milled about, sipping water rather than the usual cups of wine.

It was the first time Malach had ever seen Ameer, the youngest at thirteen, in female dress. *He* . . . no, *she* . . . looked nervous but happy, hovering close to Sister Najlah, who was her mentor.

All wore their finest: dyed feathers and golden pearls and embroidered silks. Skin glittered with perfumed powder. Wrists and earlobes winked with gems. Malach admired them for a moment, stunned at what an expert application of makeup could do to a human face.

Koko had a strict rule about keeping up appearances on the road, but the others were lazier. Malach mainly knew them from drowsy mornings around a gigantic urn of tea. Now his travel companions had been transformed into bewitching creatures that scarcely looked mortal.

Yet they all paled next to Sultana, the Bride of Azzabad.

She wore no makeup, just a hint of kohl around the eyes. Her gown was a simple low-cut white sheath, hugging a slender waist he could have circled with his hands and flaring to accommodate curving hips. The yellow claw nestled in generous cleavage.

It had to be fake, but Malach could not see how. Her olive skin was seamless and perfect in the warm firelight. Every inch voluptuous, yet she exuded an innocence that would make men weep.

The Bride caught him staring and gave the knowing half-smirk her alter ego had perfected. Malach did not smile back, only gave her a low bow. He thought for a moment, then added a curtsy for good measure, sweeping imaginary skirts wide.

Farasha laughed and shimmied her butterfly wings, which extended from a hidden harness on her back. "Well done," she said with a wink.

He sank into a chair next to the priest, who'd shaved and wasn't bad-looking. Malach found himself wondering what incarnation Alexei would take. Frumpy, he decided, with a tight bun and knee-length tweed skirt. Not nearly as hot as Lucy.

The Bride clapped her hands lightly. The murmur of conversation ceased.

"We would give you a gift," she said, looking at Malach.

The voice was higher than he was used to, yet not forced to a false timbre. It had a sweet huskiness that suited her.

"A private performance of the Blessed of the Alsakhan. Something that is normally only given to khedives or the Imperator herself." Her gaze swept the assembled company. "Treat them as you would any other dignitary, daughters. *Dazzle.*"

The others looked eager—and a touch apprehensive. Malach knew it was not him or the priest's judgment they worried about, but hers. Karl said she was a perfectionist.

Sister Najlah produced a drum and began to tap out a slowly accelerating rhythm. Ameer stepped into the ring of chairs, so terrified her hands trembled within the sleeves of her dress. She stammered out her stage name—Lady Blue. Then she launched into a complicated dance with scarves that she pulled from slits in her dress, one by one. They ranged from the bold hue of a desert sky at noon to the soft gray of a pigeon's wing. By the end, everyone was stamping their feet to the drum and her cheeks were flushed with triumph, fears evaporated in the glow of approval.

Then Farasha spun into the circle on the tips of her toes, gracing each member of the audience with a brush of the gauzy streamers tied to her wrists. Some mechanism made her wings flutter, so light and delicate she truly seemed to be flitting from flower to flower.

Sister Najlah's act was more risqué. It involved a series of ever smaller fans and ended with her perched half-naked in the priest's lap, crooning the final words of a bawdy ballad into his ear. Malach expected him to blush, but he seemed to be relaxed and enjoying the attention.

Wonders never ceased.

Most of the company also played instruments. Strings and flutes and things he had no name for. They struck up accompanying tunes or simply set the mood. Koko picked up a gourd with seeds inside, shaking it in such a manner that Malach heard the hiss and crash of ocean waves. Kareem stepped forward.

The Mermaid Queen had long emerald hair that somehow gave the impression of drifting on a salty current. Her voice was moonlight on black water, silvery and aloof. She sang a song about her father, the Mer-Lord, and how he had murdered her human lover that left everyone wiping their eyes.

Once Koko had repaired her makeup, she recited several short poems, silly ones to lift their spirits. Sultana arched a thick brow—the Bride did not pluck them to a sliver as some did. Koko gave a tiny shrug as if to say she had nothing to prove to anyone, and this earned an indulgent smile.

Next came Katy Wulf, who wore a sequined bodysuit and walked on her hands around the fire ring, so close to the licking flames that Malach's palms started to sweat. She performed a dizzying series of acrobatic feats, tying herself into knots and then exploding into handsprings that drove the small crowd wild.

Last was Nizaam/Maazin, who painted half her face as a woman and left half as a man, and sang a duet with herself in an alternating sweet soprano and rich baritone that magically seemed to harmonize in the chorus.

Afterwards, the Bride went around the circle, bestowing kisses and praise, along with the occasional whispered bit of advice for some minor improvement. The air thickened with anticipation.

Karl said she was a celebrated singer and dancer. Malach wasn't sure what to expect, but as always, she managed to surprise him.

Sultana swayed into the firelight. Her straight blue-black hair tumbled in a gleaming river across her shoulders. All eyes followed her; even usually restless Farasha sat perfectly still. When the only sound was the crackle and pop of sparks, she began to speak.

"Once upon a time," she said softly, "very long ago, when all you see around you was nothing but a lifeless void—" one arm traced a graceful arc "—there came two great beings. The Serpent and the Dragon."

Malach leaned forward. Her eyes were fixed on the middle distance, but he sensed this tale was meant for him.

"They were brother and sister and loved each other dearly. Together, they dreamt of plants and animals and suns and stars. And because their dreams had substance, these things came into being."

She danced the words, hands describing each creation. "Trees filled the empty spaces. Flowers bloomed between their roots and birds made their nests among the branches. It was all very pretty, but the Serpent decided that something was missing. She wished for children with the power of speech to tell her stories, and so she made for herself three clans, each birthed from the mouth of one of her heads."

The Bride danced slowly around the fire. "Her brother cared little for children. He built for himself a fine city and there he dwelt in peace, and his breath fed his sister's children and made them wiser. One of her clans came to love him and they settled nearby, even though the land he had chosen was hot and barren. In turn, he gifted them with a talent for music and poetry and dance so that they would always be merry."

The Bride's face grew solemn. "All was well until the Serpent's seventh son grew dissatisfied with the constraints she had laid upon him. They quarreled. Both parted with bitterness in their hearts. This bitterness grew and grew. It infected others of her children. The Serpent regretted giving them the capacity to resist her authority."

The Bride stomped a delicate foot, cheeks glistening. "She wept angry tears and from these molten droplets were birthed a fourth clan. Different from the rest in both form and temperament."

The Bride bared her even white teeth. Her body wound in a sinuous motion that raised the hair on Malach's forearms. The claw, dangling on its silver chain between her breasts, shone red in the firelight.

"The Sinn é Maz. Devoted to their mother in every respect. This new creation pleased her and she managed to forget for a time that her favorite son was estranged. In imitation of her brother, she built her own dwelling." Her hands painted it in the air. "A fortress far from his own, high in the snowy mountains."

Alexei shifted next to Malach, gaze fixed on the Bride with strange intensity.

"Time passed and the embers of rebellion smoldered until they finally set half the world aflame. A Dark Age descended upon the once peaceful land. The Serpent's daughters fled the chaos, leaving her sons to wage war on each other."

She raised an arm high, brandishing an invisible weapon. Her shoulders squared and seemed to broaden. Her mouth set in implacable lines.

"The Mother's favorite, called the Morning Star, led his brothers against the Serpent's palace and there he tried to slay her. By the time the Dragon learned of this treachery, it was too late. She had already fled, gravely wounded, into the depths of the earth."

The Bride sank to her knees, bowing her head. "The Dragon mourned the loss of his sister, but he feared the growing power of the Morning Star, who had forged a blade strong enough to fell gods. He gathered the desert children and bade them to protect his own city with their lives. Then he anointed the fiercest among them to serve as his legion. Fearing that no weapon of mortal steel could withstand the *malak*, he taught them the ways of poison."

Fingers fluttered along her slender throat. "Loyal to the death, they turned their own bodies into weapons and vowed to perish before allowing the Father's last refuge to be taken. They called it the City of Dawn for the way the sun caught the golden minarets."

The Bride lifted her face to the dark sky. "Long years they waited, ever alert, but the Morning Star did not come. Perhaps he was too busy asserting his own authority over the realm he had stolen. Or perhaps his hatred died when he banished his Mother. Generations upon generations have lived and died since those fateful events and not even the wisest *sahirs* claim to know the truth of Gavriel's end."

Her gaze settled on Malach. He stared back a challenge and she looked away, but not before he saw the speculative gleam in her onyx eyes. Then the Bride rose to her feet and the dance began again, a lively, light step now.

"Only that a day came when a ship appeared from a place

called Kvengard. The men aboard carried no weapons and sought only to trade. They knew nothing of what had transpired so long before and, being merciful, the Dragon instructed his children not to hold a grudge against the descendants of the *malak*, who had already suffered greatly for their sins."

She whirled around the fire, fingers stroking her wrists and neck as though they shone with gemstones. "The Serpent's daughters made their own place and continued to praise the Mother and pray for her return. Peace returned, although never again would they trust her sons."

The dance slowed. "And the Dragon's adopted children? Well, as their numbers grew, they spread across the desert and broke into seven tribes." She passed around the circle, touching each of her sisters' cheeks in turn. "At first, they, too, became quarrelsome. Arguing over water rights and a thousand other squabbles. But one among them convinced the rest that they must respect each other or fall into the terrible wars of the *malak*.

"This argument carried some weight, for all knew of the destruction that had rained down upon the place of mountains. A bargain was struck and the wise mystic was chosen to be the first Golden Imperator, with the promise that she would cede her throne in seven years, and that her successor would do the same. Each dispute was swiftly settled. The tribes had all agreed that during her reign, her voice would be unchallenged."

Several of the company were nodding. Everyone knew this part.

"And the Nazaré Maz?" She exhaled a drawn-out sigh. The night air up in the foothills was chilly enough that a streamer of mist drifted from her mouth. "The Breath of God held to their oath to guard the Dragon until the end of time. For without Him, all will return to the lifeless void."

The Bride threw her arms wide, head tipping back. "Blessings to the mighty Alsakhan, Father of the Ley!"

"Blessings!" the others echoed, touching fingers to throats and making a starburst. "Blessings!"

Malach imitated the gesture to be polite, though his mind was churning.

Stories, he thought, both disturbed and a little angry, though he couldn't say why.

The Bride of Azzabad bowed to thunderous applause. It had gotten cold and most of the troupe was scantily dressed. They hugged each other, giddy with the success of the rehearsal, and headed off to wash their faces and burrow beneath warm blankets. Malach thought the Bride might speak with him, but he merited only a single blown kiss before she vanished into her wagon and shut the door.

Only the priest remained, staring after her with a perplexed expression.

Malach wasn't ready to return to his pallet in Koko's wagon. He felt almost as out of sorts as he did after Nikola turned up at the Arx.

"Where's the wine?" he demanded.

Alexei didn't reply. He seemed lost in thought. Malach stalked over to the supply wagon and rummaged around until he found a bottle of something. He uncorked it and took a swig. The strong anise flavor seared his tongue, but he managed to get it down. Heat bloomed in his chest. He leaned against the wagon.

"First," he said to no one, "they claim my ancestors were holy-rolling wizards. Now it's some snake boy who hated his mother." The second gulp went down a little easier. "What a flaming load of bullshit."

"Maybe not."

He regarded the priest. The blue eyes seemed frighteningly alert now.

"Have you heard of Sinjali's Lance?" Alexei asked.

Malach walked over and sank down in the next camp chair. He handed over the bottle. The priest took a sip and coughed violently.

Malach laughed. "Have some more. Don't worry, your mouth will start to go numb."

Alexei gave him a doubtful look but tipped it to his lips again. He took a long swallow, eyes watering. "Saints," he croaked.

"It's good, isn't it?" Malach retrieved the bottle, cradling it between his knees.

"Sinjali's Lance," Alexei reminded him.

"Of course I know it. Lezarius kept Balaur locked up there."

"Well, it was built by the Praefators—"

"Not those bastards, I'm begging you."

"Just listen." Alexei eyed him seriously, as if he was about to impart some secret, mind-blowing knowledge. "It isn't just a *tower*. The whole construction works like a giant prism, splitting the ley into three streams. Blue, liminal, and red."

"You're shitting me," Malach replied without much interest.

"No. But that's not all. It was build on top of something much older. I mean *ancient*."

That got his attention. "What?"

"I went inside. The walls are covered in Wards. Not our Wards." He cleared his throat. "I mean . . . not the Curia's. Someone else's."

The wind picked up, stirring the embers of the fire. Gooseflesh dimpled Malach's exposed skin. "Hold on," he said, jogging to the wagon and returning with two blankets. They dragged their chairs nearer to the ring of stones. Alexei added another log of *bokang*. The wood burned as hot as coal but with almost no smoke. They settled the blankets around their shoulders and passed the bottle around again.

"Well, this is cozy," Malach said with a toothy smile.

Alexei raised the bottle in a mock salute. "You're right, mage. I don't even taste it anymore."

Between the roaring blaze and the alcohol, Malach felt warm inside and out. Enough to face whatever Alexei was about to tell him.

The priest held up a gloved finger. "Wasn't me that found it," he said. "It was the Reborn."

"The what?"

"The children." Alexei shook his head. "They're really weird."

"You mean the dead-not-dead ones?"

"Yeah. I think they're happy though, so that's good."

"How can you tell?"

"They smile a lot. Well, one does. His name is Will Danziger."

They paused to swap the bottle back and forth.

"So the Reborn found this . . . what?" Malach prompted.

"Big room." Alexei held his arms wide. "Big, big room. With symbols everywhere. Couldn't read them though." He frowned. "So . . . okay, remember the part in the story about the Serpent building a dwelling in the mountains?" He stabbed a finger at Malach with a knowing look. "*Yeah.*"

"I see your point." He tilted his head. "Or it could just be a very old big room with stuff in another language."

"No, no. I was *there.*"

The priest definitely sounded tipsy. Who wasn't? But he seemed certain.

"Will told me they were meant to keep something out," Alexei said in a ruminative tone. "Or something *in.* It worried me. There was power in that place."

Sparks danced like fireflies in the blackness. "Are you saying you believe all that about the Serpent and the Dragon?" Malach asked.

"Maybe not exactly. But what if some version of it *is* true?" He laughed. "I can't say I have a better explanation for why the two of us are sitting here right now. For why the ley exists. For why those things called you the Morning Star—"

Malach made a rude noise, though his heart was suddenly pounding. He had avoided thinking of the Mahadeva, but she, too, claimed he had some destiny to fulfill. Did she know all of this?

Morning Star. His own child had the ability to "talk" to the heavens, as she put it. Half her blood came from him. The other half from a witch. That's what Nikola was—he had no choice but to accept it.

Malach tipped the bottle back and was surprised to find it empty. He lowered it with a sigh.

"None of this does me any good," he pointed out. "I just want my daughter back. That's all."

"I know. For what it's worth, Falke should never have taken her. It was wrong." The priest covered a yawn. "But he's a total shit, so there you go."

Malach eyed him with surprise. "Isn't he your Pontifex?"

"Not anymore. I serve Lezarius now." His brows lowered. "Whom Falke tried to kill."

Even drunk, he said *whom*, Malach thought with wonder.

"We're out of alcohol," he remarked sadly, patting the bottle.

"S'okay," Alexei said. "I can't feel my legs anyway."

"Well, I'm glad we had this chat." He smiled, and for no reason at all, the hard kernel of rage in his chest flared to life. "Oh, and if you ever hurt my sister, I'll cut your balls off and feed them to you."

There was a brief delay as the priest processed this statement. He tried to leap to his feet and succeeded in toppling the folding chair. "You're the one who strangled her," he shouted furiously.

He writhed for a moment like a turtle on its back. Malach's smirk died as he managed to hook a foot around the camp chair. One quick jerk and he joined Alexei on the ground, just in time to catch a fist to the nose. Malach licked blood from his upper lip. *Nothing like a little brawl before bedtime.*

He was about to swing back when Koko loomed above them, a folded fan in her hand.

"Ow," Malach grumbled, rubbing the crown of his head.

"That's what you get." She pointed the fan at Alexei. "Say you're sorry. Both of you!"

They stared at each other. Malach's anger faded as swiftly as it had come. It was never directed at the priest anyway. He'd just been a convenient target.

"I'm sorry," Malach said. "I shouldn't have said that."

Alexei nodded, eyes glazed. "S'okay."

"Come on." He rose and hauled the priest to his feet. Koko gave a nod of approval, watching warily as he slung an arm under Alexei's shoulders and walked him to Karl's wagon. Alexei fell into his bunk, gave Malach an absent wave, and began to snore immediately. Karl was already out cold. After a moment, Malach tossed a blanket over Alexei's body.

"You're bleeding," Koko said when he returned.

He touched his nose. "It'll stop in a minute."

"Why do you fight with him?"

"Because I am angry."

"About the story. You think I don't know?"

She wore a belted robe, her strong, angular features clean of make-up. He smelled a hint of the lemony cream she rubbed into her skin every night.

"About many things," Malach admitted.

They walked together to the wagon. He sat at the vanity as she dipped a sponge in water and cleaned him up. There was a great deal Malach would have liked to say to her, but he lacked the words.

"I enjoy the poems you speak tonight," he told her.

"One must know when to make to make people cry and when to make them laugh," she replied.

"I don't do . . . none of these things." He knew his grammar was atrocious. "I only make people hate me."

Koko studied him. "Now you feel sorry for yourself."

"Yes," he agreed stubbornly.

"Well, I won't tell Hassan what happened. If you behave." She ruffled his hair. "But no more fighting. Lucy must look pretty when she goes on stage."

Malach stared hard at her. Koko had a tiny smile. He couldn't tell if she was making fun. His pulse beat faster.

"Are you saying yes?"

She hung her robe on a hook and crawled into bed. "I think maybe you need to be somebody else, angel boy." She blew out the candle. "Even for a little while."

Chapter Eleven

Malach woke the next morning with his skull throbbing like a bad tooth. Karl was already up and gone. Sunlight invaded the flimsy curtains like an aggressive army breaching the walls. He tugged on a clean *shawb* and found Alexei nursing a cup of tea next to the ashes of the fire. The priest seemed in a similar state. He winced when one of the guards bellowed with laughter.

"What happened to your face?" he asked, studying Malach with bloodshot eyes.

"Tripped going up the steps." Malach jerked his chin at the wagon.

Alexei gave a sympathetic nod. "I don't even remember how I got into bed."

Perfect.

Malach filled a glass with tea. His stomach rebelled at the bitter liquid, but it washed away the vile taste in his mouth. They sat in silence for a few minutes, more miserable than awkward. The tension that wired his nerves tripwire-taut whenever the former knight came near had vanished.

Through the fog of his hangover, it occurred to Malach that part of the reason was because his identity was dissolving like smoke in a brisk Novander wind. He was a mage who couldn't touch the ley. The sister whose death had stoked his hatred for thirty years was in fact alive and well. He'd turned his back on Beleth, the only person who'd ever seemed to give a fig for his wellbeing. The love of his life turned out to be a witch, and he was better at caring for small children than occupying a city.

Malach remembered every word Alexei had said the night before. How he wanted to dismiss it all as mystical nonsense! None of it had anything do with him, although Hassan clearly believed otherwise.

After they broke camp, he went back to bed. Koko mixed some concoction that nearly made him vomit, but it erased the dull ache behind his eyes. He slept like the dead, waking when she gently shook his shoulder.

"We have arrived," she said, wrinkling her broad nose. "When we reach the caravanserai, you will take a proper bath, Malach. It smells like a wine sink in here."

His stomach rumbled. "Food," he agreed. "Then bath. Then bed again."

She laughed. "That bottle you finished? It is for one small glass only. You're lucky to be alive."

"What do you call it?"

"Azo. It has a little scorpion inside." Koko laughed harder at his expression. "You didn't see it?"

"The glass is green. Too dark."

"We call it getting stung by the Azo. Now you are a true Masdari."

He sat up and pushed the curtain aside. Marath sat on a high plateau. The spine of a mountain range rose up to the east.

"That is the Jabal Harawat," Koko explained. "The Camel's Hump. It goes from Qur, a little port town at the top of Barbaroi, to the city of Marath. About five hundred Imperial leagues."

"How far in kilometers?"

She gave a careless shrug. "I don't do math."

The view on the other side of the wagon was the same monotonous desert he had seen for the last two weeks.

"How far does that go?" Malach wondered.

"Very far. To the western edge of the continent." She spoke a phrase he had trouble deciphering. *Ramaj Balanaya.*

"Ramaj is sands," he repeated, puzzling it out. "What is the other?"

"Without end."

"Ah."

"It is where you fell from the sky," Koko said, speaking slowly and using her hands to show him. "Somewhere in the middle. If you had walked in any other direction than the one you chose, you would never have found us, understand?"

Malach felt a chill. "I understand."

"Nobody goes into the Ramaj Balanaya. We met you at the edge." She eyed him in a way he didn't much like. "Very lucky."

"I cannot touch the ley," he blurted out. Their word for it was, of course, *masdar.* The root.

She tilted her head.

"I have a stone." He touched his abdomen. "Here. Kaldurite."

Her brows lifted. "Ah."

"Witches put it in me." He stood and paced, restless as the caged tiger on his left thigh. "So it is not the ley! I no use it. So it *is* luck, yes?" He patted his chest. "I have great luck always."

An utter lie, but Koko just nodded serenely. "Sure, Malach."

She began to pack her travel bag for the caravanserai, choosing her favorite cosmetics and shaking out a curly red wig.

"No, *I am sorry*?" he demanded.

She frowned over her shoulder. "For what?"

"Me!"

Her face softened. "You miss the ley?"

"Very much." Something occurred to him. "Do you see it, Koko?"

She looked startled at the question. "Of course. All around."

"With no Marks?"

"Obviously."

"Could you use it?"

Now she seemed shocked. "No! That is for very few only."

"Why?"

"It is the will of the Alsakhan." She made a shooing motion. "Better you cannot touch it here. Get us all in trouble. Now find my blue dress. And fold it nicely this time!"

An hour later, they were rolling into the city of Marath.

Luba had been a sandy blur. Everyone said it was a backwater anyway, with little to recommend it. But Marath . . . Malach felt a rush of gratitude to be back in civilization. People thronged the stone-paved streets, all wearing long robes and *kufyas* to shield them from the sun. The cloth was either black or white, but most also wore splashes of red and yellow, either on the sash, hem or along the sleeves. The colors of Marath.

Alexei had attempted to explain the different manners of dress and what it all meant. He was like a walking encyclopedia—and equally interesting. Malach had drifted off during most of the lectures. He couldn't begin to imagine what it must be like to live inside the man's head. Bryce was so prone to reverie, it was a miracle he'd managed to survive all those tours in the Void.

But the priest had another side, Malach reminded himself. The one who'd saved his ass at the khedive's palace and managed to land a punch even blind drunk. The warning *He isn't to be underestimated* automatically popped up, but it had no weight now.

Unlikely as it seemed, they'd forged their own Cold Truce and it was actually holding.

Heavy traffic—donkeys, carts, curtained palanquins, even the odd dusty automobile—slowed them to a crawl. The spicy, greasy smells of the food vendors set Malach's mouth watering. He wondered if he could haggle out the window for a kebab.

"Jawan," he said to Koko, rubbing his stomach. "You have money?"

She handed him a dry biscuit from her purse. Malach eyed it sulkily.

"We eat soon," she promised. "But it insults the master of the caravanserai to dine on street food first."

"But he never knows," Malach protested.

She raised her fan in a mock threat. He bit into the biscuit, chewing with a disgruntled air that Koko pretended not to notice.

Malach watched with regret as the busy, hodgepodge commercial district fell behind and the wagons entered a more stately area of whitewashed manor houses. They looked plain from the outside, but he caught glimpses of lush, hidden gardens beyond the walls. The caravan finally pulled into a courtyard, a very busy one. A dozen small boys dashed around, seeing to the arriving and departing guests. Malach feared they would be left waiting, but when Hassan stepped from his wagon, the innkeeper rushed up to greet him personally, bowing and scraping as if the Imperator herself had just descended.

He was a short, balding man with widely spaced, thickly-lashed brown eyes that looked perpetually anxious.

"Welcome, welcome," he said, bobbing his head. "My roof is yours, Blessed."

"You honor us," Hassan replied graciously. He looked tired. As though he, too, had not slept well.

"It is I who is honored," the innkeeper said as Hassan

kissed his cheeks. He lowered his voice. "But I have not yet inspected your rooms to ensure all is perfect! I was not expecting you for another two days."

"I'm sure they are fine."

"But if you don't mind waiting——"

"Do not trouble yourself. We are weary from the journey and would see them straight away."

He washed his hands together. "Of course, of course."

The company was whisked through a series of elegant antechambers, pausing only to leave shoes at the front door. The innkeeper did a quick head count and informed them, nearly in tears, that he had not expected two additional members of the party and the caravanserai was full up.

"You shall take my own rooms," he declared, palming sweat from his thinning black hair. "It is no trouble, no trouble at all——"

"We have shared bunks before," Hassan interrupted, eyeing a question at Koko and Karl, who wore the big straw hat he always donned when the sun was high.

"That is fine," Karl said, smiling at Alexei.

Koko met Hassan's gaze. "Lucy is my daughter now," she said. "It is tradition that she stay with me."

Shock crossed Hassan's face. Something unspoken passed between them. He was the first to turn away, faint spots of color burning his cheeks.

Alexei had followed the exchange. He wore the faraway look of a man trying to figure something out beyond his pay grade. Farasha and Kareem, who were lovers, swapped a quick whisper. All eyes watched Hassan.

"Well," he said, clearing his throat. "It seems there is no problem, then."

The innkeeper bowed with obvious relief and escorted them to the second floor. He said something about lunch, though Malach missed most of it.

The rooms were all adjacent to each other and had balconies facing a walled garden. Hassan went straight into his bedchamber, closing the door hard. Malach carried the suitcase into his and Koko's room, barely noticing the furnishings. He went out to the balcony and leaned his forearms on the balustrade, gazing at the mountains beyond. A cooling breeze swept across the plateau.

"Hassan is angry," he said to Koko, who was putting her things away in a spacious wardrobe.

"Yes, but I will speak with him."

"I don't want to make problems."

Koko checked her face in the compact mirror, powdered the tiny beads of perspiration on her nose, and came out to the balcony. She'd discarded her wig. The sunlight picked out glints of copper in her curly hair.

"Hassan thinks it is a game for you," Koko said. "That you are not serious."

Malach was quiet for a moment. "I am a man. I see myself this way. But it is not everything I am, understand?"

She nodded encouragingly.

"I have no fear to see what else is inside. *Who* else."

Koko smiled. "Then I help you find her."

He loosened his robe to show her the Broken Chain around his neck. "This is the Mark of the Via Libertas. It means freedom. I have . . . how you say sister of mother?"

"Aunt."

"Yes. She teaches me many things." He laughed. "Not a nice lady"— this time he made sure to pronounce the word correctly —"but strong. One thing she teaches is to hide nothing. To fear nothing. No part of, er . . .." He touched his forehead.

"The mind."

"Yes. And the heart. All is welcome. To be looked at and . . . taken in?"

"Embraced."

"So I would try this thing." He shrugged. "See what I feel."

"Every person has both male and female inside," Koko said. "For most, one is stronger. Some, like Hassan, are in perfect balance. I have very little masculine spirit. Since I was a young child, I knew this. But there is a reason the Alsakhan gave me this body. Life is struggle. Sometimes you must look deep inside to know who you really are."

"I already travel a long way," Malach smiled. "In the world, yes, but also in myself. I change much. But there is always more to find."

She laughed. "That is true. Lucy will give one performance. Unless she joins the company?"

Malach knew she was teasing now. He made a face of regret. "I look for my daughter. Important."

Koko sobered. "And you will get her back." She touched her breast. "This I believe."

He rested his head on her shoulder, comforted by the soft warmth of her cotton robe—and the kindness of the woman beneath. "Thank you," he whispered.

Koko laid her cheek against his hair. Then she tilted his stubbled jaw up to face her. "But first, we must discover your talent. Can you sing?"

"Yes, I like singing, but only for me." He belted out a snatch of a drinking ditty that made her wince.

"Hmmm. No stories or poems. You cannot speak well enough yet. Ideas?"

"I can dance."

"Good?"

Malach smiled. "Very good."

Koko grinned back. "Show me."

SEVERAL HOURS LATER, Malach lay in a sunken bath up to his chin, eyes half closed. He felt sore in unfamiliar places— it had been years since he'd attempted a full split—but he thought Koko was pleased.

She had spoken to Hassan. Despite Malach's pestering, she refused to repeat what was said, but when they all sat down to eat, Hassan had greeted him politely. The others followed his lead.

Even though Koko was his mentor, Malach had been adopted by the entire company. Each had a piece of advice to offer, an item of clothing or piece of jewelry to lend. Alexei seemed unsure what to make of it all, though he choked on his wine when he heard Lucy's full name.

Hassan still harbored reservations. Malach could see it in his eyes. Had he wanted to put a stop to it, he could have. Koko enjoyed her own special authority, but he was their unquestioned leader.

Malach wondered why he didn't. Whatever the reason, it only reinforced his determination to prove that he was serious.

To *dazzle*.

At the end of supper, Hassan, who had been mostly quiet, volunteered to choreograph the routine. Malach understood the honor he was being shown and had a minor attack of nerves. If he was to be one of them—at the Imperator's gala, no less—he would carry the entire troupe's reputation on his shoulders.

But he *was* a good dancer. It was not so different from fighting. You had to be quick and nimble and utterly focused —but willing to improvise. He'd always danced at Beleth's parties. His visits to Novostopol usually included an after-hours club or two.

Now Hassan and Koko were locked up in Hassan's room, plotting together. Malach wondered if Balaur would be in Qeddah. He both dreaded and longed to see his child again, but that was a separate problem.

He heard the outer door open and close softly.

"I am thinking," he called into the next room. "I should practice to walk in . . . " *Heels?* "Tall shoes. Very bad to fall down. What size you wear?"

No answer came. He sat up, peering through the archway into the dark room beyond. "Koko?"

An arrow pierced his gut, burying deep. Malach gasped and pressed a hand against his belly. The pain took his breath away, but he saw . . . nothing.

No arrow. No knife.

Just a crimson thread rising from the center of his navel. It tinted the bathwater pink.

"Hello, Malach."

The voice was cool, smug. Pewter eyes gazed down at him from a round face framed by long russet hair.

Darya.

Something tore loose inside him. It scraped past his ribs, then up the back of his throat. A hoarse croak came from his mouth. Tears stung his eyes as it slid across his tongue and into her waiting hand.

For the first time in months, Malach saw the ley. Shimmering currents of light flowing across the tiles. He'd forgotten how beautiful it was.

Darya's other hand opened. It cradled a ruby, vibrant as a beating heart against her white skin. Power sparked in the gem and he slammed back against the marble tub.

The witch's plump mouth twisted in a smile. "You wonder why my spells work against you?"

The kaldurite lay nestled in her palm, slick with blood.

His blood.

Malach lunged, sending a wave over the edge. Every Mark flared red. He met an invisible wall. Then the sensation of giant hands on his shoulders, shoving him down. The bathwater closed over his head. He thrashed, fingers groping for purchase on the slick marble. Abyssal ley pumped through his veins. It sharpened his rage to a razor's edge.

The lithomancy was stronger. It buried him under a landslide.

His chest ached. Black spots pulsed before his eyes. He distantly heard her laughing.

Darya. The one he suspected had waited a few extra minutes when he was screaming under Dr. Fithen's scalpel.

Just to teach him a lesson.

The shimmering spots merged into a long, gray tunnel. Malach knew he was seconds from blacking out. Even with his power back, he was no match for her.

I'm about to drown in a fucking bathtub, he thought with disbelief.

And then he felt it.

Her attention wavered. Only for a split second, but Malach grabbed his chance. A hair-fine tendril of abyssal ley wormed through a crack in the wall she'd built, coiling around one foot. Darya lost her balance on the wet floor. She tumbled into the bath. He locked an arm around her neck and rolled them both to the side. His head broke the surface. Malach sucked in a gulp of air. Water coursing down his face, still half-blind, he seized her will with a crushing grip that left no possibility of resistance.

Yet she did fight him. *Hard.* He caught one wrist as it tried to delve into the pouch at her waist. Bent her fingers back. Red ley poured from his skin, sinking into her flesh and then her mind.

The witch finally went limp.

He shook wet hair from his face and glanced past her. Koko stood in the archway, shock on her face.

"Help me," he croaked.

She hurried forward and heaved him upright. He sat hunched over with bent knees, ragged gasps tearing from his chest.

"Is she dead?" Koko whispered.

Darya floated on her back. Her silver eyes were open and staring at the ceiling.

Malach shook his head. "Find Hassan," he rasped. "And Bryce."

Koko touched her throat and made the starburst sign. She hurried off, locking the door behind her.

As he should have done in the first place.

Malach palpated his abdomen with shaking hands. The skin wasn't broken except for a tiny pinprick in his navel. The pain was already receding.

Darya had only removed the stone so she could kill him. A gamble she'd lost.

"Get up," Malach commanded.

Her head turned at his voice. She sat in the tub, docile as a child, while he stripped her of every stone, every scrap of metal on her person. Rings and earrings. Bracelets and anklets and buttons and coins. The pins in her hair. He even made her open her mouth and looked beneath her tongue.

Malach made a pile of them next to the bath. Then he got out and dried himself off, still shaky. It was always disorienting to feel the abyssal ley after long deprivation. He felt hot and cold. Starving and full. Horny and angry and afraid and too many other emotions to bother analyzing.

He was pulling a clean robe over his head when Hassan burst in, followed by Koko and Alexei. The priest took in the scene with soldierly calm. Hassan let out a stream of curses.

"Will more witches be coming after you?" he asked.

"Probably." Malach scooped up the mound of gems and stuffed them in his pocket.

Hassan swore again. He turned to Darya. She sat motionless in the tub, her face a perfect blank. "Why is she like that?"

"Because he controls her mind," Alexei said. "It's called compulsion. I've seen it many times. It is a thing the malak can do."

Hassan raised an unsteady hand to his forehead. "This is a disaster."

"It is not his fault," Koko exclaimed. "She tried to murder him! I walked in and saw it happening."

Hassan met Malach's eye. "I am not angry with *you*. And I am relieved you are well. But this witch used a lot of ley against you, yes? And then you used it against her in self-defense?"

Malach worked his way through the complex sentence. "You mean—"

"Yes," Hassan snapped. "The authorities will come to investigate. Are you using the ley now?"

"No. I released it."

"Good. Do not touch it again!"

"I won't, I swear."

"We must get rid of this witch." Hassan began to pace up and down. "Perhaps the hawks did not notice. Perhaps—"

He cut off as a hard knock came at the door.

Chapter Twelve

"Keep quiet," Hassan hissed.

He pulled Koko from the bathroom, shutting the door behind them. Alexei pressed an ear to the wood. He was relieved to hear the innkeeper's voice, though not the news he brought.

"The priests are here!" their host said breathlessly. "I am so sorry, Blessed. They are going door to door, questioning everyone."

"But why have they come?" Hassan asked, sounding more curious than concerned.

"They claim someone interfered with the ley. Can you imagine? It *must* be a mistake."

Hassan expressed astonishment and assured him that of course they would cooperate. "But tell me, brother. Is it the Breath of God?"

"No, thank the Root," the innkeeper replied with feeling. "Just the priests from the khedive's household."

Alexei knew he meant the khedive of Marath, not Luba, but it was still bad.

"We were just sharing a glass of wine before bed. I'll return to my own room and await them there," Hassan said.

"I'm sure it will all be straightened out. Thank you for warning us."

An instant after the outer door closed, Hassan and Koko were back, looking grim.

"This is my fault," Malach said quickly. "What can I do?"

Hassan eyed the flooded bathroom. "Clean that up, for starters. You will both keep an eye on the witch. But you must not use the ley, understand? They will sense it."

Malach nodded.

"I thought you couldn't touch the ley," Koko said with a frown.

He pointed to a glittering stone that had rolled into the corner. "That's the kaldurite the witches put inside me. Darya removed it so she could drown me with the power."

Alexei crouched down, studying the kaldurite. "How long will the compulsion last?"

Darya blinked. She raised a hand to push weakly at the wet hair plastered across her face.

"It's wearing off already," Malach said to Alexei in their native tongue. "But if you put that stone against her skin, she'll be in the same state I was. I already took her gems away, but the kaldurite is an insurance policy."

Alexei picked up the stone. The instant he touched it, the ley vanished. It was so startling, he nearly dropped it.

"Get to work," Hassan said. "I must warn the others and get back to my own room."

Malach used towels to sop up the water from the floor. After a moment's hesitation, Alexei tucked the stone into one sleeve of the witch's tightly wrapped dress. Then they used a pair of Koko's stockings to tie her up. All too soon, voices echoed down the corridor.

"The wardrobe," Koko hissed.

Alexei threw open the doors and groaned at the tight space. But there was nowhere else to hide. Malach bent down to seize Darya's arm and she scooted back across the floor. The witch was aware now—and looked furious.

"Utter one syllable and we'll give you to the priests," Malach whispered. "They don't like witches, especially ones who break the law. I'll say you attacked me and I have witnesses to back it up."

Her mouth twisted, but she gave a nod. Malach stuffed her into the wardrobe and climbed in after. Alexei had just folded himself inside next to them when a sharp knock sounded on the door. Koko latched the wardrobe shut. Her footsteps moved to the door.

"Blessed." A male voice, cool but respectful.

"Thank the Root you're here," Koko said. "Is it true that someone dared to use the ley?"

"Have you seen or heard anything unusual tonight?"

"I've been in my room," she replied. "But earlier . . . I did see a woman in the courtyard. It was getting dark and hard to tell, but . . ."

"Go on, Blessed."

"She had strange eyes. I didn't get a close look, you understand."

"Strange how?"

"Silvery gray. Very unusual."

They were crushed so tightly against each other, Alexei felt Darya's breath hitch.

"When was this?"

"An hour or so ago."

"Can you describe her?"

"Only her eyes caught the light. She was young. Dark-haired. I am sorry, I wish I could remember more."

Koko's voice was sincere and persuasive, with a hint of fear. Alexei almost found himself believing the story.

"May we have a look inside? It is just a precaution. We are searching all the rooms."

"Oh, certainly! It would set my mind at ease."

Alexei waited tensely as the priests prowled around and asked a few more questions. At last, they departed.

"Leave her in there," Malach growled as they climbed out.

Koko cast a last worried look at the witch, then closed the wardrobe. A minute later, Hassan returned.

"What do we do with her?" he wondered. "We cannot let her go, but I will not condone murder."

"I don't want her dead," Malach said. "I want to find out what she knows."

"Here's what I propose," Alexei said. "The others don't know she failed. It should buy us a little time. If we run out in the middle of the night again, it'll look suspicious. But we can't bring her to the wagons in daylight. Someone would notice."

Malach nodded impatiently.

"We take her to the wagons now. Hide her there. Tomorrow, as early as possible, we all leave together. She can be hidden again at the gates. Once we're outside the city, we can decide what to do next."

"You're sure you can control her?" Hassan asked. "Without the ley?"

"Yes," Malach said confidently. "But what about the rest of the company?"

"I will speak with them." Hassan sounded weary. "They already know witches were after you. They will keep this secret."

"I'm so sorry," Malach said. "I should have left you before."

"No." Hassan laid a hand on his shoulder. "I knew there was a risk and made my choice to help you. And I am glad you have the ley back. You will need it for your child."

"I'll repay you somehow," Malach insisted.

Hassan's face softened. "There is no price between friends." His dark eyes glinted in the candlelight. "And I, too, am curious about what this witch might say."

They waited until it was certain the priests were gone. Then Malach and Alexei snuck her out through the garden. The wagons sat in lines in another dusty walled courtyard. They brought her to Hassan's and sat her on a pallet. She stared at them warily.

"Keep an eye on her," Alexei said.

"Where are you going?"

"Rope."

Malach frowned. "She's already tied up."

"Not like I'm going to do it."

The mage cocked a brow but said nothing more. Alexei rummaged through the supply wagon and returned with a coil of tent lines.

"Does she speak Osterlish?" he asked.

Malach nodded. Alexei walked up to the witch. She had a plump, rather sulky mouth, which was drawn into a tight line.

"I'm going to tie your hands and feet," he said mildly. "The harder you try to wiggle out of the rope, the tighter the knots will get. I'm warning you now, so it will be your own fault if that happens. I won't help you. Do you understand?"

She nodded.

"I need you to say it."

Her gray eyes narrowed. "Yes, I understand."

"First, your hands will go numb. If the circulation isn't restored, they'll turn purple. Then the tissue will die and you'll lose the limb. Do you understand?"

A nod. There was a hint of fear in her eyes now.

"Say it, please."

"Yes," she answered quickly. "I understand."

"Good," Alexei said in the same conversational voice. "Turn around."

He trussed her with a series of complex knots that were virtually impossible to get out of. Malach watched closely.

"You learned that in the Beatus Laqeuo," he said in a stony voice.

"I had to complete a special three-month training course."

"What else did they teach you?"

Alexei met his gaze. "Let's just say I'm grateful that I never used half of it."

When he finished tying her up, he dropped a pillowcase over her head. It wasn't tight. She'd be able to breathe without trouble, but it would muffle sound and enhance the feeling of total helplessness.

That accomplished, they left her lying on the pallet. Alexei sat on the wagon steps. Malach leaned against one wheel.

"Why did you make her say it?" he asked after a long silence.

"Compliance must be explicit. It gets the subject used to cooperating."

"Mind fuckery, in other words."

Alexei tensed. "Are you forgetting that *you* just mind-fucked her far beyond my own humble skills?"

"Not at all. Just drawing a comparison." His jaw tightened. "I should have assumed they'd track the stone. That was a stupid mistake."

"Should we get rid of it?"

"No. We need it. And if more of them come, I'll be ready this time."

"Was she in Nantwich?"

Alexei had hardly caught a glimpse of the chamber before he was hurled halfway across the world. He remembered seeing a few witches, but the faces were a blur.

"No," Malach said. "She must have come from Dur-Athaara."

"So we don't know how many are with Balaur?"

"Not yet. I didn't have time to ask." He looked up, face catching the moonlight. "I'm sorry about your brother."

Alexei didn't reply. The remark caught him completely off guard. They had never once discussed Misha, not since that first day. But the wound hadn't healed. Had barely scabbed over.

"I did mean to help him," Malach continued softly. "To ask the Mahadeva to remove my Mark. I think she would have done it. But then everything fell apart."

"Do you know what happened to him?" Alexei asked tightly. "After you turned him?"

"Not really."

"He stopped speaking. For four years."

Malach watched him cautiously. "That's an unusual reaction."

"Yes, I'd say so!" Alexei heard his voice rising, cutting through the still night, and tried to leash his temper. "Now he's . . . I don't what he is. But he's not himself."

"I said I was sorry and I meant it. I could have killed him. I chose not to. I thought I was—"

"Being merciful by driving him mad?"

Alexei stood abruptly. Malach took a step back, hands loose at his sides.

"It was the only other option available at the time. As for the Mark itself, your brother's own personality determines the outcome. I've given my Mark to dozens of people. Many are unchanged."

"The scumbags, you mean."

Malach looked affronted. "They're not scumbags." He tilted his head, reconsidering. "Well, a few, sure, but—

"I don't believe you. Nightmarks corrupt."

"Not always." Malach's voice was calm. "I don't know your brother like you do, but it's fair to say I couldn't have predicted it would affect him so badly. I already told all this to Lezarius."

He felt betrayed. "You talked to Lezarius? About Mikhail?"

Malach nodded. "He forgave me."

Alexei gave a bitter laugh. "He forgives everyone."

"It *is* one of the Five Virtues," Malach said dryly. "The first, I believe."

Forgiveness, compassion, courage, fidelity, and honesty. Alexei himself had broken each and every one of them—all in the service of a noble dream that seemed as good as dead.

Standing in the dark courtyard with the mage he had obsessed over for years, Alexei realized that half his fury had always been directed at his brother. Misha took Malach's Mark of his own free will. Everything that followed stemmed from that one spectacularly bad decision.

In hindsight, it was obvious. Alexei had shoved his anger down, buried it deep and hoped his Marks would make it go away. What else could he do? Scream at a mute psychiatric patient in white pajamas?

But it wasn't just that. It was all of it. The seven tours in the Void. His own bad decision to join the knights of Saint Jule.

"You were right," Alexei said heavily. "What you said on Kasia's roof that night. I haven't slept right since the war. I did things I'll never forget. Or forgive."

Malach shrugged. "We all did. That's how it was."

"No. The knights were supposed to be better."

Malach smiled faintly. "Were you? I guess I missed that part."

Alexei rubbed the Raven on his neck. "Falke wanted me to go after you, back in Novostopol. He offered to make me a captain if I'd return to the Void and hunt you down."

"I'm surprised you refused the offer."

"I was tired of doing his dirty work, so I went to Kvengard instead. The only problem was that I had Marks from Feizah. And Feizah was dead."

"I didn't kill her," Malach said. "Whatever they told you—"

"I know. My brother did."

The mage's brows shot up. "Seriously?"

"Kasia was there. She saw it."

Malach looked amazed. "I always wondered who it was . . . Not in a million years did I think of the pious Captain Bryce." His expression turned wary again. "Are you saying it's my fault?"

"No. He did it for Lezarius. It's a long story. My point is that I was in rough shape by the time I got to Kvengard."

"Mark sickness?"

Alexei nodded. "I was hallucinating. The whole gruesome package. I crashed my car."

Malach looked impressed.

"That's the first time I met Luk." Alexei gave a crooked smile. "Thanks, by the way, for putting the bastard out of everyone's misery."

"It was long overdue. Truth be told, I hated him from the moment I saw him. Sanctimonious prick." Malach rubbed his arms. "It's getting chilly."

Alexei stuck his head into the wagon. Darya was lying where they'd left her, knees drawn up tight. He grabbed a blanket and tossed it over her, then came back out.

"Can I ask you something?"

"Sure." Malach seemed more relaxed now.

"Why did you help me? Back in the desert? You blamed me for what happened to Rachel. Why not leave me there? No one would have known."

"For Kasia. But also because I knew it wasn't your fault. When we landed in the desert . . . I was *furious*. And you were the only one around to vent it on."

Alexei's laughter was the faintest puff of air. "I know how that is."

"I'm not sure you do." Malach tilted his head back and studied the stars. "Nikola's done with me. Rachel is all I have left. I did . . . something terrible when I found her. She hated me, rightfully so."

Alexei knew he was speaking of the starfall at the Arx.

"Sometimes I'd look at her and think she was the only good, pure thing left in this sorry world. That if I could just keep her safe, make her forgive me, nothing else would matter. And she finally did. Or I thought she did. Seeing her smile . . . it was like the sun coming out after a long, hard winter. But that might not even have been *her*."

Alexei had no idea what to say, so he kept his mouth shut.

"I want to believe it was my daughter that I held in my arms that morning. That Balaur was hiding. Waiting for his chance to seize control. But I don't *know*." He sighed. "All I know for certain is that I've failed her utterly, in every respect. If we'd never gone to Bal Agnar—"

"You might both be dead in the Morho," Alexei interrupted gently. "I won't say I condone all your decisions, but you made the right one in the end."

"Too late," Malach muttered.

"There was no way to know that what Balaur intended was even possible," Alexei said evenly. "And the witch-queen walled her away from him?"

Malach nodded. Sudden grief twisted his face. It was a moment before he spoke. "The last thing she did."

"Then you must have faith that Rachel lives and you'll get her back. *We'll* get her back."

Malach met his eyes. "Faith. I always hated that word. It felt like an empty promise." He smiled faintly. "A panacea, to quote Lezarius. But you're right. If I love her, I cannot give up hope."

The silence lengthened, Malach lost in his own thoughts. Alexei cleared his throat. "You guard the witch. I'll take first watch."

"Okay." Malach climbed the steps to the caravan. "Bryce?"

Alexei turned back.

"I'm glad you're here."

The caravanserai was quiet as Alexei checked the

perimeter of the wagons and walked a slow circuit around the buildings. He kept to the shadows, alert for anything out of place, but part of his mind wandered to Kasia. What would she have done when they vanished into thin air? Well, it was hardly a question. She'd come after them—if she knew where they'd gone. Would her cards lead her to Qeddah? If so, he hoped she had Patryk and Natalya with her.

It had only been a week or so, but he missed them all so much it hurt. After everything they'd been through together, he had to believe they'd be reunited someday.

Faith. A slender thread but better than none at all. He knew all too well the darkness that waited when the last spark of hope guttered. He'd neared that precipice more times than he could count, yet somehow he'd never crossed the threshold. In that, the mage was right. It was love that had always pulled him back.

The strangest part was that he actually felt relieved Malach had the ley again. Neither of them could use it without alerting the priests, but if their backs were against the wall . . .

When he judged a few hours had passed, they switched places. The witch lay on her side, chest rising and falling in even breaths, but he couldn't tell if she was really asleep.

At last, the first fingers of dawn painted the sky a soft rose-quartz. Malach returned as the caravanserai shook itself awake. Sleepy-eyed boys tumbled outside and began to lead camels and horses from their quarters to the courtyard. The Blessed were among the first guests to depart. Koko brought a loaf of current bread and goat cheese, which they ate as the wagons rolled through the city.

At Alexei's insistence, Darya, too, was given food and water. She ate with brisk composure and said nothing when he retied her hands and feet. The witch had heeded his advice not to struggle. Other than a little chafing at her wrists and ankles, she was unharmed.

At the city gates, they hid her under a blanket, but the guards simply waved the wagons through. The Blessed enjoyed high rank and no one troubled them.

When Marath lay two hours behind, Hassan called a stop in a shaded gully. The traffic on the road had dwindled. They hadn't seen a Markhawk since the city limits.

"We will be in Qeddah soon," he said. "If you wish to question her with the ley, now is the time."

"You'll have to take the stone away," Malach said to Alexei. "Would you mind? I . . . I don't wish to touch it."

He nodded and plucked the kaldurite from her sleeve. This time, he slipped it into his own pocket. It still blocked the ley. The sensation was like being in the Void. Not unpleasant. Just . . . quiet. Peaceful.

Darya flinched at Malach's touch, but then her face went smooth. The pupils of her eyes dilated as if she'd just been hit with a massive dose of Sublimin.

"Where is my daughter?" he demanded.

"The Isle of Dreams."

He scowled. "No riddles—"

"It is a real place," Hassan interrupted. "I have been there countless times. The Imperator's palace is there, as well as the embassies."

Malach turned back to Darya. "How many other witches are involved?"

"Two. Heshima and Bethen."

"Can they find you?"

"No."

"Can they find the kaldurite?"

"No."

"Why not?"

"The spell that held it inside you is broken. It is just a stone now."

Some of the tension left Alexei's shoulders. One less problem to worry about.

"Could you force Balaur from Rachel's body?" Malach asked.

She hesitated. "I could break the spell that contains him to her vessel. That is the first step."

His frown deepened at the word *vessel*. "What would the second be?"

"I'm not sure. If her will was strong, she might do it herself. But she is just a child. I do not know how to reach her."

"But you could lead me to them."

"Yes," she agreed, "I could do that."

Hassan shared a look with Koko. "It will not be hard to bring you to the Isle of Dreams," he said. "We perform there tomorrow night."

Malach nodded. "Then let us have the meat of it. Why did Balaur come here? What is his interest in the Masdar League? And what is *your* interest in aiding him?"

Alexei leaned forward. Hassan pulled his robe tighter, face intent.

The tale she told, in a voice devoid of emotion, left Alexei stunned. Yet he remembered the book he had given to Kasia. *Der Cherubinischer Wandersmann by Angelus Silesius.* The picture at the end of the Dawn City.

The witch believed her deity was there—which did not make it true. But Balaur seemed to believe it, too.

"They're all crazy," Malach muttered.

He released the compulsion. The witch sagged back, her jaw slack.

Hassan rose to his feet. "I must think on this."

Alexei tried to read his expression. Concern, yes, but also a certain lack of surprise.

"Did you know any of that?" Malach demanded.

Hassan met his gaze coolly. "I collect old stories. But I did not know the City of Dawn was a god's prison."

"Nor did I," Koko breathed. "Can it be true?"

"Either way, it changes nothing," Malach said firmly. "Not for me. I don't care what the witches do. Balaur is my problem. I can assure you that whatever he told them, it's a lie. Let me rid the world of him, and you can handle the rest as you see fit."

A call came from outside. One of the guards stuck his head through the door. "Travelers," he said shortly. "Headed this way."

"Then let us continue on," Hassan said. "With haste." He shot a look at Malach. "If you *are* the Morning Star come again, then we are bound to you as surely as we are to the ley. For that is the true Covenant." His perfect face might have been carved from stone as he added grimly, "May the Alsakhan save us all."

Chapter Thirteen

Nikola held the boy's hand.

The small fingers, with their ragged, dirty nails, still felt warm. He had lapsed into unconsciousness hours before. A mercy, considering his injuries.

Caralexa finally left to get some rest. So did Patryk and Natalya, after Nikola assured them there was nothing more to do. Others came and went. Paarjini and Kasia. Valdrian. Even Cairness, who attempted to cast a spell of protection.

"I thought the ley couldn't be used to heal," Nikola said quietly.

The witch looked at her. "Tha' is true." Her gaze settled on Tristhus. For once, Nikola saw no animosity, just sadness. "But I try anyway."

If the spell did anything, Nikola couldn't tell.

Dawn had to come soon. But she knew from long years working the night shift at the Arx that it was the hour just before sunrise when the soul—if such a thing existed—often snapped its tether. Once she'd found an elderly bishop sitting in his armchair by the hearth. His body was already cool, but he had passed of natural causes with a peaceful expression on his face.

Not like the child lying before her, the sheet pulled to his chest just below the Broken Chain Mark on his collarbone. His lips were bloodless. Dark lashes fanned across chalk-white cheeks. Even asleep, pain tightened his face.

"He's dying, isn't he?"

They were the first words Sydonie had spoken in hours. She'd cried and howled when Nikola combed her hair, but ever since the attack, the girl had retreated behind a wall, stoic and dry-eyed.

"I don't know," Nikola lied.

"Yes, he is. He'll die and leave me like everyone else does."

"I won't leave you, Syd. I promise."

The child's stare was chilling. "I can take care of myself."

Alice nosed her knee, sensing her distress. Syd's features twisted in sudden rage. "It's *your* fault. Stupid dog!"

She slapped Alice's flank. The hound whimpered in confusion and pressed her tail between her legs. Syd's face crumpled. She dropped to the floor and threw her arms around Alice's neck. "I'm sorry! I didn't mean it!"

The dam burst. She wept bitter tears, pressing her cheek to the dog's dark coat. Nikola watched the scene with a numbness born of exhaustion and despair. It was wrong, all wrong. Tristhus had saved Alice's life, heedless of his own. Despite his posturing, he was just a lonely little boy. A brave one, too.

Was this the lesson? Show kindness and suffer for it?

Something snapped inside Nikola, too. Her jaw set.

"No," she muttered. "I won't allow it."

Syd looked up as Nikola drew the sheet back. She lifted the child in her arms. He weighed so little.

"What are you doing?" Syd asked, wiping her face.

"Taking him below. To the Mother."

Terror sparked in the girl's eyes. "Is he . . .?"

Nikola shook her head. "Not yet, but soon. I need your help."

Something in her voice silenced Syd's questions. She

opened the cabin door and followed Nikola down the companionway. There was a watch on deck, but everyone below was in their bunks. They entered the cargo hold, winding through crates of raw ore, chests of gems, and stores of food.

Nikola kicked aside a folded sailcloth, revealing the secret hatch. Syd struggled with it for a moment, then drew a knife and pried up the edge. Nikola maneuvered herself and the boy into the crawlspace.

"No one comes down here, understand?" she said. "Now close the hatch behind me."

Sydonie nodded. She gripped Alice's thick ruff with one hand. The hound's eyes shone like gold coins in the dim light. Then the panel slid shut, leaving Nikola in perfect darkness.

Crawling on hands and knees, she dragged the boy to the corner where the Mahadeva lay with Ashvi. He made not a sound. She hoped he was beyond pain. She sat against the wall, cradling him in her arms, head resting on her shoulder.

Malach had been healed from mortal wounds once. To her knowledge, he was the only person ever cured with ley. It was done in the grotto back in Dur-Athaara, but Nikola did not think that mattered. The power was the same. She gripped the serpent's eye stone around her neck.

"Valmitra," she whispered. "I know you thought Malach was important and that is why you intervened. This child is . . . not special. Not in the same way. But I need to have hope. To believe that you are good. If you have the ability to spare him, I beg you to do it." She hesitated. "I ... I will do anything you ask."

The darkness was absolute. She felt the boy's pulse, thready and weak. Doubt set in, gnawing with blunt, remorseless teeth. Had she chosen the wrong words? Given offense with her hubris? She debated the wisdom of taking a grievously injured child from his own bed. Wondered how Sydonie would react when Nikola returned with her brother's lifeless body.

It was she who had allowed them to come aboard. She who'd given the nod to Captain Aemlyn when the children appeared at the last minute, running along the dock at Nantwich. What the holy hell had she been thinking?

At least they knew the Morho Sarpanitum. They could have survived there. But Nikola had brought them on a hopeless quest, against an array of ruthless enemies, thinking like an idiot that it was the right thing to do.

She cursed herself and she cursed Jamila al-Jabban.

When she ran out of curses, she dabbled her toes in an ocean of other regrets. But that was not the way to the Mother.

Nikola knew better. She stilled her racing thoughts. After a time, the sounds of the ship faded. The wooden hull against her back grew moist. She touched it and found cool stone.

Like the deep shaft in the sea cliffs where she had once sat as a novice, waiting for her namestone.

Nikola laid her cheek against the boy's hair. Her eyes slid shut.

She stood in a great hall. Flaming runes covered the walls, but they were so distant the symbols seemed like tiny sparks in the darkness. A huge serpent lay coiled in the center of the chamber. Each scale resonated with a different frequency of ley. Nikola recognized the signatures of the base metals—copper, lead, and nickel. Tin, aluminum, and zinc. Gold, silver, and platinum. Others that were rarer still.

The snake was in the process of shedding its skin. All around sat mountains of gems and crystals. There was a continuous soft tinkling as more flaked off from the crevices between her scales.

She had three necks, though only two ended in heads. The third was a scarred stump, the flesh around it withered and gray. White light flowed from the other two mouths, pulsing with each breath. It flowed upward, carrying the treasure hoard at a languid pace toward the roof far above.

Nikola stood still, watching the jewels float, weightless as dandelion fluff. It was peaceful here. Beyond the reach of time or human suffering. She had a strong urge to lie down and rest in those ancient coils. To close her eyes and never open them again.

But she was a witch now and she recognized the heavy enchantments laid upon this place. Nikola shook off her lethargy and went forward until she was an arm's length away from the serpent.

"Wake up, Mother," she said boldly.

Valmitra did not stir.

Nikola reached out and touched one of the mighty jaws, which were slightly ajar. The skin was cool and rough beneath her hand. The serpent's eyes were beautiful, lustrous gold with a dark, round pupil. But they were empty of awareness. She felt a sudden rush of pity to see such a powerful being laid so low.

"Mother," she pleaded. "Please wake. We need you!"

Nikola stooped to pick up a fiery carnelian, thinking she might take a whack at the binding spells, but her fingers passed through it. She was not truly in this place. Yet she must be here for a reason. If she could not rouse Valmitra, perhaps she could take something else. Some small part of her.

The serpent's heads were so large that even though the jaws opened a mere crack, Nikola thought she might be able to fit her own skull inside the cavity. Before she could second-guess the wisdom of this approach, she pushed her face between the mighty fangs. The snake's indrawn breath whispered through her hair. The forked tongue gave a tiny flicker. It rasped against her chin. Here, inside the Mother, the planes joined.

When the long, languid exhale came, Nikola opened her own mouth and drew Valmitra's breath deep into her chest. A tingling sensation ran through her, like a dip in an icy river. She withdrew her head. Then she kissed the slumbering giant on one nose.

"Thank you, Mother," she said softly. "I will return for you."

After some searching, she found a narrow crevice leading upward. Nikola crawled through a twisted labyrinth of shafts, always seeking those that led upward. After some amount of time had passed, she emerged from a narrow cave mouth.

Wind-sculpted dunes marched to the horizon. Far in the distance, a shimmering smudge. She shaded her eyes. Buildings? She started to walk, but the city never seemed to get any closer.

The rustle of wingbeats made her spin. Five creatures alit on the sand. Four resembled lions, if they had liquid silver for fur. The last walked erect. Its face was a blur. Sometimes manlike, sometimes far more alien.

"You are a daughter of Isbail," it said.

The language was neither Osterlish nor Athaaran, yet she understood. Nikola replied in the same tongue. "My mother's name is Yana."

It lifted its head, nostrils flaring as it sniffed the air. "I recognize the bloodline. You are a Rosach."

"Thorn," she corrected. "My great-grandparents were from Nantwich."

"What is Nantwich?"

"A city on the continent."

"Which continent?"

"The Via Sancta. Surely you've heard of it."

It regarded her impassively. "Tell me your given name, *Deir Fiuracha*."

So the creature knew of the witches. Knew of the Sisterhood.

She touched the serpent's eye stone at her throat. "Nikola."

"I am Borosus."

In an eyeblink, it stood next to her. A golden-skinned hand with delicate taloned fingers reached for her shoulder—and passed straight through.

"You are not here," it said with a note of surprise.

On impulse, Nikola mimicked his gesture, trying to touch the silver breastplate covering his chest. It might have been made of mist.

"Maybe *you're* not really here," she countered.

An amused smile tugged at the corner of his thin mouth. "I am. You are dreaming. But it is a powerful one if I can speak with you." Again, the slitted nostrils flared. "If I can smell your scent."

"What are you?" she asked.

Borosus ignored the question. "We seek the Mother."

"I saw her."

"Where?"

Darkness and the drip-drip of water. A womb of stone and fiery glyphs.

"Deep in the earth," she said. "Deep in the mountain."

His alien features rearranged into something approximating a frown. He turned to the horizon. "She is inside the city, but we cannot pass the gates. The mountain, eh? Perhaps we will try another way in." Borosus studied her. "Where are the legions of the Seraphim? Where is the Morning Star?"

The phrase was *najmati kalsabah,* which also meant "dawn-bringer."

"Do you mean Gavriel?" she asked.

A terse nod.

"Dead," she replied. "A thousand years dead."

His pupils dilated. "That cannot be right. I have seen him myself!"

"Well, you're mistaken."

Borosus stepped back. Anger blazed in his cloudy blue

eyes. "Go, little sister. If you see the Rowan, tell her the Sinn é Maz have returned. Tell her that her crime will be punished."

"I don't know who the Rowan—"

He raised a hand. "Go!"

A shockwave slammed into her. Nikola woke in utter darkness. She sat up in a panic and bumped a low ceiling. For an instant, she thought she was back in the caves. Then she felt wooden planks beneath her palms. *The smuggler's hold.*

She was about to call for Sydonie to open the hatch, to bring light, but a sudden memory made her clamp her lips shut. *Don't waste it! Don't speak. Do nothing but—*

A weight lay across her chest. Nikola groped in the blackness, stars now flashing in her vision. She touched clammy flesh. A sob broke from her throat. Not too late. Not too late!

Nikola cupped the boy's cheeks. She pressed her mouth to his, releasing the serpent's breath. The small chest swelled against her. When every drop was squeezed from her lungs, Nikola sagged back. She felt on the edge of fainting. How long had she held her own breath?

There wasn't enough air in the world. It was too hot. Too close.

"Syd!" she panted, banging on the ceiling. "I'm . . . suffocating!"

Light flooded the hold. A figure crawled toward her. Silver eyes reflected like a cat's in the darkness. "Easy now," Paarjini said. "Just breathe. Nice and slow."

Valdrian came behind, and Syd. Others peered through the square hatch. Too many faces to count.

Nikola closed her eyes. Thought of nothing but following Paarjini's sound advice. Her pulse began to slow. She blinked in the light, searching for Tristhus.

He lay still as death in Valdrian's arms.

"We did as ye commanded," Paarjini said. "Left ye alone. It seemed the . . ." She cleared her throat. "Well, it seemed the only chance."

Nikola started to crawl over, tears blurring her vision. Syd intercepted her. Her expression wore a terrible resignation that was worse than blame. The girl had given up hope a long time ago.

"You tried," she whispered. "I know you did, Nikola."

"No," she said blankly. "Not one more. Not one——"

The boy made a weak sound. Everyone fell silent. Nikola scrambled over and pressed a hand to his cold forehead, smoothing the dark hair back.

"Examine him," she said in a cracked voice, too terrified to do it herself.

Valdrian drew a sharp breath through his nose. He lifted the child's bloodstained tunic. The mage's face froze, then broke into a wondering smile.

Where a ragged, festering tear had rent his flesh, the skin was now smooth and unbroken.

Syd let out a ferocious whoop. Her brother's eyes flew open. He flailed and tried to break loose from Valdrian's grip. The mage spoke to him in a soothing voice. Tristhus fell back. He started to cry.

Never had Nikola been so happy to hear a child's sobs.

"He'll need plenty o' rest," Paarjini said in brisk tones, as if a miracle had not just occurred. "And fluids. He lost a good deal o' blood."

Valdrian cast Nikola a look of awe bordering on fear and moved on his knees, hunched over with the child in his arms, to the hatch where their companions waited. Tristhus was lifted into the hold. There was much laughter and exclamations of astonishment above, punctuated by joyful barking.

We all needed this, Nikola thought, dizzy with relief. Just one victory.

If she had not been leaning against a wall, Sydonie would have knocked her flat. The girl said nothing, just squeezed her until her ribs creaked and she was breathless again. Then she darted after her brother.

When they were alone, Nikola met Paarjini's level gaze.

"I imagine ye have a story to tell," her sister said dryly.

"How long was I down here?"

"More than a day. We're almost at Qeddah."

More than a day. Nikola nodded. It could have been an hour or a week. But that seemed about right.

"You are a true *laoch*," Paarjini said with a note of admiration. "You have a warrior's heart, Nikola Thorn. Stubborn and fearless."

Once, she would have warmed at the praise. She was a full witch, but the *laoch*, the guardians, were a small, elite cadre within the sisterhood. Paarjini was formally recognizing this for the first time. But too many strange things had happened for Nikola to give her promotion more than a passing thought.

"I have news about your own child, as well," Paarjini said. "Don't get yer hopes too high. She's still in Balaur's power. But her spirit lives and for some reason, he's given her over to Kasia."

"What?" Nikola stared. "How?"

Paarjini shook her head, rueful. "Do not ask me such questions. It is a thing the aingeals have learnt. Perhaps not even all o' them. But you've heard Kasia speak o' her Garden. It is a dream place, but she has some control over what transpires there. It is . . . *real* in some way. Rachel is there." She gave a little smile. "Playin' with kittens, apparently."

Nikola covered a strangled laugh. Her emotions felt scraped raw. "Kittens?" she managed.

"Last I heard." Paarjini sighed. "I'm tellin' ye this so ye know yer little girl's all right for now. And that we *will* save her in this world. But Balaur is still the stronger o' the two. Kasia will do all she can to hold him off, but . . . "

"If he wants to harm her, he can," Nikola finished.

Paarjini gave a reluctant nod. "But he won't as long as he needs her. He *can't*. And it does tell us another thing. Heshima has not broken the spell holding him inside Rachel's body. And I know why."

Nikola thought of the Great Serpent entombed in the earth. The complex nets of enchantment binding her sleep. She'd only glimpsed them, but she knew one thing. Whoever had done it was a seriously badass witch.

The Rowan.

Nikola gripped her namestone, a spear of ice lodged in her spine.

"So do I," she said.

Chapter Fourteen

Qeddah was already the richest, most populous city in the Masdar League. With the festivities for the Golden Imperator's succession nearing their peak, it was bursting at the seams.

Boats crammed the river, flying colorful pennants. Children splashed in the shallows next to women beating their washing on flat rocks. Peddlers on bicycles sped along the narrow riverside paths, toting enormous bundles balanced on the handlebars and dangling in nets. A hubbub of shouts and laughter filled the air.

Above it all soared the Markhawks, keen eyes watching for any sudden shift in the currents of ley. Kasia tensed as one passed directly above the *Wayfarer*. Like all ley-creatures, the birds faded in and out of shadow. She wondered how many more were in the sky that she hadn't noticed at all.

"Are you sure about this?" she whispered to Paarjini.

"Not entirely," the witch admitted. "But the energy is released in the casting of the spell. That is what creates ripples in the ley. Once the illusion is in place, holding it requires only the finest thread of power. Not enough to detect from a distance."

Jamila's escape meant that their enemies would have spies at the port waiting for the ship's arrival. They had debated whether to abandon the vessel entirely, but this solution was impractical for a number of reasons.

First, because it was loaded with metals and gems the witches would need. Second, because those same spies would also be alert for a group on foot fitting their descriptions.

In the end, they'd decided to chance a spell that transformed the *Wayfarer* into a flat barge loaded with grain. Paarjini claimed the size of the object didn't matter. It was just as easy to make an apple look like an orange as to make a palace look like a hovel.

Nikola had been the one to cast it, well before they reached the outskirts of Qeddah. She kept the size of the barge precisely the same as the tall-masted carrack to prevent collisions in the channel. Since Kasia was inside the bubble of illusion, the ship looked the same as ever to her. She'd sensed the sudden burst of ley, but that's all.

"Could a witch tell the difference?" she wondered.

Nikola looked at Paarjini. Despite her inborn talent, there were clearly major gaps in her knowledge of lithomancy.

"Not unless she's very, very close," Paarjini replied. Her expression darkened. "And if Heshima does get that close, the Mother help her because she'll already be on fire."

They only had to keep the pretense going long enough to disembark. After that, Captain Aemlyn planned to sail back upriver and wait at one of the towns until they sent word.

Now Kasia watched the Markhawk trace lazy circles above the river. It did not go arrowing off to make a report to the priests, which she took as a good sign.

"Where is the Imperator's Palace?" she asked Tashtemir, craning her neck for a view past the rooftops.

The city put her in mind of a sun-warmed cat, too lazy to rise from its windowsill. Few of the buildings were more than a story or two, though they came in a variety of styles. Honey-colored stone and faded mudbrick, wood and tile, even a few with billowing fabric for walls. They crowded to the very edge of the river, where endless small piers jutted into the water.

"We are not yet at the Sa' Min-Alawm," he said. "It means the Sea of Peaceful Slumber."

"There is an inland sea?" she asked in surprise.

"More like a large lake," he amended. "The administrative buildings are on the islands. It's the center of bureaucratic power."

Kasia nodded, filing this away. "So that is where the Luban embassy will be."

"Yes, on the Isle of Dreams."

Kasia stiffened. "Why do you call it that?"

"Because the breath of the Alsakhan carries the ley and this world sprang from his dreams. Also Valmitra's. The priests worship by sitting in quiet meditation. They believe it keeps the Alsakhan content and prevents undue turbulence in the communal psyche."

He gave a short, dry laugh. "Of course, they also engage in plots of their own. Just because the League has achieved a stable form of monarchy does not mean the interests of the seven emiratis always coincide."

"The Breath of God," Kasia said slowly. "But they do not all serve Balaur or he would already have the keys he seeks."

Tashtemir nodded. "Only the Lubans, I hope. But the rest are dangerous nonetheless."

They rounded a bend and a vast body of water spread out ahead. The river itself was a muddy brown, but the Sa' Min-Alawm dazzled the eye with vivid aquamarine. It looked as crystal clear as the swimming pool at Tessaria's family mansion in Arbot Hills. Kasia saw the humps of islands, bright with flowering trees and sparkling white domes.

To the left, a busy wharf extended along the lakeshore. She feared the illusion would not hold when they sought a berth, but Captain Aemlyn assured them that the League had a free trade policy within its borders and the ship had already passed through customs at Port Sayyad. Aemlyn leapt off before the mooring ropes were secured and presented false documents to the harried official on the pier. She told him her crew would handle the offload of grain and he was happy to agree, especially when she paid in advance for the berth and made him a gift of two large rubies.

As predicted, no inspection was made of the ship. Once everything was settled, Aemlyn hired a cart to transport the most valuable gems to a large hostel that catered to foreign seafarers. She escorted it herself, along with most of her crew, leaving only her first mate behind.

The rest of them waited for dark to fall.

No one came to arrest them. No one seemed to take any special interest in the ship at all.

When the yellow moon rose and activity on the docks died down, they had a quick meeting and agreed that it was safe to go ashore. Tashtemir led the company in a circuitous route to the hotel, taking a maze of back alleys between the warehouses. Valdrian lagged behind, and such was his skill that even knowing the mage was following, Kasia couldn't spot him.

At last, they reached the hotel. It was called the Saffron Palace and also hosted a popular restaurant. Two minutes later, Valdrian appeared and reported that no one had followed. They went around back, where one of the crew was waiting at the service door. She led them into a warren of small, anonymous rooms.

They stayed only long enough to sort out sleeping arrangements. Kasia shared with Natalya again, the cots so close together they could have reached out and clasped each other's hands.

"I think it's even smaller than the ship," Natalya remarked with a laugh, rinsing her face in a basin.

But the hotel was clean and suited their purposes. Near

the lake, crowded with foreigners—including many from lands to the south that Kasia had never heard of before—and, best of all, the owner was a good friend of Captain Aemlyn's. If anyone came asking after them, he'd give a warning.

They all assembled in the witches' room. It was the largest by far, though not even Caralexa complained about that fact. The captain had changed some of the gems into local currency, which Paarjini doled out.

They'd already made a plan for how to proceed next. Tristhus was still recovering his strength. Both the hound and Sydonie refused to leave his side. Still, the children whined about being left behind until Nikola promised to buy them new Masdari-style daggers. To everyone's surprise, Caralexa volunteered to keep an eye on them. The two knights remained as well to guard the cargo.

The rest of the party went to a nearby market, where they browsed the stalls for the simple, everyday robes that were popular with all but the richest Masdaris. At Tashtemir's advice, they all bought sashes of red and purple—the colors of his homeland, Paravai.

"It is respected," he explained quietly, "but not one of the most powerful emiratis. We get on well with our neighbors." A shrug. "Or at least we did four years ago."

After a brief negotiation, Tash departed one of the stalls with armloads of new clothes and veils of various lengths and styles. The gauzy coverings could be worn by men or women. Some chose them for modesty, others to keep the sun off—or when conducting some discreet bit of business. The Masdari love of intrigues made it acceptable for anyone to veil themselves at any time, for any reason.

"I think that's sensible," Natalya whispered. "I wish we had them in Novo. I'd wear one *everywhere*."

After slipping one of the merchants a few coins for privacy, the women changed in a space at the rear of his stall, quickly tugging the robes over their heads and shedding the clothing beneath since it was far too hot for two layers. Kasia made sure her own had deep, secure pockets. She stowed her cards in one, her coin purse in the other. The loose flow of the material made them invisible.

The veil was trickier. It took her a minute to get the hang of it, until Natalya showed her the tiny slits where it hooked into her headscarf.

Then it was the men's turn. Kasia lingered at the tent flap, poking a gap with one finger. She couldn't resist a quick study of Valdrian's Marks—purely out of professional interest. The ones the nihilim gave to each other were different from the Sanctified Marks bestowed by the Curia. Wilder and stranger, like the denizens of a fevered dreamscape.

A wolverine clawed at his chest, revealing the beating heart beneath in all its purple-red glory. Springing from his navel, with roots that wound down to his thighs, was a tree with swords for branches. A black stallion stood at the trunk, riderless and fierce.

Kasia gave a thoughtful nod. She was about to turn away when he caught her spying. Their eyes met. Valdrian seemed more amused than bothered.

"Did you get a proper look?" he asked, turning in a slow circle.

Leather straps crisscrossed his muscular back like a harness. They connected with a metal brace that covered his left arm to the shoulder. The lines of more Marks were visible through the struts.

"Yes," she replied, her smile hidden by the veil. "And it's nothing I haven't seen before."

He scratched his blond beard. "I'm not sure how to take that."

"It isn't your manhood she cares about," Spassov remarked as he yanked on a pair of loose cotton trousers. "It's your Marks."

Kasia gave him a fond glance. How well he knew her.

"They're archetypes," she explained to Valdrian. "Just like my cards, only tailored to an individual psyche. I wanted to see yours so I'd know if I could trust you."

Malach would have made some cutting remark, but Valdrian was an easier-going sort. All he said was, "Ah."

She glanced at the wolverine and the naked heart. "You have a savage streak, but you're honest about it." Her gaze lowered to the tree and the horse. "You follow your own judgment. If it is wrong, you have the willingness to correct course. That is not a small thing. You are a terror to those you hate and loyal to those you love." She jerked her chin at Spassov. "Just like him."

Valdrian blinked. "You see all that?"

"It's obvious." She turned away, leaving the two men staring at each other with looks of consternation. A minute later, they both emerged in white robes. Tashtemir helped wrap the turbans. When he was done, Natalya nodded in approval.

"It suits you," she said to Patryk. "How do I look?"

"Deadly," he replied with a straight face. "Where are your knives?"

"All sorts of places. Want to look for them?"

"I prefer to keep all my fingers." He flushed as soon as he said it, shooting Valdrian a sideways look. "I mean . . ."

The mage laughed and held up his leather-capped stump. There was a faint click. A blade shot out from his sleeve. Another click and it withdrew. "This," he said, "has saved my life on countless occasions." A grin. "If I need to flip someone off, I just use the other hand."

Natalya stepped forward, awe on her face. "How did I miss that? Bloody Saints. Did you make it yourself?"

Valdrian nodded.

"Would you show me the mechanism?"

They fell into a discussion about knives. Single-edge versus double-edge, different lengths and balance points, other things

Kasia had little interest in. She turned to Spassov, who was lighting a cigarette. "Sure you don't mind hanging around? It's just that Tashtemir said only a few of us should go."

Patryk's gaze roamed to the far edge of the bazaar, where the stalls gradually merged with a carnival of entertainments. Fire-eaters and jugglers, stilt-walkers and tumblers, singers of varying skill and even the occasional burst of fireworks against the black sky.

"Not at all," he said. "I've always wanted to try Azo. It's the signature booze of the League."

"What is it?"

"No idea." He smiled. "But I plan to find out."

She almost told him not to get drunk, but what was the point? At least he held his liquor reasonably well. Unlike Natalya.

"Watch out for pickpockets," she said.

"Hopefully, they'll go for Nat first." His expression sobered. "Be careful, eh?"

"We will."

Patryk turned to Valdrian. "You coming along?"

"First round's on me," Natalya offered.

The mage eyed them both. "Sure," he said. "I'll buy the second one." He looked at Cairness, who stood by herself looking awkward. A shawl covered her auburn hair. Instead of a veil, she wore Natalya's huge sunglasses.

"Sister of the Deir Fiuracha," Valdrian called softly. "Will you join us?"

The tinted lenses made it hard to gauge Cairness's expression. To Kasia's surprise, she gave a nod. "I speak some Masdari," she said briskly. "Learnt it in school. Tashtemir's been practicin' with me. I think I can order for all of us."

It was the longest speech Kasia had ever heard her utter in a civil tone. Perhaps there was hope for them yet.

Natalya said something to the witch in Masdari, which she answered in kind, though more haltingly. They shared a smile.

"We can both practice with each other," Natalya said.

They carried their old clothes to a rubbish bin and stuffed the pile deep inside. It felt like shedding a part of herself and embracing someone new. Kasia's shoulders relaxed. They looked just like everyone else now. Balaur would never pick them out from the multitudes thronging the city.

I'm coming for you, she thought. *You'd better stay awake, Dreamer.*

Natalya pulled Kasia into a hug. "See you back at the ship." She lowered her voice. "I'll keep those boys out of trouble, don't worry."

"Said the fox about the chickens. Give me the room key. I guarantee I'll be back first."

Natalya shot her a look of mock reproach but fished in her pocket for the key. "I wish I could go with you," she said, and Kasia knew she meant it.

"Me, too. But Tashtemir said it's better if it's just Nikola, me and Paarjini." She glanced at the others. "If something goes wrong—"

"It won't," her friend said firmly. "But I know what you mean. Better we're not all in trouble."

"Exactly. So have fun, but—"

"Not too much fun." Her brown eyes were dead serious now. "A drink or two, that's all. If you do need us, we've got your back." She looked over her shoulder. The others were waiting. "Who knows? Maybe we'll pick up some useful information, too." Natalya gave her fingers a squeeze and strode off.

"I'm glad to see 'em gettin' on w' each other," Paarjini remarked, her veil puffing with each word.

"All it took was a horde of murderous assassins boarding the ship," Nikola said dryly. "Helps remind you which side you're on."

Their friends had already been swallowed up by the crowds. Paarjini turned to Tashtemir. "Ye ready?"

He stood with a faraway expression in his eyes—which was all Kasia could see of him now. She wondered how he felt being home again. The man had a quick wit—quick enough to nimbly deflect personal questions whilst giving the impression of perfect sincerity. Even Kasia, who prided herself on reading people, found Tashtemir hard to pin down.

She hoped they'd made the right choice in trusting him, because the next step in the plan could go bad in a dozen different ways—most of them ending in a prison cell.

Now Tashtemir seemed to gather his courage. He squared his shoulders and gave Paarjini a brief nod.

"We must catch a ferry," he said. "The nearest landing is this way."

Chapter Fifteen

They walked downhill to a small open-sided building at the edge of the lake, with several piers extending into the water. Tashtemir went inside and returned a few minutes later with four tokens. Oared boats with cloth sunshades were coming and going. He hailed one that had just disgorged several passengers, gave the destination, and they all climbed in, settling on wooden benches. A young woman took the tokens, dropping them in a leather pouch. She wore a sleeveless tunic, her arms corded with lean muscle. A bracelet in the shape of a dragon circled one wrist.

In a moment, they were pulling away from shore. The lakebed was composed of pure white sand, the water so clear Kasia couldn't tell how deep it was. Even at night it was an intense blue, which must come from ley flowing along the bottom. They wound through channels between the islands, passing other boats with yellow lanterns at the bow and stern. Most seemed to be hired ferries, but a few were fancier, with cabins and curtained windows that hid the occupants from view.

There was a great deal of merrymaking on the lake after dark. Groups of boats were tethered together, the occupants climbing back and forth to visit friends and share a drink. Fireworks streaked upward from every shore, to cheers of delight from the revelers.

For a moment, Kasia wished she were here with Alexei. Just two adventurers, come to raise a toast to the Golden Imperator. How romantic it would be to drift on one of the fancy boats, sipping wine and watching the lights play on the calm water, like tiny stars fallen to earth.

Of course, that made her think of Rachel. Kasia's smile faded. When she had returned to the Garden the night before, she's been relieved to find her napping on the gazebo bench. But it was strange that the child should sleep within a dream. Rachel had roused when Kasia shook her shoulder, but she seemed groggy and dull.

She feared that the child's spirit was weakening.

Kasia had chafed her icy hands, spoken to her of small, inconsequential things. Where the ripest berries grew. How to catch the frogs that clustered at the inlet of the pond. She held a little yellow flower beneath Rachel's chin and told her that it meant she liked butter.

After a time, her eyes cleared. Kasia could not bring herself to speak of anything that mattered. They did some work together, weeding the pathways. Balaur did not appear.

Kasia had departed with a promise to return every night. She woke more tired than when she went to bed, but it was a vow she meant to keep.

Now, as the boat angled toward one of the larger islands, Kasia's weariness washed away. The priests were not the only order to serve the Alsakhan. There was also a holy sanctuary dedicated to the Masdari soothsayers, all of whom were women. Tashtemir had a friend there he hoped would aid them.

Apparently, the soothsayers were on friendly terms with the witches of Dur-Athaara, although Paarjini had never dealt with them herself. All she knew was that they were cartomancers.

Kasia felt intense curiosity. She'd always believed herself to be an outlier, but this was not the case. She wished she had a year to stay and study with them. Everything she knew, she had taught herself through trial and error—and a healthy dose of intuition. But there must be so much more to it. The cartomancers had centuries of knowledge. One of the oldest orders, dating back to the Dark Ages.

As the island drew nearer, she made out a figure standing at one of the many small docks. Tashtemir, who sat on the forward bench, stared with a fixed expression. Then he gave a startled laugh.

"It is Merat," he muttered. "She must be expecting us."

"And she won't turn ye in?" Paarjini hissed. "Yer sure o' that?"

"I am sure of nothing," he admitted. "But that is not her style. She is no great admirer of the priests."

"What about the Imperator?"

"It is too late now," he said. "She has seen us."

The woman on the dock wore neither scarf nor veil. Her dark hair was short, but Kasia couldn't make out much more in the darkness. She folded her arms and took a step forward, then stopped. Yes, she had seen them.

Nikola and Paarjini exchanged a look. Kasia slid a hand into her pocket.

The boat bumped up to the dock and they climbed out. With a nod, the ferrywoman pushed off and rowed away.

Merat was tall, about Nikola's height. She wore a dress of multiple loose layers, tighter at the bodice. Her face was strong and intelligent. Also set in lines of fury.

Without a word, she strode up to Tashtemir and delivered a resounding slap that rocked him back on his heels. A tongue-lashing ensued, though since it was all in Masdari, Kasia had no idea what she was saying.

He absorbed it in silence save for a few interjections that were swiftly overridden. Merat turned to the three women.

"He is a lying worm," she declared in accented Osterlish. "But I am glad to see you. Come."

She turned without waiting for a response and stalked down a pathway.

"It's fine," Tashtemir assured them. "She got it out of her system."

Kasia doubted this but moved to follow before the woman vanished.

"Got what out of her system, exactly?" Paarjini huffed, hurrying to keep up with Merat's long strides.

"She says I left without a word, which is true." Tashtemir looked shady. "It's complicated."

"You might have mentioned this before," Nikola pointed out. "Let me see your face."

He lifted the veil. One cheek was bright red. She patted his arm. "I'm sorry she hit you."

He stared straight ahead. "I deserved it."

The isle was thickly wooded with orange and lemon trees. Merat led them to a circular stone structure with open sides and a small dome on top. Braziers piled with bokang wood cast a flickering light. Inside, curved benches formed a semi-circle. A stone table occupied the center, inlaid with a mosaic of a dragon.

They took seats facing each other, unhooking veils. Merat laid her hands flat on the table and regarded each of them calmly.

"I will tell you what I already know," she said. "You seek a powerful child. She is under the control of a mage. He, in turn, seeks the nameless city for his own gain. Is that correct?"

Paarjini nodded. "That is part of it."

Merat briefly closed her eyes. "I had hoped I was wrong, but the signs have been there for some time now. Even before we saw the twin comets." She leaned forward. "Seven years ago, I had a foretelling that the current Imperator's reign would end in dissolution. I do not speak of armed conflict but something much bigger. A fork that will set the world on a new course. Not just the Masdar League, but all of us."

"Did you see who won?" Nikola wondered.

"No, but I can tell you this. Either way, what you know now will be gone. Very soon."

They were silent. Each woman at the table understood the truth of this, but it was still a disturbing prospect.

"The Nazaré Sinn have returned, Mer," Tashtemir said quietly.

She gave him a cool look. "You hope they might aid your cause, but of course, that depends on what you do."

"I spoke to one," Nikola said. "In a dream, but I think he saw me."

For the first time, Merat looked surprised. "What did it tell you?"

"His name was Borosus. He said he was looking for the Mother. And for the Morning Star. He would not believe that Gavriel was dead."

The soothsayer hesitated. "I can tell you more about that, but first I must do a reading." She looked at Kasia. "You may do one as well, if you like."

The offer was unexpected, but Kasia was eager to consult the ley. "It's safe?"

"The ley is worked constantly on this isle. Our sanctuary is one of the few places where it's permitted. The hawks ignore the fluctuations." She eyed the witches. "Are either of you diviners?"

Nikola and Paarjini looked at each other. "I canna tell ye what will happen five minutes from now, let alone anythin' of consequence," Paarjini admitted.

"Same," Nikola added.

"Your skills lie elsewhere," Merat said with a small smile.

"We are *laoch*," Paarjini said.

A slow nod. "And I suspect you will be needed when the time comes, sisters. But for now, the mage and I will compare our approaches."

Kasia covered a jolt of shock. "I am not a mage," she said, lifting her chin. "You may call me by my name. Kasia. That's all."

"No?" Merat shrugged. "Whatever you prefer, Kasia."

They took out their decks, setting them on the stone table. The two women locked gazes, appraising each other.

"How many cards do you use?" Kasia asked.

"Thirty-six."

"Mine has twice as many."

Merat looked intrigued. "Explain."

Kasia separated the deck into five piles. "Twenty-two are called the Major Arcana," she said, turning the cards over one by one. "Also, the High Trumps. They are the most powerful. Once one is attached to a particular person, it almost never changes. In general, they speak of large events, not day-to-day questions."

"And the others?"

"Four suits. Pontifex, Cardinal, Bishop, Knight. Followed by the lesser pips. Each contains many layers of meaning that grow more complex when read in conjunction with each other."

"How many do you use?"

"It depends. Sometimes one only. Sometimes three or more. I let instinct guide the choice."

Merat frowned. "That is different indeed. Mine has no special trumps at all." She spread the deck out. "Just symbols. There are three patterns. The five-card spread. The seven-card spread. And the Grand Tableaux. It uses all thirty-six cards."

Kasia couldn't help it. Her jaw fell open. "*All* of them?"

Merat nodded. "I deal it often."

"But . . . Saints! The complexity of such a spread . . . I cannot fathom how you could read so many in tandem!"

"It *is* complex." Merat grinned. "But these things can be learned. I think perhaps there are fewer meanings to decipher in mine."

Kasia saw Nikola discreetly cover a yawn. "I would like very much to learn," she said. "But I suppose we must stay focused. Shall we do it at the same time?"

Merat nodded. "If there is room on the table."

A shadow moved on the pillar behind her. Kasia slammed her palm down on the Mage. It lit with blue ley. She heard a low, vicious snarl and readied to defend her companions.

Merat glanced over her shoulder. "Lupa will not hurt you."

A great tawny cat slunk forward, dagger fangs bared in a hiss. It was much larger than a house cat, about the same size as Alice. Long, dark tufts swept upward from the tips of its ears, which were laid flat against its head. Merat held a hand out. Lupa hissed again, then submitted to her caress.

"What is that?" Nikola asked in a level tone.

"A caracal," Tashtemir replied. "Beautiful, are they not?"

Two dark vertical stripes ran up its forehead, just above the luminous orange eyes. As if she knew they were speaking of her, Lupa's enormous tufted ears swiveled inward, giving her the look of a horned owl.

"She pretends to be fierce," Merat said fondly, "but she is soft at heart."

The cat gave them all a thorough, unblinking inspection, then sank down at her mistress's feet. A deep rumbling came from her chest.

"Now, where were we?" Merat said briskly. "I propose we each do a seven-card spread. There is still much to discuss this night, so we will keep it simple and see if the messages coincide."

Seven. It kept popping up. A potent number.

"War," Kasia muttered. "Providence, vengeance, and trouble."

"Also one's higher purpose," Merat said softly. "Symmetry, wisdom and dreams. The color of seven is violet."

Kasia frowned. "I did not know that."

She shuffled her cards, then fanned them out and chose seven at random with her left hand. Merat also shuffled but drew her cards straight off the top.

"Together," she said.

They both turned them over one at a time. Ley flared briefly along the images, then subsided.

"It is the same as before," Kasia murmured. "Exactly."

The Sun and Moon. The Serpent. The Twins.

Then the High Priestess, Fortitude, and the Wheel.

"I would draw one more," she said. "The Sun and the Moon must be counted together, as a single message."

Merat tilted her head. "I have no objection."

Kasia studied the remaining seventy-one cards. She closed her eyes and chose. When she opened them, Merat was leaning across the table.

"The Fool," she said. "Let us hear your interpretation first."

Malach. *Of course.*

"That is my brother," Kasia said dryly. "A wild card. But I can explain the others. The first pairing is the Dawn City." Kasia touched the Sun and Moon. "Together, they form twilight. A liminal time and place. The Serpent is Valmitra, of course. The Twins are Balaur and his hostage." She met Merat's eyes. "Her name is Rachel. She is my niece." She turned to Nikola. "And her daughter."

The seer's brown eyes held compassion. "I am very sorry."

"The last three . . ." Kasia sighed. "I am the High Priestess. In most decks, the Garden is called the Wheel. It stands for the turning of one's fate. Fortitude is the courage to face that destiny." She felt the usual surge of frustration when the ley chose to be opaque. "But I cannot say what mine is meant to be."

Merat nodded. "Then we will turn to the Lenormand deck."

"Why d'ye call it that?" Paarjini wondered. "It does'na sound like a Masdari word."

"Because it's not. This deck is based on the prophetic writings of one of your own sisters." Merat tilted her head. "I thought you would know that."

Paarjini looked confused. "We do not practice cartomancy."

"Not anymore. But Valmitra's daughters did once. Some, at least. The witch who invented this divination system was named Cathrynne Rowan Lenormand."

Nikola leaned forward. "Rowan? Borosus spoke of her. He said that if I saw the Rowan, I should tell her that he meant to punish her."

Merat nodded. "She was the Morning Star's consort."

Paarjini stiffened. "A *witch* aided Gavriel?"

"I already told you that," Nikola said flatly. "I felt the enchantments around the Mother. They were *spells*."

Paarjini sat back. "I hoped ye were just dreamin' that part," she said faintly.

"Then you know all," Merat said, her voice heavy. She vented a sharp breath. "It is not our fault. None of us sitting here. The deed was done generations ago by people long dead. I cannot tell you the *why* of it all. Only the *how*. The first Imperator made some covenant with Gavriel. To hold the keys to the prison of a god. A god!"

She shook her head grimly. "Madness, if you ask me." She glanced around and lowered her voice. "What I will say next is heresy of the worst sort. But I have pieced the truth together, ever since I saw the coming darkness." She paused. "There is no Alsakhan. Or, more accurately, he is the same entity as Valmitra."

"That, I did suspect," Paarjini said mildly.

The rest of them nodded. Merat seemed a bit deflated.

"Well, do not utter it where anyone can hear you. It is a fiction that our beloved deity is content. In fact, I imagine that whatever lies in that city will be very unhappy when it awakens." She looked around at them. "Unhappy with *all* of us."

"And yet we must," Paarjini said firmly.

Merat made an equivocal face. "That is the question I have wrestled with. Is it really so bad to just . . . leave the god alone?"

"Balaur will not," Kasia said. "And I fear he means to kill her. To seize the ley somehow. He has the sword."

The blood drained from Merat's face. "Truly?"

Nikola spoke for the first time in a while. "Even if he did not, I would vote to free her. I saw the Serpent myself. It was . . ." She shook her head. "It was terrible. She is being used like some magical cow that provides endless milk, but she is a thinking, feeling being! We *must* help her."

Merat was silent for a minute. "Then the only question is how."

"We will steal these keys and find the city," Kasia said. "Before Balaur does."

Merat gazed at the five cards before her. She gave a quiet laugh.

"And so it comes around," she said. "I was unsure of the meaning before, but . . . if you are to do this, you will need to leave decoys, otherwise the alarm will be raised instantly. Which presents a problem, since we do not know what they look like."

"I do," Kasia said. "One of our companions is an artist. I'll have her draw them in perfect detail."

"And I know the locksmiths who could make copies," Tashtemir said.

"Use seven different ones," Nikola suggested. "Just in case."

"I plan to."

"Who else knows about all this?" Paarjini asked. "Surely you have discussed it with your sisters."

"Two only," Merat replied. "Friends from girlhood whom I trust. But the things we speak of . . . As I said, they are heresy. I nearly went to the Imperator anyway, thinking it was my duty, but she has a new advisor. A woman from Kvengard who has long been a key trade partner with the League."

"Hanne Danziger," Kasia growled.

"The same. I misliked her the first time we met, so I did a reading." Merat's lips tightened. "I don't know *what* she is, but it isn't what she appears to be."

"The Danzigers are monsters," Kasia said flatly. "I presume her nephew is here, too? A tall, blonde man?"

The seer nodded. "I only glimpsed him once. They are both staying at the Luban compound. I fear they have some hold over the Imperator." She reached down to scratch the caracal beneath its chin. "As for my own order, I wish I could say they are all incorruptible, but that is not the case."

"Balaur walks in dreams," Kasia said. "That is how he recruited the khedive of Luba. You are wise to stay on guard."

"If you are to attempt this, tomorrow night is the time," Merat said. "It is the final night of the festivities. There will be parties everywhere. People coming and going." She eyed Nikola and Paarjini. "If you are careful, a way might be found to enter the Imperator's palace." Her gaze settled on Tashtemir. "And you have a master thief to advise you," she added coldly.

He swallowed. "Mer . . . it's not what you think."

Nikola slowly turned her head. "Tashtemir?"

"What did he tell you?" Merat asked.

"That he slept with the Imperator's wife."

She chuckled. It soon turned into full-blown laughter. "By the Root, you're an idiot," she said to him, wiping her eyes. "And they believed you?"

Paarjini's eyes narrowed. Tashtemir's widened. "Listen," he said a bit desperately. "I *was* going to tell you. But truly, it seemed irrelevant——"

"What did he steal?" Nikola wondered.

"*Tried* to steal. Eggs from a dragonet. One that belonged to the Imperator."

She eyed him in exasperation. "Why? To sell?"

Tashtemir opened his mouth, but Merat interrupted. "I think he did it to see if he could. Am I right?"

He exhaled through his nose. "Maybe. It's not like I'm a murderer."

"No," Merat agreed. "Worse. You brought shame on your entire family. Did he tell you he is the khedive youngest son?" A snort at their astonished faces. "No, of course he didn't."

Tashtemir leaned back on the bench and crossed his ankles, hands propped to either side. There was a subtle shift in his posture. A new arrogance Kasia had never seen before. Then he gave a crooked smile and seemed like the old Tash again.

"I did not ask for the honor," he said mildly. "And my father had a penchant for disappointment regardless of my actions."

"That doesn't absolve your foolishness," Merat pointed out.

Paarjini held up a finger. "Are ye talking about Paravai?" She shot him a dark look. "Or was that another lie?"

"Yes, he is from Paravai," Merat replied. "I suppose he told you it was a poor, insignificant emirati?"

Tashtemir frowned. "I never said *poor*."

"Did you say *filthy* rich?"

He shrugged.

"Is he even a veterinarian?" Nikola demanded.

"That also is true," Merat conceded. She eyed him with a mixture of fondness and irritation. "A fine one, too. He cured Lupa of mange for me once."

Tash gave the women a level look. "See? The rest is . . . " Long fingers fluttered. "Minor details."

"Why didn't ye just tell the truth?" Paarjini asked.

"Would you have trusted a thief?"

Her mouth twisted. "Maybe not."

"I did not tell Malach because I feared he would hold me for ransom. That was before I knew him well enough to realize he didn't care much about money. But the lie had stuck by then. It seemed easier to just . . . let it sit."

Kasia poked him with her toe. "Well, *Master Thief*, how would you advise us?"

"He got caught," Paarjini grumbled. "Tha' is not in his favor."

Tashtemir bristled. "Only because I misliked how the client handled the creature. He was not gentle. I decided to call off the bargain and return the dragonelle to the menagerie. *That* is when I was caught."

Merat shook her head. "You have a soft heart."

"Do you even know where the keys are?"

"I can guess. There is a room—"

Lupa suddenly rose to her feet and gave a low growl.

An instant later, Kasia heard soft footsteps on the path. The murmur of deep male voices. Merat swore under her breath and swept up her deck, motioning at Kasia to do the same. They all slipped silently from the pavilion down an opposite pathway. At a dense thicket of flowering bushes thirty meters from the pavilion, Merat signaled a halt. They crouched down.

The braziers were still burning, casting the half dozen figures in sharp relief. Kasia recognized the long belted coats from the ship. The Breath of God. Her nape prickled as one of the priests turned her way. His veil was lowered, gaze searching the darkness. The men consulted each other for a moment, then fanned out in different directions. One headed their way. He stopped in front of the thicket, so close Kasia could have reached out and touched his pant leg.

He did not carry a light—no doubt trying to get his night vision back.

A peculiar smell wafted from his garments. Sickly sweet like fermented fruit. It roiled her stomach. Kasia held her breath as he slowly drew a dagger from his belt. The ley at his feet swirled in strange patterns. Did he sense their presence?

Then something exploded from the undergrowth down the path. Kasia heard a hiss. The caracal.

The priest spun toward the sound, then continued down the pathway at a measured pace. Faint shouts echoed in the distance, but the only sound around them was the chirr of insects.

"There is a small boat at the shore," Merat whispered. "Come."

She walked at a crouch, the rest of them following. Lights shone through the trees from various buildings scattered around the isle, but Merat stuck to the dark citrus groves, avoiding the pathways. In a minute, they reached a sandy shore. A small wooden canoe sat on the beach.

"We are staying at the Saffron Palace," Paarjini whispered.

Merat nodded. "I will find you there tomorrow."

Kasia helped Tashtemir drag the boat into the water. A paddle lay on the bottom. She took a seat in the center and quickly scanned the lake. Another small isle sat nearby. If they could round the edge of it, they'd be invisible from the shore.

"Just one minute," Nikola muttered, rooting through her drawstring bag.

She fisted a stone. It flared with a spark of ley. She closed her eyes, brows drawing down in concentration.

"Now's not the time, sister," Paarjini hissed. "Come *on!*"

Nikola leapt into the canoe, climbing up to the front. Tashtemir was pushing the boat out when bobbing lights appeared to either side of the small landing.

"Go!" Merat cried. "I will hold them!"

Tashtemir turned to face her. He looked pale but determined.

"No, Mer."

He gave the boat a hard shove. The canoe drifted out from shore. Then he turned and ran toward the lights, bellowing in Masdari. The lanterns followed, the priest's harsh cries fading as they took off in pursuit.

"You idiot," Merat whispered angrily, staring after them.

Nikola reached into her pouch again. Paarjini caught her wrist.

"If we take on those priests, we might get him back. *Might*." Her gaze followed a burst of fireworks as it arced upward, branching into a dozen sparkling streamers. "But the projective spells will look like *that* to whoever's watchin'—and ye can be sure they are. The Masdari made his choice. It'll do him no good if we're all caught."

They both knew she was right. "Tomorrow," Kasia called softly to Merat, who gave a grim nod. She dug the paddle into the water, making for the small island. In another minute, they reached the tip. She glanced back over her shoulder. The seer was gone.

"It's my fault," Nikola said as the canoe slid around a rocky point and the Isle of the Soothsayers disappeared from view. "Dammit!" She slammed a fist on her thigh. "But I had to try."

"Did ye find him at least?" Paarjini asked, and Kasia realized that Nikola had taken the opportunity to track Malach's kaldurite.

"No." Now she looked utterly miserable. "It was all for nothing. The spell around the stone . . . it's *gone*."

Kasia went cold. "What does that mean? Is he dead?"

"Not necessarily," Paarjini said. "Keep paddlin'."

Kasia realized she was sitting there, staring into space. She dug the oar into the water, aiming for the near shore. Small buildings crowded the edge, most with rickety docks.

"He could have gotten rid of it somehow," Paarjini continued, though she looked troubled. "He's tried it before."

"And nearly killed himself," Nikola muttered.

Kasia was silent, focused on getting them to safety, but her hopes were crumbling to dust. How would they ever find each other now? If only she could dream walk like Balaur! But she had no clue how to find a particular person and Alexei never dreamed anyway.

"We were betrayed," she muttered. "And Tashtemir knows everything. They'll probably torture him."

"I won't leave him to his fate," Nikola said. "Even if he did lie to us. We have to find out where they've taken him."

The boat entered the shallows. Sand scraped beneath the oar. Kasia dug in and propelled them to one of the docks.

"We already have an impossible task," she said with a sigh. "What's one more?"

Chapter Sixteen

Jule Danziger walked precisely six steps behind the Imperator. She was fat and gray-haired and wore a heavy silk robe embroidered with golden-maned dragons. The train was so long he'd be in danger of stepping on it if he came any closer.

Jule imagined the explosion of rage as she jerked to a stop, his boot planted firmly on the ridiculous garment. What would she do? Have him executed? He was already dead by most measures.

His aunt glanced back with a frown, as if reading his thoughts. He wiped the grin from his face. *Hanne* walked next to her. They were best fucking friends, weren't they? While he was shunted to the rear like a servant.

Well, he had his own friends. When it came to Balaur, none stood higher than Jule. He'd been faithful from the very beginning. And soon he would collect his reward. Then both of those bitches would be bowing and scraping to *him*.

He itched all over, a maddening sensation that burrowed into the bone, but Jule didn't dare to scratch. Not in front of the Imperator's own priests. They flanked the procession, three on each side. If they sensed the taint in him, they gave no sign of it. Perhaps their own flesh was too corrupted.

Every morning, he drank a vile-tasting restorative that Hanne brewed in her makeshift laboratory. It held them both together—to a degree—but he desperately needed something stronger. The true Elixir of Immortality. It would give him a diamond body like those brats back in Kvengard who'd slipped through his fingers.

His own cousin Willem had been granted the gift of the Magnum Opus. The Great Work of transmutation from base flesh to cold radiance. To power beyond comprehension. And what did the stupid little shit do with it? He'd defied his maker and driven Balaur from Jalghuth.

Well, Jule would serve more faithfully.

He slipped into a daydream of what he would do once he became immortal. Kasia Novak topped the list. He wouldn't kill her. No, that was too easy. He'd make her slave. His concubine—

Something iridescent hummed past his face. Jule startled, raising a hand to slap it away. One of the priests glared at him and he swallowed an oath. They had been invited to view the Imperator's famous menagerie, a dome of steel and glass enclosing a section of the palace grounds. He'd expected a few exotic animals, not these fucking *flying lizards*.

"I import my pets from all over the world," the Imperator was saying, "but my greatest treasures are the dragonelles."

Some were the size of insects, others as big as birds of prey. Hanne made sounds of amazement as they flitted from perch to perch, scales gleaming in the sunlight.

"The lesser children of the Alsakhan," the Imperator continued. "You will not find them anywhere else." She held an arm out. One of the dragonelles alit on her wrist. A tiny puff of flame came from its jaws. She snapped her fingers at a handler clad in leathers, who fed it a scrap of meat.

Jule studied the yellow eye. A shiver of excitement pulsed through him. *Soon your father will be dead. A new father will rise from the ashes. One to make nations tremble.*

Old allegiances would crumble and new ones be forged. An empire to last until the end of time.

The party moved on. Hanne steered their conversation to the succession. The topic bored him to tears, but he forced himself to listen. A pity the Imperator could not simply be compelled, but she never went anywhere without her priests in attendance.

"The khedive of Luba is a child," the Imperator said.

"She is twenty-five," Hanne replied. "Since her father's accident, she has exercised sound judgment in the governing of Luba. I am certain she would be more than equal to the responsibility. And, forgive me, but it would appease those who say the succession is not fair."

"Not fair?" the Imperator said sharply.

"I know you value my honesty, O Holiest Anointed One. I am an outsider with little to gain either way. But we have known each a long time, *ja*? I may speak freely?"

"Go on." The Imperator stopped abruptly at a crossing pathway. Jule caught himself mid-stride, narrowly avoiding a collision with one of the priests. He hooked a finger in his sweat-soaked collar. It was humid as a jungle inside the dome.

"It has not gone unremarked upon that the last nine Imperators came from the wealthiest and most powerful emiratis," Hanne said carefully. "In choosing Luba, you would send a message that the system is equitable. It would be part of your magnificent legacy to the people."

"But I have already made insinuations to Yan Kish." She regarded his aunt with a level gaze. "Why should I change my mind at this late hour?"

"I am willing to finance a new deep-water port in Marath," Hanne said. "To ensure that you continue to prosper after you leave office. It would rival Port Sayyad."

Marath was the Imperator's own emirati, which was locked in a centuries-old rivalry with its neighbor, Barbaroi.

The Imperator gave a thin smile. "I want it to be even bigger."

Hanne bowed her head. "Of course. And there will be a more substantial reward once you have named Luba as your successor."

"So you keep saying," the Imperator replied dryly. "Yet I see no evidence of this treasure hoard."

"It is on the way." Hanne lowered her voice. "The rumors of the sword are true. It must be a sign that Luba is destined for greatness."

"Gavriel's blade," the Imperator said slowly. "Are you certain of its authenticity?"

"There is no doubt. She has consulted with the wise men on the Isle of Mystics. Their records have drawings of the sword. If you saw it—"

They all turned at a stir by the door. A group of Luban priests were speaking with the Imperator's guards. They surrounded a disheveled man in chains. The Imperator's expression froze.

"A gift, Anointed One," Hanne said with satisfaction.

The Imperator's head slowly turned. "Gift? He already belongs to me."

Hanne swallowed. "Naturally, I did not mean—"

She raised a hand. Hanne cut off. "Where did you find him?" she demanded.

A priest stepped forward. "At the Soothsayers' Sanctuary. We received an anonymous report that he had returned to the League."

"Was he with anyone?"

"No, Holiness. He was alone. Shall we take him to the water cells?"

The Imperator locked eyes with the prisoner, who inclined his head.

"No. He shall remain here, where he can contemplate his

misdeeds." She gave a chilling smile. "You look well, Tashtemir."

The prisoner bowed, chains clanking. "Thank you, Holiness. In truth, I am a shadow of my former self. I endured the most dreadful exile. The mages abused me at every opportunity."

"So that's where you were," she said thoughtfully.

"Oh, you wouldn't believe the torments they exacted," he said quickly. "Truly, you would have been most pleased, Holiness. It is hardly necessary for you to repeat them. I learned my lesson tenfold."

"Why were you on the soothsayers' isle?"

His back straightened. "I went there to warn them of a conspiracy against you, Holiness. I knew you would not listen to me, but I hoped to convince them. I risked a great deal." He looked fierce. "You *must* heed me, the Danzigers are not—"

"Must?" the Imperator hissed. "A traitor and thief, making base accusations to save his own hide?"

One of the priests kicked him in the kneecap. The prisoner yelped and fell to the ground.

"Summon Yagbu," she said. "Tell him I have another pet to add to my collection, though this one will not be staying long." Her gaze lifted to the apex of the enormous dome. "Suspend him from the roof. Yes, in a cage, I think, until I have further need of him."

The priests bowed low. One ran off to fetch Yagbu. The prisoner had paled at the name—for good reason. Jule had heard of the man. He was the Imperator's torturer.

"You should not have returned, Tashtemir," she said. "But you were always overconfident. I suggest you spend your time in prayer. If the Alsakhan is merciful, perhaps your heart will give out before Yagbu is finished with you."

The Imperator strode off without a backward glance. When they had turned a corner of the path, she laughed. "I had given up hope of finding him. I wonder why he came back? Well, it matters not. He will be executed on the morrow, just before the ceremony. Let him spend the night imagining his end." She laid a hand on Hanne's arm. "Now, I would see this sword."

"SHE'S COMING!"

The khedive gestured curtly from the doorway. Heshima gave her a cold look. The woman had played the part of Jamila al-Jabban, but her true name was Tawfiq al-Mirza, the last living heir to the throne of Luba. A shallow creature driven by boundless ambition, she spoke only of power and riches and revenge on those who had snubbed her.

Valmitra would give the khedive her just reward, of that Heshima had no doubt.

But until then, they had to play the game. Heshima beckoned to Bethen and cloaked them both in a spell of invisibility. It merely bent the light. Once it was fixed in place, the priests wouldn't notice it.

She had agreed to allow the Imperator to view the blade, but only if the witches remained present. It belonged to Dur Athaara now.

Four of the veiled killers entered first. Jaundiced eyes flicked over the room, ensuring it was safe—the fools. Then the Danzigers entered with the Imperator and the khedive.

"Is that it?" The Imperator asked, pointing to the wrapped bundle in the corner.

"The Sword of Gavriel," Tawfik concurred.

"Show me."

The group moved closer. Heshima pressed against the wall, tugging the young witch with her. The khedive drew on a pair of thick, padded gloves and lifted it by the hilt. As the blade slid from the scabbard, Heshima felt the wrongness of it in every nerve ending. First, the odd shape. Broad and curved in the center and tapering to a fine point at the end. Then, the hilt. Inset with jewels and an elaborate gold quillion that resembled the wingtips of a bird.

"What a wondrous object," the Imperator whispered.

Her haughty tone had dissolved into awe. The fey light of the runes flickered across her face, painting it with fire.

"It lay buried in the sands for untold centuries," the khedive replied. "A storm uncovered it just as one of my caravans was passing. Surely it wanted to be found."

"Still, the relic is dangerous. If the witches knew, they might try to lay claim to it. They can be militant on matters of history."

You've no idea, Heshima thought grimly.

"I will keep it well hidden," Tawfik promised.

The Imperator reached for the blade, but the khedive drew it away.

"Forgive me, but it must not be touched." She licked her lips. "The steel is poison."

The Imperator hastily drew her fingers back. "What do the runes say?"

"It is called *Anathema*. The inscription reads: *My heart is light as a feather and heavy as an iron gate*."

"So Gavriel was conflicted?"

"I do not know, Holiness. Perhaps."

The khedive sheathed the blade. The Imperator stared at it for a long moment, then turned, her expression intent.

"To wear the dragon mantle is a grave responsibility. There are mysteries you know nothing of. Are you prepared to face them? To carry out your duty despite what you think you believe?"

The khedive swallowed. "I am, Holiness."

The Imperator kissed her on both cheeks. "I will make the announcement first thing in the morning. Now we must talk.

Of Gavriel and . . . other matters. There is much I must prepare you for."

The khedive curtsied, cheeks flushed with triumph. "I am honored, Holiness. You will not regret your decision."

The party left. Heshima released the invisibility spell just as the door opened again and Balaur skipped inside. He wore a pretty knee-length dress and green slippers. A rag doll was clutched in one chubby fist. If he would only behave as the man he was . . . but no, he seemed to relish playing the part of an innocent child.

"I hear it is done," he said with a smile. "Aren't you pleased, Heshima?"

"I will be pleased when we reach the city." She paused. "So you gave her the Masdari?"

"To sweeten the pot." He laughed merrily. "I think she cares more about punishing him than the sword."

"I still mislike this plan. What if he tells her everything?"

"Between screams?" Balaur said dryly. "I think not."

"There is more." She crossed to the window. "Darya went looking for Malach two days ago. When I tried to track his kaldurite myself, I found nothing. It is gone from his body. Since she has not returned, I can only assume Darya failed. Which means she is likely dead herself."

"Now that *is* a shame," Balaur said with false sympathy.

Heshima rounded on him. "What will you do about it?"

"If he no longer has the stone, then I can pay him a visit myself. It was the only thing blocking me from his dreams."

"He has the ability to cause a great deal of trouble," Heshima muttered. "And we are too close to suffer his interference. What exactly can you accomplish by spying on his dreams? We need him dead!"

"Just leave it to me," Balaur said.

Bethen's wide blue eyes followed him as he threw himself into a chair and hooked his legs over the armrest. She always went mute in his presence. Heshima had planned to leave

Darya guarding the blade. Now she had no choice but to give the task to Bethen, Valmitra save them.

"And no more *displaying* the sword to anyone," she snapped. "It is unspeakably dangerous and it belongs to us now."

"I told you," he replied acidly, "you can keep it!"

Heshima studied the child's face. She wondered if Rachel was dead or still clinging to life.

And which would be worse.

"How did the khedive even know what the blade was?" Heshima asked.

"Not her. The *sahir*. There is an old book on the Isle of the Mystics. It has a rendering of the Morning Star and his blade, *Anathema*."

"You've seen it?"

A nod. "The detail is very fine. There is no mistaking the runes, the shape and hilt. Gavriel is kneeling. A flaxen-haired witch stands above him, casting her sorceries." He laughed at Heshima's expression. "Dur-Athaara erased her from their histories, but she was real."

Heshima scowled. "They are both long dead now."

"And we will have the keys in hand tomorrow at midnight. It is tradition that they be formally transferred to the new Imperator prior to his or her official inauguration. A secret ceremony, for obvious reasons."

"Perhaps we should question Tashtemir ourselves. Learn their plans."

Balaur chuckled. "How do you think we found him in the first place?"

"What do you mean?"

"I have an ally among those who oppose us."

The khedive had told her who was on the ship. Heshima didn't care about the rest of them, but Paarjini and Nikola worried her.

"Who?" she demanded.

He smiled. "It doesn't matter. They are reliable and report everything to me in the dreamworld. We do not need the Masdari. Let the Imperator dispose of him as she likes."

"I would still know the name of your informant," Heshima said. "This is not a game."

"But it is," he replied silkily. "And one we will win. I'm afraid my informant is confidential."

"Then tell me where the keys are being held."

"So you can take them and leave me behind?" Balaur shook his head. "Patience, witch. Patience."

It took all her willpower not to blast him on the spot.

"One more day," she said through gritted teeth. "That is all I will give you."

"I will keep our bargain." He got to his feet. "I'm sure everyone will be satisfied with the outcome."

Heshima watched him leave. She beckoned to Bethen. The golden-haired acolyte sank down next to her, face solemn.

"Is Darya dead?" she whispered.

"I fear so," Heshima replied. "We will have to manage without her. Now, let us continue our training. You must be strong when the time comes."

Bethen nodded. "I will not allow anyone to take the sword. But . . . what will you do with it? After?"

Heshima turned to the relic. The magic buzzed in her head, a low frequency static that set her teeth on edge. "When we sail home," she said, "we will drop it in the deepest part of the sea."

Chapter Seventeen

Fireworks burst in the dark sky above, shooting sparkling streamers in all directions. All around, Qeddah sang and danced and feasted with abandon. Not so long ago, Malach would have joined the revelry, trawling for prey like a barracuda swimming through the shallows.

Now, all he could think about was his daughter and how he would feel when he saw her again.

"Which is the Isle of Dreams?" he asked Koko.

She pointed off the bow. The company was crossing the lake in three sleek launches. Malach stared at the large isle at the center. Lights shone through the dense vegetation. It was too dark to see clearly, but he got the impression of palatial buildings in clusters along its length.

"Is that where you came from?" he asked softly, leaning over the witch, who sat at his feet with her hands bound in front of her.

Darya wore a light cloak with the hood up. She gave a brief nod, eyes cast down.

He frowned. "Are you depressed?"

She looked up at him sharply. It was most satisfying.

"I know you're unhappy," said Malach, who recalled every

condescending remark she'd made during his time in the Pit. "But the sooner you accept your situation, the swifter the time will pass."

"I do accept it," she whispered. "I have no choice. If you just let me guide you to the City of Dawn——"

Malach laughed. "Wander in circles around the desert with you? I think not."

"I can show you where it is, I swear. Balaur will come——"

"No, Darya, you will take me to him. And then you will help me drive him out. *That* is what will happen."

She lowered her face. "As you say."

He shared a look with Koko. The witch pretended to be cowed. He knew she wasn't, not yet, but she would be. He would erase her will completely if that's what it took. Leave her a drooling wreck without the impetus to feed herself. And he would feel not a moment's regret.

A quarter hour later, the launch chugged up to the Isle of the Blessed. Servants appeared at the dock to collect the baggage, greeting everyone with warm smiles. Malach and Alexei waited with Koko in the launch's cabin. When the last of them was gone, he untied Darya's feet and they walked up a short hill to the company's chapter house, an airy, three-story stucco building. Koko said there were three others like it on the isle, as well as a larger meeting house where they could all gather for special performances.

This one belonged only to Hassan's company. They were taking the situation well, Malach thought, perhaps because he only planned to keep his prisoner there a single night. Or perhaps—as Koko claimed—because they had grown fond of him and were eager to see Lucy perform. Hassan had not told them all of what the witch said. It was too blasphemous. They were, after all, the Blessed of the Alsakhan. If their god did not even exist—or if he was something else entirely—well, the eve of the Imperator's succession was not the right time to share this news.

Alexei took charge of Darya while Koko showed him around. The downstairs had a communal gathering area strewn with cushions and low tables, as well as a rehearsal space, music room, kitchen and dining hall. The second and third floors were sleeping quarters.

Malach made sure Darya's bonds were secure, the kaldurite nestled in her own gem pouch around her neck. He left her locked in an empty storage closet. Then he and Alexei joined Hassan on a wide veranda overlooking the lake. Tall bamboo in pots provided screens between the different sitting areas.

"It's a pretty view, yes?" Hassan said, bracing his elbows on the balustrade. "One would never suspect the corruption that eats at the heart of the capital."

"I'm sorry our own troubles have spilled over to your country," Alexei said.

"Spilled over?" he laughed softly. "Balaur brought matters to a head, but they have festered for centuries. Now I know why only priests and soothsayers are allowed to touch the ley. They fear that too much disturbance might wake whatever is bound in the desert."

"You already knew that part, didn't you?" Malach guessed.

A brief nod. "Not all, but about the keys, yes. I always wondered why they existed. We were told that it was to keep marauders from trying to plunder the city, but that made little sense. If a god lived there, why could he not do it himself?"

"We?" Malach prompted. "You mean the Blessed?"

Hassan was quiet for a long moment. At last, he sighed deeply. "I suppose the time for secrets is past." He lifted his sleeve, exposing a faint scar on his inner arm. "This is the brand of the Nazaré Maz. The Breath of God. I was one of them."

Malach stared in disbelief. The flawless olive skin and perfect white teeth. "But you are not . . . "

"Disfigured? No, I ran away when I was still very young.

Before the training began in earnest." He gazed out at the water. "I was one of those boys whose families sent them to the priests in Qeddah. My parents were poor and had too many children. When the recruiters came to our village, the priests convinced them it would be an honor. They also paid my parents a large sum. Too much to turn down."

"They sold you," Malach said flatly.

Hassan shrugged. "It was not so bad at first. After my dusty village, the capital seemed a paradise. We were well fed. Given soft beds and clean clothes. Our duties were light. Working in the kitchens, keeping the incense burning in the sanctuaries. If only I had remained with the regular priests, I would likely still be one of them."

Malach joined him at the balustrade. A soft breeze swept Hassan's straight black hair from his forehead. The Isle of Dreams sat just across a narrow channel, lights twinkling. Close enough to hear a sudden snatch of drunken laughter.

"But then, one day about six months after I arrived, the Nazaré Maz came to inspect the boys and choose new acolytes. A handful volunteered for it. But the rest of us . . . we had heard the rumors. That only half the boys survived the initiation rites and those who did were never the same. They wore veils, but what I could see was enough.

"I hung to the back of the crowd, keeping my head down. But they took me anyway." His voice was calm, but Malach could only imagine the terror of a young boy about to be inducted into such an order.

"Do you know why?" Alexei asked.

Hassan shrugged. "Later, one of them told me that they deliberately choose the prettiest boys. It makes their dedication to the god that much more of a sacrifice."

Malach muttered a soft oath. Yet another reason he despised organized religion.

"I ran away after a few months. It was that or kill myself. I made it into the city and survived on the streets for a while."

"Did they come looking for you?" Malach asked.

"Oh, yes." A dry laugh. "I knew too many of their secrets by then. And I would have been caught if not for Sarea. She ran a club where some of the sisters performed for fun. Sarea dressed me as a girl when the priests came and they were never the wiser. But she helped me to discover my true talents."

He smiled. "When I grew old enough, she brought me to the Isle of the Blessed. They hold open auditions every year. I was to their liking. And so I came to live within sight of my old tormenters." He pointed to a dark shape in the distance. "That is the Citadel of the Breath of God."

They all regarded the island, which now took on a distinctly sinister cast. Unlike the others, few lights burned.

"All this was nearly twenty years ago," Hassan said. "But I do not mind the procession through the countryside. It takes me away from their long shadow."

His intense fear when the priests had arrived in Marath made sense now.

"Does Koko know?"

"Of course. But not the others." He gave them both a level look. "No one else knows."

"Thank you for trusting us with your story," Malach said, impulsively leaning over to kiss his smooth cheek.

Hassan's smile broadened. "It's almost as terrible as yours."

Malach jerked a chin at Alexei. "His is pretty awful, too. Ask him to tell you sometime."

Alexei laughed, and the pall the tale had left over them all seemed to lift.

"The khedive of Luba is a wicked woman and her allies are even worse," Hassan said. "I will do whatever I can to aid you." He paused, gaze intent. "Aren't you afraid? I know you are not Gavriel, but the Teeth of God mistook you for him. What if Valmitra does as well?"

"I hope I never meet Valmitra," Malach replied honestly. "Or any god at all. I just want my daughter back."

"Of course." He fingered the claw around his neck. "But I wonder if it will be that simple, Malach."

"It is," he said stubbornly. "I am a mage of Bal Kirith, nothing more. But there is one thing more that I want. To perform tomorrow. And I would have your blessing for it."

Hassan frowned. "You still wish to?"

A fair question. Didn't he have enough on his plate? But he could feel Lucy, under his skin. Dying to step out in a pair of vicious stilettos. To turn every head. To make them *swoon*.

"It's hard to explain." He exhaled a short, sharp breath, pulse racing. "I just want to."

"Then you should," Hassan said with a smile. "I think the timing might work. If you give the first performance, you will be done by eight. Then you can take this witch and go to the Luban embassy."

"And if you're recognized?" Alexei asked in a low voice. "On stage?"

"I'll hide my Marks," Malach said, though it pained him. "I'll be wearing a wig, full make-up, all of it. Just let me try. If you still think you'd know me, I'll call it off."

"And you will not be performing for the Imperator herself," Hassan interjected. "Not even for the major dignitaries. Let us be clear on that. The main program has been decided for months in advance. But I could add you to one of the smaller venues."

"That's fine," Malach said quickly. "Better."

Alexei nodded slowly. "Fair enough. Now, as for the rest of it, Darya will be known to the guards."

"And she'll do whatever I tell her to do," Malach agreed.

"Can you really compel her to use lithomancy?"

"We'll find out."

Alexei looked dubious, but Malach felt lighter of heart knowing they had a plan—even if it was a sketchy one. But once he got inside the Luban embassy, he could turn the guards against each other. Turn the witches against each other. Let them find out what happened when a mage in his full powers was running loose.

"Then you must rise early to practice," Hassan said sternly, pushing off the balustrade. "I will not have you embarrass me, daughter."

THE MIGHTY REGNUM tree soared a hundred meters above the forest floor. Nikola was already far ahead, lost in the golden dagger-shaped leaves. Malach hurried to climb the rope ladder. By the time he reached the wide upper branch, she was already lying on her side, head propped on one hand, grinning up at him.

Malach sank down next to her. The Morho Sarpanitum spread out in a dense green canopy. Streamers of mist wound through it like a network of rivers. Nikola's eyes were chestnut brown again and glinting with mischief.

"The last time we were here," she said, "you refused my advances."

"Only to keep you from leaving."

"And now?"

He bent his head and kissed her. "I'm feeling much better."

She tugged her head scarf loose. The action made her white shift slip from a slender brown shoulder. "Maybe I don't want you anymore," she teased.

"But you do," he whispered, nuzzling her neck. "I know you do."

"How?" she asked, laughing and pushing him away— though not very hard.

"Because you're mine," he said seriously. "And you'll always be mine."

213

As he spoke the words, he knew they were true. Had been true since the first time he saw her, sitting alone in a cafe. He loved his daughter with a fierce protectiveness, but what he felt for Nikola . . . She brought out the best and the worst in him. He would love her always, to the end of his days, whether she stayed with him or not. It was bittersweet knowledge.

"Catch me, then," she said, and moved so quickly that his hand caught only empty air.

"Wait!" Malach cried.

His heart stopped as she slipped soundlessly over the edge . . .

The forest vanished. Malach stood in a lavish chamber with thick carpets and furnishings inlaid with pearl and ivory. Birds sang through an open window. A sword sat in the corner. It was sheathed in a leather scabbard. Only the hilt was visible, long and chased with gold filigree.

"You may touch it."

He turned.

A woman stood in the doorway. Alabaster skin and hair of spun silver, chin-length and falling in loose waves. She looked younger than him by ten years, but she had the presence and composure of a woman twice her age. The pewter eyes triggered a warning buzz, but it faded when she spoke in a gentle voice.

"You are the son and the heir. It is *yours*."

He hesitated. A distant memory stirred. Bodies sprawled beneath an empty pedestal in Luba. Monstrous creatures seeking a sword.

"Few can wield it safely," she said. "But you are one such. Balaur is another."

He frowned at the name. "How do you know him? Who are you?"

"Cathrynne Rowan." Her voice sank to a whisper. "I came to tell you this. You can kill him with it. You can save your daughter."

"How?"

"The blade has the power to do many things, including to force him from Rachel's body. Draw ley through the runes and cast him out. Then you can slay Balaur's spirit." She eyed the sword. "I helped Gavriel make it. For an aeon it was lost. But you are his closest heir. The sword seeks you now."

"Why did he do it?" Malach asked. "Why did he rebel?"

A cynical smile touched the corner of Cathrynne Rowan's mouth. "Is that really what you want to know?"

A witch. She is a witch. Our age-old enemies . . .

"No," he admitted. "It is this. Why did you help him?"

The smile died. "Because I wanted to." She leaned forward and kissed his lips. She looked over her shoulder, eyes wide . . . and faded away.

Footsteps approached. Slow and heavy, each one resounding like a hammer blow. A trickle of plaster sifted down from the ceiling.

"Anut najmati kalsabah," a voice bellowed. *"Anut alkhayin!"*

He reached for the sword. Something burst into the chamber behind him. Heat seared his skin, peeling it off in charred strips—

MALACH SAT UP, drenched in icy sweat. The sheets were tangled around his legs. He kicked them off, heart pounding. The moon had set. Starlight came through the window, faintly illuminating the black expanse of the lake beyond.

He stumbled to a water pitcher and drained it, wiping his mouth with the back of his arm.

His chamber was on the top floor, a large, comfortable room with simple but well-made furniture. He dragged a chair out to the narrow terrace and sat with his head in his hands, bits and pieces of the dream floating around. It had been so long since he'd dreamt at all. The kaldurite had done something to his subconscious mind. Now that the dam had broken, it was all flooding out.

Nikola, who he thought of constantly. So that much made sense. The Sinn é Maz. Again, no surprise that they would haunt his nightmares. But the sword . . . and the woman.

A witch. That much was clear from her eyes.

She was not from Dur-Athaara. He would know if he'd seen her before. A figment of his imagination, then. Yet she was so striking.

Then it hit him.

"I am you," he whispered, dumbfounded. "You are Lucy."

Chapter Eighteen

"Every performance tells a story," Koko said. "So what is yours?"

Morning sun spilled into a large rehearsal room with a polished wood floor. Mirrors ran the length of three walls, giving reflections from every angle. Koko sat crosslegged on a cushion, sipping tea, as Malach practiced walking in heels.

"I'm not sure," he admitted, trying to keep his ankles from wobbling. "This is harder than it looks."

"It just takes practice," she said. "Heel first, then toe. Small steps. Keep your shoulders back . . . yes! Much better. Aim for the centerline, not straight ahead. I want a *strut*, not a plod."

Hassan was warming up at a long rail by the windows. He wore a plain white dress with thin straps that crossed on his strong, slender back. The abundant black hair was wound into a topknot. His feet were bare, and even those were beautiful, perfectly formed with high arches and small, even toes.

"The song you chose is fast, yes?" he asked.

Malach gave him the beat with one heel and Hassan tried out a bit of choreography. It was like watching silk slide across skin or bright water rush down a riverbed. That smooth. That mesmerizing. Hassan's alter ego, Sultana, might be famous for her voice, but she could dance her ass off, too.

The routine picked up speed—and complexity. At last, he spun to a stop, gleaming with perspiration. "Too hard?" he asked.

"Lucy can handle it," Koko said, winking at Malach.

He nodded, eager to try. "Yes. I'm sure I can learn it."

Hassan smiled. "Good. But Koko is right. It should be personal. What about the women in your life? The ones who influenced you?"

"I have a sister. For many years, I thought she was dead. Then I found her again."

The words came easily now. He no longer translated in his mind; the sentences simply spilled out. Masdari was rooted in the Old Tongue, just like Osterlish. Once he'd realized that, it was like a key turning in a lock. Even unfamiliar words became decipherable.

If nothing else, he thought in amusement, *at least I've picked up two new languages in this pilgrimage around the globe.*

Koko gave an encouraging smile. "I'm happy for you."

"Her name is Kasia. She's very good at reading people, though she herself is hard to know. She hides her feelings, but she can explode if you push her too far." He tried out a low kick. "She's the most dangerous woman I've ever met, and trust me, I've known my share."

"I like her already," Koko said.

"Then there's my cousin, Dantarion. Also dangerous, but she flaunts it." He decided not to mention his *other* child. "And Nikola Thorn. She's Rachel's mother."

"Ah. What is she like?"

"Beautiful. Dark like you. She has a silver tooth."

"And as a person?" Koko prompted.

For a moment, Malach was tongue-tied. He could talk about her for hours and still not convey what she meant to him. Some of it was beyond words. Nikola lived in his heart.

"She does not think enough of herself," he said at last. "But she is resourceful and kind and she fears very little."

"What about your mother?"

"She died when I was four." He did a sharp turn on one toe and managed not to fall.

Koko frowned. "I'm sorry. But think of them when you are Lucy. You must show the softer, feminine qualities but also the strength. Ah, it is time for your fitting."

Four seamstresses bustled inside and took his measurements. Koko was fingering various fabrics when Karl wandered in, covering a yawn. He brightened when he saw what they were up to.

"What do you think?" Malach asked.

"Lucy Fur makes me think of a tiger," Karl said, curling his fingers. "With long claws. How about a jungle print?"

"I like that," Malach said slowly. "But I want to do something witchy, too."

Hassan stopped dancing and stared at him in surprise.

"Charbaz?" Karl exclaimed. "I thought you hated them."

"Not all. I want to cast a spell. Can I have some glitter to throw around?"

Koko arched a brow. "Not in here, you can't. But for the routine . . . why not?"

Hassan stepped up to Malach's side. "Here's what I'm thinking," he said. "Watch me in the mirror. We'll take it in pieces, just try to follow along . . ."

———

AFTER LUNCH, Alexei dressed in the white robe of a servant and took a launch with Hassan to the Isle of Dreams to inspect the performance venue. It occupied a large clearing near the palace, with a stage in the middle. A curtained alcove had stairs leading to underground dressing rooms and tunnels through which performers and props could travel without being seen by the audience.

"After Lucy performs, you can use these tunnels," Hassan said softly, leading him through the warren of chambers and corridors. "The Luban embassy is on the eastern side." He pointed. "That tunnel will lead you to an exit not far from it."

Alexei sketched a map in his mind and marked the spot. "Can I take a quick look now? I won't get too close."

"Go ahead. I must speak with the musicians, the prop master, and many others." He gave a harried smile. "They won't be thrilled with the last-minute schedule change, but I'll call in some favors. Meet me back here in an hour?"

Alexei clasped his arm and took the tight spiral stairs two at a time. He headed in the direction Hassan had indicated, following paths that meandered among groves of trees and flowering shrubs. It was the last night of the Imperator's seven-year reign and servants rushed everywhere with a purposeful air. He asked for directions and was sent past a number of stately buildings to the edge of the southern lakeshore.

The Luban embassy was smaller than the rest, though elegantly proportioned and in good repair. Four stories of pink stone, with wrought-iron balconies on the upper two levels, surrounded by well-tended gardens. He made a circuit of the grounds. Then he sat on a bench that was partly screened by trees and watched the front doors, learning the rhythm of the place.

There were no guards stationed outside. They must be in the antechamber. He watched the servants wreathe all the balconies in festive chains of flowers. Watched them light the lamps on every floor. It all seemed perfectly ordinary.

The low angle of the sun signaled that his hour had nearly passed when the doors opened and a sleek blond man emerged with a petite older woman on his arm. Kasia had warned him, but a jolt of shock still ran through Alexei to see the Danzigers again. The last time he'd set eyes on them, Hanne had been lying dead on the floor of her own drawing room amid the putrid wreckage of her nephew. Yet here they were, finely dressed and—

His breath caught as a small child ran out to join them. Her hair was cut short on the sides, leaving a longer strip down the middle like the crest of a bird. She had golden brown skin and a lovely, heart-shaped face, but his skin went cold. He remembered that horrible voice coming from the child's mouth. *Let me go!*

Four veiled priests took up the rear as the party walked along one of the wide pathways leading toward the palace. Alexei turned away, watching from the corner of his eye. He considered following, but it would be a disaster if he tipped their hand too soon.

Well, at least he knew who else was here.

He rose and hurried back to the performance venue, glad to have confirmed the witch's claim—and gladder still that Malach hadn't been with him.

Chapter Nineteen

"How do we know this soothsayer isn't the one who betrayed you?" Natalya asked.

"We don't," Kasia conceded. "She said she was expecting us. She could have alerted the priests."

"But they didn't arrest all of you," Patryk said, scratching his day-old stubble.

"Which is the smart thing to do," Natalya pointed out. "It makes it seem like she didn't rat you out." She sighed. "I still say the whole plan is blown now. They have Tashtemir, who knows *everything*."

"Not necessarily." Kasia crossed her arms and eyed Paarjini, who nodded. "Let's see if Merat shows up."

"Or the Imperator's guards," Patryk added.

They'd taken the precaution of moving to a different inn the night before. The *Wayfarer* sailed upriver to await word. Valdrian and Cairness were watching the Saffron Palace, which wasn't far from their new lodgings. Odd as it seemed, the mage and witch seemed to have struck up a friendship.

Nikola eyed her companions seriously. "We can't just sit here while Balaur gets those keys. We must do something!"

"We will," Kasia promised. "But we must be cautious, too. What's your gut instinct about Merat?"

"I trust her," Nikola said. "I don't think she's the one who sold Tashtemir out."

"Why not?" Caralexa demanded. "She's the obvious choice."

"You didn't see the way they looked at each other. He's in love with her. She's still angry at him for leaving, but she loves him, too."

"It seemed that way," Kasia agreed. "Though I don't discount that she's a convincing liar."

"Well, let's hope she's on our side," Paarjini said, "because we need her. None of us have ever set foot on the Imperator's isle. We know nothin' about the palace or the guards or any of it. We barely speak the language—"

They turned as Cairness slipped through the door. "She's here," the witch whispered.

Caralexa rose and took a place behind the door. An instant later, Merat entered. The soothsayer looked as though she hadn't slept. Her short dark hair was rumpled, her eyes red above the veil. She carried a leather satchel over one shoulder.

"Please, sit." Paarjini gestured to an empty chair.

Merat sank down and unhooked her veil. "I am still willing to aid you, but I want something in return." Her chin rose. "Free Tashtemir."

"He's still alive?" Kasia said. "That's good news!"

"Yes," Merat replied bitterly, "but his execution is scheduled for tomorrow morning."

Kasia and Natalya exchanged a worried look.

"Where are they keeping him?" Natalya asked.

"In the Imperator's menagerie. They have him in a cage." Her mouth tightened. "A hundred feet off the ground."

"How is he?" Paarjini asked.

"Unharmed for now. Will you help?"

"We wouldna abandon a friend." Paarjini leaned forward. "But tell me, did the priests give *ye* any trouble?"

Cairness fingered her ruby bracelet. Caralexa's hand fell to her sword hilt. Natalya began to casually trim her fingernails with one of Tess's knives. Spassov rested his hamhock forearms on the table and smiled.

"Are you accusing me of summoning the priests?" Merat asked angrily.

"No one is accusing you of anything," Kasia said. "But it is a fair question. Did they realize you were with him? With *us*?"

Merat shook her head. "I made it back to the chapter house without being seen. We were all questioned briefly, but the priests showed no special interest in me."

"We don't think she was followed here," Cairness conceded. She glanced at Valdrian, who had silently entered and stood next to the other mage. He shook his head in confirmation.

"No one knew we'd gone to the Soothsayers' Isle," Paarjini said. "If it wasn't you, then who gave us away?"

"I could ask the same thing," Merat retorted. Her gaze swept the room. "There are many more of *you*. How do I know one of you did not tip them off?"

"It wasn't any of us," Cairness said hotly, cheeks flushing. The young witch wore her temper like the rubies she favored —fiery red and out in the open.

Merat shrugged. "I cannot make you believe me."

"But ye will not leave this room until we do!" Cairness erupted, jumping to her feet.

It might have gotten bad then, but the sudden loud tolling of bells outside silenced the argument. Kasia feared it might be a signal for the priests to swoop down on the inn until she realized that they were pealing across the city. Just like when the Curia chose a new Pontifex.

"The next Imperator has been announced," Merat said.

Cairness scowled and sat back down.

"You don't seem surprised," Nikola said.

"Because I already know who it is." Merat gave a mirthless smile. "Not because I am a soothsayer, but because the rumors started flying last night. By morning, everyone on the lake knew a decision had been reached." She unfolded a flimsy piece of paper and pressed it flat on the table. "The khedive of Luba."

They all leaned forward. Kasia couldn't read the Masdari script, but there was no mistaking the woman's portrait. She wore a confident smile and elegant beaded *abbaz*, her hair caught back in a silver circlet.

"Jamila," Paarjini muttered in disgust.

Merat raised a brow.

"That's what she called herself," Kasia explained. "We had her captive until a few days ago. I suspect she deliberately allowed herself to be taken prisoner."

"I despise the woman," Natalya said, "but it *was* a bold move."

"Her real name is Tawfik al-Mirza," Merat said. "I know little about her except that her father was the last khedive and he died a few years ago."

"Well, we know she made it to Qeddah," Nikola said, fingering the poster. "Where did you get this?"

"They are being plastered on every tavern wall and street corner," Merat replied. "So the citizens may look upon their new Imperator. Only the court attends the actual succession ceremony."

She opened the leather satchel and dropped a dozen metal tokens on top of the picture. "These will permit you access to the Isle of Dreams. Tonight's festivities require hundreds of cooks, porters, servants, carpenters, and entertainers who have their own retinues. The royal guard will be checking tokens at the docks, but once you are on the Isle, it should not be difficult to blend with the crowds."

Merat withdrew another small pouch. It rattled as she set it down. "Beads in the color of the Imperator's household servants. You cannot find these in the market, but if you sew them to the hems of simple white garments, they will give you an excuse to come and go from the palace itself."

"Thank you," Kasia said. "You have risked a great deal."

"Not nearly as much as you will."

"We need one more thing." She set a stack of sketches on the table. "Replicas of the seven keys. Tashtemir was going to do it, but . . ."

She and Natalya had stayed up half the night working on them. If there was any hope of fooling the Imperator, they had to be perfect.

"I can manage that," Merat said. "We will meet beforehand."

"Do you know when the handover happens?" Kasia asked.

"Not exactly, but it can't be before midnight. I have seen the schedule of events. The Imperator and her successor will dine together at nine with all the other ambassadors. After that, they receive gifts and well wishes from foreign delegations. Then the local power brokers. Merchants, mystics, the Blessed, the priests—"

"Priests? Is it possible the keys would be exchanged then?"

"These are not private meetings. They're held in the main audience chamber in full view of the entire court." She smiled. "I attended the last two. They're interminable. Neither ended before eleven, usually closer to midnight."

"Then we will meet you at nine o'clock," Kasia proposed. "It will be full dark by then."

"What about Tashtemir?"

"We need him to find the keys, so he will be freed first."

"And if the alarm is sounded?"

"I can delay that," Paarjini said. "All we'll need is an hour or so. He'll guide us to the keys, we make our escape and leave the city."

"All right," Merat said, tucking Kasia's sketches into the satchel. "I will meet you with the replicas. There's a garden on the south side of the palace. It has a stream with a bridge and a small wood. I will come to the bridge at nine."

"And the menagerie?"

"On the western side. It's enclosed by a brick wall and a glass dome. There's only one way in and you can be sure it will be well-guarded." Merat smiled. "But here's a piece of news you will like. There is no ban against using ley on the Isle of Dreams. If you are discreet, no one should notice."

"Thank you," Paarjini said, clasping her hand. "We will be there."

Merat squeezed her fingers. "May the Alsakhan grant you success. Tashtemir made a mistake, but I believe he has paid for it. The Imperator is a cruel woman." Her mouth tightened as she rose. "I will not be sorry to see her gone."

Once she'd left the room, Cairness and Valdrian slipped out to follow.

"Well, the course is set," Paarjini said. "We have a few hours to get ready. Who knows how to sew?"

"I do," Nikola said.

"So do I," Kasia added.

Tess had made her learn. She'd never done much more than mend stockings or sew on errant buttons, but she doubted anyone would look too closely.

"Then you two can manage the beads. I'm thinkin' it's best to work in teams." She eyed Natalya and Patryk. "Any thoughts about how to get Tashtemir out o' this menagerie?"

"A few," Nat said. "I'll discuss it with Valdrian and Cairness." She turned to Caralexa. "And you, if you're willing."

The mage nodded. "Tashtemir patched me up a few times when I was injured. And we need him. You can count on me."

Natalya nodded. "That gives us two mages, a witch . . ." She glanced at Patryk. "And a big addle-pated bear of a priest."

He lit a cigarette and blew smoke at the ceiling. "Sounds about right."

"What about the knights?" Kasia asked.

There were three left: Ashe from Nantwich, Klaus from Kvengard, and Naresha from Jalghuth. Since the attack on the ship, the men had forged a close bond. Now they were outside, guarding the inn.

"Klaus knows a bit o' Masdari. We'll send him to hire a boat for the evening. They can wait for us in one o' the coves for when it's time to go."

Nikola cleared her throat. "Paarjini. We'll have to force. You do realize that?"

The witch's face hardened. "We promised the Mahadeva we wouldn't."

"That was before we knew everything. But there's too much at stake now. Surely you can see that."

Nikola had an air of such quiet authority, it was easy to forget she'd been a char not long ago. Then again, didn't it take strength and courage to toil each day for a pittance? Certainly more than the soft lives of their paymasters.

Things were already changing in Nantwich, where the Mistress of Chars, Lucie Moss, had organized the Arx workers into a union. Kasia hoped the rebellion would spread to Kvengard and Novostopol, too. It was past time the Curia practiced what it preached.

She tuned back in to the argument, which seemed to be going in circles.

"It's one thing to get all the way inside the palace unseen, but to get out again?" Nikola was saying in an exasperated tone. "Impossible."

"We'll use invisibility spells," Paarjibi shot back. "And force t'where, exactly? Ye don't even know where yer goin'!"

"Jamila told us. The Ceaseless Sands."

"Which are hundreds o' kilometers across. We could end up anywhere."

"She has a point," Caralexa added. "I say we hire the boat. Fuck those magic boxes. That witch back at the Arx was cut in half."

"I agree," said Kasia, who remembered every detail of the bloody scene. "Forcing is too dangerous."

Nikola gave them each a hard stare. Then she nodded unhappily. "Fine." A mutter under her breath: "But you'll see I'm right."

"What about the kids?" Paarjini asked. "They won't like being left behind. And if they try to follow, it'll be a disaster."

Sydonie and Tristhus. They should never have been allowed to come. The boy had nearly died once already. And —even though she was probably an awful person for thinking it—Kasia still didn't entirely trust them.

Malach had found them living at Bal Agnar. What if they'd been Balaur's little moles all along? *Someone* had tipped off those priests. Probably the same someone who set up the ambush on the river. Just because Tristhus had been injured didn't mean he was innocent.

"We shouldn't tell them anything," Kasia said. "Nothing important, I mean. Can't we just . . . lock them in their room?"

Nikola shot her a troubled look, as if she knew exactly what Kasia was thinking. "You think those kids wouldn't find a way out? No, we'll say they have a very important task. Guarding the cargo from thieves. They might go for it."

"You can be the one to tell 'em," Paarjini said dryly.

Lexa rose to her feet and nodded at Natalya and Patryk, who were whispering with their heads bent together.

"Let's go hammer out the details of this jailbreak," she said.

The three of them left. Paarjini went looking for Valdrian and Cairness, while Kasia and Nikola found needles and thread and began sewing beads onto the hems of their robes.

"I've been meaning to ask," Nikola said with a quick sideways glance. "Is there any way I could visit this Garden of yours?"

"I wish there were. But bringing another person into my dream . . . I don't know how such a thing would be done." Kasia frowned. "Not without the ley, and we cannot risk using it until tonight."

"But you saw her?" Nikola asked anxiously.

"Rachel is well." Kasia smiled, hoping she'd believe the lie. "I told her that her mother and father love her very much."

"I do," Nikola said quietly. "Love her, I mean. I didn't want to because I knew I couldn't keep her. I'd promised her to Malach, you see. It was the price of our bargain. He would help me leave Novostopol and I would give him a child."

"I didn't know that." Kasia kept her eyes on the beadwork.

Nikola snorted. "Of course it all went to hell. He'd promised Falke a child, too. Did you know *that*?"

She nodded. "Falke hinted at it, though he never said it outright."

"Anyway, I just . . . " Nikola sighed. "I just want to do right by them both, but Rachel especially. She's been through so much."

"She's strong. Like her mother."

Nikola looked down, quickly wiping away a tear.

"My adopted parents never wanted me," Kasia said matter-of-factly. "They only did it because Falke ordered them to. I suppose he paid them well to take me in. The Reverend Mother Clavis claimed they didn't know who I really was, but I always had the sense that my mother disliked me. She never said so directly, and she never laid a finger on me. But I just knew. I can't remember her touching me, except if she had to."

Nikola winced. "Sounds awful."

"It was odd." She picked up another bead and ran her

needle through the hole. "My father was kinder. Him, I cared for very much."

"He's gone, I take it."

She nodded. "Heart attack. It was shortly after I failed the Probatio tests. My mother said the shame of it killed him."

Nikola shook her head. "What a load of horseshit!"

"I ran away after that. How did *your* parents take it when you failed?"

"Shocked beyond belief."

"Were you?"

"Not really," Nikola admitted. "I didn't care that much. Of course, I didn't know how difficult life would actually be."

"I wasn't surprised, either. I expected to fail."

They eyed each other in commiseration.

"What did your parents do?" Kasia asked.

Nikola returned to her sewing, each stitch neat and precise —unlike Kasia's uneven lines.

"They didn't kick me out. In fact, they hugged me and tried to be reassuring. But they never looked at me the same again. It's like I was some sketchy stray they'd taken in and they weren't sure I could be trusted around the kids."

"Do you have brothers and sisters?"

"Two of each. They all passed. We haven't spoken in years."

"Well, the tests are useless," Kasia muttered, biting off a thread. "Mario Karolo passed them. So did Luk. He was a pontifex!"

"And they were both soulless killers without a shred of decency," Nikola agreed. "Saints, we'd better hurry. How many of these robes are there?"

"Eight, I think."

They bent to their task in silence after that. The neighborhood was much rowdier than the more expensive ones on the lakeshore. As the afternoon lengthened, the hubbub grew louder. Drunken arguments mingled with bicycle horns, firecrackers, shrieking children, squawking chickens, and the thin, piercing cries of circling Markhawks.

By five-thirty, the last silver bead was sewn on and they each donned an abaya. Natalya stashed a dozen throwing knives in hidden sheaths about her person. The witches stuffed their gem pouches to bursting. Valdrian oiled his spring-blade mechanism and Caralexa practiced squats and handsprings in the dusty yard, sending the chickens scattering with frightened clucks.

At Nikola's coaxing, the children agreed to stay and "guard the treasure," along with Alice. The hound would protect them if anything went wrong, and Kasia wouldn't risk her on the Isle of Dreams, where a single nip of a priest's poisoned flesh could kill her.

The three knights procured a boat, which they would anchor in a cove of the nearby Isle of Cats should a swift getaway be needed.

Kasia found a narrow stair that led to the roof of the inn. She sat on the tiles and watched the sun set. Lights shimmered along the length of the Isle of Dreams, reflecting in the lake like drowned stars.

Kasia shuffled her deck and dealt a reading.

The Sun and Moon. The Serpent. The Twins.

Then The High Priestess, The Fool, and Fortitude.

All the same—but with one change.

Instead of The Wheel, the last card was The Tower. It perched atop a mountain of bare rock. Jagged lightning struck the golden dome on top, which was shaped like a crown. Two people tumbled from the narrow windows, chased by gouts of flame. One wore a blue cloak, one a red cloak.

Danger and catastrophe. A sudden reversal of fate. Hubris and excessive ambition punished from on high.

It was a terrifying image, but—like Death—The Tower wasn't always bad news. Sometimes it meant liberation from psychological constraints. A blinding flash of insight that shattered the illusions of the material world.

Kasia shuffled and fanned the cards again. Closed her eyes and chose at random. Seven more times. Each produced the same cards in precisely the same order.

Even after so many years practicing cartomancy, even believing wholeheartedly as she did, it raised the hair on her arms.

The final spread.

She knew it wouldn't change until Balaur was dead—or she was.

───────────

MALACH CLOSED his eyes as Koko swept shadow over his lids.

"Don't squeeze them shut," she muttered. "Just pretend you're sleeping."

"Sorry."

She'd been working on him for over an hour. Foundation, then an array of creams and powders. Earlier that afternoon, after he'd rinsed off the sweat from Hassan's brutal rehearsal, Karl had given him the closest shave of his life, then tweezed his thick brows. That was the only painful part. The rest made him feel like a block of granite being patiently shaped into something delicate and pretty.

"When can I look?" he demanded.

"Not yet." She outlined his lips with a pencil.

"Is that red?"

"The reddest red." She painted them with a tiny brush and ordered him to kiss a blotter.

"Priest," he called over. "What do you think?"

Koko made a tsking noise. "That's cheating."

"Smoking hot," Alexei called from across the dressing room.

Malach smiled. "I bet I am."

"You don't lack confidence at least," Hassan said dryly. "That's good. Confidence will cover any mistake."

Both he and Koko had already given private performances to the Golden Imperator. Malach understood the honor he was being shown to have two of the most famous Blessed in the country overseeing his debut. Yet the nerves that had plagued him that morning were gone.

He felt—there really was no other word for it—*joy*. A fierce, heart-pounding exhilaration, as if anything at all might happen. As if the last horrible year was just a dream and he'd awoken to find himself living another life entirely.

One that was fucking fabulous.

"We're ready for hair," Koko announced.

"Blonde," he said immediately.

"Yes, I know, but there are many possibilities."

"The lightest you have. Not long or short. Medium-length. And I want a bit of curl."

"I know just the one," Karl said, jumping to his feet.

Malach tried to peek over his shoulder at the mirror, but Koko swiftly blocked his view. "Only when she's perfect."

He waited impatiently as she set the wig on his head, tugging it down and adjusting the hairline. Expert fingers fluffed his hair. She let out a sigh.

"I'm a genius," she said. "You can't deny it."

Karl was grinning like a maniac. He ran into the hall and gathered the rest of the company, who had been waiting outside the dressing room. They surrounded him in a cloud of perfume and exclamations of delight. Farasha fluttered her butterfly wings. She blew him an air kiss so she wouldn't ruin his makeup.

"Stunning," she whispered.

Now Malach's nerves did kick in. He swallowed with a dry mouth. Koko swept an arm with dramatic flair. "Say hello to Miss Lucy Fur!"

She swung the chair around to face the mirror, bursting

into pleased laughter at his expression. "I see you're in love with yourself now. Well, it's time for the final touch. The *tuck*."

"Tuck?" he echoed, still staring dumbstruck into the mirror.

"That thing between your legs?" She flicked her fingers distastefully. "It's got to go, daughter."

Chapter Twenty

On this, the last night of the Golden Imperator's seven-year reign, no expense had been spared in living up to the Isle of Dreams' lofty name.

Strings of twinkling white lights adorned the boughs of the fruit trees. Flower petals covered the ground like drifts of snow. Torches and braziers burned along every pathway. The weather was perfect, balmy and clear.

Knots of courtiers in their finest silk robes moved between the embassies, each of which was hosting its own gala. More entertainments filled the spaces between—jugglers and acrobats, storytellers and singers. The scents of spiced food and sugary confections filled the air.

Nikola took it all in through her gauzy veil, paying particular attention to any tall, dark-skinned women. Heshima must be here somewhere. Bethen, too, though Nikola thought she could handle her fellow novice easily if it came down to a fight.

The tokens Merat gave them had worked and the guards at the bridge waved them all through without any questions. The rescue team had headed for the menagerie to free Tashtemir, leaving Nikola, Kasia and Paarjini to mingle with the crowds and keep an eye out for their enemies. So far, they'd seen no sign of anyone from the Luban compound.

My daughter is here somewhere, too.

Nikola knew it wasn't really Rachel, but the thought of seeing her brought a wave of dread. Easier to focus on Heshima, to stoke her rage at the betrayal. Her former mentor was strong, but Nikola had learned a trick or two. Setting her on fire would be just the beginning—

"Where shall we go?" Kasia whispered in her ear.

"How much time until we meet Merat?"

"About an hour," Paarjini said. "Can we eat something?"

"Yes, I'm starved." Kasia linked her arms in theirs and steered them all over to a groaning buffet table.

"How do we eat with the veils?" Paarjini hissed.

"Carefully." Kasia laughed softly. "Watch him."

A tall man at the end of the table was casually slipping morsels of food beneath his own veil, which he held from his face with one hand.

"I don't know how either of you can think of food," Nikola muttered.

"I don't know how you *cannot*," Paarjini said, stuffing a pastry into her mouth.

They were dressed as servants and a few of the guests cast them admonishing looks.

"At least be discreet," Nikola whispered.

Paarjini pretended to rearrange the platters, snagging orange-glazed shrimp when no one was looking and popping them under her veil. Kasia boldly heaped a plate high with food as though she meant to take it to her mistress, then hid behind a date palm, returning with an empty plate and bulging gut.

Nikola's own stomach churned. She kept thinking of Tashtemir. He was the only one who knew where in the palace the keys were kept. And besides that, if the others failed, he would be executed in the morning.

"Don't fret," Kasia said, sensing her black mood. "Patryk and Natalya make a fine team. Plus they have the two mages. And Cairness."

"Don't say it'll be easy," Nikola warned. "You'll jinx them."

"I wasn't going to. But you must trust them. You believe in Valmitra, don't you?"

"How can I not? I've seen her myself."

"Well, I say that she's guiding events even in sleep. Remember what I said about the ley working in spirals? We've been brought here for a reason. And now we must have faith."

"I do," Paarjini mumbled around a mouthful of honeyed rice balls. She tossed one to an aggressive peacock, which snapped it up.

Nikola smiled, realized Kasia couldn't see it, and squeezed her hand. "You talk sense, as always."

They drifted away from the buffet and spent a few minutes watching two young girls with trained cats that pranced across see-saws and leapt through a series of ever-higher platforms. Then a troupe of contortionists who made Nikola's back ache just looking at them. Some of the sooth-sayers had a table at which they were reading fortunes. Merat was not there and they continued on, past games of chance and verdigris-painted human statues and half-naked boys conducting foot races while onlookers cheered or howled as their favorites lost.

Servants moved unobtrusively through the crowds, refilling goblets and whisking away empty plates. They saw no sign of the Imperator herself, though that was hardly surprising. She would be enjoying private entertainments inside the palace.

"What's going on over there?" Kasia craned her neck. "I think I know that song."

A crowd had gathered around a nearby stage. All the tables were full, so they joined the throngs standing at the back.

"So do I," Nikola said in surprise. "What's it called again?"

The musicians were playing a cover of a pop song that used to be popular at the clubs in Novo, but with twangy Masdari acoustic instruments.

"Um . . ." Kasia swayed to the thumping beat. "Isn't it. . .*Cold-Hearted Bitch?*"

Nikola laughed. "Yes!"

She started humming along as a spotlight hit the stage. Potted palms and ropy vines created a jungle motif. Cheers erupted as a blonde woman in a leopard print robe crawled out from between two of the trees. She slunk across the stage with feline grace, head low, shoulders loose. When she reached the very edge, she arched her back and howled in time with the refrain.

Then, in a single lithe movement, she leapt to her feet. A quick jerk of the sash and the robe slid from her shoulders. She wore a tight, shimmering dress similar to the wrapped garments of the witches, but much shorter and swelling to accommodate generous cleavage. Her fingers sprang open, tossing handfuls of glittery powder into the air. It drifted down, gilding her bare skin, her hair, and the entire front row of the audience.

The crowd, which had been drinking since noon, went insane.

The beat started to build toward the second chorus as she stalked up and down, hips swaying in a taunt, finger waving for the lyric: *Boy, you asked for trouble.* One hand traced her hourglass waist and hip.

"And now you found it," Nikola mouthed. "But boy, you got more than you bargained for. 'Cause I'm a—"

"Cold-hearted bitch!" Kasia finished loudly.

No one even turned to look. The dancer's raw charisma had them all spellbound and she knew it. *Owned it.* Nikola hooted with the rest of them as she leapt down from the stage and prowled through the tables, cupping cheeks with her long crimson nails, then shoving the owners back in their seats.

Feet stomped, hands clapped, as she slipped back into the dance, each movement precisely choreographed but utterly abandoned at the same time. It heated the blood just to watch. Nikola had rarely gone to the clubs. They were too sweaty. Too packed. But now she missed it. The press of bodies. The anonymous thrill of merging physically with total strangers.

The dancer threw more glitter around, conjuring magic with the flick of a wrist, the bat of a long lash. At last she paused in front of a plump middle-aged man. A dagger-heeled shoe planted itself on the table. He stared up at her, starstruck. She tossed her hair back and pivoted, sweeping one leg clear over his turban. He clutched his chest as though he might have a heart attack, though he wore a thrilled smile to be singled out.

"Look at her thighs," Nikola whispered. "I wish I had legs like that."

Paarjini squinted. An odd grin twisted her mouth. "Tha's Malach."

Nikola assumed she'd misheard. "What?"

"Yes, it is." A firm nod. "Tha's the aingeal."

Nikola laughed. Then she took another look. A long, good one.

Every movement was light and feminine. Not an exagger-ated pantomime, either. She seemed perfectly at home with her voluptuous curves, with the clothes, the shoes, all of it. Yet the rather heavy set of her shoulders . . . the chiseled profile . . . and, let's be honest, the attitude . . .

"Thirteen bloody hells," Nikola said in delight. "It is!"

"I told ye."

She glanced over at Kasia. Saints, but the woman could give lessons in composure to the Pontifex Feizah herself! She looked completely unsurprised by this chance meeting—and the latest incarnation of her brother. All she said was, "I wonder what happened to his Marks?"

Paarjini shrugged. "Makeup? But I have to say, I think I like him better as a woman."

Nikola watched in amazement as he—she?—dropped into a full split and bounced up again, spinning away to wild applause.

"We need to find a way backstage," Kasia whispered. "Wait for him there."

Nikola nodded, unable to tear her eyes away. What road had led him to this place? A million questions swirled in her mind. But she knew one thing for sure. He'd just ripped her heart out and tucked it into his pocket.

Or maybe his bra.

"I love him so much," she said to Paarjini, tears in her eyes.

The witch looked resigned. "I know ye do, sister."

THE CHEERS of the crowd filtered down the stairwell, accompanied by the thumping rhythm of drums. Alexei would have given a great deal to watch, but someone needed to mind the witch and the task had fallen to him.

He studied himself in the vanity mirror. It was all a bit surreal. If anyone had told him a year ago—Saints, *two weeks ago*—that he'd be sitting in a dressing room in Qeddah while his sworn enemy performed in drag, he would have laughed. And yet here he was, not only feeling left out but admiring Malach's courage.

He caught Darya's reflection. She sat on the floor, watching him with an unreadable expression.

"I saw the Danzigers today," he said. "You keep interesting company, witch."

"As do you," she replied. "What is a Raven priest of the Via Sancta doing with an aingeal dian?"

He frowned at the unfamiliar term.

"A Fallen One," she clarified. "I thought you hated them as much as we do."

He ignored the remark. "Did you know that the Danzigers were dead a few months ago?" Just like that, his blood started to simmer. "That they led the Order of the Black Sun in Kvengard? I spent months searching for missing children, only to find they'd been murdered at the Danzigers' manor house. Is your goddess worth *that*?"

She recoiled slightly. "I've nothing to do with it!"

"You ally yourself with the man who ordered it. So you'll have to come up with something better." He shook his head in disgust. "Say you did free this deity. Do you honestly believe Valmitra will look kindly on you, after all you've done? Stood by while your own queen was slain at Balaur's hand? And if you think he won't betray you at the last, you are a fool as well as a murderer."

Her face had gone very pale. "You know nothing, priest—"

"I know this." He found an icy calm. "Your plans will fail. And you will all go down in history as the greatest traitors Dur-Athaara has ever seen."

"We are heroes," she spat. "But you are descended from the aingeals. Why should I expect you to understand?"

"The fallen ones?" He laughed. "Yes, I fought them for years. But none of them—not a one except Balaur!—ever stooped as low as you have. Malach has far more of a conscience than you do." He expelled a forceful breath. "Never mind. Why am I bothering? Just know that soon enough, you will be the instrument of your sisters' downfall."

She glared daggers at him. "I will enjoy watching Heshima flay you, piece by piece—"

The door burst open. Karl stood there. His eyes were huge. "You must come. Koko . . ."

Alexei leapt to his feet. "What happened?"

"I found her in one of the corridors," Karl said tonelessly. "She has been stabbed. I don't——"

Alexei barely heard the rest of his words. He glanced at Darya. She was trussed in such a web of knots, there was no chance she'd go anywhere. He gripped Karl's arm. "Take me there."

He had to push the boy to get him going. Costumed performers of every variety crowded the other dressing rooms and spilled into the corridor, waiting for their turns to go on stage. A few gave them curious stares as they pushed their way through to one of the distant tunnels. The echo of voices and pulse of the music dimmed.

"Did you see who did it?" Alexei asked, heart pounding. "How bad is she?"

Karl stared straight ahead. He seemed lost to shock. "Just a little farther."

They went a dozen more steps. The tunnel ahead was dark and empty. Alexei's scalp tingled. *Wrong. Something is wrong.* He drew Karl to an abrupt halt and turned the boy to face him. His features were slack, the pupils dilated to black buttons.

The knowledge struck like a fist to his gut. *Compulsion.*

"A message for you." Karl's grin was a rictus, as if fine threads pulled at the corners of his mouth. "It's too late."

Alexei spun away and sprinted back down the tunnel. The door to Malach's dressing room was slightly ajar. He kicked it wide. Darya lay on her side. The hilt of a knife jutted from her breast. Blood trickled from the corner of her open mouth. He turned back to the door, scanning the warren of tunnels, but whoever had done it was gone.

"Priest," she croaked.

He sank down next to her. He had seen many battlefield

injuries and knew immediately that the wound was a fatal one. Not through the heart, or she'd already be gone, but close enough.

They'd been found out somehow. Betrayed.

"Who was it?" he whispered urgently. "Who came here?"

Her mouth split in a red smile. The ley around her swirled, gathered, slid into the steel blade. A fiery dose of adrenaline hit a second before his mind registered the danger. His gaze flicked to her neck. The drawstring bag holding the kaldurite was gone.

Alexei tensed to flee and was thrown violently backwards. The mirror cracked as he slammed into the vanity. He tumbled off in a shower of tubes and bottles. Invisible hands gripped his throat. Squeezing tighter, tighter. He kicked, over-turning a chair.

Above them, the audience clapped and roared. It merged with the buzzing in his ears.

He tried to crawl to Darya, to yank the blade from her flesh, but the brutal vise around his throat made his move-ments sluggish. The witch was bleeding out. Her eyes were half-closed. Yet she watched him struggle with a stubborn gleam.

His last conscious thought was to wonder which of them would die first.

Chapter Twenty-One

Nikola watched Malach take a bow, flushed and exultant. A group of gorgeous women in costume blew kisses at him and tossed several bouquets, which he scooped up and pressed to his chest. He looked as happy as she'd ever seen him. It made her heart skip.

You deserve this, she thought. *You really do.*

She realized that she hadn't thought of Rachel or Balaur or Tashtemir or any of it for at least twenty minutes. But her friends were risking their lives in the Imperator's menagerie at that very moment. Nikola's smile died.

At least I found him. I found him, and I'll never lose him again.

If he still wants me—

"There's a stairway. It must lead to the dressing rooms!"

Nikola turned. Kasia tugged at her hand. Paarjini followed as they made their way around the fringes of the crowd to a curtained alcove near the stage. A regal, dark-skinned woman stood at the edge, watching Malach with a look of pride.

Nikola smiled and tried to walk by. The woman blocked her path and said something politely in Masdari. No doubt informing her that she wasn't permitted backstage.

"I know him," Nikola replied in Osterlish, pointing at Malach. "We're good friends."

He was still basking in the glow and hadn't spotted them yet.

The woman shook her head with a helpless shrug. Two burly bouncer-types ambled over, standing to either side of her. They looked distinctly less friendly.

Then she felt it. A projective spell being worked somewhere close by. Paarjini muttered a furious oath. One hand dropped to the pouch at her waist. Nikola grabbed her wrist, shaking her head.

"Wait," she hissed. "There's too many people."

Kasia tore her veil off and took a step towards the stage. One of the guards seized her arm. He spoke sternly and pointed at the exit.

"Malach!" she yelled, but the musicians struck up an encore and her voice was drowned out.

The world unfocused as Nikola opened all her senses to the magic. It was like following faint strains of music. It resonated most strongly . . . directly below her feet.

"You have to let us through," she cried, lifting her own veil. "Please!"

The woman jerked back. *My eyes.* Naturally, they had reason to fear witches. Then the woman's gaze swung to Kasia. Narrowed and fixed on Nikola again. She tapped her canine tooth. It took a moment to realize what she wanted. Nikola bared her teeth in a big fake smile, the way little kids did for photographs.

The woman nodded to herself and gestured to the guards to step back. Before she could change her mind, Paarjini barreled through the gap, flying down a set of spiral stairs with Nikola and Kasia at her heels. Clusters of people waited at the bottom. They elbowed their way through to a chorus of affronted murmurs. The spell pulsed in Nikola's head now, so strong she could hardly believe none of them felt it.

The source was behind the fifth door on the right.

By the time Nikola reached it, Paarjini was already inside. The awful scene drew her up short. A witch lay in a pool of blood, wrists and ankles bound, the hilt of a knife buried in her chest. A man sprawled beside her, unmoving. Kasia ran to his side. Her reserve finally cracked. She looked gutted as she sank down to her knees and cupped his face.

Nikola quickly closed the door before anyone else saw. She didn't recognize the witch, but Paarjini obviously did. They locked eyes with mutual animosity. How the woman could still be alive, Nikola didn't know. She'd lost so much blood . . .

Paarjini thrust out a hand. A summoning spell ignited in her carnelian ring. The knife flew across the room, slapping hilt-first into her palm. The instant the metal left the witch's body, she shuddered and went still.

Her magic died with her.

Yet the man didn't stir. His lips were blue, his skin ashen. Alexei Bryce, Nikola guessed. The priest who had been forced in the box with Malach.

"No," Kasia whispered. She dragged Alexei upright and shook him. "Breathe, damn you!"

Paarjini crouched down. "Is he . . ."

"Not yet!" Kasia slapped his face, a ringing crack that made Nikola wince. Blue eyes shot open, wide and panicked. He gasped—a huge, sucking breath like he'd just surfaced from a deep plunge in arctic waters. Then he burst into a fit of hoarse coughing. Kasia held his shoulders, murmuring soft words. One of his cheeks bore a livid handprint, but he didn't seem to have any other injuries.

At least, he gathered himself and stared at her in wonder. "How—?"

Kasia's fierce embrace practically knocked him over again. She was laughing and crying at the same time. The priest closed his eyes and buried his face in her hair. They held each other tightly, not speaking.

Nikola turned away to give them privacy, glad but also envious. Their love seemed so *easy*. So simple and straightforward. Not like her own complicated mess of a life.

Paarjini stalked to the door and peered through the crack.

"What's her name?" Nikola asked, eyeing the dead witch.

"Darya. One o' those who minded Malach at the Pit."

Nikola was still trying to make sense of it all when Paarjini grinned. "Speakin' o' the devil herself." She stood back from the door.

The rapid click of high heels approached in the corridor. Nikola straightened her back, suddenly nervous. The last time she'd come with her sisters to Malach's rescue, it hadn't worked out well, to say the least. Would he be angry? Relieved to see her? Or did he hate *all* witches now? She braced for an outburst.

But when he stepped through the door, Malach hesitated in a manner that was entirely unlike him. He must already have known she was there. The tall woman was with him— the one who'd asked to see Nikola's silver tooth. So he'd told his friends about her. She couldn't help wondering what he'd said.

A quick glance told him that Darya was dead and Alexei was alive. He brightened a little at Kasia's smile, but his eyes were serious as he regarded Nikola.

"I'm so sorry," he whispered. "Sorry for all of it."

She stepped up to him, heart beating fast. "It doesn't matter." She kissed him and tasted lipstick. He lifted her up, crushing her against his impressive bosom.

"I never caught your stage name, by the way," she whispered in his ear.

"Lucy Fur."

She laughed. "Of course."

He pulled back. "You saw?"

She nodded.

"What did you think?" He didn't seem worried, just curious.

She touched his perfectly contoured cheek. "I thought you were *hot*, Lucy."

His eyes twinkled. "She's a lesbian, in case you were wondering —"

"All right," Paarjini interjected. "Ye make a fine woman, aingeal, I dinna deny it. But there's naught time for singin' yer praises. A friend o' yers is in hot water and we came to save him, among other things." She glanced pointedly at Nikola. "Time's runnin' out."

Malach peeled off the blonde wig and scrubbed a hand through his hair. "Friend?" he echoed in bewilderment. "Who?"

———

TASHTEMIR PEERED down through the narrow bars of his cage. Every movement sent it swaying over a hundred feet of empty air.

If he could pick the lock and leap out, the fall would kill him—but perhaps not instantly. If his skull failed to crack open, he might lie there broken and bleeding for a while. It was not an appetizing prospect.

"My friend!" he called down. "Sorry to bother you!"

Fat Yagbu craned his thick neck up at the cage. "Not at all, old friend. What troubles you?"

He had a cultured, melodious voice that sounded like it belonged to another man entirely. Someone two hundred pounds lighter and with far fewer scars.

"I was wondering if the Imperator meant what she said about the Forty-Nine Agonies?"

"When *doesn't* she mean what she says?" Yagbu replied mildly. He ran a palm over his bald head. "I cannot recall a single instance of that."

"Nor I," Tash admitted. "It just seems excessive. I will be executed tomorrow anyway."

Yagbu's regretful smile was visible even at a distance. "If it were up to me, I would cut off your head and be done with it." His massive shoulders hitched. "But I am merely the Imperator's instrument of justice. Nothing personal."

"Of course not," Tash agreed. "I've always had the utmost respect for your work ethic and even temperament. But . . . what if I were to have an unfortunate accident?"

For all his physical menace, Yagbu had the face of a scholar. He wore thick, round, black-framed spectacles, through which brown eyes blinked shrewdly at the world. "You mean if you were to fall from your cage?"

Tashtemir regarded the loose shackles around his ankles. He'd opened them with a key lifted from one of the guards just before they threw him inside. "Well, yes. Such a thing could hardly be foreseeable. My question—theoretical, naturally—is whether you would put me out of my misery should I fail to die quickly?"

It was early evening, the time of day when the dragonelles slept. The menagerie was so quiet, Tashtemir heard the sharp puff of air from Yagbu's nostrils.

"The Imperator would be most displeased with me either way," he said. "Public executions serve a civic purpose, both punitive and as a deterrent to other would-be criminals." The stool creaked under his bulk. "The torture beforehand is for entertainment. If you die, she is deprived of both."

"That would be terrible," Tashtemir agreed quickly. "Forget I asked."

He started to whistle a melancholy tune.

Yagbu rose to his feet. He lumbered toward the chain that hoisted the cage into the air. "I hate to say it, old friend, but this kind of talk makes me nervous."

"Wait!" Tashtemir cried. "I have no designs to escape! It would be impossible."

"That is true, but we both know you are not speaking about physical escape. And if I fail, it could be me sitting in that birdcage next." He slapped the horsehide whip called a *sawt* against his leather-clad thigh. "I do not like heights, Tashtemir."

"Nor do I."

"Then I propose that we bring you down, safe and sound."

"I wouldn't mind." He paused. "Yet I sense a proviso coming."

The last fading rays of sunlight glinted from Yagbu's glasses as he peered up at the dome. "How right you are, dearest. To pass the time, I thought I might warm up my skills. It's been a few months since I was called upon to perform the full scourging."

Tashtemir went cold. "Really, it's not necessary."

The chain wound around a winch. Yagbu jammed the whip into his belt and turned the crank. The cage began to sink.

"I thought we were friends!" Tash protested.

"You should not have stolen from the Imperator."

"Listen." He licked his lips. "My father would pay dearly—"

"A lie and we both know it." Yagbu's voice turned sympathetic. "He's an unforgiving man. I can see why you turned out the way you did."

"Yagbu, there is a conspiracy afoot. You must listen—"

A rich chuckle. "There's always a conspiracy."

From high above, the torturer looked like a fairly large man. But as the cage descended, he took on the proportions of a fleshy mountain. He wore a leather vest and pants, mottled with old stains. Tufts of gray hair rose from the cannonballs he called shoulders. Fat Yagbu *was* fat, certainly, but it was layered over slabs of unyielding muscle. Thick metal cuffs girded each wrist, each blazoned with a dragon.

"Look, I'll give you a choice for the first agony," he said reasonably. "Ants or spiders?"

"That's a tough one," Tashtemir said, working feverishly on the shackle around his left wrist. "Are they the biting kind?"

Yagbu paused to look up again. The cage swayed in a slow arc. "Do you really have to ask?"

"Yes, of course they are. But won't the Imperator be angry if you start without her?" The key was sticking. The angle was awkward. And his fingers were slippery with sweat—

"She's a busy woman. I doubt she'll count them all. And I'll save the best parts for later. Fire. Acid. The long prong that —Never mind. I don't want to spoil the surprise." He started cranking again.

"I've never seen them all," Tashtemir said, coughing at the same instant the lock gave with a sharp *click*. "It must be tiring for you to torture someone for so long. I assume we're talking hours."

"Why, you're the first person who's ever expressed concern for me, Tashtemir," Yagbu replied. "I appreciate it. And yes, it does take a toll." He sounded philosophical. "But that is the world we live in, my friend. Callous and cruel. Someone has to do it, and I would rather be the person holding the whip than the one receiving the lashes."

"Entirely sensible," Tashtemir said, as he started on the second wrist. The cage was halfway down now. Within another ten seconds or so, Yagbu would see what he was up to. "And you have the natural physique for it, too."

Yagbu took one hand from the chain to slap his protruding belly, also generously covered with hair. The cage suddenly dropped another ten feet, sending Tashtemir's stomach hurtling up into his ribcage, before abruptly halting again. "Would you believe I was three weeks premature? My mother fed me sheep's milk and pureed chicken livers."

"She must have been very devoted." He gave a hard twist, born of desperation. The key snapped off in the lock.

"Quite an unpleasant woman, actually," Yagbu corrected. "But she had a hard life."

Another few turns and the cage dangled at eye level—which for Yagbu was still seven feet off the ground. He fixed the chain in place and plodded over.

"I see you already removed three of the shackles," he observed, squinting through the thick lenses, which magnified his eyes to an unnerving size. "What happened with the last one?"

Tashtemir showed him the lock. "Key broke off. Rotten luck." He tried a smile. "Not that I could have bested you even if I were free."

Yagbu nodded. "It was a good effort, though." He gave the cage a gentle push. Tashtemir swung away and back, away, then back. "Now, this is interesting," he remarked. "I think . . . yes. We'll work this into my repertoire."

His heavy steps receded. Tashtemir drew his knees to his chest. He regarded the dozing dragonelles on their perches. Such marvelous creatures. He'd tended them happily for years. Mended torn wings and soothed scale-rot with honey baths. They fed exclusively on the nuts from the bokang trees, which resembled yellow pearls. They preferred to dine on the wing and he'd spent many a pleasant evening tossing the nuts into the air and watching them dive and swoop and turn-barrel rolls in pursuit of a morsel.

Then, a foolish debt—followed by an even more foolish plan to get out of it.

He'd only been caught because he misliked how the client handled the young dragonelles and called the deal off. It was in the process of returning them to the menagerie that he'd been discovered.

If you get away with something, never go back.

A lesson I clearly failed to learn, he thought glumly as he waited for Fat Yagbu to return.

Chapter Twenty-Two

✦❧✦

Malach exhaled as Koko unlaced his corset.

"Ah, Tash," he muttered. "Dammit."

"Will ye come with us?" Paarjini asked. "We could use another aingeal."

He met her gaze. "I'm sorry, but I can't."

"Why not?"

"I'm going to the Luban embassy to get my daughter."

She stared at him. "Are ye mad? They know yer here!"

"And they know you're here, too," he pointed out. "But I don't see you giving up on your plan."

She spluttered but found no answer to this.

"The key business is none of my concern," he said. "Rachel is."

Kasia touched his arm. "Malach—"

"You won't change my mind," he said in a harder tone. "I'm not letting her slip through my fingers again. What if Balaur runs? They could force to anywhere in the world."

"If you go blundering into that embassy, ye'll tip off the Lubans. Ye'll get us all killed!"

"I won't. I promise you, I won't interfere with anyone else, as long as they stay out of my way. It'll be fast and quiet."

"What exactly do ye mean to do with Rachel, even if ye do manage to find her?" Paarjini asked—not without a note of sympathy. "If we free Valmitra, I am certain the Mother will fix matters. She'll unleash her vengeance on Balaur."

He met her gray eyes. "And how can you be sure she won't unleash it on *all* of us?"

Paarjini hesitated for an instant. "I dinna think she will."

"Now that's a ringing endorsement."

He picked up a sponge and started wiping his makeup off. The fifteen minutes as Lucy Fur had been one of the purest, sweetest adrenaline rushes of his entire life. Now all that energy had ebbed away and he felt exhausted.

"Have you considered the fact that it might be best to simply take these keys back to Dur-Athaara? Keep them safe and just go on as you always have?" he asked. "Maybe Valmitra was bound for a reason. Maybe she's not as nice as you think she is."

Paarjini frowned. "She saved yer life. And ye would leave her imprisoned?"

"I'm grateful for that," he said carefully, thinking of the silver-skinned creatures who had attacked him. "But without knowing the circumstances in which Gavriel did this, it seems rash. Once your god is free, I doubt there's any power on this earth that can cage her again—"

He broke off as Hassan entered with Karl. They both looked sick when they saw Darya. Karl covered his mouth.

"It's my fault," he mumbled.

"No, it's not," Alexei replied firmly. "No one can withstand compulsion. But do you remember who did it? What they looked like? Anything would help."

Karl shook his head. "I don't remember a thing after leaving the chapter house."

"It wasn't Valdrian," Malach said. "Or Lexa. I can vouch for that."

"A witch?

"Then another mage we don't know," Kasia said. Her expression darkened. "Or the Danzigers. Who knows what they're capable of?"

"Why didn't they kill Malach?" Alexei wondered. "And me? Why just the witch?"

Everyone was silent. Paarjini glanced at a cheap wrist-watch she'd bought at the bazaar. "We're out o' time," she said. "So be it, aingeal. You go your way, we'll go ours."

"Where are you meeting the others?" Malach asked, kneeling down to help Karl and Koko clean up the scattered cosmetics. Hassan laid a towel over Darya's face and started to sweep up the broken glass.

When no one replied, Malach looked over one shoulder. "You can speak in front of the Blessed," he said. "They already know everything. I trust them completely."

Alexei made formal introductions. Hands were warmly clasped, cheeks kissed in the Masdari way. All the while, the priest hovered protectively at his sister's side. Malach knew he wouldn't be leaving her again and felt relieved. Alexei was as dangerous as his sister. They'd keep each other safe.

"The rendezvous point is a bridge on the south side of the palace," Kasia said. "In ten minutes."

"I have to go," Alexei told him gravely. "I'm sorry."

"I expected you would." He pulled a shirt over his head. "I'll give you a head start before I enter the embassy. Fair enough?"

Paarjini and Kasia nodded.

"You can bring Rachel to the Isle of the Blessed," Hassan said. "Take the private launch. I'll wait for you there."

Malach took his hand. "Thank you."

Hassan squeezed it. "You made me proud tonight, daughter."

"And I," Koko whispered.

Malach smiled. A second wind stirred his sails.

"If we are successful, we will find you there," Paarjini said.

He turned to Nikola, who hadn't said a word. "I'll bring her back."

She shook her head. "No, you won't."

Malach frowned. "Please don't make this hard—"

Silver eyes flashed. "*We* will, Malach. I'm going with you."

Paarjini opened her mouth, then closed it again at a sharp look from Kasia.

"It's her right," Kasia said firmly. "We will manage without her. But his chances of success are much greater with a witch at his side, don't you think?"

"Aye," Paarjini conceded. "They are. Valmitra shelter ye both."

He embraced Kasia and shared a taut nod with Alexei. Then the three of them slipped out the door.

Nikola pulled him close. "I'm going to make us invisible." Her voice held amusement. "Does that fit with your plans?"

He nodded, throat tight. "Thank you. For staying."

"You don't have to do everything alone, Malach," she said gently. "One day you'll realize that."

He tore his gaze away and looked at Hassan. "What about Darya?"

"I'll lock the door when we leave," he replied. "She won't be discovered until tomorrow." A strange, wistful expression crossed his beautiful face. "And I think that by then . . . everything will be different, yes? One way or another."

THEY SLIPPED across the Isle of Dreams together, hand in hand. Wild music skirled through the trees, its strains mingling with human voices raised in talk and laughter. A hundred heady scents tickled his nose. Pickled fish and perfumed throats. Smoke from the braziers and the crisp citrus notes of orange blossoms.

Lucy had drawn every eye, but now he was nothing and

no one. A ghost drifting through the revelries, passing so close he felt the heat of their bodies. So close he could have reached out and plucked the sugared treats from their fingers.

They avoided the busiest pathways where large groups reeled along together, arms linked, debating which entertainment to indulge in next. Had his aunt Beleth been here, she would be among them, unable to resist the debauchery.

Balaur was different. A spider who was most at home lurking in the center of his web. Malach knew he would be at the Luban embassy. Expecting visitors.

When the compound appeared ahead, he pulled Nikola into a cluster of date palms at the lakeshore. The ley bent the light around them, but he could see her face clearly in the moonlight. So beautiful it thickened the blood in his veins, made him both sluggish and painfully aware.

"I thought of you," he murmured. "On stage."

She gazed up at him warily. "Not because I'm a cold-hearted bitch, I hope."

"The contrary." Her hands were warm in his. "I just liked the beat."

Nikola laughed. "Here I was, so worried about you, and you were traveling with gorgeous, kind-hearted drag queens."

"They're called the Blessed here. And they make my own meager talents dwindle in comparison. I hope you can see Sultana perform someday. And Koko. They're amazing."

"What about Alexei?"

"We've moved on."

"I'm glad to hear it." She hesitated. "And us?"

"I would do anything for you, Nikola," he said carefully. "I just want you to be happy."

"Same here. You, I mean."

"Is there any chance these two happy lives might coincide?"

The silver pirate tooth gleamed as her smile widened. "I rule nothing out."

He bent his head and kissed her. She smoothed the hair back from his brow. A smile curled the corner of her mouth. "Okay, Lucy."

He felt completely at ease with her. As if every harsh word and colossal mistake had happened to other people. They hadn't, of course, but that was the magic of love. It let you wipe the slate clean, again and again.

"You're my best friend, you know," he said. "My favorite person in the whole world."

She blinked in surprise. A bullfrog's baritone sang in the rushes, answered by a chorus of harmonic chirps that rang like silvery bells against the surface of the lake.

"I remember that sound from Bal Kirith," she said. "It kept me awake at night."

"Peepers." Malach smiled. "Beleth called them the *chorum nocturno*. The night choir."

"I like that." She spread her palm over his heart. "I hated it there, but I never regretted going with you, Malach."

He covered her hand with his own. He hadn't bothered to take off the long red nails. In fact, he thought he might keep them.

"Because you adore me. You always have and you always—"

"All right," she laughed. "No need to rub it in."

A sudden scream made them both stiffen. It was followed by smothered laughter and scolding voices, but the moment of intimacy faded. He gathered his thoughts.

"Can you put Balaur to sleep? Like you did to the knights in the Arx?"

"Yes, and I can keep him that way. But I don't know how to kick him out of Rachel's body. Or how to kill him even if I could."

"There must be a way."

"Valmitra is real. If she is freed . . ." Nikola trailed off, studying his face. "Why are you so afraid of her?"

"Why aren't *you*?" he countered.

"I saw her. I'm sure she's benevolent."

"You saw her? How?"

"In a dream," Nikola admitted. "But it was more than a dream."

"Did you speak to her?"

"No."

"Then how can you know for sure?" He held her close, resting his chin on her head scarf. "My ancestor went to great lengths to lock her up. What if he had good cause?"

"Balaur means to kill Valmitra, Malach. To take control of the ley."

It didn't surprise him, though he doubted such a thing would be possible. Balaur was a madman.

"Which is why we're going to stop him," Malach said.

She pulled back to look at his face. "You promised to let Paarjini take those keys to the city. Not to interfere. I hope you meant it."

"I did," he said reluctantly. "But I don't want to be anywhere near when this goddess of yours does break free."

He nearly told her about being mistaken for Gavriel but decided to wait. Not because he didn't trust her, but because it was ludicrous.

"We should go," he said. "Once Balaur is asleep, we'll take him to the launch. Lock him up and figure out what to do next. But Darya told me there were two more witches working with Balaur."

"I'll deal with them," Nikola said fiercely. "Kasia promised me that Rachel is in a safe place. I can't explain it, but she's still with us."

"I've never stopped believing that," he said. "Now let's get our daughter. Hopefully for the last time."

They circled around to the embassy's rear lawns. Lanterns hung from the trees and candles in red glass globes flickered on two dozen tables. Musicians played on a dais as the Luban entourage drank and dined and celebrated their khedive's ascension.

Malach and Nikola slipped through the open doors of the long stone terrace and entered the embassy's reception chamber. The party was going full swing inside, wine fumes mingling with the huge floral bouquets in every corner. Malach jerked his head at the stairs and Nikola nodded. A pair of veiled priests guarded the first floor landing, hard eyes scanning the guests. They shifted uneasily as Malach and Nikola ghosted past them, but neither raised an alarm.

The second floor seemed deserted. Faint voices and music drifted up as they explored a long corridor, checking the rooms to either side. All were empty, except for the last. A sweet voice was singing softly on the other side.

"Bethen," Nikola mouthed.

Malach gave a taut nod. She chose a red stone from her pouch and laid a hand on the knob. The expression on her face made him glad they were on the same side.

Nikola flung the door open.

A young fair-haired witch sat by the window. She leapt to her feet, but Nikola was quicker. The spell knocked Bethen onto her ass. Another burst of ley and the young witch's own pouch tore loose, along with the clips in her hair, the rings around her fingers. Malach threw an arm up as a tornado of gems and coins flew through the air. He pounced before she could recover, pinning her hands to the rug.

"Don't fucking move," he snarled. "Where is everyone?"

Bethen's eyes darted to Nikola, wide with terror.

"They left!" she cried. "I'm the only one here."

Nikola stalked over, kicking bits of jewelry out of the way.

"It's over, Bethen. Where is Balaur? And Heshima?"

"Gone." She swallowed. "I am supposed to guard the sword until they return."

Malach pulled the sash from her waist and bound her wrists.

"Where," Nikola said furiously, "did they go?"

Bethen began to stammer an explanation, but his attention had shifted to a cloth-wrapped bundle in the corner. The long hilt of a sword stuck out. Chased with gold. Quillions like the feathers of an eagle. Exactly like the one he'd dreamt of.

Malach walked over, heart pounding.

"No!" Bethen screamed. "You must not—"

Nikola must have planted a hand over her mouth for the protests grew muffled.

Malach's hand closed around the hilt. The ley in his palm surged to meet it. A mild electric shock ran up his arm. The pommel was hot to the touch, as if it had been lying near a fire. He loosed the bindings and drew the sword halfway from its leather scabbard.

Runes danced along the steel. Sharp lines and angles. He squinted in the sudden brightness. They were unfamiliar, yet he could almost read them.

"Leave that alone, Malach," Nikola said in a hard voice.

"Why?" His own voice sounded distant.

"Because it's poison! Jamila said the one who carried it died!"

"It won't hurt me," Malach replied absently.

"How can you possibly—"

She cut off as a sudden breeze swept the room.

Wingbeats.

Malach spun around, Gavriel's blade gripped in both hands.

A creature alit on the narrow wrought-iron balcony. One graceful leap and it stood inside the room. Bethen squeaked and scrabbled away.

"I have learned the tongue you speak now, Deceiver," it hissed, furling its wings. A breastplate of ornately etched gold covered its chest. "You eluded me once, but now we face each other again." Slitted nostrils widened, scenting the air. "Where are your legions, war-bringer? Have they abandoned you?"

"I am not the Morning Star," Malach grated. "Leave me be!"

Draconic eyes bored into him. They swirled with yellow and bronze and rust red. Wisps of smoke rose from the stone under its feet.

"I've come for the sword." It took a step closer. Liquid mercury shimmered along its skin, flowing like water. "Give it to me."

"No."

Nikola rose to her feet. "Borosus," she said calmly. "It is you, isn't it?"

Its head swung toward her, lowering in irritation. "So you are a traitor, too, Nikola Thorn."

"You're mistaken," she said firmly. "I already told you that. This man's name is Malach. Gavriel is dead."

"Then why does he hold Gavriel's blade?"

"We just found it." She shot Malach an incredulous look. "Don't be stubborn. Give it up."

He eyed them both. Nikola *knew* this thing? What else had she failed to tell him?

"We are locked out of the dawn city," Borosus said. "What of the palace at Mount Meru? I had a sending from the Cherubim, but it was faint."

Nikola shook her head. "I do not know that place. But we seek to free the Mother, Borosus. We are not enemies."

Speak for yourself, Malach thought, but he was wise enough not to say it. He lowered the blade.

Borosus studied them both for a long minute. "Perhaps it is as you say," he replied at last. "Much has changed since last I walked this earth."

His features were alien, yet the way he blinked slowly, his gaze unfocused, conveyed a pitiful confusion. Then he turned back to Malach, sharp again. "Yet I will not allow you to keep that blade."

Malach looked down at the sword in his hand. What was

he doing? He didn't want it. *Did he?* The woman had claimed he could kill Balaur with it. Just a dream . . .

He was about to lay the blade down when light filled the chamber. He staggered back and saw Bethen, a gem raised high, her face terrified but determined. The golden breast-plate tolled like an enormous bell struck by a mallet. Borosus snarled and raked his talons across her throat. She fell, a spray of bright red droplets hissing where they struck the creature's molten skin.

Borosus rounded on Nikola, enraged. Flames licked at his tongue.

In three desperate strides, Malach reached her side. He shielded her with his body as a sheet of flame erupted from Borosus's mouth. Malach expected to be incinerated, but the assault met an invisible barrier. The bracelets around Nikola's arms flared in a protective spell.

A roar of frustration. Then the Sinn é Maz started to change. Its body swelled to fill the chamber, a mountain of scaled flesh and gnashing teeth. The great armored tail lashed, sweeping heavy furniture before it in an explosion of cracking wood. The curtains were already alight. A wild wind rose, fanning the flames. In an instant, the carpet caught. Smoke filled Malach's throat.

"Morning Star!" an unearthly voice bellowed. "*Betrayer!*"

A serpentine head rose above them, brushing the ceiling. Jaws gaped wide. A sulfurous blast of air foretold what was about to happen.

Nikola grasped his free hand. A clap of silent thunder rattled Malach's ribcage. The ground fell away beneath his feet.

They landed in a heap of tangled limbs, him on top, Nikola's breath warm on his neck. It was so quiet he could hear his own blood rushing in his ears. Feel her heart banging against his chest in the same staccato rhythm. She wheezed and he worried he was crushing her so he rolled off, but then he realized she was *laughing*.

It had a hysterical edge, but the choked guffaws were irresistible and he started to laugh with her, until tears ran down his cheeks and his gut ached.

"I thought we were dead," she said, when she managed to speak again. "I really did."

They were somewhere in the deep desert. Not a breath of wind stirred. The sky was thick with bright stars. He felt a little nauseous, but not too bad. Nikola was getting better at this.

"How many times have you forced?" he asked, rolling to his side in the sand.

"Too many." She lay on her back, arms and legs spread wide. "The Maid told me that every time a witch uses unnatural magic, it tears the fabric of reality." She held her fingers a hair apart. "Just a small one, but still. Not good."

His brows lifted.

"Apparently, they did it all the time during the last Dark Age. That shit adds up." Her head turned to him. "But we're still here, so I guess I didn't blow up the universe."

He looked around at the sea of darkness. "Why this spot, Nikola?"

"It's the Ceaseless Sands," she replied softly.

He felt a chill. "We could be anywhere in the League—"

"I don't think so." A pause. "I let the ley choose."

The chill deepened, sinking into his marrow. "What if we'd ended up at the bottom of the sea? Or in the middle of a mountain?"

"But we didn't."

He still had the sword. It lay at his feet, the edge of the blade catching the starlight.

"Balaur will go to the dawn city whether he has the keys or not," Nikola said. "We'll find him there. That's what the Crone told me just before she died."

Malach felt threads of fate binding him tight. It was infuriating. Why couldn't the ley just let him be?

"If I must go, then I'm bringing this," he said, gripping the hilt. "And if Paarjini fails, I'll find a way to finish him."

Nikola sat up. "You plan to greet Valmitra brandishing Gavriel's blade? Have you lost your wits?"

"I don't want to greet her at all," he replied with equal heat. "But I won't go empty-handed. How did you know Borosus?"

"I met him in a dream. It was brief."

"What does he want?"

"To free her." Nikola's eyes narrowed. "He said you eluded him once. I had the distinct impression he meant you personally—not Gavriel."

"We did meet before," Malach admitted. "In Luba."

He told her about going to the khedive's compound and Alexei following. The dead priests and arrival of the Teeth of God.

"So he saved your ass," she said.

"He did indeed."

"Why? From what I understand, he loathes you, Malach."

He sighed. "Because I'd saved his. Do you want to hear the whole story?"

"Are you kidding?" She brushed sand from herself. "Of course I do. You can tell me while we walk. Then I'll tell you mine." Her gaze lit on the sword. "I still say it's a terrible idea to bring that."

"So why was it discovered, eh? Coincidence?"

She stared at him, stone-faced.

"I won't leave it. And I feel perfectly fine. It doesn't hurt me." He looked around at the wasteland that stretched in all directions. "Which way?"

"I don't know." She blew out a breath. "If you insist on keeping that vile thing, can you at least try to read those runes?"

He hesitated, then drew on the abyssal ley. He'd been around enough witches to realize there was lithomancy in the blade. Tangled skeins of ley that wrapped the sword from pommel to tip. They tried to repel his assault, but then the spells seemed to recognize him, parting like mist. The runes turned from white to bloody red. A single blue stone inlaid in the pommel ignited with power.

He saw the witch from his dream. Curling hair of pale ash blonde, roughly cut off at her jawline. Alabaster skin and silver eyes. She should have been as cold and remote as moonlight, but her face was too mobile. It held warmth and mischief and keen intelligence.

Watching her was like watching a gem held to fire, each facet throwing back a different emotion. Rings circled her fingers, stacked three and four high. A dagger was thrust through her belt, and a coiled whip. She held a slim deck of cards with an intricate pattern of thorns and birds.

He saw a deeply tanned man who might have been his own brother, except that he had wings the same blue-black as his hair.

The angel knelt at the witch's feet, glossy feathers trailing behind him in the snow. Their eyes locked. They weren't doing much, but the emotion laced through the sweven was potent, like bitter salt in a morsel of cake. A sorrow so vast it nearly wrenched him from his moorings.

The witch turned to Malach. "The red star of the Seventh Gate," she said, her voice low and urgent. "That is where it ends."

The angel frowned. He had stern, unyielding features, but they softened as he looked up at the witch. "Whom do you speak to, Cat? There is no one."

The witch seemed to stare directly at Malach. "Follow the labyrinth to its heart."

The sweven faded. His head spun at the implications.

Could she have foreseen this moment a thousand years into the future? Planted a message for him—

He dropped the blade and took a step back. The runes died.

Nikola laid a hand on his arm. "What did you see?"

"Gavriel. And a witch—"

"Cathrynne Rowan. They were lovers."

He remembered Hassan pressing him about the women who were important to him on the morning before he performed. For some unfathomable reason, he had chosen to be *her*.

The fight bled out of him. He would face whatever waited in the dawn city. What choice did he have? Malach picked up the sword and pointed the tip at a red star low on the horizon. An arch of brighter stars twinkled around it. The Seventh Gate.

"That way," he said.

Chapter Twenty-Three

"You son of a *bitch*! My own sister?"

Patryk loomed over her, features twisted into sulky anger. "At least she appreciates me. You've been clammy as week-old fish since I forgot our anniversary."

The slap sent him rocking back against the small gate set into the bestiary's brick wall. Natalya seized his robes and slammed him again, just in case the guards hadn't heard it.

"Listen to me, you great oaf," she yelled. "I ought to cut your balls off and serve them to you in a pudding."

"You already have!" he roared. "I'm a laughing-stock! You think I don't know about Rahim?"

His accent was terrible and he got half the words wrong, but his voice was so slurred, she doubted the guards would be able to tell the difference.

She suppressed a grin. "Here they come. I'll pretend to knee you in the crotch—"

He looked alarmed as her knee violently came up—and halted just shy of its target. Patryk croaked and rattled the gate again.

The menagerie guards wore tunics with the palace livery

and loose trousers tucked into supple, calf-high boots. Each carried a curved dagger at his belt. They looked annoyed.

Just a little closer, she thought.

But the guards stopped about a meter away and made shooing motions.

Natalya pressed her face to the gate. "Tell him I hate him!" she hissed. "Tell him he's a motherless pig!"

They grimaced at each other. She'd dumped a glass of wine down the front of her abaya so the fumes would be unmistakable.

A terse command was issued in Masdari to leave before they were both forcibly ejected from the festivities.

Natalya kicked the gate, rattling it again. She planted a foot on Patryk's rear and toppled him over—which wasn't hard since he was panting with his hands braced on his knees. Then she burst into tears, clinging to the bars. "I'm sorry," she sobbed. "I'm sorry!"

They exchanged another look. The first guard took a step forward, pity on his face. "Look, why don't you just take him home? Make up there?"

She wiped her cheeks on a sleeve. Then she pointed to the ground. A gold ring lay in the grass, where she'd tossed it through the ornate ironwork.

"Can I just have that back?" A huge sniffle.

The guard bent down and picked it up. He strode to the gate and reached through, pressing it into her palm. Beside her, the grass bent beneath invisible feet. The guard gave a sharp inhale of surprise as Valdrian's own hand closed around his wrist. Natalya didn't see it happen, but she did see the compulsion take effect. A rapid dilation of the pupils. A slackening of the muscles of his face.

He withdrew a key from the pocket of his trousers and fitted it into the gate. The other guard protested in a harsh tone, rushing forward. The instant he came within reach—a second compulsion.

It was awful to witness. As if they had both been trans-formed into mindless puppets. Natalya shared Kasia's distaste for the trick, though she couldn't imagine how they'd get inside without it.

She looked around as the gate swung wide. "Where's Caralexa?"

The purple-haired mage had volunteered to keep an eye out and discourage the roaming gangs of tipsy courtiers from approaching the lawn around the gate. She was supposed to listen for the argument that signaled stage one of the plan.

"I don't know," Cairness whispered in Natalya's ear. "But we can't wait."

Caralexa's absence troubled her, but Natalya nodded and slunk through the gate, Spassov at her side. "Leave it unlocked," she said. "Hopefully she'll find us."

Cairness eased the gate shut behind them. She scanned the sky for Markhawks, but it looked clear. Natalya wondered if the fireworks had driven them away.

"Step up close," Cairness whispered. "I'll make the illusion big enough for all of us."

Natalya pressed against her, jostling another warm body on the way.

"Sorry," she muttered, as Valdrian popped into view, followed by Spassov.

The mage grinned through his blonde beard. "That was simple enough."

The two guards were standing like automatons just inside the gate. Cairness thumbed a milky white stone set into one of her rings and they both sank to the ground. Once the snoring bodies had been hauled out of sight and deposited under a bush, they started through the grounds of the menagerie.

Dark shapes flitted overhead. Here and there, tiny tongues of flame flashed like cigarette lighters. Kasia had told her about the dragonelles. She wished she could see them clearly. Her sole Mark was of a golden-maned dragon and she wondered if it was even remotely accurate. Ah, to have a single afternoon in which she could sit and sketch them!

She kept a hand resting on Cairness's shoulder as they shuffled along a brick walkway that wound through trees and shrubs, some potted, others growing out of the sandy soil. Odd geometric shapes thrust upward at intervals. As her eyes adjusted, she saw they were platforms on poles, upon which the tenants of the bestiary roosted. Small, luminous eyes tracked their passage. They might be invisible to humans, but they weren't going unnoticed by the dragonelles. She just hoped the creatures wouldn't screech a warning.

The menagerie was larger than it looked from the outside, a private jungle—and equally humid. The air smelled of damp earth and another tangy, nutty scent whose source was revealed when a soft splat hit her sleeve. Natalya grimaced and held it toward Spassov, who quivered with silent laughter.

Starlight filtering through the dome overhead provided the only light, but as they rounded a curve, she saw a yellow flare. A chain as thick as her arm descended from the apex of the steel-girded dome. She'd expected to find Tashtemir dangling high above her head, but his cage had been lowered to a point about two meters off the ground. Cairness drew to a halt at the edge of the light, forcing them all to stop with her.

A lacquered cabinet on wheels stood off to the side. It held dozens of drawers, some very small, others quite large. Each bore a brass plaque.

The cage was describing a gentle arc, swinging to and fro. A giant stood at the perimeter. He was clad in a dark leather vest, which parted to reveal an impressive gut and a hoop winking at his navel.

One scarred fist gripped a flaming brand, which he swiped at the bars every time the cage drifted near.

"Mercy, Yagbu!" Tashtemir cried hoarsely as the cage swung away. "This is a most dreadful punishment you have devised! I cannot bear it another moment—"

Laughter rang out. There was nothing especially cruel about it. More like they were sharing a joke. "I've barely managed to singe you, dearest. You are too quick."

The giant's voice was at odds with his appearance, mild and cultured.

"No, no, look at this welt." Tashtemir pulled his sleeve up. "It stings terribly."

Yagbu gripped the bars and drew the cage to a stop. He lowered the torch to inspect the prisoner's arm. Firelight glinted on a pair of thick black spectacles. "I've had worse frying dumplings."

"How long have we been at it?"

"Half an hour or so. Shall we try the spiders now?"

"I already told you, I prefer the ants." A pause. "But the torch is rather exciting. I wouldn't mind continuing."

"Dearest," the giant said gently. "We have at least a dozen agonies to get through before midnight."

"One mustn't rush these things."

"True, but there *is* a schedule to keep. I refer to your pending execution, of course." He gave a desultory swipe with the brand, sending Tashtemir scrambling to the opposite side of the cage. "And this is not nearly as entertaining as I expected it to be."

Yagbu jammed the torch in a bracket and stumped over to the cabinet. Meaty fingers walked across the drawers. "Ah yes, here we are."

A medium-sized drawer slid open. He held up a glass globe, half full with dark, sloshing liquid. Or no . . . not liquid. *Insects*.

A dragonelle swooped low to examine it. Natalya caught a flash of shimmering blue-green scales before Yagbu drew the globe protectively to his chest. "Not for you, lovelies," he pronounced.

The dragonelle hovered for an instant, then zipped away.

"I suppose you'll have to tie me up," Tashtemir said. "It won't work very well if I'm able to slap at them."

"Correct you are. Which means I'll have to open the door to your cage. So no funny business."

"I wouldn't dream of it, old friend. What would be the point?"

"None whatsoever," Yagbu agreed. "I might be fat, but I can run like a *fenak*." He gently set the globe back in its drawer. "A moment while I fetch the restraints."

He began walking toward the place where Natalya and the others stood concealed by Cairness's spell. Behind him, the torch flickered, sending shadows dancing against the wall.

Shadows.

A spear of acid stabbed her gut. The witch had neglected to hide the four long silhouettes stretching down the brick pathway.

In one sudden, blurring movement, Yagbu drew a whip from his belt. His arm extended straight up, then fell with practiced ease. A crack rent the air. Valdrian clutched his cheek, blood blooming between the fingers.

The next moments were chaos. An avalanche of hairy flesh bearing down in ground-eating strides. Patryk stepping in front of her. The bright glint of a blade in her hand, though she didn't recall drawing it. Cairness haloed by a burst of ley. The giant thudding to the ground at her feet, his glasses askew across his nose.

Natalya took a hasty step back, readying her knives.

"Don't kill him!" Tashtemir cried, clutching the bars of his cage.

Cairness turned. She was breathing hard. "You're welcome," she said tartly.

He gave a wild laugh. "I am grateful, believe me. But truly, I'm barely harmed. Yagbu is an honest man. I would see him treated courteously." He studied Valdrian with concern. "Assuming he did not put your eye out, of course."

Valdrian drew his hand away. A centimeter-long cut crossed his cheek. "I got lucky," he announced with a feral smile. "The scar'll make a good tale, though."

Cairness clucked and dabbed at the trickle of blood with her sleeve.

"The key is in Yagbu's vest pocket," Tashtemir said.

Natalya located the pocket and unlocked the cage. She tried various keys until she found one that fit the manacle around his ankle. Tashtemir dropped down with a wince. His black hair stuck up like a disheveled porcupine. Spassov threw an arm around his shoulders.

"Steady," he said in a kindly tone. "Cramps?"

"Not too bad," Tashtemir replied, chafing his thighs. "I'll walk it off."

Natalya eyed Yagbu's limp form. He hadn't stirred. A lump the size of a pigeon's egg rose from his bald head.

"Do you think we can get him into the cage?" she wondered. "It would look better if *someone* was up there in case any guards happen by. We need at least an hour or two before the alarm is raised."

It took all five of them to drag Yagbu over, mush him inside, and hoist him up. They only got the cage halfway to the ceiling before they gave up, dripping in sweat, but it was better than nothing.

"Farewell, old friend," Tashtemir whispered with a crisp salute. "I do hope we never meet again."

They followed the path back toward the outer wall, Cairness in the lead. Tashtemir fell in next to Valdrian, who clapped him heartily on the back, then grabbed his arm when the Masdari nearly fell over.

"Right on schedule," Natalya said softly to Patryk. "You were perfect."

"My face still stings," he grumbled, rubbing his jaw. "Why did I have to wed such a violent woman?"

"It's not my fault if you like hotheads." Natalya scanned

the darkness, blades ready in each hand. "You shouldn't have cheated on me."

"If you'd shown me the slightest bit of love or respect, I wouldn't have had to," he replied in a wounded tone. "Would it kill you to admit that?"

"And would it kill *you* to admit that with all the late nights you've been working, leaving me alone with Rahim, the strapping young gardener . . ."

She trailed off at a look from Cairness. "We'll finish this later," she hissed.

"That's what you always say," he hissed back.

They were nearly at the wall when a lone figure slipped from a pool of darkness next to the gate. Natalya tensed, then saw it was Caralexa. The strip of purple hair sticking up like a stiff brush made the mage impossible to miss. Her green cloak swirled around her boots as she trotted over.

"What happened to ye?" Cairness demanded softly.

A shrug. "I thought I saw Malach and followed, but it wasn't him. You were already through by the time I reached the gate. I must have just missed you." Her gaze found Tashtemir. "It's good to see you again, Masdari. A patrol just passed. We'd better move fast."

Caralexa stepped closer. Something didn't feel right. The mage wasn't looking around. She hadn't even lowered her voice. Natalya was reaching for one of her knives when Caralexa grabbed Cairness by her red hair, yanking the witch's head back. A knife pressed to her throat.

"None of you fucking move," Caralexa growled.

Two dozen shadows rose up from hiding places behind trees and shrubs. Moonlight glinted on steel as guards in the livery of Luba swiftly surrounded them, cutting off every escape route. Natalya inched closer to Patryk, whose eyes had gone narrow and flinty. Tashtemir muttered something in Masdari.

She's been Balaur's creature from the start. Oh Saints, Kasia and Alexei...

Natalya turned to Valdrian, expecting him to be in on it, too. But his expression was one of enraged disbelief.

"What have you done?" he demanded, fists clenching. "Lex—"

"On your knees!" she snapped. "Now! All of you!"

Natalya shared a tight look with Patryk. She knew they were both thinking the same thing. What value was there in keeping any of them alive at this point? If they surrendered, they were as good as dead. Except for Tashtemir, whom the Imperator wanted to execute herself.

"Don't do it," Cairness gasped, before Caralexa slammed her with a compulsion and her eyes rolled back in her head.

Natalya drew a knife and was calculating the odds of cutting their way out when a flare of crackling black light erupted. She fell, every muscle cramping hard. The blade slid from her fingers. Hot needles pricked her flesh. Through blurred eyes, she saw her friends writhing on the ground.

The guards stepped up, stripping everyone of their weapons. Slowly, slowly, the pain ebbed. She thought Caralexa had done it, but then she saw a plump, matronly figure standing next to the mage, peering down with bright, birdlike eyes.

Memories of Danziger Haus crashed down. Hanne with her big gardening shears and straw sun hat. Hanne promising to find them passage on a ship bound for Nantwich. Hanne drugging her and Tess with the intention of murdering them both. And finally, Jule disemboweling his aunt with a sweep of black claws.

Natalya stared at her with loathing. "Just can't stay dead, can you?"

Hanne's expression froze. Darkness crawled across her eyes. "And you can't seem to stay where you belong, Domina

Anderle." The Kven accent gave each word a sharp edge. "But this time I'll put you to good use."

"What does that mean?" Natalya demanded.

Hanne's smile was chilling. "I have a makeshift laboratory in Qeddah. Right here on the Isle of Dreams. I've been studying the techniques of the Breath of God, among other things."

Her mouth pursed in annoyance. "But it hasn't been easy to find subjects. Not willing ones, at least. So I must thank you for delivering yourselves to me. I've always been curious about the anatomical differences between witches and mages." Hanne tapped her forehead. "I'll have to dissect their brains to find the answer, but it's all in the name of science, *ja?*"

A dry chuckle. "Of course, you are neither witch nor mage." She glanced at Patryk, then back to Natalya. "But there are uses for healthy human flesh, as well. If I am to be immortal, I'd prefer a younger body." Her lips tightened. "This one is failing."

Hanne waved a hand at the Luban guards. "Take them to the cells. All except Tashtemir Kelevan. The Imperator wants him herself."

Natalya tried to stand and earned a boot to the face, then another kick in the gut. She rolled to her side, gasping, as Hanne walked away, sensible heels clicking on the stone pathway.

Chapter Twenty-Four

Lights gleamed in every window of the palace, casting a yellow glow across the perfectly manicured lawns. Courtiers strolled through the jasmine-scented night, serenaded by a group of musicians in a gazebo. Here in the palace grounds, a greater degree of decorum prevailed. The mood seemed mellow and reflective.

The Imperator's final banquet with her successor, Tawfik al-Mirza, and all the highest-ranking members of the court would be well underway by now.

Kasia studied the ornate facade, searching for anything amiss. The palace was more imposing than the embassies, graced with numerous domes, cupolas, and minarets with tall spires reaching heavenward. Enormous stone dragons flanked the main entrance. They looked disturbingly like the one she had seen from the ship.

She'd expected heavy security, but the Masdar League had known peace for a thousand years. No one had ever attempted to disrupt the succession and the guards at the main doors looked relaxed.

Kasia, Alexei and Paarjini headed to the designated meeting point, a bridge over a small stream with a stone bench at one end. She was relieved to see Merat waiting. The tall soothsayer rose as they approached. She wore an ankle-length robe of midnight blue with stars and moons embroidered along the sleeves.

"Any word about Tashtemir?" she asked anxiously.

"Not yet," Kasia replied. "What time is it?"

Paarjini checked her watch. "Almost nine o'clock."

"Surely we'd know if it had gone wrong," Alexei said, eying the guards, who leaned on spears, chatting with each other.

"Did you bring the keys?" Paarjini asked.

Merat patted a cloth pouch. "In here. Exactly to the specifications you gave me."

"May I see them?" Kasia asked.

"The moment I see Tashtemir alive and well," she replied firmly.

Kasia gave a reluctant nod. She wondered how Malach and Nikola were faring.

Merat's sharp eyes fixed on Alexei's Raven Mark. "You are a priest of the Via Sancta," she said with a note of surprise.

He nodded. "I didn't come here willingly." A glance at Kasia. "But fate has brought us all back together."

"I sense a tale," Merat said wryly, regarding them both.

"Too long to relate," Alexei agreed. "You're a cartomancer, too?"

She laughed. "We do not call it that, but yes." Another quick look at his Mark. "The ley works through many different mediums."

They settled on the bench, watching people come and go from the palace. The minutes slipped past. Paarjini kept checking her watch, one foot tapping against the bench.

"They're late," she said.

Kasia turned to Alexei. "Let's walk around to the menagerie. Have a look."

Merat pointed. "It's that way. Do you see the glass dome on the far side?"

"We'll stay in case they show up," Paarjini said. "Don't be long."

They strolled casually through the grounds. Within a few minutes, they reached a high, circular brick wall. It had a gate halfway around. Alexei kept watch while Kasia sidled over and gave it a push. Locked. She peered through the bars into an enclosure thick with vegetation. Nothing looked amiss, though it was too dark to see far.

Surely if they'd been caught, extra guards would be posted.

"I don't like this," Alexei said softly, when she returned. "Where are they?"

"If they did fail, it's over," she replied grimly. "What should we do?"

He exhaled through his nose. "I think Malach had the right of it, going after Balaur himself. If we can't stop the handover of the keys, at least we can stop him from getting them himself."

"Assuming Balaur was even at the embassy. He might not be."

They watched the gate in silence for a moment.

"Natalya came up with the plan," Kasia said, feeling sick. "It was a good one, too. They had Valdrian and Caralexa. Cairness, too. She's a witch."

"And Patryk," Alexei murmured.

"I thought they could deal with anything that came up." She shook her head. "None of them liked each other at first. But that changed. They were solid, you know? So how is it that not even one of them got away?" She looked around. "Should we try to break in?"

Alexei stared into the dark menagerie. "No," he said at last. "We don't know what's waiting in there. We need to warn Paarjini."

Kasia gave a reluctant nod and they started back.

"It makes no sense that only Darya was targeted," Alexei said. "I think there's a game being played here. And we're all being used."

"That would be like Balaur," she agreed bitterly. "He enjoys being a puppet-master. But I'm not entirely sure he's the one influencing events. Or not the only one, at least."

"What do the cards tell you?"

"That a final confrontation is coming. That I must stay strong and remember who I am."

He drew her to a stop, strong fingers clasping her own. "I will stand with you, whatever you decide."

Kasia pulled him into an embrace against the shadow of the wall. She could still scarcely believe she had him back, and felt a moment's sympathy for Merat. She knew all too well the agony of waiting.

"I hope you mean that, Bryce."

He looked down at her with an injured look. "Why wouldn't I? I love you more than life itself."

She sighed. "I don't doubt that. And I love you, too. But I fear we will both face choices not to our liking."

"There's nothing new in that," he replied dryly.

She grinned. "True enough. I just want it to be over. To have Rachel back safely. Balaur gone forever. And, I suppose, Valmitra freed, if that is best."

"Do you . . . ever wonder about that last part?"

"Of course. It's different for Paarjini. But we never worshipped a god. I'm not even sure what the word means."

"Nor I," Alexei admitted. "The essence of my faith is individual choice. Answering to one's conscience and choosing right for its own sake, without reward or threat of punishment."

She drank in the lines of his face. So serious. So earnest. "And we will continue to keep that faith until proven otherwise."

They were nearly back when a figure detached from the trees, heading straight for them. Kasia tensed until she recognized Hassan. He strode up to Alexei and spoke in an urgent tone, hands gesticulating.

"He's been looking for us," Alexei told her. "A fire broke out at the Luban embassy. The priests doused the flames and sealed it off. They claim it was set accidentally, but he doesn't believe them."

"Malach?" she asked, a sharp stone lodging in her heart. "And Nikola?"

"He has no word."

She steeled herself. Now wasn't the time to fall to pieces. "Will Hassan come? We must tell Paarjini and Merat. Get them out of there immediately."

Alexei posed the question and Hassan agreed. They hurried back to the bridge. The whole way, Kasia feared the two women would have vanished as well, but they were still waiting. When the soothsayer saw Hassan, she rose to her feet and bowed, a flustered look on her face. Hassan returned the bow. They eyed each other uncertainly.

"We're all friends here," Paarjini said with an edge of impatience. "It's nearly ten. Did ye learn anything?"

Kasia glanced around. "Not here," she whispered.

They walked across the wide lawn, her back tingling the entire way. It wasn't until they were deep in a stand of date palms that Kasia relaxed a little. The palace was still visible in the distance, but none of the guards were looking over.

"What did ye find out?" Paarjini asked.

"Hassan says the Luban embassy caught fire," Alexei replied. "We saw no sign of Tashtemir or anyone else. No sign they were caught either, but I think we must assume so."

The soothsayer blanched at the news. Her gaze turned in the direction of the menagerie. It was hidden by trees and she took a half step toward it before stopping.

"It's all goin' to shite," Paarjini muttered. "I hate to say it, but it's time to call it off. Leave the isle, regroup, and decide what to do."

"Not just yet," Kasia said.

Merat gathered herself and gave Kasia a nod of under-standing.

"A reading first," she said tensely.

They retreated to another lawn behind the trees and sat down in a circle on the grass. Usually Kasia approached her cards with focused deliberation, but she felt suddenly impul-sive. She looked around, gaze catching on a burst of fireworks above the palace. It streaked toward the firmament in a sparkling white blaze. With a series of thunderous pops, it broke into hibiscus blossoms of red, blue, violet, yellow and pink. They unfurled across the dark sky, hovering suspended for a long moment before falling back to earth.

Five flowers. Five petals.

"If I choose, it will be the same reading as always." She looked at Alexei. "We need a fresh perspective. Will you do it?"

"If you think it will help," he replied.

"Five cards," she said, fanning the deck across the lawn.

He drew quickly, without hesitation, and turned them over.

The Knight. The High Priestess. The Seven of Keys. The Nine of Ravens. The Sorceress. It took only an instant to deci-pher the meaning.

She pushed the Knight toward Alexei. "You."

He nodded, familiar with the archetype the ley had given him from previous readings.

The Seven of Keys she pressed into Hassan's hand.

"You," she said.

It showed a beautiful woman in a flowing white gown, dark hair spilling down her back. She held three keys in one hand, four in the other. Rays of shining light framed her head. *Blessed.* Hassan stared down at the image in shock.

"You," she said, offering the Nine of Ravens to Merat.

The card showed another woman, this one with a cap of short hair and nine cards arrayed before her on a table. Each held one simple image. The Lenormand deck. Her chin was propped on one hand as she studied the spread with a slight frown. A tawny caracal crouched at her feet, its tail wound around her ankle.

"And you," she said, giving the last to Paarjini. "The final card of the Major Arcana."

The Sorceress stood on a white beach, long foam-tipped combers breaking behind her. Jewels winked in her chestnut hair. A lump of Fool's Gold shone at her throat.

"I'm the High Priestess," Kasia said, as the silence lengthened. "Never has the ley been more direct. We must finish this ourselves."

Paarjini opened her mouth, then closed it again. She scrutinized her own card again, then leaned forward to examine the others.

"Tha is eerie," she said at last. "But how? Without Tashtemir, we have no knowledge o' the palace or where the keys are kept." She handed the card back. "I'm sorry, Kasia, but I won't undertake a suicide mission. Not even if the ley commands it."

Merat looked thoughtful. "I could probably get you inside," she said. "The outer court is more loosely guarded than the inner."

"Tha is a kind offer." Paarjini patted her hand. "But it still leaves the problem of where we must go. Do ye ken?"

Merat shook her head with regret. "The soothsayers are not privy to such things."

Kasia stared at Hassan. "But you are, Blessed," she said softly. "Am I wrong?"

His dark eyes lifted. "No," he said in a thick accent. "You are not."

"Then the only question is whether you will help us."

His hand stole to a yellow claw that hung on a chain around his neck. "It seems I have no choice," he said faintly.

Alexei didn't look happy. They spoke together in Masdari. At length, he turned back. "It is a great deal you ask of him. More than you realize."

"I know." She could see it in the shadows behind his eyes.

"I told him that we would not hold it against him if he said no, but he is willing. He said . . . it is no coincidence that he was shown the place we seek when he was a young boy. Only once, but he remembers—"

Hassan raised a hand. "The chamber lies at the heart of the palace," he said in halting Osterlish. "Guarded by the Nazaré Maz, the Breath of God."

"I've met them," Paarjini said.

Hassan turned to her. His elegant features might have been carved from granite. "Then you know what they can do."

"Aye. And I have some ideas about how to manage them."

She sounded confident, but Hassan still looked like he faced an executioner wielding a dull axe. Kasia would have refused him if she weren't certain they were meant to do this.

"We have two hours," she said. "Will that be enough time?"

Hassan seemed to have exhausted his supply of Osterlish. He replied in Masdari, with Alexei translating.

"To steal the Imperator's greatest treasure out from under her nose? Yes, I suppose so. The palace is not that large. If I walked directly to the chamber, it would take ten minutes at a leisurely pace." Hassan gave a hollow laugh. "It is what we will encounter along the way that worries me."

Chapter Twenty-Five

Brass standing lamps cast a mellow light on the stone walls. Laughter and voices drifted through the arcaded porticos, carried on air scented with a hundred savory dishes.

Getting inside the palace had proved surprisingly easy. Merat and Hassan were both known to the guards. Paarjini and Kasia were already dressed as palace servants, with silver beads sewn into the hems of their abayas, and Alexei had been glamoured to look like a steward bearing gifts for the new Imperator.

Apparently, there was an entire chamber set aside for these inaugural presents, which struck Kasia more like bribes than expressions of goodwill. She could only imagine what sort of Imperator Jamila would make. Or Tawfik al-Mirza—whatever her real name was.

Alexei ducked his head whenever they passed someone coming from the opposite direction. Paarjini had warned them that it was almost impossible to fool the eye up close— not when it came to something as mobile and complex as a human face. With luck, the illusion would pass casual scrutiny.

When they reached the first ring of guards to the inner palace, Paarjini used a moonstone to induce a light waking trance. They still stood at their post, but their eyes stared straight ahead as the party passed through the double doors.

"How long will it last?" Kasia whispered.

"Twenty minutes, perhaps," Paarjini replied.

"That's not much time. I think Nikola was right. Once we find the keys, you might have to force us out."

The witch sighed. "I'll do what I must. Let's hurry."

Hassan led the way through the multitude of corridors laid out on an east-west axis. Mosaics spangled with azure and gold covered the walls. Motifs of lilies were painted on the vaulted ceiling. Natalya would have loved to see the palace, Kasia thought. She could probably have given an entire history lesson on Masdari art and architecture.

Saints, let her and Patryk be safe somewhere.

They got through a second ring of soldiers the same way, these wearing tunics of gold with dragons on the breast and funny-looking conical helmets. The Imperator's personal guard.

Kasia was starting to believe they might make it when they rounded a corner and ran straight into one of the priests. He must have moved in perfect silence for she hadn't heard a single footfall.

Merat recovered quickly, making a starburst gesture of respect and standing aside to let him pass, with the rest of them quickly following.

He was a huge man, bald as an egg, with thick lips seamed by pink scar tissue that was visible even through the veil. The priest snapped something at Merat in a harsh voice. Again, she made a gesture of humility, quietly repeating the apology with downcast gaze.

He nodded once, sourly, and started to walk by when his obsidian eyes landed on Hassan, who had furtively tucked something into his robe. The priest halted and barked a command.

Hassan slowly withdrew the yellowed claw that hung from

a chain around his neck. The priest stared at it. Then he spoke again in Masdari, gesturing at Hassan's sleeve.

Hassan lifted his chin. Kasia was struck by how noble and brave he looked at that moment, like the old tale of Davindra and Golgath.

"Ka," he said defiantly, which she knew meant *no*.

The priest's face twisted in rage. He repeated the command.

Merat stepped in, clearly attempting to be polite and sort the situation out. But the Breath of God only grew angrier. His arm snaked out, reaching for Hassan. Kasia didn't see Alexei move, but the next instant he'd yanked the priest's curved dagger from its waist-sheath and slashed it across his throat. A jet of blood arced through the air. Paarjini screamed as it struck her sleeve.

The priest sank to the ground, a dark river spreading outward from his body. It *smoked*. Kasia stepped back before it touched her slipper.

"Cut the cloth away," Hassan cried.

Alexei wiped the blade on the priest's robe and used the edge to roughly sever Paarjini's sleeve. The flesh beneath was raw, the skin bubbling. Her face drew tight in agony. Kasia tore her veil from its clasps and started to bind the arm. Paarjini was trembling all over.

"No!" Hassan pulled the veil from her hands. "That will only make it worse. The material will melt into her flesh."

"How do we stop the burn?" Kasia asked.

"There are herbs," Merat said quickly. "I must get her to my sisters before she loses . . ." The soothsayer trailed off. "It can be treated, but there is little time."

"Go," Alexei said. "Hurry."

"I'm sorry," Paarjini whispered, tears in her eyes.

"It was my fault," Alexei said. "I didn't think. We'll continue alone. How much farther?"

"Only a little way," Hassan said, wrapping an arm around

Paarjini's waist. She leaned against him, panting. "Left, then right, then two lefts." He glanced with hatred at the dead priest. "Be prepared for more. They are like roaches. If you see one, you can be sure the rest are not far off, hiding in the woodwork."

"I'll need the fake keys," Kasia said.

Merat thrust the cloth pouch into her hands.

"Do not fail," Paarjini rasped, squeezing Kasia's fingers.

"We won't," Kasia promised, though she wondered how they would get past the Breath of God guarding the chamber. She couldn't compel them—that required touching bare skin. And spilling their blood was equally dangerous.

Merat and Hassan set off at a brisk pace, carrying Paarjini between them. The witch looked back once before they vanished around a corner. Kasia turned to Alexei. "What exactly happened?"

"Hassan was sold to the Breath of God as a boy. He ran away and made a new life. That priest recognized him. He has a brand on his arm that would have proven it." Alexei shook his head. "From what I understood, he was the same man Hassan had been given to for training. What are the odds, Kasia?"

She felt the threads of ley around them twisting, tightening. "Astronomical. I'm glad you killed him. But somehow I knew it would come to this in the end. Just the two of us."

"The sword and the ley," he said softly.

She rose up on her toes and kissed him, hoping it wasn't for the last time.

"The sword and the ley," she agreed.

He gripped the priest's blade. Kasia readied her cards. Together, they strode swiftly down the corridor. Left, then right and left again.

At the final juncture, they slowed and approached on silent feet. Without Paarjini, there would be no forcing to safety. But if she could just swap out the keys and hide the originals before they were caught . . .

Voices drifted around the corner. A pair, at least.

"Do you have gloves?" she mouthed silently.

He pulled a pair from his pocket and tugged them on.

She fanned her deck, pausing at a blindfolded woman driving a chariot drawn by a pair of Marksteeds. The Chariot of Justice. Morvana Ziegler's card. The Kven bishop was a devout believer—yet the opposite of mindless fanatics like the Nazaré Maz. Kasia smiled.

Let these priests have a taste of their own true nature.

She mimed for Alexei to wait. He shook his head, jaw setting stubbornly. She drew him close. "You must," she whispered in his ear. "Else you will lose your sight."

He looked startled, then gave a nod. She counted down from three with her fingers and stepped around the corner.

Seven Breath of God were waiting for her. None wore veils. Mottled, gray-skinned faces turned in unison. Their eyes were set into deep sockets that absorbed the torchlight like water seeping into an open grave. Their mouths were slashes, the lips stained red. They didn't make a sound. Just swarmed down the corridor, black robes flapping like wings.

Kasia waited, resisting the terror that froze her limbs. Their cowls fell back, revealing bone-white, hairless skulls. Steel whispered against leather scabbards. She smelled them now, a sharp, sickly-sweet aroma that made her think of the hospital where her father died. Disinfectant covering the stench of sickness.

She forced herself to wait until she thought they were close enough. Then she raised the Chariot of Justice. The power roared up through the soles of her feet like an electric current. *Let them see the light!*

She squeezed her own eyes tight and raised an arm. It burst through her lids like an exploding star. The world turned white. She staggered into the stone wall. The priests were shouting and crashing against each other.

One by one, they fell silent.

Kasia pressed the heels of her hands against her eyes. Her skin felt flayed. Alexei's face swam into focus. It doubled, queasily.

Hands cupped her face. "Kasia!"

She blinked and the images slid together.

"I can see," she said.

The seven priests lay motionless. Not a drop of blood marred the white marble. She realized that Alexei had snapped their necks.

It had to be done. *She* had called the ley to blind them. *She* had told him to don his gloves. The Breath of God were monstrous. Yet she fought down a shudder at the cold efficiency of it. Sometimes she forgot that he had been a member of Falke's Beatus Laqueo. The Order of the Holy Noose, trained to hunt and kill mages.

"Paarjini's illusions might have gone undetected," she said, "but this won't. We must hurry."

He met her gaze, then led the way through the bodies to the end of the corridor. An archway opened into an octagonal chamber. Even if the priests had not been guarding it, she would have known it held something powerful. The ley dashed in violent waves against seven pedestals, each holding a lacquered wooden box. Her gaze rose to the dome above. It was painted with a fresco depicting seven gates.

Kasia handed Alexei the cloth bag and opened the first box.

A large key of iron nested in a cutout. The bow had a lattice of ornate curlicues. He rummaged through the bag and found its match. Kasia held them up, side by side. The locksmith had followed the design precisely. She saw no difference between the two keys. She pocketed the first and placed the fake in the box. It snugged into the velvet lining.

The next box held a key of mellow gold, with wings on the shaft and a heart-shaped bow. She didn't waste time comparing them. Again, the replica fit the box's cutout perfectly.

Alexei slipped to the door and peered down the corridor, then hurried back. Next came silver, then mercury, copper, and lead. Each key was unique, with a different bit and bow. Silver had a crescent moon, mercury a flame, copper a teardrop, lead a rose with thorns twining around the shaft.

The last key was tin. A gargoyle gripped the bow with tiny talons. Kasia dropped it into her pocket and shut the lid just as a dark-skinned woman with eyes like storm clouds appeared in the archway.

The deck of cards was wrenched from her fingers. The next thing she knew, her body was hurtling upward with sickening speed. She stopped just short of the dome and rotated in midair until her feet were above her head. She hung suspended for a few seconds, writhing like a fish in a net.

"Let me go!" she yelled.

The woman laughed. "Sure."

The invisible grip slackened. The ground rushed to meet her.

Kasia jerked to a stop above one of the pedestals, so close her hair brushed the marble. From her upside-down vantage point, she saw a child step into the chamber. Rachel's body— but the ley knew him for what he was. It surged at his feet, an angry red.

"The soldier is useless," Balaur said. "Get rid of him."

Kasia twisted and saw Alexei, blade up, surrounded by a dozen Breath of God. An instant later, he dropped the sword with a cry of pain. The hilt blazed white-hot. He sank to one knee, tearing at a glove. The witch flicked a finger. He skidded along the ground and slammed hard into the stone wall. The priests lifted their veils. She caught a whiff of death.

"Wait!" Kasia cried.

Balaur held up a hand.

"I will make a bargain with you," she said.

"You have nothing I want," he replied. "Only the keys, and they are mine for the taking."

A force pinned her arms to her sides. A hand fished in her pocket and withdrew the keys, one by one. Balaur walked along the pedestals, examining each box.

"These might fool the Imperator," he said. "But they would not have fooled me. Can't you feel the power in them?"

The blood rushing to her head made it hard to focus.

"I do have something you want," Kasia said, twisting to catch his eye.

"And what is that?"

"Me. This body. It is young and strong. I'll give it to you willingly."

She heard Alexei's sharp intake of breath.

"What do I need it for?" Balaur asked. "Once I have the elixir, I'll be restored—"

"Are you sure of that?" she pressed. "What if you simply gain immortality in the body you currently occupy?"

Her vision was swimming, but she thought Balaur frowned slightly.

"What if you're trapped inside Rachel forever?" she asked softly. "A frail little girl. The process might be irreversible. Is that the body to make nations tremble?"

Balaur said nothing. She decided to sweeten the offer.

"I have no Marks, but you won't need them. Not if you command the very source of the ley." A pause. "Imagine the punishment of existing as you do, but with no body to call home. An eternity in which to contemplate my defeat and humiliation. A Nigredo with no hope of redemption. Only everlasting darkness."

The witch shifted uneasily. "Make your decision," she snapped. "I agreed to come here so we could leave immediately. I have waited long enough!"

Balaur walked over to Kasia. He rose up on tiptoes so they were eye to eye. Rachel had the same green-gold irises as her father, the same as Kasia, but an evil intelligence peered through them.

"You would do this of your own free will?"

"Yes," she said firmly. "With one other condition. I want to see this city for myself first. I want to know what lives there. And I want Alexei to come with me. Once we arrive, you will let him go. And I will cede my body to you."

"No," he said at once. "I will release the priest. But you will give me your body *now*."

The witch stepped forward. "That violates our terms," she said coldly. "I will not break the spell containing you until we reach the city. It isn't negotiable."

Rage flashed across his face. Then he nodded and smiled.

"Of course, Heshima. I had forgotten. Forgive the lapse."

All this time, the witch had been fisting a stone from which the ley flowed. Its light winked out. Kasia dropped abruptly to the marble floor, landing on her shoulder and hip. She curled into a ball, teeth gritted.

"Easy," Balaur admonished. "I'd thank you not to damage my new vessel."

Heshima muttered something.

"Get up," Balaur ordered.

Kasia clambered painfully to her feet. She caught Alexei's gaze. He stared at her without expression.

Balaur turned to the priests. "Dispose of the bodies outside and set seven of your brothers to guard the chamber. Invent some story to explain the burst of ley. All must appear undisturbed."

The next minutes were a blur of twisting corridors. Six Breath of God accompanied them. She was terrified that Alexei would try to escape and die in the attempt, but he walked ahead of her with a straight spine. Anger rolled off him in waves. She understood, yet her own rage had been quenched by an icy calm.

She'd bought them time the only way she knew how—by appealing to Balaur's sadistic nature. Planting the seed of doubt about his vessel had helped, but she knew why he had agreed. To savor her humiliation.

They exited the palace into an empty patch of ground somewhere on the opposite side from the main entrance. Sounds of revelry drifted over. Music and singing, laughter and more bouts of fireworks. Heshima ordered them all to draw close while she formed a box of ley.

Kasia tried to stand next to Alexei, but the priests moved between them. Then: the earth spinning, falling away. Pressure so hard she thought her bones would snap. Kasia came back to herself on soft, cool sand, stomach heaving. She crawled to Alexei. He pulled her tight, wordlessly rocking them both like one might cradle an infant. The lights of the city twinkled in the distance.

"What are they doing here?" an imperious voice demanded.

The khedive of Luba stalked over. Behind her, Kasia saw a row of wagons and two dozen hard-faced men.

Balaur stood with Heshima. Neither showed any ill effects from the forcing. "They are my prisoners," he replied. "Bind them and make space in one of the wagons."

Kasia still thought of her as Jamila, though the resemblance was scant. Her black hair was gleaming, her robes embroidered with colorful birds that must have taken an army of seamstresses weeks to finish. "That was not the plan—"

"It has changed," Heshima interrupted. "Do as he says."

The khedive scowled. "Where are the keys?"

"I have them," Balaur said.

Her face stilled. "Show me."

He took the keys out. Greedy eyes devoured them. "We could have just waited until they were given to me." Her lips formed a pout. "I was forced to feign illness to leave the dinner early. The Imperator was not pleased."

"But she could hardly change her mind at this late hour," Balaur pointed out. "And now we have the last of your enemies in our hands." A chuckle. "They even left fakes so she will be none the wiser. And when you ascend the throne tomorrow, it will not be for seven years. Luba's reign will last forever."

She stared at him for a long moment, gaze distant. "And all those who stood in my way will learn penitence. But I must be back in time for the ceremony tomorrow. That is crucial."

"You will be," Balaur promised. "Where is Herr Danziger?"

A tall figure stepped into the moonlight from between two of the wagons. Kasia and Alexei stood, hands laced together. A fierce rush of satisfaction buoyed her spirits.

His blonde hair was falling out in clumps, the skull beneath not white but brown, like an ancient fossil. His face had waxy sheen. When he raised a hand to jam a cigarette between his lips, the flayed fingers left a reddish smear on the paper.

"You're not looking so well, Jule," she said.

Pearly teeth shone against black gums. "Well, now, you should see the rest of me, Kasia."

He wore an expensive tailored suit, the shirt buttoned to the top. Jule drew on the cigarette. A thread of smoke drifted out of one ear.

"Don't you worry," he said. "I'll be better soon. Then we can spend some time together."

Balaur cast him a disgusted glance that Jule failed to notice.

"Where's your aunt, Danziger?" Alexei asked coldly.

Jule turned to him. "Hanne? She's with your friends. Cutting them to pieces and sewing them into new shapes right now. Or maybe she's testing poisons. She has quite the imagination."

He spun away and limped into the darkness. Four of the guards bound Kasia and Alexei, while others unloaded crates from one of the wagons. Judging by the effortless way they tossed them out, she knew they were empty. Waiting to hold the khedive's plunder.

She and Alexei were trussed with ropes and dumped onto a heap of burlap sacks. Harness jingled. The wagon lurched into motion. From between the slats, she saw Balaur riding a mule alongside Heshima. The khedive sat with a stooped, white-bearded old man.

"Kasia," Alexei whispered.

She twisted around to face him. His eyes were tight.

"Did you know this would happen?"

"No," she answered truthfully. "Of course not. I would never keep such a thing from you."

The weight of the betrayal nearly sunk her then. She'd always believed the ley was on their side. Tried to obey its commands.

Yet at every turn, it favored Balaur.

Now Hanne Danziger had Patryk and Natalya, and the others. Kasia remembered the woman's glittering dark eyes and false cheer. The monstrous underground laboratory she'd presided over in Kvengard. She fought a wave of terror for their friends.

"I must think," she whispered.

Alexei nodded and shifted closer, sharing his warmth.

How many hours until dawn?

Her eyes grew heavy, but she didn't dare fall asleep. Somehow, she had misread everything. And if she didn't find the right answer before the sun rose, little else mattered.

Chapter Twenty-Six

A bitter wind howled down from the mountain peaks, flapping Morvana Ziegler's woolen cloak. She clutched the hood, tucking her chin and fixing her gaze on the ground ahead. A chessboard of seams stitched the frozen surface of Lake Khotang where the ice had buckled into blade-sharp ridges. They looked like tiny versions of the Sundar Kush range that rose like an impassable wall in the distance.

"Is this normal for Maia month?" Morvana asked, her words snatched away on a cloud of vapor.

In Kvengard, the dogwoods would be in full bloom, the grass thick with robins.

Lezarius glanced over. Frost rimed his bushy brows. "Not usually," he said, voice muffled through a blue scarf. "Spring is late this year."

The Northern Curia was beautiful but stark, a monochromatic landscape of black basalt and varieties of frozen water. Even the sky was washed out, leaden with clouds that promised more snow before nightfall. The only splash of color lay ahead, where two figures stood next to a parley flag, crimson robes rippling like bloodstains against the snow.

Captain Mikhail Bryce strode ahead, one hand resting on his sword hilt, scanning the terrain as if he expected more mages to leap out of crevices in the ice. He wore no helm and the wind lashed his dark hair. She noticed new threads of silver at the temples. New lines of weariness at the corners of his blue eyes.

During the journey from Nantwich, he would twist and mutter in his sleep—on the rare occasions she nagged him into resting. Most nights, he paced endless circuits around the camp. At first, he'd allowed her to join him. He had a keen intellect and enjoyed debating the finer points of the *Meliora*. Morvana enjoyed his company and thought he felt the same.

But as they neared Jalghuth, he withdrew into himself, rebuffing everyone except for Lezarius. She hadn't seen him eat in days.

It worried her—though not as much as what awaited them. She glanced past the two mages to the camp that sprawled along the forested edge of the Morho Sarpanitum, stretching all the way to the lakeshore. Smoke from hundreds of fires stained the sky. A standard with the Broken Chain of Bal Kirith fluttered from a pole at the center of the camp. Every so often, the wind shifted, carrying the stench of rotten meat from the tents. She'd thought their rations had spoiled until Mikhail explained that it was the Perditae soldiers. In the Old Tongue, the name meant Lost Ones.

Many were knights who had been sent to reclaim Bal Agnar. Instead of taking the city, they had defected to the nihilim.

Lezarius thought they could still be saved. But Morvana's scouts had returned with dire reports. The knights' pupils had changed to horizontal slits. They communicated in grunts and gestures as often as speech. She remembered what the two young mages, Sydonie and Tristhus, had told her in chillingly matter-of-fact tones. That the Perditae were monsters born from the tainted ley in the Morho.

They try to eat you up. Sometimes they eat each other.

Morvana tore her eyes from the camp. It had been madness to come here. But the Reverend Mother Clavis was somewhere among those tents. A hostage, badly wounded. They couldn't abandon her.

She heard the snap of the white parley flag now. It echoed the pops and groans of the contracting ice as the mountains' shadow lengthened and the temperature plunged. The pale sun had already dropped behind Khumbu glacier. They had perhaps an hour of daylight left.

Mikhail stopped so abruptly that Morvana almost walked into him.

"That's not Beleth," he said in a low voice.

Lezarius peered at the two mages. "I see Dantarion. We are not friends, but not exactly enemies either. The other . . ."

"Cadmael Jarrah," Mikhail said. "A high-priority fugitive during the war. He always slipped through our fingers. Jarrah is a brutal bastard, Reverend Father."

Lezarius puffed out a breath. "Unfortunate," he replied calmly. "Let us see what they want."

The mages watched them approach in silence. That was another unnerving feature of the far north. The hushed, enveloping quiet, as if they had reached the edge of the world. The squeak of Morvana's waterproof boots against the snow-pack sounded far too loud as she trailed the pontifex and his captain to the parley flag.

It stood midway between the two camps. Their own—far smaller—cluster of tents sat across a long, narrow arm of the lake, just below the black tower known as Sinjali's Lance. Several kilometers to the west, Jalghuth perched in the foothills. A wooden palisade surrounded the small city. The gates were barred. No one had come out to challenge the army camped at the other end of the lake.

"That's far enough!"

A woman's voice rang across the ice. She walked forward,

hood falling to her shoulders. She had clear green eyes and auburn hair pulled back into a loose ponytail. Her face was youthful, hardly older than Morvana. Freckles scattered across an upturned nose.

"Lezarius," she said, inclining her head.

"Dantarion," he replied gravely.

The mage stopped twelve paces away, as if reaching an invisible border. "Who have you brought?"

"Bishop Zeigler from Kvengard. Captain Bryce of my personal guard."

Her gaze locked on Mikhail. Morvana got the strong impression they'd met before.

"Lay down your blade, knight," Dantarion said. "This is a parley."

Mikhail slowly drew his sword. He stabbed it point-down in the snow, then stepped aside. "What about you?" he asked.

"I am unarmed." She smiled. "But you're welcome to search me."

The mage wore no gloves. Mikhail regarded her bare hands for a moment. "I'll take your word, bishop."

A hawk wheeled overhead, so high it was just a dark speck against the clouds. It let out a screech and sped away for the mountains.

"Very well," Dantarion announced in a bored tone. "Let us settle the terms of this accord."

The second mage walked up. He ignored Morvana and Mikhail, focusing on Lezarius with open animosity. "I am Cardinal Jarrah." A yellow-toothed sneer. "And you are the mighty Lion of the North."

He had the bloated look of a heavy drinker. Thinning ginger hair swept back from a high, pale brow. A lifetime of excess and cruelty could be read in the sagging jowls, small, suspicious eyes, and permanently downturned mouth.

"Why has Beleth not come herself?" Lezarius asked.

"The Reverend Mother is resting from the journey," Dantarion answered. "She sends Jarrah in her stead."

"I see. And Clavis, is she well?"

"She's alive," Jarrah said.

"I would like to see her," Lezarius said mildly.

"You will see her when you give us Dmitry Falke."

"I hoped we could reach a new arrangement." He pulled a sheaf of papers from his cloak. Jarrah snatched them away.

"What is this?" he muttered, scanning the parchment.

"The agreement Falke signed in Nantwich with Cardinal Malach of Bal Kirith. It formally gives the city back to mage control. It also provides for assistance in rebuilding, and the return of looted relics."

"We're already aware of this." Jarrah thrust the papers at Dantarion. "It changes nothing. Beleth's left hand was severed by Falke's knights and she wants his in return."

"I want to speak to her in person," Lezarius said.

"That's not possible," Jarrah replied. "And I'm not here to negotiate. You have until tomorrow morning to give us Falke." A nasty smile. "I'll even allow him to choose which hand he will lose. Tonight, he can jerk off, play the flute, whatever he likes."

He made a chopping motion with his forearm. "Then we even the score. I have no quarrel with the rest of you. In fact, I hope we can coexist in perfect harmony."

Morvana regarded the man's flat, devious eyes. "How will this exchange be carried out?" she asked. "And what happens to Falke afterwards?"

"It's simple," Dantarion replied. "We meet here at daybreak. You bring Falke. We bring Clavis. When the severing is finished, you get Falke back, plus the rest of Clavis's knights. Then we leave. But if the gates of Jalghuth open for any reason, we will overrun your camp." Her gaze rested on Lezarius. "The knights would never reach you in time."

It was why Beleth had insisted on camping at the eastern

end of the lake. Within sight of Jalghuth—but too far to quickly summon aid.

"What guarantee do we have that you'll return Falke alive?" Morvana pressed.

"My word as a cardinal of the Via Libertas," Jarrah replied. He raised the hood of his red cloak. "Tomorrow. Or we will send you a piece of Clavis each hour until Falke appears. First the hands, then the feet, then the head."

Dantarion lifted her chin. She tore the treaty in half and dropped it on the snow. "Don't be late," she snapped, striding after Cardinal Jarrah.

Dusk painted the mountains in shades of arctic blue. The deepening chill burrowed beneath Morvana's cloak.

"Why did Falke's knights have to sever Beleth?" Lezarius muttered. "Why couldn't they just have taken her captive?"

"They were afraid of her," Mikhail replied. "And they wanted to make an example for the rest."

"It's a barbaric practice," Morvana said.

"Yes. But what's done is done." His measuring stare followed the two mages as they made their way towards the camp. "Jarrah is lying."

"About which part?" Lezarius asked.

"We know Clavis is alive," Morvana put in. "Rycroft proves that."

Miles Rycroft was a knight from Nantwich, one of those held prisoner at Westfield Stadium. He'd volunteered to come north. The Crossed Keys on his neck had been given by Clavis herself. If she'd been dead, Rycroft would be hallucinating, but he showed no symptoms of Mark sickness.

"Not about Clavis," Mikhail agreed. "But he won't give Falke back. That I can promise you."

"Why?" Lezarius asked. "Don't they want Bal Kirith to be restored? There's a real chance for peace. The first in decades!"

"Jarrah doesn't think that far ahead. He hates Falke with a

passion. Once he has him . . ." Mikhail shook his head. "He won't stop with a hand."

"Then it's time we visit the Lance," Lezarius said firmly. "The Reborn are our only hope now."

Morvana felt an icy chill that had little to do with the weather. She'd spent months searching for the missing Kven children only to learn that they were dead . . . No, not dead. *Transformed*. But into what?

Lezarius had hoped that the purity of the ley here would return the Curia soldiers to their senses, but something was wrong. It was barely a trickle.

They headed away from the lake, entering the pine forest that hugged the lower slopes of Mount Ogo. The snow was deeper here. Jays flitted through the branches, letting out raucous warning cries. She saw the leaping tracks of squirrels and a few larger trails that might have been wolves or bobcats. Lezarius paused at an icy stream.

"I need you to return to camp," he told Mikhail. "Relay what the mages said. Morvana and I will join you shortly."

Mikhail frowned. "I'll go with you."

"It's not necessary," Lezarius said quickly. "The Lance is safe. And our companions will worry if none of us return from the parley."

"But—"

"That's an order, captain."

Mikhail gave him a long, searching look. Then he turned to Morvana. "Guard your thoughts," he said quietly. "The Reborn can read minds."

"I have nothing to hide," she replied, though it was an unsettling prospect.

He gave her a brief nod. Morvana watched him disappear into the trees. She could smell the smoke from their own campfires, just over the rise. A dozen or so against the hundreds of Perditae.

Lezarius turned without a word and began to clamber up

the slope. For a time, the only sound was the wet plop of snow sliding from fir boughs and their own laboring breath. At last, they topped a hill and emerged onto a road. The snow looked pristine as though no one had passed this way in weeks. Sinjali's Lance loomed ahead, a black spike against the stars. She saw not a glimmer of light.

"Are you certain they're still here?" she asked.

"Where else would they go?" Lezarius replied. "This is the wellspring of the ley. Willem Danziger speaks for the other children. He told me they were brought here to protect the source. That is their purpose."

"Protect it from Balaur, you mean?"

"He reversed the Wards on the walls. When I arrived with Dantarion, they all shone red."

Morvana stared in astonishment. "I did not realize such a thing was possible."

"Nor did I. It was my undoing." Lezarius shook his head. "I'd planned to make another Void here at Jalghuth and drive Balaur out, but I couldn't banish the ley. The abyssal was too strong."

"What happened?"

"Mikhail saved me. He brought the Reborn with him. They broke through the barrier Balaur had built." His gaze turned inward. "The torrent of ley burned me out. I cannot touch it at all anymore. But it sent Balaur scurrying away like a rat before a broom—"

The elderly pontifex lost his footing on a patch of black ice. Morvana steadied him, then linked their arms. "We can hold each other up, Reverend Father," she said.

He smiled and Morvana felt a rush of fondness. She'd served Luk for her entire life, until he turned traitor. She had always respected him, but he was a reserved, aloof man. And Falke . . . well, she admired his courage and loyalty to Clavis, but she didn't *like* him.

Lezarius had more human warmth and decency than the

two of them put together. She understood why Mikhail seemed to worship him.

"I used to be nimble as a goat on these trails," he said ruefully. "But we are nearly there." He pointed. "One more turning."

They picked their way around a hairpin bend. The Lance came into view again, perched almost directly above. The road led to a narrow bridge that spanned a chasm too deep to see its bottom.

Morvana's pulse ticked up as they approached the huge doors, which were half buried in drifts. The only one of the missing children she'd met was Sofie Arnault. The girl had been traumatized but physically unharmed. The alchemists had not yet begun their experiments on her.

As for the others, she knew only what Lezarius had told her. That the children claimed to be purified by the ley. *Immortal.* Morvana wasn't sure what she believed, but she needed to see them. To know that they were not suffering.

Lezarius banged a fist on the doors. High on the mountain, the wind was a razor flaying every inch of exposed flesh. Long minutes passed. Morvana stomped her feet in a futile effort to bring sensation to her toes. Lezarius shot her a worried look and pounded again. This time, she joined him, striking several hard blows.

What if something had happened? What if they were wrong about the children? Or worse, what if it wasn't the children who lived here now? What if it were something else entirely—

She heard the patter of rapid footsteps. The doors flung wide.

A boy of about thirteen stood on the threshold. She knew him from a painting she'd seen at his home, but the boy in that picture had dark hair and blue eyes like Mikhail Bryce. This one had white hair, white eyelashes, white lips, white skin. He wore a thin, ragged t-shirt, blue jeans, and red sneakers. One eye swirled with color. The other was flat black.

She'd been warned about Will's appearance and kept her expression neutral, but some deep part of her recoiled.

"Lezarius," the boy exclaimed. "Come inside."

They entered a stark antechamber that was barely warmer than the mountain. Staircases of reflective black stone spiraled upward to dizzying heights within the hollow interior of the tower.

"This is—"

"Bishop Morvana Ziegler," the boy finished. "We know."

She forced a smile. "Hello, Will."

A faint aroma of flowers permeated the frigid air. It took her a moment to realize it was coming from the boy.

"I thought you'd be expecting me," Lezarius said.

Will cocked his head. "We've been busy."

"With the Wards?"

The boy nodded.

"There are matters I must speak with you about, Will. Urgent matters. Can we go to the study?"

The child regarded him without emotion. "I want to show you some things first."

"What things?"

"Come see."

Lezarius looked at Morvana and sighed. "All right, Will."

He led them into a downward-sloping corridor. Morvana tried to follow Mikhail's advice and keep her mind blank, despite her mounting unease.

"Have you seen Greylight?" Lezarius asked.

Will glanced over his shoulder. "Not in a while. She doesn't come around anymore."

"Who is Greylight?" Morvana asked.

"My cat," Lezarius replied. He looked troubled.

Gooseflesh rose on Morvana's arms as they entered a dim

chamber. A jagged crevice rent the floor. The top of a ladder poked out.

"I went down there once with Alexei," Lezarius said. "Just before we left for Nantwich." He drew a crumpled paper from his pocket. "Do you recall when Jamila al-Jabban sketched the runes of Gavriel's sword? They are the same."

She glanced at the paper. When she looked up, Will was already gone.

"What's down there, Reverend Father?" she whispered.

"The ruins of an older structure. The Reborn have been studying it."

She glanced at the ladder, curious despite herself. "All right. Let's have a look."

Morvana helped Lezarius gain his footing on the rungs. She held the ladder steady as he descended, then followed him down.

The circular chamber below occupied the entire width of Sinjali's Lance. Distant archways led off in different directions. A few symbols lined the pearly stone walls, traced with glowing white light. In a superficial way, they resembled the alchemical signs she'd seen in the laboratory, but these were simpler. Curving glyphs that might have been numbers or letters.

Six more children sat on the floor, staring intently at the Wards.

Lezarius frowned. "What happened to the rest, Will? There were dozens."

"We broke them," the boy replied serenely.

"You promised you wouldn't!"

"I said we couldn't," the child corrected. "But we have learned since you left."

"What have you learned?" Lezarius demanded. "Is this why the ley is so weak?"

A nod. "We triggered some kind of defenses."

"You must stop!"

The boy regarded him, unruffled by the stern tone. "An angel came, Lezarius. He said we woke him from a long slumber."

"Angel?"

"His name is Borosus. He is radiant."

Lezarius and Morvana exchanged a look. "What else did he say?"

"That we are doing the work of the ley. We must continue."

All this time, the other Reborn had not moved or spoken, or even glanced in their direction. They were fixated on the Wards. But Morvana recognized them. Anna-Rose Laurent. Wandy Keller. Noach Beitz. Karl Josef Zelig. Eddi Haas. Ursula Fellbach. Some were bloodless like Will. The rest had pink cheeks and ruby lips, like perfect little dolls. She could not tell if they were happy or sad. If they felt anything at all.

"What is the work of the ley?" she asked.

Will laid his palm against one of the Wards. The light flared blindingly bright for a moment, then faded. "In the olden days," he said, "when the world was young and the Dark Ages had not yet come to pass, Mount Ogo was called Mount Meru. The high seat of the Empyrium."

Morvana knew other nations had existed before the Via Sancta. Remnants could be found across the continent, weathered jumbles of stone that hinted at former glory, but their names had been lost. She'd never heard of the Empyrium. Judging by Lezarius's intent expression, neither had he.

"Sinjali's Lance was built atop an ancient palace. It is one of only two places in the world where the ley emerges," Will continued. "The other is in the Masdar League. They are different but the same."

Lezarius shook his head. "I'm sorry, I don't understand."

Will made two folds in his t-shirt, then pressed them together. "They are almost touching, you see. Just a hair apart."

"Like the undercity in Nantwich," Morvana said thoughtfully. "Do you mean a liminal space, Will?"

Colors swirled in his left eye. It was mesmerizing, hypnotic. She tore her gaze away, examining the Wards again.

"The in-between," he agreed.

"Are the Wards guarding a doorway?"

"Something like that."

"What will happen if it opens?" Morvana wondered. "If the places join?"

Will smiled. "The Mother will wake."

She swallowed, mouth dry. "Who is the Mother?"

A long moment passed before he replied. "You seek our help, but we cannot give it." His eyes lifted to the ceiling. "What happens in the world above is none of our concern."

"All I ask is that you come out," Lezarius pleaded. "Show yourself to the mages. Visit their camp. They cannot hurt you. But your presence might heal the knights, just as you healed me. Please, we are desperate!"

Will laid a hand on his shoulder. "You are welcome to shelter inside the Lance. Bar the doors behind you. But we cannot spare the time. The Red King is coming."

"Who is the Red King?" Morvana asked.

"He means Balaur," Lezarius said wearily.

"He is coming *here*?"

"To the other tower," Will clarified. "The one in the Masdar League. But if he seizes that one, he will control the Lance as well." Impatience tinged his voice. "I cannot explain it to you. Have faith, Lezarius. We are on the same side."

"How close are you to shattering the final Wards?" Lezarius asked.

Four still blazed. When Morvana looked closely, she could make out the dark etchings of those the children had broken.

"The last are complex." Will's pale brows furrowed. "I am not sure how long it will take. You must leave us now." He wandered away, joining the others cross-legged on the ground.

Lezarius eyed him with slumped shoulders. "I feared this might happen."

"What do you think is behind those Wards?" Morvana whispered. "Who is this Mother he speaks of?"

"I'm not sure I want to find out," he admitted. "But I don't know how to stop them. Do you?"

Chapter Twenty-Seven

Green fir boughs crackled and popped in the fire. Morvana held her hands to the flames, savoring the warmth. She'd barely tasted the hot meal Mikhail had handed them on their return. Pasta in red sauce, a fruit bar, chocolate with nuts, and a waxy box of apple cider. The packaging promised a perfect balance of fat and carbohydrates for cold-weather conditions. She'd forced it all down and felt energy returning to her numbed limbs.

"What would you have me do?" Dmitry Falke asked. "If I sneak off, they'll kill Clavis. And, most likely, they'd catch me in the Morho anyway."

No one spoke for a minute. Half the Kven knights huddled around the fire. The others patrolled the perimeter. Across the arm of the lake, she could see the lights of Beleth's camp, twinkling like votive candles along the dark altar of the lake.

"I hate to say it, but he's right," Miles Rycroft said heavily. "We're out of options."

Falke gazed down at his hands. An unkempt white beard covered his cheeks. Dark pouches hung beneath his eyes. Yet the head of the Eastern Curia still exuded the calm, resolute authority that had commanded legions on the battlefield.

"I'm right-handed," he said. "By tradition, that is the one on which the pontifical ring is worn. So I need not debate the question. I will cede my left."

Morvana felt ill. She snatched her own hands back, tucking them under her arms. Was there no decency left in the world? Since Luk, she had struggled to keep her faith. The ideals of compassion and mercy had never seemed more ludicrous. There would always be one more grudge to settle. One more grievance to avenge.

"I'm so sorry," Lezarius said. "I truly believed the children would aid us."

"I know you did." Falke looked resigned. "Clavis is young. I am old. If I can trade my hand for her, I give it willingly."

"There must be another way," Lezarius persisted. "If I could only speak with Beleth—"

"She might be dead."

"No. Dantarion wasn't grieving her loss. I would have known."

Falke raised an eyebrow.

"I know what you think of her," Lezarius continued, "but Dantarion saved the children from Jann Danziger. She is not altogether mercenary." He squared his shoulders. "Let me go to their camp. Make a last appeal—"

"No," Falke snapped. "We will not give them another hostage."

"They could have taken me at the parley," Lezarius pointed out.

"They're toying with us," Falke muttered. "But I see no good coming of it." His voice hardened. "Let me do this. You never approved of my conduct before. In fact, you openly denounced me. Consider it atonement."

Lezarius frowned. He opened his mouth to argue when

Mikhail stepped into the firelight. Snowflakes dusted his dark hair. He looked at Morvana, his expression unreadable.

"May we speak privately, Your Grace?" he asked in a low voice.

She'd been excommunicated by Luk, but he insisted on using her title in front of the knights. Morvana had given up objecting.

"Certainly," she agreed, wondering what he wanted. Captain Bryce had taken the news with his usual stoicism, then departed to check on the horses. He seemed to prefer their company to people. All things considered, she could hardly blame him.

She followed him past the picket lines and ducked inside his tent. The furnishings were bare bones—a cot and folding chair. A muddy tarp to cover the slush. He lit a lamp. Mikhail was a tall man, but they stood nearly eye to eye.

"I have a proposal," he said. "Let me infiltrate the camp and free Clavis myself. Tonight."

Kasia had warned her that Mikhail was suicidal. She'd seen no concrete evidence of it—until now.

"That's a brave offer, captain," she said. "But the answer is no. It's impossible. They have too many sentries."

"I might be able to fool them."

"Fool them?" She frowned. "How?"

He unclasped the heavy wool cloak and tossed it to the cot. Then he lifted his tabard and undertunic. Faded bruises tinged his skin.

"This is how." Mikhail watched her warily. "I'm practically one of them."

The image on his chest was unmistakably a Nightmark. A blindfolded man with a knife to his throat and an ecstatic, disturbing smile. Morvana stared in shocked fascination. She'd never actually seen one before.

"I should have told you before," he said roughly, letting the garments fall. "I'm sorry."

"That is . . ." She cleared her throat. "That is the Mark that was inverted?"

He nodded. Everything suddenly made sense.

"Malach gave it to me. Four years ago, when Alexei and I served together in Falke's Beatus Laqueo. It was before the Cold Truce. The fighting was hot then." He sighed. "Alexei joined because of me. If he had died . . . it would have been my fault. So I struck a bargain. My brother's life for the mage's Nightmark."

Another jolt of surprise. *Malach*. Balaur's regent—who had turned against him. "I see," she said quietly.

"I'm tired of living with it, Your Grace." His blue eyes bored into her. "*Please*. This is my choice."

She drew a breath. "To throw your life away because you made a mistake?"

He didn't answer. She felt suddenly furious.

"You don't like Falke *or* Clavis," she exclaimed. "It is Lezarius you're loyal to. Both of them wanted him dead! Why do their fates matter so much to you?"

"Because I have a chance to succeed," he replied evenly. "Perditae operate largely by smell. The corrupted knights might view me as one of their own."

She leaned forward and sniffed. "You smell normal to me, captain. A bit ripe, but we all are."

"Their senses are more acute than yours. And I'm not talking about my body."

"Your soul?" She scowled. "This is ridiculous!"

"Then let me test it," he said stubbornly.

She threw her hands up. "You planned this all along, didn't you?"

"As a last resort," he admitted. "But Alexei confided in me about the Reborn. He feared something like this might happen." Mikhail looked away. "If I can kill Cadmael Jarrah while I'm at it, I'll do that, too. Consider it a bonus."

Morvana shook her head. "Do you believe peace is possible, captain?"

His attention snapped back. He looked mildly affronted. "Of course. That is the founding doctrine of the Via Sancta."

"I don't mean some theoretical, perfect, eternal peace when we are all flawless individuals," she replied tartly. "I mean *now*. In this lifetime."

He met her gaze. "All peace requires is that both sides grow so tired of fighting each other that they stop. I think we're all tired. Even the mages."

Morvana was opening her mouth to reply when Miles Rycroft stuck his head in the flap. Melting snowflakes glistened against his brown skin. "We have a visitor," he said, eyes gleaming. "In red."

They exchanged a quick look and hurried outside.

A hooded figure stood by the campfire. She turned at their approach.

"It's the skeleton," Dantarion said in a cheerful tone. "You put on some weight since I saw you last."

Mikhail grunted. "What do you want?"

"To strike a bargain. My child is in that camp. So is my mother. I want them both out, with a guarantee that the treaty ceding Bal Kirith will be honored."

"The one you tore up?" Falke asked.

Her cold gaze turned to him. "I won't pretend I care what happens to you. You still severed Beleth."

Falke stiffened. "I didn't—"

"Give the order personally? Maybe you didn't and maybe you did. I have no way of knowing. I trust you about as much as I trust Jarrah, which is to say not at all." She turned to Lezarius. "But I do trust *him*."

Lezarius inclined his head. "Thank you, Dantarion," he said solemnly. "I appreciate that."

Her lips curled in a smile. "I know you, old lion. You actually believe what you preach. I saw it myself when you pulled me from the lake." Her smile died. "Jarrah means to kill you all and then breach the walls of Jalghuth. The only thing stopping him is that you are camped so close to the Lance. He fears what Balaur created. I haven't told him that the children can't harm a living soul."

The wind picked up, whistling through the guy lines of the tents and sending flurries of embers into the sky. Dantarion shook her head in amazement. "I didn't think you'd come. The last pontifices of the Via Sancta. What a gift you've made him. All three! You might as well put ribbons on yourselves."

Falke stared at her. "I doubt you can comprehend it, mage, but we're loyal to our own."

She held her palms to the fire. "That's heartwarming, Dmitry," she said in an acid tone. "You have my undying admiration. But once he lures you out, he means to lead his forces in an assault. Jarrah is a fool. He can barely control the Perditae as it is. Once they get a taste of blood . . . Well, it is no place for my son."

A smile split Lezarius's seamed face. "A boy, then. What is his name?"

"Felix. It means lucky in the Old Tongue." Her brow knit. "I gave birth to him alone in the Morho. There were Perditae nearby. I tried to be quiet, but they caught my scent. I almost . . ." She drew a shuddering breath. "I hate them," she said in an empty voice. "You've no idea how much."

Morvana felt a stab of pity. The ordeal sounded unimaginable.

"What about your mother?" Lezarius asked.

"She had a stroke," Dantarion said. "Two days ago. Her health was already poor after what was done to her. She can walk, even speak, but her mind is not what it was."

"Perhaps for the best," Falke muttered.

"She was never like Balaur!" Dantarion said angrily. "You know that. They weren't even allies."

He regarded her stonily. "She marched on Novostopol."

318

"After you excommunicated her and led an assault on Bal Kirith." Dantarion's jaw set. "Do you know what she told me? She *knew* Balaur was alive. For all those years! He came to her dreams and pleaded for her to rescue him from Jalghuth. She told him to fuck off!"

Falke blinked in surprise. "Did she?"

"Yes! She never liked him." The mage turned to Lezarius. "You should have killed him when you had the chance. You can only blame yourself."

The pontifex looked troubled. "I accept responsibility for my mistakes," he said. "But your mother did not govern Bal Kirith with compassion or sound judgment."

She snorted. "I suppose you'll say it was a cesspool of vice. But Bal Agnar was a whole other level of misery."

To Morvana's surprise, it was Falke who nodded. "That much is true."

Dantarion stared at him. "If Beleth was still in charge, I wouldn't be here. She would have kept her word. Taken your hand and let you go. She's a hard woman, but she just wanted justice. That's all."

"And if we take you hostage instead?" Falke asked mildly.

Lezarius shot him a glare, but Dantarion only laughed. "First, I'd like to see you try. Second, no one over there gives a shit what happens to me. In fact, Jarrah would be relieved to see me dead."

Morvana cleared her throat. "No one is taking anyone hostage," she said firmly. "I am willing to try your proposal, but how can it be done?"

"Not by a frontal assault, that's for certain," Dantarion replied, eying their meager numbers.

"We need intelligence," Mikhail said. "Where the hostages are kept, how the patrols operate, all of it."

"I can give you that."

"The children said they would open the Lance if we sought asylum there," Lezarius ventured.

"You're sure they'd take Beleth?" Dantarion asked.

"They never lie."

"That's not the same thing."

Lezarius produced a hand-rolled cigarette and lit it with a twig from the fire. "To be honest, I doubt they care what we do. They're . . ." He took a long drag and exhaled a stream of smoke. "Focused on something else."

She nodded reluctantly. "That's been my main problem. There's nowhere to go around here. Nowhere safe, anyway. Bal Agnar is even worse. Why do you think we left?"

Falke leaned forward. "So all the knights there . . ."

"Dead or scattered," she said grimly. "It's a tomb."

A ripple of shock went through the group. Morvana didn't know how many knights had gone over, but it must have been hundreds. She whispered a brief litany for their souls.

"I wish I'd listened to the envoy Malach sent," Dantarion continued wearily. "Jessiel begged us to go with her. All the younger ones left. They were glad to take the offer."

"Why didn't you?" Lezarius asked.

"Beleth refused."

"And you wouldn't leave her," he said gently, with a pointed look at Falke.

Dantarion straightened her back. "It's too late now. All I want is a home in Bal Kirith. To join my cousins there. Do we have a deal?"

Morvana nodded. "Let it end here," she said. "The ley willing we all survive the night."

Falke and Lezarius made noises of assent. Rycroft nodded, his expression grim. What choice was there? If any of the pontifices died, everyone they'd Marked would be in trouble. There used to be plenty of other clergy ready to take over the Marks, just as she had done with Alexei. But most were old, like Falke and Lezarius. Their numbers had steadily dwindled in the last decade or so. Few had the ability anymore. It was why Luk had struck his devil's bargain with the mages—or part of the reason.

Now she contemplated what would happen if *all three of them* died.

"The rest of you should head up to the Lance immediately," Mikhail said. He looked almost eager. "Take the horses. Leave a few knights to move around the campfire in case they're watching. I'll go with Dantarion."

She eyed him appraisingly. "Just you?"

"I'll be enough," he replied. "If you're willing to use abyssal ley to invert the Perditae's Marks."

A flicker of surprise. "Drive them even crazier, you mean?"

"Exactly." His gaze moved to the distant camp. "Let's kick that anthill."

Dantarion gave a bark of incredulous laughter. "You're one of Malach's, aren't you? He always knew how to pick the fucking psychopaths."

A hush fell over the campfire. The light of the flames danced in the hollows of Mikhail's face. "Do you want me or not?"

"Oh, I want you," she said, amused. "In the two days since we arrived, twelve of the Perditae are dead—all at each other's hands. It won't take much to tip them over the edge."

Morvana thought of the howls and screams she'd heard the night before—some abruptly cut off. Her skin crawled.

"I'm coming with you," she heard herself say.

Mikhail blanched. "No," he grated. "I forbid it!"

She arched a brow and he amended his tone, though she could see he was struggling. "Your Grace. I respectfully submit that your presence is not needed in this rescue mission. It would only complicate matters."

"How?"

He visibly swallowed. "Because I would be obligated to protect you."

"You're not obligated to do anything, captain," she replied. "And last I checked, I was leading this mission. The Wolves answer to me. Must I have you arrested for insubordination?"

Her knights stood up, hands dropping to their swords.

"No," Mikhail said stonily.

"Then your objections are noted and overruled."

"What use will you be?" Dantarion wondered. "You're Kven, aren't you?"

"I won't carry a weapon," Morvana responded, "but I can carry a child."

Dantarion went very still. "You think I'd trust you with my son?"

"You might have to."

The mage studied her. "You do look strong. Will you swear on the *Meliora* that you mean us no harm?"

"Yes," Morvana responded immediately.

"I'll come, as well," Falke said.

Dantarion shook her head. "Absolutely not. You'd only be a liability."

"I can still hold a sword!"

"And the answer is still no."

"So I'm supposed to go cower inside the Lance?" he asked disdainfully.

"Yes. Go pack your bags."

"She's right," Lezarius said. "This will be done by stealth or not at all. And like you said, Dmitry, we are old men."

Falke glowered. "What about Clavis's knights?" he asked gruffly.

"Seven are still alive. They're wearing Warded shackles so they can't touch the ley." Dantarion dangled something silver from her fingers. "But I lifted the keys from Cardinal Shithead."

"Won't he notice?" Morvana asked.

"Jarrah's been drinking since this morning." She tucked

the keys back in a pocket. "Getting into the camp shouldn't be too hard. It's getting out again that concerns me."

Rycroft raised a hand. "I have a few ideas."

"We can discuss them in my tent," Mikhail said tightly.

He threw Morvana a baleful look and strode off. The horses seemed to sense his mood, nickering uneasily along the picket line.

Dantarion chuckled. "I think the knight fancies you."

"I hold his brother's Marks," Morvana said, hating the flush that rose to her cheeks. "That's all."

"Sure, whatever you say." The mage tipped her freckled face to the sky. "Great. It's fucking snowing again."

Chapter Twenty-Eight

By the time Morvana stepped out of Mikhail's tent, the snowfall had reached near whiteout conditions. She clasped hands with Lezarius, then watched as he and Falke vanished into the treeline. Six knights escorted them, leading half the horses.

"I'll wait for the signal," Rycroft shouted over the wind.

She nodded and followed Mikhail and Dantarion into the storm.

They skirted the lakeshore, crossing the frozen no man's land between the camps. The sudden squall was to their benefit, but the wind and sleet cut visibility to a few paces ahead. Bryce was just a dark silhouette in the gloom, though he paused occasionally to glance back and make sure she was still there.

She knew little about Nightmarks. Only that they represented an unholy pact with the abyssal ley. You traded your conscience, your *humanity*, for some desire that could only be satisfied by a mage. But Mikhail had taken the bargain for selfless reasons. Did that make a difference?

She had never known a man who took his duty so seriously. The conflict must be tearing him apart. She wished

Kasia had been honest with her, but understood why she'd withheld the truth. She'd thought Morvana would be afraid. And, in all fairness, the man had held a knife to her throat the first time they met. Perhaps she *ought* to fear him.

Yet she didn't. The Mark might be tugging at him, but she felt sure he was stronger than he believed. The only thing that frightened her was his plan to martyr himself.

Falke and Lezarius had known. Neither looked surprised when Dantarion called him *one of Malach's*.

Lezarius made sense. The two of them were as close as father and son. But Falke? She suspected he had more to do with it than Mikhail admitted. No doubt Falke had tried to use him to further his own ends. Her fists clenched. That scheming—

Morvana's thoughts stilled as she glimpsed dark figures ahead. The first line of sentries.

Mikhail fell back. He clamped a hand around her arm, dragging her forward. Dantarion let her hood slip down. The wind whipped loose strands of auburn hair around her face.

"Mox nox!" she shouted in an imperious tone. "It's Bishop Dantarion! We found this one sneaking around."

The five knights surged forward, wading silently through knee-deep drifts. Snow dusted their armor.

"I'm bringing her in," Dantarion said. "Stand aside."

The knights came closer, spreading out in a semicircle. Their breastplates were engraved with the Raven of Novostopol. Through the bars of their helms, she saw goat-like eyes with horizontal pupils. One growled and drew his blade.

"*Jalghuth*," he rasped in a guttural voice.

Mikhail let go of her and stepped forward, his face calm. "Brother," he said, holding his palms out.

The tip of the blade flicked to his throat. The knight leaned forward slightly. A low, rumbling sound came from his throat. It was, Morvana thought queasily, not unlike the purr of a contented cat.

"You see?" Mikhail said, as the blade slowly lowered. "We serve the same masters."

The knight stood aside. Mikhail was turning to her when movement blurred at the corner of her eye. Steel sang as his own blade swept from the scabbard. She took a startled step back, crashing into something behind. She tumbled into the snow. Scrabbled away from grasping hands. They were slug-white, tipped with ragged, dirty nails.

Bodies thrashed in the blizzard. There was no clash of metal, no cries, just a series of meaty thunks and gurgles.

Morvana blinked sleet from her eyes. Someone hoisted her to her feet. Dantarion. The mage's other hand held a bloody sword. A few meters away, Mikhail kicked one of the knights from his own blade. It had gone through the gap in the gorget.

The rest lay sprawled in the snow.

He hurried to Morvana's side. "Are you hurt?"

She wordlessly shook her head. There was blood in his beard. On his lips. A fine spray across his forehead, black in the darkness. Mikhail seemed to interpret her expression as an accusation, because the concern on his face evaporated. He stepped back as though slapped.

"Thank you," she said quickly. "You did what you had to."

He gave her a brusque nod.

"I told you," Dantarion muttered, wiping her blade on a cloak. "The bastards don't listen to anyone." Her gaze flicked to Morvana. "Not when they're hungry."

"Will the next patrol find them?" Mikhail asked.

"Yes." She sheathed her sword. "But they might not even sound the alarm."

They eat you. Sometimes they eat each other.

Morvana shoved the thought away.

"And if they do?" she asked. "How long do we have?"

"Fifteen, twenty minutes."

Mikhail nodded. "There's nowhere to hide the bodies. Let's move."

They followed the trail the knights had broken. Thankfully, the next patrol didn't come as close. Dantarion called out the passphrase, *Mox Nox*, and they retreated into the darkness.

Lights beckoned ahead, though most glimmered deeper in the camp. The oil for the lanterns was running short, and the Perditae had acute night vision anyway. Morvana hunched into her hood as they reached the first tents, pitched pell-mell in clusters. Dantarion said they were starting to form clans, each with a rudimentary leader. Jarrah had failed to plan for adequate supplies and his troops were already turning on each other.

Dantarion and Mikhail flanked her as they hurried along, the snow here churned to slush by hundreds of boots. It was quiet except for the flapping of canvas and thick, bleating snores from inside the tents. Drift-covered mounds dotted the ground at irregular intervals. She paid them little attention until she saw a pale hand poking out and realized they were corpses. Even through the snow, the coppery tang of blood filled her nose.

Morvana realized, in a detached way, that she had never been more afraid in her life. She had known such things existed—but only in theory. Her life as Luk's nuncio had been orderly and routine, each day planned down to the minute. Meetings and reports, punctuated by the occasional visit to another city for more meetings and reports. But monsters were real.

Luk had been one of them.

Yet he was a more civilized brand of monster than the abject souls who occupied this camp. There was something singularly unnerving about people who had, not so long ago, been just like her, and were now killing and eating each other without a second thought.

She wanted to insist she could never be one of them. Not

under any circumstances. But part of her didn't believe it. Not anymore.

"Stop it," she muttered to herself. "Never cede hope. For once you do, then——"

"All that is good will be lost," Mikhail finished in a low voice.

The third Sutra of the *Meliora*.

He stared straight ahead. How he'd heard her over the howling wind, she couldn't fathom. Were his senses more acute, here in this place of death? On impulse, she reached for his hand. The heat of it soaked right through his glove, as though he burned with fever. Blue eyes widened as she gave his fingers a squeeze.

"Courage, captain," she said, amazed at how calm she sounded.

She thought of the child, Felix, and what his mother was risking to save him. She thought of Clavis, who lay wounded, and her knights, who the mage said were still loyal. Still human. Maybe it was the Warded manacles that kept them from touching the tainted ley. Or maybe their love for the Reverend Mother protected them. Morvana knew the young pontifex was practically a saint to her knights.

Mikhail squeezed her hand back, very gently as if he feared his own strength, and withdrew his fingers, curling them around his sword hilt again.

"Nearly there," Dantarion whispered. "Get behind me and stay close."

The tents with lanterns lay just ahead. Knights patrolled in pairs, but they knew Dantarion and seemed scared of her. No one challenged them as they slipped through the flaps of a large tent with two poles that sat off to the side.

The sudden warmth and light left Morvana blinking like a mole dug from its burrow. A small figure ran over and threw its arms around Dantarion's waist. She hoisted him up to one hip, planting a kiss on his tousled dark hair. He took one look at Mikhail and buried his face in her shoulder.

"Where have you been?" a quavering voice demanded.

A gaunt, elderly woman rose to her feet. She wore a graying braid over one shoulder. Beleth's left hand gripped the edge of a table. The stump of the right was hidden in the sleeve of a fur-lined cloak.

"I brought friends, Reverend Mother," Dantarion said in a placating tone.

"Friends? I don't know these people!"

Her face was pasty white, although her hand looked deeply tanned. Morvana realized that she wore a thick layer of powder. Pale blue eyes, almost colorless, peered out from beneath arched brows that had been drawn on her face with what looked like a black marker. One was a good inch higher than the other.

"They're here to help," Dantarion said. "We must go."

Beleth's mismatched brows furrowed. "Go where?" The words came out slightly slurred.

"I'll explain later." She set the boy on his feet and blew a lock of auburn hair from her face. "Everything is fine."

"Fine?" Beleth's voice rose. "I want my books. My manifestos! Where have you hidden them?"

The tent was a jumble of crumpled chip packets, soda cans, and nests of blankets mingled with discarded clothing.

"I'm taking you to them," Dantarion replied. "Back to your study. You'd like that, wouldn't you?"

Her face soured. "Don't treat me like a child."

Mikhail glanced through the crack in the flap. He shot Dantarion a pointed look. The mage hurried to her mother, whispering urgently in her ear.

"Hello, Felix," Morvana said. She tried a smile, wishing she were better with small children. The boy stared back, green eyes watchful. He had Dantarion's fair coloring, though his hair was a shade darker.

"Do you want to leave this place, Felix? I bet you do."

His chubby hands knotted together. He looked anxiously at his mother and gave the barest nod.

"We're going to take you someplace safe," she promised.

Felix seemed doubtful. Mikhail crouched down and held out a hand. He'd wiped the blood from his face at some point, but the boy still shied away, darting to Dantarion's side.

"It's the armor," Morvana said softly. "Not you."

He wasn't wearing full plate, just greaves and a cuirass—but that was enough.

"I know." He sighed and stood up. "We'll get you clear. Take the child and run."

"If she lets me."

"I think she will." He sounded sad. "If only the two of you make it, I'd be content."

She frowned. "We're all making it, captain."

Dantarion had succeeded in prodding Beleth toward the flap. But she moved stiffly—and with strident protests.

"Mother," Dantarion said through gritted teeth. "You must heed me now. Malach has retaken Bal Kirith. If you don't return, he will declare himself pontifex. Is that what you want?"

"Malach? He lives?"

"Yes, I told you that before. You were angry at him for leaving you. Remember?"

To Morvana's astonishment, tears welled up in Beleth's pale eyes, gouging tracks through the face powder. "I would like to see him again," she muttered.

"Then we must go. And if you put up a fuss, Jarrah will catch us."

"Jarrah." Her chin trembled, this time with rage. "I'll have him executed! Thrown to the crocodilians!"

"Yes, yes," Dantarion snapped. "But later. I promise!"

The former pontifex of Bal Kirith gave a brisk nod. Her gaze seemed sharper. It swept over Morvana and Mikhail, but

Dantarion must have already explained their presence for she said nothing more.

Felix tugged at Dantarion's cloak. "Mama?" he asked softly.

"Yes, love?"

"Are you coming, too?"

"Of course. But you must go with Morvana. I'll join you afterwards. Grandmama will go with you."

His face crumpled. "I want to stay with you!"

She swept him up. "Be brave for me now. Can you do that?"

He sniffled.

"Yes, you can." She pressed her forehead to his, rubbing noses. "Everything will be better soon."

"Don't coddle," Beleth said. "It ruins them."

"I'm not letting him turn out like Syd and Trist," Dantarion hissed.

Beleth emitted a rusty cackle. "You were always a docile child, Dante. Too docile. Cried at the drop of a hat. But those two have spirit!"

Dantarion flushed. *Docile?* Morvana thought. Then she had an idea.

"I know your cousins," she blurted.

The boy eyed her skeptically.

"Sydonie has a Mark of a doll on her arm. She calls it . . ." Morvana groped for the name. "Mirabelle!"

"You *know* the hellspawn?" Dantarion asked with a note of amazement.

"We're good friends." She kept her gaze on Felix. "I'll keep you safe, I promise."

The boy drew a deep breath. "Okay," he whispered.

Morvana held her arms out. Dantarion gave him a last kiss and handed him over. He wrapped his legs around her waist. His hair smelled like woodsmoke and boy. A clean scent that instantly dragged her back to her own childhood.

She had two little brothers, much younger. Being book-
ish, she'd mostly ignored them. But sometimes, if her mother
was busy in the mornings, she would brush their silky blond
hair before school. They hated it, and she had hated doing it,
but now she missed them. They must be worried sick
about her.

Morvana adjusted Felix on her hip. It was about two kilometers to their camp if she cut straight across the ice.

She wondered how fast Beleth could run.

By dumb luck, the prisoner tent was at the edge of the
lake. Jarrah had chosen it because there was no cover on the
frozen expanse, no way to sneak across without being seen. He
didn't expect a rescue to come from inside the camp itself.

They stepped outside. The wind struck her like a slap.
Shapes moved ahead, the sentries around the prisoner tent.
Once Dantarion started inverting their Marks, it would be
chaos. So far, she'd seen no sign of the other mages, but now
loud laughter erupted from inside a pavilion of scarlet silk.
The lamplight made it glow like a beacon. She pictured them
gathered in their red cloaks, gloating over their coming
victory. Too arrogant to realize the army they'd brought was
quietly going rabid.

They moved swiftly, Dantarion half dragging Beleth. The
black void of the lake loomed ahead. Timing was everything.
As soon as she started to cross, the sentries would notice. Most
of the rest were sleeping.

She hoped.

Who knew what was going on in those darkened tents?

She gripped Felix with frozen arms. He was looking
around, his face taut. "Mama don't let me go outside," he
whispered.

"Because she loves you," Morvana whispered back. "Now
hush."

He scrunched his eyes against the snow. "They're
coming."

She cradled his head, pressing him tighter against her. "Don't look."

In her peripheral vision, she saw the knights drawing closer. Silent, save for the soft clink of their armor. The urge to flee lit every nerve ending. Dantarion peeled off, barking a brief order.

The knights crowded around her. She wasn't a big woman. They all stood more than a head taller. With the helms and heavy plate, they were hulking. She regarded them with contempt—though she had to look up to do it.

"Someone killed four of the sentries," Dantarion snapped. "I want them found!"

"Keep going," Mikhail urged Morvana softly. "We'll manage."

Her mouth was so dry, she could only nod. She took two steps toward the lakeshore and paused as the flaps of the pavilion stirred. Cadmael Jarrah stepped out. He was flanked by four other mages, white-haired but dangerous nonetheless.

"Beleth," he cried in a jovial tone. "You've decided to join us!"

Morvana suppressed a shudder as their eyes crawled over her and Felix. Glittering with cold amusement.

Jarrah frowned. "Or were you going somewhere? It's a poor night for a swim."

"Fuck you, Cadmael!" Beleth bellowed, her stringy hair fluttering in the wind. She shook her stump in the air. "You fucking back-stabbing snake!"

"Easy now," Dantarion said, striding over. "I can explain, Your Eminence."

Jarrah watched her with a smirk. He showed not an iota of surprise. Not until she drew her sword mid-stride and ran him through. His mouth gaped as he sank to his knees in the snow. Jarrah toppled slowly to the side. Before he hit, her blade found one of his companions. The others scurried back into the tent.

"*Go!*" Dantarion shouted.

Morvana lurched past the knights. A blade flashed down —and met Mikhail's with a clash. He pivoted into the gap, shielding her from the others. She ran with the single-minded focus of a rabbit from a pack of dogs, bounding over the tent lines. Shouts chased her, and the clamor of battle. Then her boots skidded on ice and she knew she'd reached the lake. Where Beleth had gone, she had no idea.

"Mama!" Felix cried.

Morvana glanced over her shoulder. Dozens of figures milled along the shore. Bursts of red light erupted like flaring coals. Abyssal ley. She prayed it was Dantarion and not the mages.

Then one of the figures broke loose in pursuit. Saints, but it moved fast! She tore her gaze away and sprinted, breath whooshing in and out. A few centimeters of snow coated the lake farther out, but the wind had swept patches of the ice clean. In the black night, it was impossible to tell the difference. She hit one and went down like a lightning-struck tree. Instinct kept her from dropping the child, but the burden made the fall that much harder. She winced and set him on his feet.

"Take my hand," she gasped. "We run together, *ja?*"

Another glance told her the knight had halved the distance. His armor made him heavy. *Let him step on a thin patch. Let him go through.*

But she knew there were no thin patches. Lezarius said the ice would hold the weight of an armored transport, sometimes until Juven month.

Without the boy in her arms, she should have been faster. But she'd landed on one knee. It throbbed with each step. They reached the middle, the fire of her own camp burning in the distance. A tiny flicker of light. *Too far.* She could hear the knight's panting now. The steady, ground-eating thud of his boots. Another fifty meters—maybe less—and he'd be on them.

"Run ahead!" she urged Felix, giving him a little push. "Run to the fire! The people there will help you."

He was so terrified, he didn't hesitate. She watched his small silhouette vanish into the snow. Then she turned to face the knight.

I will slow him down, she thought wildly. *Buy the boy time to reach the fire.*

She sank to the ground and fumbled with her gloves. Her hands were so cold they'd stopped working. She used her teeth to pull one off, pressing a palm to the ice. The ley was just a ghostly sheen, down on the lakebed. She tried to summon it from the depths but felt nothing.

She looked up just as the knight spotted her. His steps slowed. He flipped his helm up. His eyes were almost normal. *Almost.* But not quite. Somehow it was worse than the full Perditae.

"Please," she said, raising her trembling hands.

A muscle in his cheek twitched. He tried to speak, but only a groan emerged.

"Let me go." She slowly rose to her feet. "I am a bishop of Kvengard. My name is Morvana Ziegler. You can . . . you can fight this!"

He tilted his head. She saw anguish. And naked hunger. The Raven on his neck pulsed red. On and off. On and off. Like the traffic lights in Novostopol.

Stop . . . go . . . stop . . . go.

The knight sprang. Something buzzed past her ear. He jerked away, a white-fletched arrow jutting from his throat. Miles Rycroft ran toward her, slinging the bow over his shoulder. He barely spared a glance for the fallen knight.

"Do you have the boy?" she asked, legs watery with relief.

"Yes." He searched her face. "What of Clavis?"

"I don't know. They were trying to free her. Did Mikhail radio?"

"No." He gazed at the mage camp. "It's time to hit them hard." He nodded at a metal tube lying on the ice. "It's over there . . . Your Grace?"

Morvana looked back. Rycroft was staring at her in confusion.

"Aren't you going to the Lance? Your horse is waiting."

"Not yet," she said wearily.

"But—"

Morvana waved over her shoulder and started limping back across the ice.

Chapter Twenty-Nine

The stabbing pain in her knee dulled as she picked her way across the frozen lake—with greater caution this time. The joint felt stiff, but it was just bruised. A low roar drifted from the camp ahead. It reminded her of the morby matches in Kvengard. The stadium wasn't far from the Arx and on warm summer evenings she could hear the fans cheering through the open window of her office.

But as Morvana drew closer, shrill screams rose above the din. The howls of maddened voices in unison, like a choir of wolves. Part of her—a large part—couldn't believe she was going back. How could she possibly help now?

Yet her feet kept trudging along. A hundred yards from the southern shore, fire bloomed in the camp. A split second later, she heard a whooshing, whirring *thump*. Rycroft had fired a shoulder-launched shell. Its trajectory had hit the center of the camp, well away from the prisoners. In the light of the burning tents, she saw a writhing mass of bodies. Some of the knights fought each other. Others ran in all directions, a few of them naked. She stopped, her throat tight. It looked like a scene from the Second Dark Age. Perfect, unbridled mayhem.

Then a small group broke loose. Half a dozen people clustered together. The tallest cradled a limp body in his arms.

Snow crunched beneath her boots as she ran forward. Mikhail swam into focus, streaked with blood. Their eyes met. Stark relief flashed across his face. The young, dark-skinned woman he held was Clavis. Her eyes were closed, cheek pressed to his shoulder.

Dantarion took the rear, red cloak swirling as she cut down pursuers. The rest wore the green and yellow tabards of Nantwich. They stumbled along like sleepwalkers. Morvana met them a short way out, catching one of the knights as his knees buckled. He was skin and bones.

"Where's my son?" Dantarion shouted over the din.

"Safe," Morvana called back. "He's at the Lance by now."

She nodded. "Take him to Bal Kirith. Give him to Malach."

"Aren't you coming?"

"Not without my mother. The stupid old bitch took off." She gave Morvana a savage smile. "Go now. I'll hold them."

A pack of Perditae had gone still, watching. One lifted his face. His mouth opened. A tongue slithered out, tasting the air. He yelped and loped forward. Dantarion turned to meet them. She pressed a hand to her side, then grunted and raised her blade. Blood dripped from her fingers.

"Is she hurt?" Morvana demanded.

"You heard the mage," Mikhail said. He sounded angry. "Stay and we all die."

She knew what he was thinking. If he didn't have to carry Clavis, he would fight at her side. Dantarion could have grabbed Beleth and vanished. But she'd kept her word and helped to free the hostages.

Morvana eyed his burden. A child was one thing, but she knew she could never carry a full-grown woman across the lake. Clavis's men were in no state to help.

She slung her arm around the wobbly knight and together

they blundered across the lake. The others helped each other as best they could. Mikhail plodded along with a fixed expression. His radio crackled, but he didn't stop to dig it out. The snowfall was finally tapering off, the wind dying. A deeper, killing cold blanketed her limbs, wicking away sweat the instant it left her body. The near-vertical wall of the Sundar Kush rose ahead. A scattering of stars twinkled above its high crags.

"Wh . . . what's . . . y-your n-ame?" she asked the knight.

His face was blade-thin, as though every spare bit had been carved away. Dark, tilted eyes lifted. "Beech."

"M-Morvana," she stammered.

She didn't try speaking again, just pointed. A spark glowed in the distance. The campfire was still there. He gave a weary nod.

She looked back. Perditae were boiling from the camp. A full moon shone through racing shreds of cloud. It glinted on their armor as they swarmed across the ice, like the carapaces of scurrying beetles. She saw no sign of Dantarion. But she knew what the mage would tell her to do.

"Where's the radio?" she asked through chattering teeth.

"My belt." Mikhail followed her gaze to the horde and swore softly.

She groped under his cloak and pulled it from a leather pouch. "How do I w-work it?"

He adjusted Clavis in his arms. Frost rimed the beard around his mouth. "Press the green button."

A burst of static. "Rycroft?"

There was a pause. "*Verum*," a tinny voice replied. "Bryce?"

"The lake," she said. "Shell it."

A longer pause. "Come again?"

"Shell the lake!"

"What about . . . vis?"

"Clavis is w-with us."

More static. "I didn't . . . that."

She fumbled with the radio, cursing as it slid from her fingers and bounced along the ice. She dropped to all fours and crawled over, praying it wasn't broken. The first lines of the Perditae were two hundred yards out, coming fast. Morvana hit the green button. "We have her! We have Clavis!"

She stood and held up the radio, waving it over her head.

On the far edge, she thought she saw a figure waving back.

Mikhail stared at her. "Are you crazy?"

She didn't bother answering, just threw her arm around Beech and dragged him onward. Mikhael started to run, chivvying the other knights along. A minute passed. Two. She started to wonder if her transmission had failed. Rycroft would never fire if he thought his pontifex was—

A tremendous crack rolled through the valley like thunder. The shockwave sent her skidding forward on the ice. She somehow managed not to fall, but then the ice lurched under her feet and she realized it was breaking into plates, pushed by a frothing wave. About half the Perditae were gone, swallowed by the lake. Icy water rose around her boots. She found Beech's hand, scrambling toward shore.

Fresh cracks webbed outward with every step. She looked for Mikhail and found him ten meters to the right, on his feet with Clavis, hunched over and sprinting. The rush of water filled her ears. It raced forward like an incoming tide, sweeping fragments of ice before it. The whole surface was undulating now, bucking up and down, tearing apart with crackling pops. One of the knights ahead fell through, but two of his companions caught his arms and pulled him back out.

She looked back just in time. A black gap yawned ahead. Widening by the second.

"Jump!" she screamed.

Together, she and Beech leapt across, sliding onto the sheet beyond. It listed but felt marginally sturdier than the one they'd just left. They reached the far side just as the wave hit, washing across the ice. Then snow crunched under her heels. They clambered up a rocky bank, panting. The others stumbled behind. She did a quick head count. All accounted for.

A horse whinnied in the darkness. Miles Rycroft and four Kven knights rode up, leading the rest of the mounts. Rycroft's lips were moving as he trotted over to Mikhail, though she didn't hear the words. A prayer of thanks, perhaps.

"Lizzie Brown," she whispered, picking out her chestnut mare. The horse was trembling, spooked by the blast. Morvana patted her muzzle. "I know how you feel," she muttered.

One of her knights took charge of Beech, throwing a blanket around his shoulders and leading him off. Voices swam in and out. Morvana knew they were far from safe. Many of the Perditae had escaped. They wouldn't stop. She got one foot in the stirrup and clung to the reins for a moment, trying to find the gumption to go further. Hands circled her waist, lifting her up.

She flung a leg over the saddle. Mikhail regarded her. "That was a good call, Your Grace."

"Was it?"

"Yes." His gaze flicked into the darkness. "Mounted, we'll beat them to the Lance."

She waited for him to swing astride his black charger, then followed the party at a canter up into the hills. The horses were fresh and muscled through the drifts at a brisk pace. Bright moonlight cast everything in a silvery glow. Lizzie's warmth thawed her somewhat and Morvana's spirits lifted until she thought of Dantarion. Even Beleth, as surprising as that was. She'd been scared spitless at the time, but now the recollection of the old pontifex cursing Cadmael Jarrah brought a stiff smile. All told, Morvana preferred Beleth to Luk. At least she was honest.

She fell into a waking doze, loosely holding the reins as

Lizzie plodded beneath pine boughs heavy with snow. They forded a shallow stream and began to climb. The sound of the horses' hooves changed and she shook herself from her stupor. They'd reached the ice road. The lead riders broke into a canter. Several winding turns and the narrow stone bridge to Sinjali's Lance appeared. She eyed the tower beyond, seamless save for the great doors. It would hold against the Perditae.

They galloped the last stretch, reining up in front. Rycroft leapt down and banged on the doors. Surely there would be a fire inside. She had forgotten what being warm felt like.

Miles was lifting his fist to bang again when they swung wide. Lezarius flew out, a joyful expression on his face. "I watched from the tower ramparts, but it was too dark to see what was happening!"

Falke followed. His white hair stood up in wild tufts, as if he'd been repeatedly tugging on it. "Thank the Saints," he exclaimed with more feeling than she'd ever heard. "And you found Clavis!"

She slumped on one of the packhorses, riding with a burly Kven knight. Her eyes cracked at his booming voice. She gave a pained smile. "Dmitry," she whispered hoarsely.

"You can tell us all about this heroic rescue once we're inside," Lezarius said, briskly rubbing his hands. "There are still some old supplies from the days when I was living here. And we have the rations from camp. It should keep us for a while. I'll find a way to summon aid from Jalghuth." He stepped to the side. "Bring the horses through. We've set up a makeshift stable."

The arched doors could have accommodated a giant with room to spare. One by one, the knights rode straight into the Lance, hooves echoing within the dim interior. Mikhael and Morvana were the last. She'd nearly reached the doors when a pale figure materialized in the gap.

"We're sorry," Will Danziger said, looking past her to Mikhail. "Not him."

Morvana reined up. The words made no sense. She assumed she'd misheard. "What?"

"He's not welcome here."

"Why not?" she demanded.

"He is impure."

The sheer outrageousness of this statement robbed her of speech for a moment. "Are you telling me," she asked slowly, "that the man who just risked his life to save these men, to save a *pontifex*, isn't good enough for you?"

The other children had gathered behind him, blocking the way. Alive, they had ranged in age from eight to fifteen. Some were dark, some fair. But they had an unsettling sameness now. Neither hostile nor friendly. Just implacable.

Their ranks parted to allow Lezarius to squeeze through. "What's going on?"

"They're not letting Mikhail inside," she snapped. "Do something!"

His face went slack with surprise. He turned to Will. "Is this true?"

"I told you the same before, Lezarius." He sounded regretful. "Nothing has changed."

"Nothing has changed?" the pontifex exclaimed. "How can you say that?"

"If anything, it is worse now," Will said calmly. "I warned you, but you wouldn't heed me. You cannot save him. He is on the brink."

"The brink of what?" Lezarius looked at Mikhail, then back at the boy. His voice firmed. "You are wrong, Will. I have been with him every day these past weeks! There are no signs . . ."

"Not that you can see." The boy's jaw set. "I'll put it in terms you can understand, Lezarius. You are a geologist by training, yes?"

The pontifex nodded impatiently.

"When two plates come together, it creates a line of invisible stress. The pressure grows and grows, deep in the earth. On the surface, all appears normal. But then one day, without warning, the pressure becomes intolerable. In a few catastrophic seconds, destruction is unleashed."

Lezarius shook his head. "This is pure speculation——"

"It's fine," Mikhail interrupted. His icy indifference made her neck prickle. "Bar the doors." He wheeled his charger around.

"No!" Morvana shouted. She'd never been so furious in her life.

He slackened the reins, meeting her eye. "Go," he said in a gentler tone. "I'll be fine."

"I won't!" She dug her knees into Lizzie's flanks, guiding her away from the tower. She trotted to his side and glared at him, daring him to speak.

"Your Grace——"

"Those kids . . . " Her jaw clenched. "They are full of *scheisse!*"

Lezarius seemed bewildered. "Captain, I . . ."

Lizzie danced to the left, snorting. Mikhail's warhorse was more disciplined, but it rolled its eyes and gave a low whinny.

"They're coming." He cast her an exasperated look. "Don't be a fool. Go with the others."

She peered down the ice road. A line of Perditae marched on the Lance, rank upon rank. Lezarius was speaking in urgent tones to Will. She could see his pleas were falling on deaf ears.

"Do you have Felix?" she called. "Dantarion's boy?"

Lezarius looked up. "What? Oh, yes. He is safe. But——"

"Then do as the captain says," she said, with a final withering stare at Will. "Bar the doors."

She urged Lizzie forward, up the ice road. Mikhail's hoofbeats rang out behind. In an instant, he was galloping next to her.

"How far does this go?" she shouted, leaning over the mount, urging her on.

"I don't know!" he shouted back. "I've never come this way!"

The black mass of Mount Ogo loomed above them, its lower reaches blanketed with snow. The lights of Jalghuth twinkled in the distance. But it lay at the other end of the ice road, which was currently occupied by an army of lunatics.

The answer came soon enough. Half a kilometer on, the road simply ended. Rolling terrain lay beyond, a mix of woods and steep ravines. They drew up and looked at each other.

"What now?" she wondered. Her breath formed a cloud of white crystals.

"We seek shelter in the trees." He swung from the saddle.

Morvana gazed at the dark forest. "Yes," she said. "That is what we shall do." She half fell from the horse. Mikhail caught her.

They stood face to face for a moment. It was so still, she could hear the wind sighing in the pines. No sounds of pursuit yet. With luck, the Perditae would vent their wrath on Sinjali's Lance for a while.

Luck. She hoped they hadn't used it all up.

"At least *you're* warm," she said with a mirthless laugh.

Heat rolled off him in waves, like he was burning up from the inside out. Burning straight down to the wick. But his blue eyes were clear as he handed her Lizzie's reins. "Can you make it?"

She snorted. "I am Kven. Of course I can make it."

Mikhail grinned. He was so stern most of the time, she barely recalled what he looked like when he forgot himself enough to smile. Younger. Even more handsome.

"I've never met a bishop like you before," he said.

"That's probably a good thing," she said seriously. "I doubt my superiors would approve of a single decision I've made since I left the Arx."

A muscle twitched in his cheek. "Did you just make a joke, Your Grace?"

"No." She frowned. "Are you teasing me?"

"No." He turned away, but she saw his shoulders shaking with silent laughter.

Morvana poked his back. "You are!"

"No," he insisted in a choked voice. "Your Grace——"

"Oh, enough with *Your Grace!*" she exclaimed, laughing herself now. "Do you know what you sound like? Ridiculous!"

He put a finger to his lips and she clapped a hand over her mouth. "*Ja,*" she whispered through her fingers. "The cannibals."

Mikhail shook his head. He drew a sobering breath through his nose. "We must keep moving."

Her own giddy mirth faded. "Lead on, captain."

"Misha," he said.

She nodded, surprised and pleased. In Novostopol, they often used nicknames with family, or very close friends. It felt like a gift.

"Misha," she repeated, liking the sound of it. Softer than the jagged syllables of his given name.

A light, sugary snow sifted down as she took up Lizzie's reins and followed him into the darkness.

Chapter Thirty

Kasia saw each card in her mind's eye.

The Sun and Moon. The Serpent. The Twins.

The High Priestess and The Fool. Fortitude and The Tower.

The first two went together. The Dawn City, obviously. But what if it was more than that? Dawn and dusk were liminal times. Boundaries between light and dark. It could refer to the liminal ley itself, which supported her theory that part of Balaur's spirit still drifted in limbo.

The Serpent was Valmitra. The Twins . . . She'd always assumed that they referred to Balaur and Rachel. But what if it meant Balaur and herself? Were they more alike than she cared to admit? And if so, how could she use that to her advantage?

She felt as though she stood on a great height staring down into a fathomless pit. He had always bested her. He was stronger in the liminal realm.

Yet Fortitude spoke otherwise. It told her she had a chance. And that perhaps she would not be alone.

Enter The Fool.

Well, she'd always known her brother had a crucial part to

play. The Mahadeva had known it, too. His fate had drawn him to this place. If he was still with Nikola, if they had survived the fire at the Luban embassy, the two of them would be following.

Her thoughts turned to the witch, Cathrynne Rowen, and the prophecy she had spoken more than a thousand years ago.

Whomever drinks the elixir cannot be killed by Marked or Unmarked, man or woman, during the night or day, awake or asleep, inside or outside, with a weapon nor by bare hands.

That sounded damned close to immortality.

But what *was* this elixir? Who had made it, and why? Not Gavriel or surely he would have drunk it himself.

Nothing made sense.

She rewound the reels of her memories, searching desperately for clues. Chance events took on new significance.

The shell that fell on Bal Kirith, sparing both her and Malach but setting them on different paths.

Natalya getting sick the night of Ferran Massot's party and Kasia going in her place.

Alexei and Spassov being on duty the night Massot's Mark turned.

Malach meeting Tashtemir at the docks in Novo. Choosing Nikola Thorn to carry his child—out of a city of a hundred thousand people.

If any one of these things had not happened, *any single one*, it all would have played out differently.

Her skin prickled. Was it all truly random? Or was she being swept along by ancient currents of ley that inexorably led to riding in this wagon, on this night?

If that were the case—and she desperately needed to have faith it was—the fight would be won or lost in the liminal world.

"I must see Rachel," she whispered. "Prepare her."

Alexei gazed at her in the darkness. "I'll watch over you."

Considering that he was trussed hand and foot, the statement ought to have sounded ridiculous. But it gave her comfort.

Kasia closed her eyes. The wagon swayed, sand hissing beneath its wheels. She emptied her mind. Her breathing grew deep and even.

RAIN.

She tipped her face up, opened her mouth, and let it trickle down her parched throat. It dimpled the pond, where a white heron stood motionless in the reeds, unperturbed at the deluge. Rachel was nowhere to be seen.

Kasia called her name, striding along the tangle of gravel paths. The air smelled of rich black earth and growing things, but also a faint miasma of rot. The blight she had carefully pruned was worse, she noticed. Yellow-brown spots marred many of the leaves.

He's been here.

She checked the gazebo and raspberry patch. Climbed the ladder to the elaborate treehouse she'd created. It had a carpet and cozy window seat, dolls and a silver tea set. The hook for a yellow rain slicker was empty.

No Rachel.

Kasia started to run, panic blooming in her chest. If Balaur had taken her away, back to the dark place . . .

Her dress was soaked through by the time she careened around a bend and saw the child. Kasia shivered with relief, hugging her arms around herself. Rachel looked up with dull eyes as she approached.

"Why didn't you answer?" Kasia demanded. "I was worried."

The girl was leaning over the lip of an old moss-furred well. Kasia took her hand and pulled her back.

"That's dangerous," she scolded. "You might have fallen in!"

Rachel stared at the well. "What's down there?"

She vented a breath. In the next instant, boards covered the dark opening. "There," she said. "It's safe now. Where are your kittens?"

Rachel blinked slowly. "What kittens?"

Kasia cast about and found the basket a short way off. She peeked inside and was greeted with weak mewling. She frowned, focusing, and five full-grown cats leapt from the basket. They wound around her legs and she crouched to stroke their ears. The rain was tapering off.

"Go catch some mice," she told them.

The cats stalked away. One problem disposed of.

"Walk with me," Kasia said, holding out her hand.

Rachel stared after the cats for a moment, then clasped Kasia's fingers, eying her solemnly. "You made them grow up." She bit her lip. "Could you do the same for me? Make me big and strong for when grandpapa comes back?" A flicker of fear. "I don't like him."

"Nor do I," Kasia replied, drawing her away from the well. "But you are different. I'm afraid I can't."

They walked together back to the pond, Rachel's steps clumsy and stumbling. Kasia's neck prickled as she scanned the dripping trees for an old man with a staff. Paranoia? Or were they being watched?

A dinghy waited in the rushes. Kasia baled rainwater from the bottom. She climbed in and sat Rachel in the stern. Then she rowed them out to the middle, shipped the oars, and let the boat drift.

Let him eavesdrop now.

"I made a bargain with grandpapa," she whispered. "So you can leave this place and go back to the real world."

Rachel slumped on the bench. Her face looked pinched,

the shadows beneath her eyes dark as bruises. "Will I see Malach?"

"I hope so, yes. Both your parents love you very much. They want you back."

"Nikola, too?" she asked uncertainly.

"Of course. But when you do go back, there is something you must do for me. Something only you can do."

The urgent tone made her suddenly alert. "I won't hurt anyone," she said with a tight expression.

"And I would never ask that of you." She felt time slipping away. "It won't hurt anybody." *Except maybe Balaur.* "Will you promise to do it for me?"

"Okay," Rachel whispered. "What is it?"

Kasia explained what she had in mind. She feared it might be impossible. The child had summoned a starfall—but this was something else. Something even bigger.

Rachel tilted her head, considering. "I think I can," she said at last. "Will you be there, too?" She looked anxious.

"I hope so. But it is possible . . ." She cleared her throat. "I might not be. And if I'm not, then it's even more important that you do it."

The child looked puzzled, but gave a firm nod. "I will. But . . . when?"

"The instant you wake. You'll be in a strange place, but don't be afraid."

She licked dry lips. "The dark place?"

"I can't tell you what it looks like, Rachel. I'm not there yet. But I will be. Very soon."

None of it made much sense, but the child seemed to accept this explanation. "Will it hurt?" she asked. "Going back?"

"I don't know. Did it hurt when grandpapa took you away?"

A brief, weary nod. Kasia felt a surge of anger.

"Maybe going back will be easier. But even if it does hurt,

you must go back. When the moment comes, don't resist. Just let go—"

Rachel's face shimmered, turned to gauze. Gray mist crept across the pond.

"The instant you wake," Kasia cried. "Don't forget—"

———

HER EYES FLEW WIDE. Alexei was nudging her with his knee, saying her name. She peered through the slats of the cart.

The wagons had stopped. The sky was lightening.

"Did you find her?" he asked in a low voice.

Kasia turned back. "Yes. She knows. When the time comes, I will do my best to fight him off." Her heart beat painfully in her chest. "But you will not be there to see it."

"What?"

"You will leave first. It's the only way."

"Kasia—"

"Just listen!" she hissed. "The child is *dying*, Alexei. Slipping away. He *must* give her up. If he takes me, so be it. I'll find another way."

Alexei was shaking his head. "No, no—"

Kasia rode over him. "I need you to have faith. Do you believe in the ley? That it is a force of good?"

He didn't answer.

"Do you *believe*?"

His gaze burned. "Yes," he muttered. "All right, yes!"

"It told me Malach would come. How, I don't know, but he will. And when he does, you will let him pass the gates. You will wait for the sign. Then you will find him and send him to me. To *me*, not Balaur."

Footsteps approached the wagon. She tried to gather her thoughts. So many threads tangled together. One wrong stitch and it would all fall apart.

"What sign?" Alexei demanded. "Send Malach where?"

"The liminal plane——" She cut off as Heshima and Balaur appeared with four mercenaries. He gestured and one took out a knife. Her heart sank as the man leapt into the wagon, but he only cut her bindings and jumped out again.

"Stand up," Balaur ordered. "I want you to bear witness."

Kasia chafed her wrists, stretching cramped legs. A thin band of light glowed on the eastern horizon. The sky above was still dark, but the stars had grown fainter.

"Are you sure this is the correct spot?" the khedive demanded, robes swishing as she glided over.

They were somewhere in the middle of the Ceaseless Sands. Moment by moment, the dunes were shifting from featureless gray to a pale, delicate pink, their crisp peaks and valleys stretching in every direction. Kasia saw no landmarks of any kind. As its name suggested, the desert was continually reshaped by the wind into new formations, changeable as the surface of the sea.

"It is not the place that matters, but the keys and the time," Balaur snapped. "Now be quiet!"

A fraught silence fell.

The band of light grew brighter. Redder. Streaks of rose bled upward, merging with a widening stripe of yellow that gilded the edges of the clouds. Kasia could see the exact point where the sun waited behind the dunes. A halo of fiery orange, deepening as the gears of the world slowly turned.

The halo intensified, searing her eyes now, but she couldn't look away. Then the leading edge of the star broke over the dunes in a molten flash. She blinked, half blinded, and gripped the edge of the wagon with white knuckles.

The khedive gave a wordless cry.

Where empty desert had been just a moment before, the domes and spires of a magnificent city rose ahead, so close she could see pennants snapping in a stiff breeze, although no wind stirred the air outside its shining white walls. Every banner had a golden starburst against a blue field.

"Hurry! Before it vanishes!" Balaur raced forward. Heshima lifted her skirts and ran after him.

The khedive scrambled for her wagon, barking orders. One of her men shoved Kasia down to the burlap sacks and climbed up. The wagons lurched forward. She sat down next to Alexei, hauling him upright. "Don't forget what I said," she whispered. "When Rachel——"

The guard drew his knife, growling at them in Masdari. He made a slashing motion. She stopped talking. He watched them the rest of the way through lowered brows. It was only a minute or two before the wagon halted. She stood and peered over the edge. They were at the first gate. A monstrous iron-clad door without adornment save for a keyhole in the center.

"Balaur!" she cried.

He turned, the iron key ready.

"Let the priest go now," she shouted. "Give him a mule. And water."

Rachel's hazel eyes narrowed.

"Just do it," Heshima urged. "Or let me have the keys! There's no time to waste."

"Very well," he snapped. "Send him on his way."

Balaur did not pause to watch, fearful perhaps that the gate would vanish. He thrust the iron key into the lock, twisting it with an audible thunk. For a moment, nothing happened. Then a line of violet light split the door into two halves. They soundlessly parted, revealing another door beyond, this one bright argent. The Silver Gate.

Balaur capered, clapping Rachel's small hands together. Heshima showed more dignity, but her face shone with an otherworldly fervor like the paintings of martyrs at the Arx. The khedive whispered with her aged advisor. He seemed frightened now, as if he were having second thoughts about plundering the seat of a god.

"Hoi!" the khedive cried. Her wagon trundled into the gap.

Kasia turned to Alexei. His bonds had been cut. He rose stiffly to his feet. Before the guard could object, she pulled him into a tight embrace.

"If you love me, do as I ask," she whispered in his ear.

She felt his reluctance in the tense lines of his body. It went against every part of him to leave her there. She knew Alexei would give his life for her in an instant, but what she needed from him was worse.

To walk away.

"Find my brother," she hissed, as the guards pulled them apart.

He turned his head, holding her gaze as they prodded him to the mule. He was still angry, and deeply afraid, but she thought she saw a spark of something else. He *did* believe in her. He wouldn't have gone otherwise.

She watched him ride off, away from the rising sun. When she was certain no one intended to pursue, she hurried to catch up with the party of wagons, two guards jogging at her side. Iron, silver, and copper already stood open. It was odd because the outer curtain wall didn't look very thick, certainly not wide enough to accommodate a series of gates. Yet there they were behind her, each separated by a broad antechamber.

The Mercury Gate came next, gleaming and reflective like the chrome ravens on clergy cars. A distorted mirror image of tangled black hair and pale skin reflected back as she walked past. She wondered if it would be the last time she ever saw herself. If different eyes would soon be looking out at the world.

A disquieting thought. But she had demanded Alexei's faith; the least she could do was return it. Rachel had courage and strength, but she was just a little girl. Balaur would not find his own daughter such easy prey.

The wagons pressed on, stopping and then rolling forward again as the doors gave way in succession. Lead followed, then tin. At each gate, Balaur produced the matching key and the liminal ley recognized it.

The final gate was lustrous gold. The only one with any markings—a huge starburst like the one on the pennants—and dead in its center, the last keyhole.

Kasia stood near the back of the group, but she saw Balaur's hand tremble slightly as he fitted the golden key to the lock.

"We keep to the bargain, witch," he said, looking up at Heshima. "You get your god, I get the elixir."

"And I get the treasure!" the khedive added in shrill tones.

Heshima gave a taut nod.

"You will break the binding spell," Balaur pressed.

"Yes," the witch burst out. "Don't toy with us. Open it!"

He turned the key. The violet light shimmered, then grew so bright Kasia was forced to throw an arm up. It filled her vision and died.

The last gate swung open.

Chapter Thirty-One

Kasia shuffled forward, snared in the press of sweaty male bodies. As she stepped through the gate, a rush of sounds filled her ears. The front rank—Balaur and Heshima, presumably— stopped dead, jamming up the wagons. Kasia quietly slipped through gaps, a damp wind stirring her hair. It smelled of the sea and other things, too. Cinnamon and sandalwood. Grass. A tang of woodsmoke.

She braced a foot in the spokes of a wagon wheel and climbed up for a better look. No one tried to yank her down. The guards were all dumbstruck and staring in amazement.

Kasia had expected an empty shell. A gilded cage. But this was a living, breathing city. People strolled arm and arm through green parks, bustled along wide thoroughfares. They wore colorful costumes in many different styles, like flocks of exotic birds. Others rode tawny caracal cats five times the size of Lupa. Gulls flashed white overhead, emitting rusty shrieks and diving to squabble over scraps in the gutter.

The gate had opened into a wide plaza. The gray stone buildings surrounding it had elaborate terra cotta friezes and cornices of marble, with open platforms extending from the upper stories. Tiny figures took off and alit on the platforms. She squinted, but they were too far off to make out clearly.

One structure stood above the rest. A pearly white tower in the distance with a golden cupola on top.

The mercenaries spread out with hands on swords as a group of hard-looking women approached. Identical smoke-colored eyes named them witches, but none had any gemstones that Kasia could see. Each carried a knife and a coiled whip at her belt. They wore tight trousers and gleaming silver bodices with a gold starburst on the breast. She thought it was chainmail until they drew closer and she saw it was some kind of stiff, metallic cloth. One of the huge caracals padded along beside them. The dark tufts on its ears were as long as her hand.

Heshima's back stiffened. Balaur ducked behind her skirts.

The women were obviously soldiers. Or maybe prison guards. Kasia waited for them to call out a challenge, but they walked past without a glance. They were speaking a foreign tongue that sounded similar to Masdari. A brown-skinned witch with her hair woven into elaborate braids laughed and looked straight at Kasia. Straight *through* her.

"Illusion," Heshima said with a note of awe. "None of this is real."

"What do you mean?" the khedive demanded. Her men parted to let her through. Spots of furious color burned in her cheeks. "Where's my treasure? I was promised gold! Jewels!"

Heshima stared at her for a long moment, expressionless. Then she smiled. "I meant the people. The rest is real enough." She pointed a finger. "Follow that street. There is a vast hoard in the building at the end of it. Enough to fill these wagons a dozen times over. It will be guarded by fear-some beasts, but they are just phantoms to frighten off thieves."

Greed lit the khedive's eyes. She climbed back into her cart, squinting into the distance. "Are you certain?"

"I am a witch," Heshima assured her. "We can sense these things."

"Come, stand at my side, Kasia," Balaur called in a jovial voice. "We can't have you running off, can we?"

She thought of the sickly child waiting in the Garden. Balaur had cared for her body at least. The girl looking at her now had plump, ruddy cheeks and bright eyes. She wondered if he would leave some taint behind but thought not. Whatever his spirit consisted of, it would depart wholesale. The rest was just flesh and bone.

The wagons with the khedive and her mercenaries trundled off, leaving only one. Jule Danziger clambered out, his movements awkward and sluggish. A white haze covered one blue eye. The other rolled blearily in the socket.

"Where is the elixir?" he croaked. "I need it."

Balaur ignored him, looking up at Heshima. "It is time, witch. Free me from this vessel."

She took a step back—out of his reach. "Not yet. I suspect we are both going to the same place." She gazed at the white tower. "I will do it there."

He scowled. "That was not our bargain."

"And you never specified where," she shot back. "But I swear by Valmitra that I will liberate you once we arrive."

His mouth twisted. Balaur gave a sour nod. "Very well." He gazed after the khedive, whose wagons had already disappeared. "Did you really sense a hoard of treasure?"

She laughed. "No. Let her discover the truth for herself. By the time she does, it will not matter."

During this exchange, Jule Danziger had been standing with a befuddled expression on his decaying face. When he realized they weren't at their destination, he cursed roundly and crawled back into the wagon bed, huddling there in a wretched heap. Balaur and Kasia took the bench, Heshima walking beside the mules.

All this time, the city was still humming around them, its

inhabitants going about their business in carefree fashion. It seemed like the utopia the Via Sancta had promised, with no signs of poverty, inequality, or violence. Kasia didn't spot any more witch patrols—yet she remembered the daggers and whips. What were they guarding against?

Despite the icy fear-sweat pooling at her nape, she felt curious. If a witch—or witches—had devised this panorama, most likely they'd based it on a place they knew. A place that was *real*, though lost to the ages now.

"Can't you dispel these illusions?" Balaur asked petulantly, as a gang of high-spirited teenagers darted in front of the wagons, causing the mules to balk. "They are distracting."

"No," Heshima replied without turning. "The weavings of ley are too complex. I wouldn't know where to begin."

He turned to Kasia, reading her thoughts. "Well, it's all fascinating, isn't it, my dear? Pre-Dark Ages!" He waved a hand. "*This* is what I want for humanity. To restore us to a state of perfect bliss."

She snorted. "I'm sure."

He chuckled, in a good humor again. "Look at those lacquered coaches! Drawn by cats, no less. It is like a children's tale." His gaze rose to one of the fluttering standards. "The Morning Star. We descend from nobility, Kasia."

Heshima's jaw tightened, but she said nothing. The bewildered mules had decided to treat the traffic as if it were real, plodding along at a cautious pace despite Balaur's oaths and shaking of the reins. Kasia didn't blame them. The illusion was extraordinarily convincing. Wheels clattered, dogs barked, cups at the sidewalk cafes clinked gently against saucers. The tantalizing scent of hot pastry drifted through the air.

Balaur stiffened as three pale forms glided across their path. Deathly white skin, with eyes of swirling color. The Reborn! Kasia drew a breath to cry for help, but then she saw their faces. None were the children she'd met in Kvengard.

These had wings of iridescent pearl, like the tower, and they flew on without pausing.

Illusions, like all the rest of it.

Balaur stared after them, looking almost as bloodless.

"What were those creatures, witch?" he demanded hoarsely.

She shrugged. "There were different orders of your kind," she replied. "Or so I was told. In the end, they turned against each other."

The wagon crossed an arching stone bridge above a canal. Narrow, poled boats glided through its green waters. Balaur twisted around on the seat, but the trio had vanished. "That particular order of angels. What was it?"

"The Cherubim, I expect. They looked like children. The Mahadeva said—" She abruptly fell silent. The witch's face was smooth, but her fingers twitched at her sides. Balaur didn't notice. All he said was, "How peculiar."

But Kasia sensed his sudden unease. She leaned toward him, pitching her voice low. "I met the children you murdered. They will come for you, Balaur."

He cast her a sharp look. "They cannot harm me. Not now or ever."

"Are you certain of that? They were not what you expected." A cold smile. "You didn't even know what they were. Maybe someone else sent them, eh? Maybe you were just a tool in the Mother's hand."

"Be quiet," he snapped. "Or I will compel you to be quiet!"

The witch looked over with a slight frown. Kasia fell silent.

They rode on, each district more magnificent than the last. Mellow lamplight glowed through oval windows. She caught the strains of alien music. Glimpsed women wearing feathered masks and tight-waisted brocade gowns. A tall man in profile, ebony wings folded against his back, gesturing with a goblet.

At first, she recoiled at the masks, remembering the Lethe

Club, but there was no cruelty in the laughter that drifted from the open balconies. The slow pace of the wagon allowed her to observe her surroundings at leisure. A handsome couple emerged from one house, holding hands, and entered the next one, where they were warmly greeted. Perhaps it was a festival day like Caristia, when everyone went visiting. They all looked so happy, it made her chest ache. Kasia wished she could step into the dream. Don a mask and pretend to be one of them.

For a moment, she half-convinced herself that they were real and she was the illusion. A ghost haunting the fringes.

How could all this have been lost? she wondered, a bitter taste at the back of her throat. Her gaze lifted to the starburst unfurling from a spire above, snapped by the salt wind.

It was Gavriel's fault. He'd destroyed everything.

Was that why he had left this simulacrum? A memorial to the people he'd betrayed?

A few streets later, she saw the same couple come out of a house. The same greeting and the same black and white cat—normal-sized—winding between their legs as they entered the house next door. She realized it was on a loop. The fantasy popped like a soap bubble and she just felt inexplicably sorry for them all.

A mist rose. Fine tendrils above the cobbles at first but thickening to pea soup as they drew near the tower. It muffled all sound except the creaking of the wagon.

Kasia gathered herself. She had to be sure he'd left Rachel's body before fighting back. Whatever else happened, at least she could save the child. Then a horrible thought struck her. Would Rachel know the way back? Or might she get lost? And what would happen to her body then? How long could it survive without a soul?

If only she knew what Balaur had done. *How* he had done it. She might have some idea what to expect.

"We are here," he hissed, grabbing her arm. "I can feel the power."

Lacking her cards, Kasia felt nothing. The paved street gave way to desert sands. Then the mists parted and the white tower appeared just ahead, soaring aloft like a divine pillar supporting the arch of the sky. The wagon jerked to a stop. Every muscle involuntarily clenched in primal terror.

An enormous serpent coiled around the base. It had two heads and jaws that could have swallowed the mules whole. The eyes were open, gleaming with ancient malice. The scales dazzled, each encrusted with gold and silver and precious gems. It was the treasure hoard the khedive sought.

Balaur's hand tightened painfully, the small fingers digging into her arm. Heshima gave a soft gasp.

A minute passed. The witch sank to the ground, hands raised in supplication. Kasia's terror eased when the serpent didn't react to their presence.

"Is it . . ." She swallowed dust. "Is it an illusion?"

"No," Balaur replied, gaze fixed on the tower. "I can see the ley streaming from her mouth. It surges with each breath." There was an ugly, covetous edge to his voice. "Behold the true power in this world, Kasia."

She studied the being the witches had named Valmitra and the Masdaris called the Alsakhan. The great triangular head rested on drifting sands. What Kasia had taken for malice now looked like emptiness.

"She sleeps?" Kasia ventured.

"She is bound by spells," Heshima replied with an edge of anger.

"Can you break them?" Balaur asked.

The witch turned to him. "I must."

"Then free me so I may go seek the elixir." He gazed at the tower. "It is inside."

Heshima turned to Kasia. "You do this willingly?"

She lifted her chin. "I would rather he take me than allow Rachel's spirit to wither and die."

The witch nodded. "It has never sat well with me that he

occupies a child." She shot Balaur a cool, inscrutable look. "I do this for the girl, not you."

He stared at her. "We had a bargain. As long as you keep your end, I don't care why you do it." Cruel delight lit in his eyes. He sauntered over to Kasia. She felt a slight tug on the pocket of her robe. "On your knees."

"Is that necessary?" Heshima frowned. "She already said—"

"Yes," he interrupted savagely. "She will kneel to me."

Heshima fell silent. Her gaze found Kasia, then flicked to the serpent and back to Balaur.

Kasia understood. She believed Valmitra would handle the problem of Balaur herself once she woke.

If the witch could rouse her.

She might fail. In which case, Balaur would probably kill Heshima, too.

Kasia sank to her knees. It didn't require much effort to make herself tremble. "Go ahead. Release him."

Heshima took a stone from her pouch, face intent. Her fingers sprang open. Rachel's body shuddered. Her eyes rolled back, showing only the whites. She made a sound between a sigh and a groan. An inky shadow pooled around her feet and stretched across the sand. It reached out like skeletal fingers. Kasia fought the urge to run. She had to be sure he was fully out of the child.

Rachel shambled over, legs stiff and jerky. A small hand gripped Kasia's hair, so tightly her scalp stung and tears pricked her eyes. She braced herself.

The assault came an instant later, an alien presence prying at her mind. Agonizing pain split her forehead like a hatchet blow. In the corner of her eye, she saw something big and hunched over, neither man nor beast, that vanished to gray smoke when she tried to look at it directly.

"Kill him!" she screamed at the witch.

The tower blurred and tilted on its axis. Rachel slumped

to the ground like a marionette with its strings cut. Through a haze of briny tears, Kasia saw Heshima drag her away toward the tower, toward the dozing god.

A vise squeezed her body. Red rage swirled around her, a maelstrom of chaos and desperation.

And fear.

As she had surmised, he was a between-thing now. A ghost trapped in the liminal plane. His roiling emotions nearly swept her up, but she found an inner eye of calm amidst the storm.

She heard Tess's dying words. *I love you, girl. Remember, you can choose. No one can take that from you.*

She thought of a squalling infant in the arms of a knight —one who would one day be pontifex.

I am more Falke's daughter than I am Balaur's.

The shadow buffeted her with great dark wings. When that did not work, it turned to writhing vines, twining around her limbs, seeking any hairline crack in which to put down roots.

I am not a mage.

Her jaw clenched.

I am not your blood. I renounce you.

Kasia bit down on her own tongue and tasted blood.

I renounce you.

Nails dug into her fisted palms.

The shadow keened in wordless fury. It thrashed and whipped, tentacles circling her throat.

I renounce you!

Chapter Thirty-Two

❦

The sun sat two hands above the horizon when Malach and Nikola arrived at the Iron Gate.

They had followed the red star through the night, a cool wind at their backs. The desert was silent save for the distant barking of a fenak fox—an eerie sound like a crying baby—and later, the thin cry of a Markhawk. The bird circled above them once, twice, then sped away to the east.

Perhaps it was a spy for Balaur. If so, there was little Malach could do about it. As they walked, he told Nikola everything that happened since he came to the League. Then she shared her own tale.

When he heard what happened to Tristhus and how she'd saved the boy, Malach was surprised at the depth of his relief. He realized that he loved both Trist and Syd despite the fact that they were holy terrors.

It was the khedive's priests who attacked the ship, but Balaur's hand guided them all. Another debt Malach planned to repay with interest.

This day would be the final reckoning. As much as he resisted the idea of destiny, he could feel it pulling at him. What else could explain the sudden appearance of a full-fledged city where a moment ago there had been nothing but dunes? He feared what they might find beyond the walls, but having Nikola at his side lent him courage.

They paused at the huge metal-bound door, peering through the series of six more gates that opened beyond, one after the next.

"Cathrynne Rowan told me to follow the labyrinth to its heart," he said.

Nikola looked at him sharply. "You spoke to her?"

"She left a sweven in the sword. I saw her and Gavriel, but I don't think he knew what she was doing." He adjusted his grip on the blade, which rested on one shoulder. "It was a message. She looked right at me. Like she knew I'd find it someday. Or someone would."

Nikola's gaze lifted to the white spire in the distance. "The tower," she said softly. "That's where they went."

Malach took her hand. "Are you ready?"

Her silver incisor caught the sunlight as she smiled. "No, but what the hell, let's go anyway."

Together, they walked through the seven gates. When they passed the last, which was made of gold, a sudden cacophony of sound drew Malach up short. People clogged the sidewalks, alongside lacquered coaches drawn by strange beasts. Fountains burbled, hawkers cried their wares, wheels jounced against pavement.

He turned to Nikola and mouthed *What the hell?*

She was looking around with an odd expression he couldn't place. Surprise mingled with grudging admiration.

"It's fake," she said. "All of it, I think. Definitely the people."

He frowned. "Why bother?"

"I have no idea."

She stepped into the path of a fast-moving coach. Malach's gut clenched. Every detail of the conveyance looked solid and real. The sunlight reflecting on the windows, half-hidden behind curtains. The driver, a fat, balding man in a loose ankle-length robe and sandals. The pair of tawny, tuft-eared cats that drew it along with lithe, springing steps of their great paws.

Malach's pulse beat in his throat. "Nikola——"

She waved at him as the coach rattled straight through the spot where she stood. He swore softly. "Do *not* do that again, please."

"I can't imagine how they pulled this off," she said. "I've never seen an illusion that comes close."

He looked past her. "Is that an illusion?"

Nikola followed his gaze. A mule-drawn wagon was trotting in their direction. A familiar figure sat on the bench—Jamila al-Jabban. Her attention was fixed on the gates, every line of her face drawn tight with fury. An old man sat next to her, looking equally unhappy.

Malach hesitated. He owed Jamila a debt, too, one he would love to pay back right now. Judging by the look in Nikola's eye, she felt the same. But a dozen leather-vested mercenary types were crammed into the wagon bed. He couldn't take them all on at once. And he wouldn't risk losing Rachel.

Another moment and Jamila would see them. He took Nikola's arm and steered them into the flow of fake people moving through the plaza. The khedive rode straight past and out the gates without a second glance.

"She thought she'd get rich," Nikola said. "But the treasure was just an illusion."

Malach was about to say it served her right for believing Balaur's bullshit, but then he remembered how he had done the same at Bal Agnar, heard only what he wanted to hear, and kept his mouth shut.

They hurried in silence for the tower, scanning every face. Amid the hustle and bustle, it would be all too easy for Heshima to sneak up on them and unleash some nasty spell. But they encountered only specters until they passed through a bank of fog and emerged in front of the white tower. An enormous two-headed snake coiled around the base. Malach wanted to believe it was another illusion, but he could see the ley pulsing from its mouth. The severed stump where a third head had once sprouted.

Kasia stood next to the serpent. Stark relief crossed her face as she saw them, but Malach hardly noticed. His daughter lay on the ground at her feet like a wilted flower.

"Thanks the Saints you came," Kasia said. "Balaur left her body and tried to take mine, but I fought him off. I think he entered the witch. She cursed me and ran away." Tears sprang to her eyes. "I don't know, but Rachel isn't breathing—"

A rush of blood in his ears drowned the rest. Malach ran to his daughter. The sword slipped from his fingers as he knelt in the dust and pressed an ear to Rachel's chest. The cradle of her ribs felt tiny in his hands.

He listened for ten seconds. Twenty. The child was lifeless.

He drew on the ley, knowing it couldn't heal but desperate enough to try anyway. It flowed from the earth into his hands as he laid them over her heart, thinking wildly that he might compel it to start beating again. He knew Rachel was dead when the power wouldn't enter her body. Abyssal ley could only be used on the living.

It shimmered along his skin and sank back into the sand.

"How long has she been like this?" he demanded. "How long?"

Part of him was insane with grief that they came too late, but it would not help his daughter to lose control and he would not give up yet.

"Only a few minutes," Kasia said quickly.

He looked for Nikola. She'd run to the Serpent. He felt a surge of despairing anger that she would choose Valmitra, but then he saw her lean forward as if she meant to kiss those terrible jaws and he remembered the story she had told him about Tristhus.

Nikola ran back and blew into Rachel's mouth. The child's chest rose, filling with breath. Nikola tucked a blue stone into Rachel's left hand. It glowed softly, the light streaming between her fingers.

"Come back, Rachel," Malach whispered. "We're here. We've come for you."

How pale and still she was in his arms.

A minute later, their daughter stirred, a tiny movement. Her cheeks were flushed, hair damp against her brow. She didn't open her eyes, but a weak pulse fluttered beneath his fingers.

"Thank the Mother," Nikola whispered.

The three of them held each other, Malach shaking with relief.

Then, movement in the corner of his eye. Heshima stepped out from the fog. She raised a hand and force exploded outward, sending them all tumbling backwards. He slammed into something and heard the dry snap of bone. A lance of agony tore through his right leg. Nikola groaned a short distance away. Rachel lay unmoving.

He cursed through gritted teeth and assessed the damage. His pants were torn and white bone poked through the skin. An open fracture—those were bad. His whole leg was on on fire, but adrenaline kicked in and everything became clear and sharp.

Besides the witch, Kasia was the only one still standing. She must have grabbed Gavriel's sword for she held it up before her, glaring daggers.

"I knew you would betray me," Heshima said in a wintry voice. "You used him to bring the Morning Star's blade."

"Betray *you*?" Kasia shook her head in amazement. "You're the traitor."

"Give it to me. Give me Gavriel's sword or I will tear you limb from limb."

"No."

The witch closed her fist, then flung her arm outward, fingers splaying. A line of force rippled across the sand. It raised violent whirlwinds that swept past Kasia without seeming to touch her. Heshima's calm shattered. She gave a guttural growl. Ley burst from every ring and bracelet. From the buckles on her shoes and the woven silver of her belt. From her buttons and pouch and the necklace around her slender throat.

It raised a choking storm of dust. When the air cleared, Kasia was untouched. She held up a stone. Even from a distance, Malach knew what it was.

"The kaldurite you put into my brother. I found it in Rachel's pocket. Balaur must have taken it from your dead sister Darya."

"You *are* Balaur!" Heshima spat.

Those words gave Malach pause. But no, the witch was wrong, how could that possibly be? Kasia was too strong, too smart, she would never allow it. She would never . . .

Kasia strode forward with a grim face and Malach thought she meant to finish the witch, but then she turned and stabbed the sword into the serpent's great jaws. Valmitra reared up with a terrible hiss. Amber liquid spilled from the wound, thick like honey. The serpent uncoiled and lashed its tail, knocking Heshima down. Then it slithered inside the white tower, smashing the doors from their hinges.

Malach pulled himself toward Rachel, keeping his weight off the broken leg. He could feel the upper femur swinging back and forth inside his thigh while the rest of it just stayed there. He tried to push through the shock and get a grip on what was happening, but nothing made any sense.

Rachel lay in a heap. He just wanted to reach her, to protect her, but it was taking him too long to get there. Nikola moved weakly some distance away, and Heshima was climbing to her feet with a stunned look, but Kasia . . . she hunched on hands and knees, lapping at the amber pool, the sword clutched in one hand. Black hair obscured her face, but it wasn't her, he knew that now.

Her shadow looked wrong. He should have seen that before. Should have noticed.

Then she stood up—*he* stood up—and slowly turned to regard them, eyes shining like burnished gold.

"I can feel it in my veins," Balaur exulted. "The purest essence of the ley!"

"What have you done?" Heshima screamed.

"I have drunk the venom of your god, witch." He tossed the kaldurite away. "Test it." He spread his arms wide. "Try to kill me."

Bitter hatred etched Heshima's face. She raised a hand. Ley gathered around her, then exploded outward. It enclosed Balaur like a halo, pulsing for a long moment. Then the spell rebounded. Heshima flew backward like she'd been hit by a battering ram. Her body bounced—actually *bounced*—and sprawled akimbo like a discarded doll.

Balaur started to laugh. A mockery of ley billowed from his mouth, gray and dull like smoke from a funeral pyre.

"It is done," he cried. "It is done and it can never be undone. I am a god!" He walked to Heshima, peering down at her body. "You were a fool. It was I who came to your dreams in the guise of Valmitra. I who guided your every step." He slashed the sword through the air. "I manipulated all of you! And you were none the wiser until it was too late. This was all meant to be! I am Gavriel's true heir and I will finish what he began."

Covetous eyes fixed on Rachel. "Now I will take my grandchild. If she is obedient, I will even let her drink the elixir."

A red veil dimmed Malach's eyes. He dragged himself forward. Balaur did nothing, just watched. When he drew close enough, Malach grabbed his ankle and tried to compel him. After a minute, Balaur delivered a casual backhand that sent him sprawling, the copper tang of blood on his lips and agony exploding in his leg.

"You planned to use this sword on me," he said, the words distorted by the ringing in Malach's ears. "So I will use it on *you*, my feckless son."

The twisted shadow fell over him.

"Stop!" Nikola screamed. "Just wait!"

Malach shook his head to clear it.

Someone else was here, moving across the open ground. He hoped it was the priest come to save them. Kasia's valiant knight.

But in the harsh morning light, he saw it was only another nightmare.

Chapter Thirty-Three

Nikola turned at a scuffing, dragging sound behind her.

It was coming from the wagon. Or rather, the wagon bed, where a man-shaped creature had just emerged from the piles of burlap sacks.

For an awful moment, she thought Balaur had raised the dead—torn the veil asunder and called demons to serve him.

The thing that approached with a hitching gait looked like it had crawled out of a muddy grave. Putrid strands of blond hair clung to its scalp. White teeth gleamed through shriveled lips. It wore a fashionable jacket and trousers, now stained with nameless fluids. One eye resembled a hard-boiled egg. The other was blue and burning with need.

It sank to its knees, crawling to the pool of amber liquid. Kasia's eyes followed with amusement.

"Reward," the thing rasped. "For my years of service. You promised."

"Yes, of course, Jule." A slow, indulgent smile. "Drink your fill."

Nikola remembered the name. The man who had killed Kasia's mentor, Tessaria Foy.

A black tongue snaked out, lapping at the puddle like a

cat over a dish of cream, though it wasn't a dainty meal, as a cat would make; no, he slurped and smacked his withered lips.

Nikola gazed up at the tower, fervently wishing Valmitra would return and take her vengeance on them both, but the Great Serpent had vanished.

"Have you ever experienced the like?" Balaur asked. "Sweeter than any nectar, more nourishing than Mother's milk." He laughed at his own pun. "Some would be afraid to taste the Great Serpent's venom, but we are cut from a different cloth, aren't we, Jule? We take what we want. What we deserve!"

The Kven made some garbled response. A soft glow enveloped him. When he straightened, he had been transformed. Flaxen hair gleamed. Smooth, tanned skin radiated health. He cracked his neck and sprang to his feet, grinning.

"What shall I do to them, eh?" he asked. "Name it. Name it and I'll do it."

Balaur said nothing, only watched with a monster's patient, curious eyes.

"The ecstasy," Jule whispered with a shiver. His eyes rolled up to the whites, then snapped back into place. He turned to Nikola. "I'm going to kill your family first, while you watch. Then I'm going to kill that bitch of a snake. And then . . ." He cleared his throat. "Then I'm going to . . ." He swallowed. "It's fucking *hot*."

"Is something amiss?" Balaur asked.

Jule coughed. A fine spray of blood came out.

"What?" he muttered.

Balaur approached with awkward, ungainly steps, as though he hadn't yet mastered the mechanics of Kasia's body.

"You don't look well," he said with a frown. "Not at all."

Jule hacked as though something was tearing loose deep inside him. "Burns . . ."

"Oh dear. Oh me, oh my." Balaur chuckled.

"What?" Jule repeated like a hoarse parrot. "What? What?"

He was sweating profusely now.

"I wonder . . . " Balaur laid a finger against his nose, head tilting quizzically. "Is the elixir turning to poison in your veins? That must be terrible. I cannot even imagine it."

Jule sank to his knees. His face was a bruised purple now, eyes bulging from their sockets. Wisps of smoke rose from his collar.

"Here's what I think." Balaur nudged Danziger with one foot, toppling him. "I think you have been naive. Did you honestly believe you could become like *me*? You are not an angel, Jule. Not even the lowest order."

Jule gave a whimper of protest. His fingers clawed furrows in the sand, mouth agape and features contorted into a rictus. Nikola wished the real Kasia could see his rage and fear and pain and humiliation.

"You have been a loyal servant," Balaur continued mildly, "but that is all you are. Unfortunately, you seem to have forgotten your place." He clucked his tongue. "Well, you cannot blame me. This is your own doing. Your aunt is not so stupid. She suspected this might happen, *ja*? That is why she seeks an alchemical solution for her failing body. That is why she will live to serve me and you will die screaming, Jule."

Danziger croaked in dismay.

Once when Nikola was nine, she'd gotten mad and thrown one of her dolls at the ceiling. It landed behind the radiator and she'd forgotten all about it until winter came and the heat turned on. She still remembered the smell of burning plastic. By the time her mother located the source, the doll was melted and half-bald, pretty locks singed to a blackened stubble. Her lidless eyes stared accusingly. It had given Nikola nightmares for weeks.

Jule looked like the doll, except worse, because instead of

burning plastic, he smelled like a cooked ham. Weeping blisters pebbled his throat.

"What?" he croaked. "What?"

When his hair caught and his eyes burst, Nikola looked away, stomach churning.

"Bloody hells," she whispered to Malach, who held their daughter's limp hand. His face was the shade of curdled milk, his leg a red ruin.

"It's the least the bastard deserved," he whispered back. "I can't walk, but you must get Rachel out of here. Run back to the gates. Go, now, before he——"

"Before I what?"

The thing inside Kasia was staring at them both. Jule had stopped thrashing and lay steaming in the sun, his empty eye sockets turned to the sky.

Nikola got to her feet, moving to stand in front of her family. She could not think of Balaur as *he* or *him* anymore. The spirit wasn't human or angel or anything recognizable.

It was a cold empty void. A devouring darkness.

"I meant to thank you for bringing this," it said to Malach, hefting the sword. "Perhaps you realize now that it was I who came to your dream in the guise of Cathrynne Rowan. The kaldurite shielded your mind for a long time, but once it was gone, you were defenseless. And you played the part of my errand boy to perfection."

Its gaze swiveled to Nikola. "But you *burned* me. I have not forgotten that." Lips twisted in sudden rage. "Do you know what it feels like to die in shriveling flames?"

"No," she replied honestly, "but I hope it was really fucking painful."

The sword slashed the air, then pointed at her. "This cannot be used against me now. You heard the prophecy. No weapon can harm me." It glanced at the tower. "Unlike Valmitra. Gavriel used it to cut off one of her heads. Let us see if it works on the other two."

"If you kill her," Nikola growled, "you have no idea what will happen."

"I will be this world's new god." It came nearer, the sword dragging a line in the sand. "You think I do not know you, Nikola Thorn, but I do, I know you better than you know yourself. You call yourself a witch when you are nothing but a char. Tell me, do your knees still ache from scrubbing floors?"

If it thought the barb would sting, it was sadly mistaken. She felt no shame for her past anymore. No shame for who she was.

"At least it's honest work."

"My mother was a woman in gray. I would not call her honest." The lip curled. "She was a whore, too, so you have much in common."

"Shut your fucking mouth," Malach snarled.

"And if I don't? What will you do now? You served your purpose. You brought me the Morning Star's blade. You have been a good dog. Now you are worthless, just like Herr Danziger."

It adjusted its grip on the sword.

Nikola eyed Malach, then Rachel. *How can I possibly choose between them?*

"If you kill her father, the child will know," Nikola said. "She'll hate you forever."

Kasia's icy, beautiful face gave nothing away, but—as incredible as it seemed—Nikola thought she'd struck a nerve.

A hand extended. "Then give me the child of your own will. I will care for her."

"You're afraid to be alone," Nikola said softly.

"I am afraid of nothing."

"No, you are. You're afraid that everyone else will die and you will be the last thing left on this earth, so you want my daughter to keep you company."

"It is a gift! She has the angel blood. Half is enough—I

am proof of that. I will give her immortality. But you will help me. You will make her drink the elixir."

"Nikola, no." Malach gazed at her in horror. "I'd rather die—"

"Shut up," the thing spat. "I will spare you both if you make her mine. Mine forever."

Nikola pretended to think it over as she bent down next to Rachel.

"Do you promise to treat her well?"

"As I would my own daughter."

The profound irony of this statement seemed to be lost on Balaur.

For all his cunning, all his obsessive plotting, he'd fallen victim to his own lies.

Malach opened his mouth to object again and Nikola shot him a quelling look. "I never wanted her anyway," she said. "So I will give her to you, if you give me Malach. He cannot harm you."

She found Rachel's hand. The small fingers still gripped the chunk of blue lapis, a restorative for memory and concentration. Nikola found the heart of the stone and loosed the ley inside.

"Wake, love," she whispered.

"What are you doing?" Balaur demanded.

Rachel's eyes fluttered open. She sat up and turned to Balaur, eerily composed and alert.

"You took her," she said. "You took Auntie."

The thing looked back at her with a strange expression.

"She gave herself to me." He beckoned. "Leave them. Come and I will make you my heir, Rachel."

"Why would I want that?"

"Because I will spare your parents if you do."

Rachel tried to rise. Malach caught her wrist.

"Let go, let go!" she screamed.

He tried to hold on, but he was badly hurt and she fought free of him.

"For fuck's sake, stop her!" he shouted as she ran to the Balaur-thing.

Nikola shook her head. Their daughter would not accept this offer. She knew it in her heart.

The child stopped just short of the Beast of Bal Agnar. She began to sway, chin tilted toward the sky.

"What are you doing?" it hissed.

"Go," Rachel replied. "Go, and I will call the Black Sun."

He eyed her distrustfully. "You must drink the elixir first."

"When the Serpent is dead. I am afraid of her." She smiled. "We are blood, grandfather. Closer than blood. Return to me when it is done." She cast a sly look at Nikola and Malach. "I will manage my parents, but if you harm them, it will make me angry. I might have to destroy this city."

Balaur studied the heavens, his expression wary. Then he turned and lurched into the tower, feet stumbling as though Kasia's body fought him.

Rachel said nothing to either of them. Just closed her eyes and returned to her humming and swaying

"Stay with her," Nikola said.

"Where are you going?" Malach demanded.

"To stop him from killing Valmitra."

"How? You can't go after him alone. Nikola!"

Her serpent's eye namestone shimmered redly against the sand. She ran over and retrieved it. The chain had snapped so she thrust it into a pocket.

"You saw what just happened!" Malach yelled. He tried to climb to his feet and gasped in pain. "Dammit. Whatever you do to him will rebound on you!"

"We both know I have to. There isn't anyone else left. But I won't try any spells, I promise."

He stared up at her mutinously. "Liar."

She kissed his sweaty forehead. "How bad is the pain?"

"Not too bad."

Nikola smiled. "Liar. Stay here."

He gave a strained laugh. "Where else would I go?"

She stood up and walked to their daughter. "Do you know what you're doing?" Nikola asked softly.

Rachel gave the tiniest nod.

"Okay. Take care of your father."

If the girl heard, she gave no sign.

Nikola's gems had been hurled far and wide by Heshima's projective magic. She spotted an amethyst and a chunk of carnelian and swept them up. Then a bracelet with olivine and sardonyx, and—miracle of miracles—one of her spare pouches, which held tourmaline, beryl, and selenite. It wasn't nearly enough, but there was no time to search for the rest.

"*Sister.*"

Nikola spun, readying a defensive spell in her right hand. She'd thought Heshima was dead, but the witch's eyes cracked open and she lifted a trembling hand to the bloodstone around her neck. It was dark green with flecks of red.

Her namestone.

"Touch that and I'll blow you halfway to Qeddah," Nikola said.

Heshima let her hand fall. She swallowed. A line of dried blood ran from the corner of her mouth.

"There is . . . still power in it," she whispered. "Take it. Use it all."

A trick to lure her closer? Maybe. But bloodstone was potent. Projective with a strong element of fire. She couldn't afford to leave it behind.

Nikola approached warily and ripped it from her neck, snapping the chain just as Heshima had once done to her.

"Soon you will face the Mother's judgment," she said. "I do not think it will be in your favor."

"You must . . . save her."

Nikola stared at the woman she had hated, then grudgingly respected, then hated again. Without Heshima's training, she might never have had her breakthrough. For a moment, she remembered that day on the beach when Heshima had set her hair on fire. Nikola doused the flames by summoning a wave that soaked them both to the skin. The first exhilarating taste of her own power.

She wanted to say something cruel, but she could see the witch was dying and that she was only holding on so there would be some power left in her namestone.

"I do not forgive you," Nikola said. "But I will honor this sacrifice."

Heshima gave a grateful nod and closed her eyes.

Nikola checked her pouch for more gems. They were all depleted, but Kasia's deck of cards was in there. Nikola wasn't sure what she could do with them—they weren't reservoirs of power like the stones—but she took them anyway, unwilling to leave them with Heshima.

Then she ran through the shattered doors into the tower, having lost at least five precious minutes. But Malach was right. She'd lied. There was no way she'd go after Balaur without any magic at her disposal. She'd just have to be careful.

The interior of the tower was a soaring, awe-inspiring space, with arched buttresses far above like the great basilica at the Arx in Novostopol. Shafts of sunlight speared down through stained glass windows two stories tall. The middle was hollow and she could see all the way up to the top, a dizzying spiral of white stone stairs and ornate pillared landings.

The walls were pearly like marble but more reflective. Her own blurred shadow chased her as she followed a trail of amber droplets and the smudged prints of a woman's foot— Balaur. They ascended one of the twisting staircases.

Nikola took the worn risers two at a time, breath rasping like a bellows. The staircase grew more cramped as the tower tapered. She skidded around a curve and saw a monstrous shadow ahead. Heshima's bloodstone ignited in her fist. A blast of fiery projective power shot up the staircase. She heard a cry and a thud. Nikola hurried up and peeked around the curving stone wall.

Borosus hunched over on the next landing, wings furled against his back. He turned her way, chalcedony eyes catching the dim light. Silver blood dripped from one taloned hand. His mouth opened and she glimpsed the red furnace of his throat. Nikola pulled back an instant before a gout of flame licked the wall.

She beat a hasty retreat, pausing three landings down.

What to do? The creature was blocking her way.

He'd killed the novice witch Bethen back in Qeddah—though that was no great loss—and tried to kill both Nikola and Malach. What was he doing here?

She ground her teeth. The timing couldn't be worse.

"Borosus!" she shouted. "It's Nikola Thorn! Don't—"

A second fireball rolled down the staircase, this one even bigger. The heat of it singed her hair before she threw up a protective shield.

"Najmati kalsabah!" Borosus thundered. "Where is the Morning Star?"

Chapter Thirty-Four

A wall of dense fog sliced across the cobbled street just ahead. The mule's ears twitched. It stopped in its tracks. Alexei urged it forward with his knees, but the animal refused to move.

"Come along," he said wearily, sliding from its back. "I can't leave you here."

The mule cast him an accusing look. Alexei stroked its dappled hide, releasing a trickle of calming blue ley through his palm. When he took up the bridle, the animal flicked its tail and plodded along again, hooves ringing in the silence.

Yet at the edge of the fog, he found himself balking like his four-legged companion. It was peculiar, rising up to the second story of the buildings along a perfectly straight line. Another illusion? Probably . . . but what waited on the other side?

"I don't like this either," he muttered. "But we can't get around and this is the way we must go."

Some distance ahead, the gilded dome of a white tower pierced the sky. Except for the color, it was a close twin of Sinjali's Lance. Alexei had no doubt it was where Balaur had gone.

When he'd first passed the gates, he'd been astonished by the convincing appearance of a vibrant, living city, but it was unraveling now. All the people stood motionless, flickering and slightly transparent. An eerie twilight veiled the sky. A gathering darkness.

Alexei wasn't sure he believed the ley was inherently good anymore, but he did believe in Kasia. She'd predicted Malach would follow and he had—with Nikola Thorn.

Alexei had been hiding behind a dune when he saw them appear from the south and go through the Iron Gate. Shortly afterward, the khedive's wagon emerged at a rollicking speed, making haste back to Qeddah.

As instructed, he'd hurried to the gate. Whatever Kasia planned, she couldn't do it alone. She said she needed her brother.

You will wait for the sign. Then you will find him and send him to me. To me, not Balaur. To the liminal plane.

He'd puzzled over those words for the last hour. How was he supposed to send Malach to the liminal plane?

The twilight thickened. Alexei squinted up at the tower. The light was gradually dimming, though the sky was cloudless. He frowned, blinking dazzled eyes. It was like the sun was . . . *shrinking.*

A finger of dread traced his spine.

Or turning black.

Wait for the sign, she'd said.

Alexei had a feeling this was it.

He mounted the mule and dug his heels in, plunging through the wall of fog. Sound ceased and visibility dropped to near-zero. The mist soaked his cassock and beaded his lashes. After a few minutes, it ended abruptly. One instant, he could hardly see the bridle in his hands. The next, the mule stepped through into clear air. The base of the white tower sat just ahead, and near it, two people.

The mule's hindquarters went rigid. A ripple of terror ran

from its tail to its head. Alexei thought the animal would bolt, but it stood stock still as he slid from his back.

"Bryce?" Malach called weakly. "Is that you?"

"It's me." He hurried over. Malach was a bloody mess. He'd used strips of his own pants to cinch a tourniquet around a broken femur. The leg looked swollen and discolored. Rachel stood next to her father. She was humming to herself, eyes fixed on the sky, and gave no sign that she knew Alexei was there.

"Is she . . . ?" He studied the girl. "Is she herself again?"

Malach nodded. "But Balaur drank the elixir. It was Valmitra's venom. The fucker is probably immortal, or close enough it makes no difference. He went into the tower to finish the job. Nikola went after him."

Alexei looked around. Heshima lay dead, eyes open and staring. The smell of broiled meat hung in the air. It came from another corpse, this one unmistakably Jule Danziger.

The phrase *Valmitra's venom* rolled around in his head for a minute. And *probably immortal*.

Alexei licked dry lips. "Where's Kasia?"

Malach stared up at the tower with a grim expression. Alexei realized then that she'd lost the battle. A black wave washed over him. He braced his hands on his knees, trying to breathe, but there wasn't enough air in the world.

"You already knew," Malach said softly. "How?"

Alexei rubbed his face, pulled himself together. "Balaur caught us in the palace. Inside the chamber with the keys. He had a dozen priests with him. He was going to kill us both, but Kasia offered to trade herself for Rachel. He agreed. She did it to save your daughter."

Malach's jaw tightened. Unshed tears stood in his eyes.

"She made him bring us both here first. They let me go at the gates, ordered me to ride into the desert." He remembered his last sight of her, against the rising sun. "I hoped she might be able to fight him off. But she warned me that . . . well, that he might win."

"Nikola went after her," Malach said roughly. "You should go, too." He reached up and gripped Alexei's arm. "We'll fix this somehow. There's got to be a way."

Alexei looked at Rachel, still swaying to silent music. It was nearly dusk now. As impossible as it seemed, he realized it was *her*. The child had summoned an eclipse.

Summoned the Black Sun.

His fragile control slipped its moorings. He was tired of not understanding what the hell was going on. Tired of losing at every turn.

"Why is she doing that?" he demanded. "Does she serve Balaur now?"

Malach stared back, brows furrowed. "What? No, you dumb bastard! She says Kasia told her to do it. When they met in the Garden."

The Garden.

The place she went when she slept; when she dreamt.

A liminal place.

Could she have fled there when Balaur took her body? Yes, he thought, hope stirring. Where else could she hide?

When you find Malach, send him to me.

To me, not Balaur.

She had foreseen that her body wouldn't be her own anymore.

Send him to me...

But Malach wouldn't go willingly. He would never leave his daughter's side now—even if it meant that Balaur won.

Which means I'll have to be a sneaky bastard.

". . . my fault," Malach was rambling, obviously half-delirious from the pain. "I brought the sword." A bleak laugh. "It was a stupid thing to do, but I thought I could use it against him. See, I had a dream, Bryce. About a woman. A witch, I mean, with silver hair like Lucy. I thought . . ." He trailed off, eyes glazed. "Now Nikola's gone. I'm not sure Balaur can *ever* be fucking killed. And I think he means to finish what he started—"

Alexei raised a hand. "I don't blame you. But I have a message from your sister."

Malach blinked. "Okay."

Alexei stared past him. His eyes widened. "What the hell?"

Malach turned to look.

"Sorry," Alexei muttered.

He hauled a fist back and punched him in the face.

Chapter Thirty-Five

White clouds drifted across a deep blue sky.

Kasia sat up. She smelled strawberries.

Alexei lay on his back, lips stained with juice. Before she could speak, he rolled over and pulled her into his arms. Kissed her until her head spun.

They lay on a blanket, a picnic basket nearby. A loaf of crusty bread poked out next to a wheel of yellow cheese. Bees hummed in the clover. A happy shout made her reluctantly pull away, propping herself on one elbow.

Rachel was playing croquet with her parents on the vast emerald lawn. Malach waved, then whacked his ball. It went hurtling into the lake and vanished with a splash. Rachel collapsed into giggles.

"Looks like you're going swimming!" he cried, scooping her up and running for the strip of sandy beach. Nikola followed at a slower pace, yellow sundress billowing around her.

Kasia frowned. A stone manor house sat at the top of the lawn.

"How long are they visiting?" she heard herself ask.

"Just the weekend." Alexei's gaze wandered down to her

lips. "I thought we might take a nap, hmmm? We all stayed up so late last night."

He wore a white linen shirt, open at the throat. For a split second, she thought she saw a Raven on one side, Crossed Keys on the other. She stared for a moment, disconcerted. Then he curled his fingers in hers.

"What's the matter, Kasia? If you're wondering about the breakfast dishes, I already did them. The laundry, too." Alexei smiled. "Don't worry about a thing, my love."

"No," she replied absently. "I won't worry."

She gazed up at the house. It was perfect, not too big and not too small. One side had a bay window, and she remembered reading a novel there in a worn armchair with a knitted throw across her knees. It must have been the previous winter because snow drifted down outside and a blaze crackled in the hearth.

The back had a porch overlooking the lake. Wicker furniture and planters trailing bright red blooms. Stairs led down to the lawn.

Five cats sat on the lowest step, staring at her. There was something accusing in their unblinking yellow eyes. She eyed the picnic basket. Heard a faint mewling. Not now—but before . . .

An alarm buzzed in her mind.

"Kasia?" Alexei sounded hurt now. "Are you angry at me? I'll do anything you want—"

"No," she said roughly. "No!"

She squeezed her eyes shut, a sob trapped in her throat. When she opened them, he was gone. She sat alone in the gazebo, the murky pond ahead. It was the same bench where she'd met Balaur so many times in his guise as a pilgrim. Kasia's fists clenched.

He won. Of course he did.

She watched the heron wade through the rushes, slow and patient and utterly focused.

But I was strong enough to flee here. To save a piece of my Garden. That's worth something.

Better than endless darkness.

With a single thought, she could have it all back. The perfect life, surrounded by everyone she loved. She could bring Natalya and Patryk. Tessaria Foy. Build them their own fancy manors. Be the goddess of her own little realm forever and ever—or as long as her unhoused spirit endured. In time, she would forget it wasn't real. Just like the happy people in the dawn city.

The heron's head stabbed down. A frog dangled from its beak. Three gulps and it moved on, hunting again. Rain dimpled the surface of the pond.

And what is Balaur doing while I sit here? Is he killing a god?

She wondered how he meant to do it. He would need Gavriel's sword, but it wasn't in the wagon. Heshima wouldn't have permitted—

Kasia sat up straight. She swore softly. Balaur would use someone to bring the blade to him. Probably the same confederate who had betrayed them in Qeddah.

But if he didn't have the sword yet, there was still time.

She leapt to her feet, determined to find a way out. Grass sweet with the scent of clover ran in a strip along the high brick wall that bounded the Garden. She followed the wall, imagining that she would find an open gate and walk through it into the city.

Within a few minutes, she found herself back at the gazebo. The wall was unbroken.

"All right," she muttered. "I'll find another way."

Kasia followed the path to the old well where she threw blight cuttings. The boards across the opening were gone. A ladder led down into the depths. She braced her hands on the mossy edge and leaned over, just as Rachel once did.

What's down there? the child had asked.

Kasia peered into the darkness. A whisper of stale air brushed her cheek.

"Nothing but rotting junk," she muttered. "But it might be a way out."

She felt a bit foolish since the ladder wasn't real, but she couldn't help giving it a hard shake to make sure the rungs would hold her weight. The wood felt solid enough. She hoisted herself over the edge and climbed down, the scrape of her shoes echoing in the darkness. Only a meter down, the temperature started to drop. She exhaled and saw her own breath, puffs of white in the dank air.

Kasia shivered and kept climbing. It smelled like she imagined a cave would, a mingling of water and minerals and decaying plant matter. When only a tiny circle of daylight showed above, her feet touched solid ground. The bottom of the well was dry, though spongy with wet leaves. Three low passages led away from the circular shaft.

Kasia's spirits lifted. She *had* found a way out!

But they all looked the same. Which one?

She chose a tunnel at random, stepped through, and—

SMOKE.

The screams of men and horses—but distant.

Much louder is the ringing clash of steel.

Two men circle each other in a huge chamber with a black sun laid out in tiles on the floor, its twelve jagged rays stretching to the far walls. Next to you is a silver throne on a dais, polished to a high gleam. You stare at the distorted reflection.

Waist-length hair spills over a ruby-red gown. Marks cover your bare arms. A Broken Chain circles your neck. The Mark of Bal Kirith, but that is not where you are now.

This is Bal Agnar. The innermost sanctum of the Arx, its

doors torn from their hinges and guarded by hateful knights
of the Curia.

"Yield!" a deep voice grates.

You turn to the pair locked in combat. Both young, one
dark-haired and dark-eyed, the other fair with eyes of blue
and wearing the pristine white silk of a pontifex. The first has
a Raven on his swirling cloak. He is stronger and faster.
Steadily beating his opponent back.

"Father!" you scream.

The blond man doesn't spare you a glance. He gets his
blade up, but it's battered down, swept away, sliding across the
floor. A vicious slash and he grunts, skin ashen. A glint of gold
as something flies through the air. He is clutching his own
bloody hand and you see that the blade severed his fingers,
including the one with the insignia ring.

He sinks down. The tip of the dark-haired man's blade
finds his throat—

KASIA BLINKED. She was back in the well's central shaft, mossy
walls looming around her.

Falke and Balaur.

Both decades younger, but she knew the tale. Everyone
did. The single combat at Bal Agnar that led to Balaur's
capture.

She bit her lip. Not a sweven.

Or—not one from somebody else.

*It was me watching from the dais. Not really me, but a version of me
if I'd been raised by the mages.*

She eyed the tunnels, hopes fading. Were any of them a
way out of her prison? Or were they just dark daydreams of
futures that never came to pass?

Kasia gathered her courage and stepped through the next
doorway.

In this sweven, she was the Pontifex of Bal Kirith, ruling alongside her dissolute brother until Clavis came with an army of knights and killed them both.

In the next, Tessaria never found her and she ended up selling her Unmarked body in the streets of Novostopol.

There was one where she simply grew old and bitter, like her mother, and worked as a char at the Batavia Institute, where she saw a handsome priest from the Interfectorem sometimes but never dared to speak to him.

One where Natalya went to Dr. Massot's house on that fateful night and was murdered by him, and Kasia attended her funeral.

After the last, which ended standing over the grave, snotty and ravaged and sobbing hysterically, Kasia decided she'd had enough.

She stood in the damp, cold well, hugging herself with goosefleshed arms.

"No wonder I threw this shit down here. It's rubbish. All of it!"

Kasia took hold of the ladder and climbed out so fast she skinned her knuckles on the rock. When she reached the top, reached the light, she threw herself onto the grass and lay there for a minute, letting the rain wash her face.

"That was a stupid idea to go down there," she declared, liking the bright anger in her voice. "Stupid!"

The word echoed through the quiet Garden.

After a few minutes, she sat up and pulled herself together. Well, it did mean something—something beyond the obvious that those were all things she feared.

"I'm supposed to see beneath the surface," she muttered. "It's my one fogging talent in life. So let's look at them collectively. What do they have in common?"

Her own words came back to her.

Fortitude.

She'd been in the ship's hold with Nikola and Paarjini the

first time she drew the card, which had an image of a woman taming a lion. The energy of the unconscious mind.

To conquer our demons, we must venture beyond the ego. Sometimes into dangerous waters.

Again and again, Balaur had pushed her to claim her birthright as a mage. She had been so desperate to reject him that she had rejected part of herself, too.

Master of lies.

But oh, he was subtle, wasn't he?

"I'm only weaker because he convinced me it was true," she said softly. "For what is the ley if not a dream within a dream?"

She listened to the drone of insects, the hush of rain.

"I am tired of other people's labels," she muttered. "Marked and Unmarked. Nihilim and human. Good and evil. I think I will simply be myself from now on."

How empowering! Yet here she still was, trapped in her gilded cage.

She needed Malach, but what she'd told Nikola back at the inn was true—she had no idea how to bring another person into her dream.

Balaur knew how. He brought Rachel. Came himself whenever he felt like it.

It was possible.

She tried the obvious first—shouting Malach's name at the sky.

That didn't work and was also faintly embarrassing.

Kasia thought hard, all too aware that time was running out. She refused to consider the possibility that Balaur had won already. If Valmitra was dead, Kasia felt sure her Garden would be gone.

She would be gone.

The Serpent made the ley and, Balaur's delusions of grandeur aside, if she were dead there would be no more.

Yet the end was close. Kasia could feel it.

Then an idea came to her. She closed her eyes and pictured what she wanted, just as she had with the kittens. When she opened them, The Fool was resting precariously on the lip of the well. She snatched the card up before it fell in. Warmed it between her palms for a moment—because here they were still warm—and then held it up for scrutiny.

Yes, every detail looked right.

The little white dog nipping at his heels. The cliff and crashing waves. The Fool himself, sauntering along with a merry air, heedless of where he stepped—

Kasia leaned closer. "That's new," she said.

Instead of a cloth-wrapped bundle on a pole, a sword rested over his right shoulder.

Then she heard someone muttering down one of the paths.

Kasia hurried toward the sound, chin tucked against the downpour. Malach sat on a bench, a bewildered expression on his face.

He wasn't actually wearing the Fool's garb, which consisted of an old-fashioned green-and-yellow doublet with flowing, severely dagged sleeves over tight pantaloons and yellow boots.

Kasia would have paid good money to see *that*.

No, he wore a tan raincoat over a rumpled suit and tie. A briefcase sat between his polished black dress shoes. When he saw her, he jumped to his feet.

"Kasia!"

Malach ran up and crushed her to his chest. She hugged him back, surprised by the intense rush of affection. A short time ago, she had hated his guts. Not as much as Jule Danziger, but it was definitely hate.

How much we've both changed.

"I feared you were gone forever." He studied her face. "It is you, I hope?"

"It's me, Malach." She smoothed strands of wet hair back

from his forehead with a chuckle. It was short and parted on the right.

"What's so funny?" he demanded.

"You look just as you did when we first met. Like an accountant."

He seemed to notice the suit and tie for the first time. "Why am I like this?"

"Because this is a dream within a dream, and it is a memory of mine." She smoothed his lapels. "So Alexei found you."

Malach rubbed his jaw. "He did. In fact, he just punched me in the face. Really hard."

Kasia hadn't expected that—but it had worked.

"He only did it to bring you here, as I instructed him to do."

Malach looked alarmed. "Rachel. I left her there—"

"Alexei will watch over her," Kasia said gently. "He is the Knight. The Protector. He will guard her with his life, I can promise you that. But brother, we have bigger fish to catch."

She could see him struggling with this and plunged ahead before he tried to wake himself. "Listen to me, Malach."

"What?"

"Did Balaur drink the elixir?"

He blinked, focusing on her again. "The venom of a giant snake deity? Why, yes, he did."

"Venom?" She frowned. "So that's what it was . . ."

"Danziger drank it, too. It killed him. Fucking horribly, you'll be glad to know. Trust me when I say he won't be coming back."

Jule was dead. She savored the news for a moment, enjoying the warm glow, but Danziger was just a lapdog. It was his master she meant to destroy.

"What about Balaur? How did it affect him?"

It felt strange asking that question, because *her* lips had tasted the venom. It flowed through *her* veins now.

"Heshima tried to kill him," Malach replied. "The spell bounced right off. I think the bastard might really be immortal." His mouth set. "We're screwed. Utterly and without reservation."

"Maybe not."

"How so?"

"Because we can now meet the very specific conditions under which he *can* be killed."

Malach eyed her skeptically. "Conditions?"

"You don't know about Cathrynne Rowan's prophecy?"

He shook his head.

"It's all very peculiar," Kasia mused. "How could she have seen so far into the future? Yet it makes sense. Though I'm not sure—"

"The conditions," Malach said impatiently. "What are they? And how can we do anything to him when we're stuck here?"

Kasia tried to gather her thoughts. Her mind felt adrift, bobbing like a gull on a pretty blue sea.

Damnit. The same thing had happened to Rachel. A slow untethering.

Too much time outside one's body was not good for devising complex plots. Kasia ran her thumb along the crisp edge of the card, digging until it hurt.

Focus.

"It was on the *Wayfarer*. There was a storm. Valdrian compelled Jamila al-Jabban to confess and this is what she told us."

If not for her uncanny memory, the words of the prophesy would have been lost. But she managed to dredge them up and speak them in the proper order.

"That's it?" Malach frowned.

"That's it."

"Sounds like a children's rhyme."

"Nikola said the same."

"I suppose you have a plan."

Kasia nodded and briefly laid it out, feeling more alert now.

"Fair enough," he said when she was done. "But here's the problem. Even if we can exploit Balaur's weakness, make him mortal again, he's inside your body, Kasia. To kill him, we'd have to . . ." Malach trailed off. "Are you still anchored to it?"

She nodded. "By a thread, but I must be. If I weren't, all this," she waved a hand at their surroundings, "would not exist."

Malach sank to the bench again, holding his head in his hands. "Can you kick him out?"

"I will try." She gave a wry smile, though she felt afraid. "But if I fail, you must take the sword and use it on my body." She took his hand and pressed it to her chest. "Here."

Malach snatched his hand back. He stared at her. "You can't ask that of me!"

"One life for all the rest? It's simple math."

He snorted in exasperation. "You aren't just *one life*, Kasia. You're my sister! I lost you once already. I will *not* kill you—"

"What about Rachel, eh?" she pressed ruthlessly. "What about Nikola? Will you do it for them?"

His brows drew down. "Don't, Kasia. Don't make me choose."

"There's no choice to be made. It's my body, Malach. I get to decide—not you, understand?"

He eyed her mutinously.

"But I promise you that I'll do my best to draw him out," she added.

"How?"

"I'm not sure yet."

Malach was quiet for a long minute. "There's something I must tell you. I'm not sure it's true, but you deserve to know. Balaur claimed he was our father."

"I know. He told me himself."

Malach vented an angry breath. "Do you think he really is?"

"I *know* he is. It's how he stole Rachel. He said he needed his own bloodline to occupy a vessel." She sat down next to him on the bench. "But we can use our blood ties against him. You don't have any special ability related to dreams, but I do."

"This place."

"Yes. I kept Rachel here. It's real in some way, Malach." She sighed. "I denied my connection to Balaur because I hated him so much. Denied the legacy he gave me. But that's exactly what he wanted. It made me weaker. I must own this power if I am to wield it as he does."

"How can I help you, Kasia?" He searched her face. "Why did you bring me here?"

Kasia thought of The Fool, the leap of blind faith he represented.

"It began a long time ago. All the way back to the day Falke spared us both and our paths diverged. But they came together again, didn't they?"

"I am glad they did," he said hoarsely. "Not a day passed that I didn't think of you. It was a festering thorn in my heart."

She clasped his hand. "And not a day passed that I didn't wish for a family who loved me, and who I loved back."

She gazed at him, so earnest and unguarded, and understood that Falke was right. That's all Malach wanted, too. Then her thoughts got slippery again and she roped them back before they escaped into the rain.

"Listen to me, now," she said. "That lithomantic box dropped you exactly where you needed to be. I won't claim it was all fated. There are always choices that carry consequences. But you met the Blessed for a reason, Malach. To discover another part of yourself. And, perhaps, to be changed by it forever." She held his gaze. "Do you understand?"

He was quiet for a minute. "I think so. The prophecy—"

She touched a finger to his lips. "Don't speak of it again. It's ill luck. We know what must be done." She frowned. "There is only one part I am uncertain about, but we will discover the truth for ourselves when the time arrives."

"Which part?"

"The sword. *Anathema*." Kasia stood. "Now we must find a way out of the Garden and pray we are not too late." She tugged him to his feet. It felt natural to hold his hand, to stand shoulder to shoulder, his dark hair and hazel eyes a mirror of her own.

"I wish we had known each other when we were children," she said.

He squeezed her fingers. "So do I."

Together, they walked to the high wall, choked with ivy. Kasia tore the vines apart and laid her palm against the bricks. The clock stood at a minute to midnight, yet she felt strangely at peace. Comfortable in her own skin.

Ready to break this rusty cage wide open.

"Violet is the color of seven," she whispered, threads flowing from her fingertips, winding into the crevices. "Seven is a gate. Violet is a gate."

The wall shimmered before her. The outline of an arbor appeared, heavy with wild grapes.

I am a Dreamer. All doors open to me.

Pictures spun through her mind. A black-haired angel sounding a trumpet and the dead rising to heed his call.

In some decks, the seventh trump was called Judgment.

She turned to Malach. "Wait for me here. Watch and wait until you are needed."

"Take me with you."

Kasia shook her head. "I have already been unhoused from my body. I don't know what might happen if I dragged your spirit back to the living world with me. You might wake in your own body. Or you might die. We can't risk it."

He bit his lip, then hugged her one last time. "I'll be here."

Kasia followed a fine thread of awareness to her body on the earthly plane. For a moment, she had the sense of being in two places at once. Of a deep gulf falling away on all sides and a hot wind on her cheek.

The arbor shimmered with liminal ley.

Kasia stepped through.

Chapter Thirty-Six

Through the liminal archway, Kasia saw a circular chamber with open arches all the way around and a golden dome above. Wind-sculpted sands stretched to the horizon, now cloaked in an unsettling twilight. The Great Serpent lay coiled at the far edge, her two heads resting on the stone.

She was so still Kasia feared she was dead.

A figure stood over her, leaning on the sword of the Morning Star, which was propped point-down. Kasia glimpsed her own profile, half hidden by a veil of black hair.

Balaur was talking to Valmitra. A rambling, disjointed monologue about alchemy and the ley, his divine right to godhood, and why she must absolve him for murdering her. It was only then that Kasia realized—with no small measure of relief—that he had not yet done the deed.

Ley trickled from the snake's great jaws, ebbing and flowing with each breath. Her eyes—burnished gold with a large black pupil at the center—showed no sign of life, but the wound to her cheek had stopped bleeding venom. A single Ward etched into the stone blazed with a steady white light.

A dream within a dream . . .

KAT ROSS

"Mother," Balaur wailed in a self-pitying tone, tears streaming down his cheeks. "Forgive me. Forgive me!"

Kasia knuckled her forehead. The numbness was creeping over her again. He *was* mad. Did he believe himself to be Gavriel? Was it all some bizarre pantomime? Perhaps he was only play-acting—

But Balaur was raising the blade now. It glinted in the dying light.

The dying light . . .

Kasia peered out at the desert. The sun had gone queer, the sky dark in all the wrong places, and she remembered what she had told Rachel to do. Remembered why it was important.

I am only weak because he convinced me it was true.

And that is the secret of a good liar. You must believe the lie yourself.

Balaur had fallen for his own deceits. But his tricks were nothing but smoke and mirrors.

"Father!" she called.

He spun around and froze in surprise, then lowered the sword.

"What are you doing here?" he demanded.

Her jaw tightened. "Stopping you."

"You cannot escape the dream. It is impossible—"

Kasia gathered her will and tried to pass through the gate. It was like wading chest-deep against an inrushing tide. She leaned forward, straining, and managed to take a single step. Balaur laughed. The sound of her own mocking voice made Kasia furious.

"Look at you," he exclaimed. "You are nothing but a specter!"

Kasia glanced down. Her form was a frail shadow, the white stone of the tower clearly visible through her body.

"But I am flesh and blood," he crowed. "Far more than that. Watch!"

He drew the angel blade across one pale forearm, wincing

404

as it bit deep. Blood pattered to the floor, but the wound closed within seconds. He examined the unbroken skin, then held up the arm with a wide, manic grin.

"You see? Not even the mighty sword of the Morning Star can harm me!"

Balaur turned away, squinting up at the sky. The fiery corona was shrinking fast. Only a sliver remained. With no eyes to blind, Kasia was able to look at it directly, though Balaur shielded his gaze with a hand. They stood together in silence as totality arrived. A final dazzling flare . . . and then Luna threw her mantle across Sol's face, casting the tower into uncanny darkness.

"The Black Sun has risen," he crowed. "All is happening as it is meant to be. Even the heavens embrace my ascension! Kneel, Kasia. Kneel to your new god." Teeth bared. "Else I will end your exile with pain and fire. I will hunt you to your Garden and destroy it!"

Kasia looked at Valmitra's gleaming, gem-studded coils. Wounded and disoriented, the serpent had fled as far as she could. Then the Ward had entranced her again. She was helpless. If she died, the ley would die. Kasia knew it in her bones.

Fortitude. The lion tamer. Why had she drawn it over and over? The deeper meaning was not simply courage but honesty. Turn your back on the beast in yourself and it would grow ever more ravenous. She understood that the card was not just for her but for *him.* Balaur could not face his own fears —and in the end they devoured him.

"It is you who dreams now," she said. "Behold, Father."

She knelt and scooped Valmitra's breath into her palm.

I have the power to do anything I wish, she thought, willing herself to believe it. *That is fact.*

The stone firmed beneath her knees. Her hand looked a little more solid. For the first time, she felt a hot, dry wind on her brow.

"What are you doing, you stupid girl?" he snapped.

Kasia closed her fist with a flourish like a magician about to make a coin disappear. When she opened it, she held a card between her thumb and first finger.

"The Twins," she said, holding it out. "Take it."

Balaur's mouth worked as though he chewed something unpleasant. He took a step back.

"No?" She arched a brow. "I will show you then."

She'd drawn The Twins many times before. They were posed in a mirror image of each other with androgynous features and mismatched eyes, one blue, one hazel. No matter which way you held the card, one was upright, the other inverted.

Just like the turning of The Wheel. For one to win, the other must lose.

But now the image was different.

The top half was the High Priestess. She lounged on a throne of red roses, jet hair tumbling across her shoulders. A diadem circled her brow. Behind her, two pillars marked the entrance to a temple. One was white and one was black, symbolizing the polarities of masculine and feminine, light and dark.

The bottom half was a stooped old man standing in a dry riverbed. A forest of dead, skeletal trees lay in the distance, and the shattered ruin of a tower. One hand clutched a black-ened vial, the other a ring of keys. It wasn't his advanced age that made him disagreeable to look at but his temperament, which was stamped across his features. Small, cold eyes. Harsh lines of disappointment and bitterness bracketing his mouth.

Balaur scowled. "Put that away!"

"You don't like what you see?" She dropped the card. "All right."

It fluttered toward the ground—and stopped halfway. The card floated in midair for a moment. Then it grew bigger and bigger until it stood on end between them, life-sized. Balaur stared like a man gazing at his own reflection and seeing the first signs of a fatal disease.

"No," he growled. "It is false. An illusion like the rest!" He hefted the sword above his head. Ley shimmered along the razor-sharp edge. It reflected in the serpent's sightless eye. Then the sword slashed down in a vicious arc, severing the card in two.

The pieces fell away and faded to nothing. He was breathing hard, cheeks flushed.

"I have had enough of you," he said in a low voice. "You could have stayed hidden in your Garden, but you chose to interfere. I think Gavriel's sword can end you, daughter. Let us find out."

The tip found her throat, digging into the tender juncture of her jaw. Kasia's pulse beat swiftly against the steel. The sour taste of fear flooded her mouth.

Then the realization struck. *I have a heartbeat . . .*

Balaur made a terrible sound. The arm holding the blade trembled and sank as though it had grown unbearably heavy. His face began to melt. To change.

"It is impossible," he spluttered hoarsely.

Strength flowed into her. Kasia soaked it up like rain on a parched field.

"Nothing is impossible in dreams," she replied. "Rejoice. You are yourself again, Father."

This new incarnation was not the twinkly-eyed, silver-haired grandfather who used to haunt her Garden. Nor was it the distinguished middle-aged pontifex who strode confidently into the throne room at Nantwich. It was not even the man-hag from The Twins, which had been her artistic creation.

All were close, but this one's face was even crueler and emptier. Like the other versions of Balaur, his eyes were blue, but they held low cunning more than genuine intelligence. Sagging jowls pulled the corners of his mouth into a permanent scowl. He had the aspect of a miser who could never hoard enough coin. Of a tyrant who saw assassins behind every bush. A man who would die alone and unloved because he hated himself even more than he hated everyone else.

"The ley has given you your true form," Kasia said.

Balaur howled as she grabbed his bony arm and twisted the sword from his grasp. She tossed it through the arch of the trellis, then dragged him along toward the Garden.

"I am still immortal!" he shrieked. "Not you! Whatever body I have, I am still a god!"

"You think the Black Sun heralds your return," she panted, as he writhed and spat and kicked. "I foresee the opposite. It spells your doom."

She saw that he understood. Not all, but some. He was working through Cathrynne Rowan's prophecy, trying to find the flaw in his divinity, but he didn't believe it was over.

Not yet.

"Let us speak the words together," she said.

Balaur wrenched himself free. "No!"

Kasia caught the sleeve of his robe as he tried to flee, reeling him back. The eclipse was still in totality, a strange amalgam of dawn and dusk, but it wouldn't last long. Kasia had to hurry.

"*Not in the night or the day,*" she whispered.

The heady fragrance of grapevines met her nose as she hauled Balaur into the bower's arch.

"*Not inside or outside.*"

He clawed at her eyes. She grabbed his wrists. They struggled and grunted, rustling the leaves. She managed to pin his arms.

"*Not by Marked or Unmarked.*"

His gaze narrowed. "You are——"

"Neither," she panted, blowing a strand of hair from her face. "And both. My cards are my Marks. I am a mage." She said it without shame now. "But I am also officially Unmarked."

Balaur recoiled, gnashing his brown, broken teeth. "It matters not!" he screeched. "I cannot die!"

"*Not awake or asleep,*" she hissed.

The mist concealing the Garden dissolved. Here, in the liminal doorway, she smelled the rich loam of dirt. Heard the steady patter of rain and chirping of frogs. But Malach was nowhere to be seen. Doubt crept in. What if he'd woken too soon?

Then we're done for.

"Not by man or woman," she finished in a rush. "Not by a weapon or bare hands."

Balaur sneered. "There. It is over, Kasia. You lack the last two conditions! And now"—the mouth yawned into a dark cavern—"now you will die, daughter!"

Gray fog spilled out, wrapping around them both. It stank of acrid chemicals. Kasia saw the world under its new god. A place without birdsong or hope or green growing things. A place with pointless machines that ran all day and night, pumping sterile water from their pipes and leaden smoke from their chimneys.

And him roaming the wasteland of his own making, never pausing, half-deaf from the clamor and entirely insane.

But the mockery of ley that flowed from him had its own potency. Now it was Balaur who pinned *her* against the trellis, his rank breath in her face.

"I should have strangled you in the cradle," he hissed. "Should have strangled you both—"

He cut off as a faint but distinct sound drifted through the archway.

Stiletto heels crunching on gravel.

A figure approached from one of the paths, light and graceful like a dancer but with the prowling swagger of a caracal. Hair and brows black as a moonless night. Face bare of cosmetics and achingly beautiful. A dagger Mark ran down one bronzed, muscular arm, its tip brushing the third knuckle.

Not Lucy. Not Malach.

Both at once.

A liminal spirit who embodied the masculine and feminine in perfect harmony. Perfect union. Perfect balance.

Balaur stared. A muscle jumped in his cheek. *"You,"* he said with contempt as the figure sank to one knee in the downpour and grasped the hilt of Gavriel's sword. Long lacquered nails gleamed like droplets of blood in the stormlight.

"Go ahead," Balaur spat. "The terms are unambiguous. No weapon can hurt me—"

Kasia pulled herself free and stepped out of the way as the blade ran him through.

"It's cold," Balaur gasped with a note of surprise.

He tilted against the trellis. Then he sat heavily and gazed down in bewilderment.

"How did you know? How did you . . ."

The words were swallowed by a wracking, red cough.

"Because it had to be," Kasia said.

There would be no returning this time. All the potions and elixirs in the world couldn't save him from the noose of his own fate.

He gazed up at her, blue eyes filming over. "Why?"

The question did not strike her as some rhetorical lament. At the end, he wanted an answer.

How did I come so far, only to fail? Why can't I have what I want?

"Because a long time ago, a witch named Cathrynne Rowan saw you coming," Kasia said. "Or maybe Valmitra did, through her. I doubt we will never know the truth of it. But you took the bait she left and now the trap has snapped shut."

Balaur smiled through bloody lips. He raised his mutilated left hand in a salute—or a rude gesture. With the missing fingers, it was hard to tell.

"Well done," he croaked.

Then he lay down and died.

An instant later, the moon's umbral shadow swept onward. Kasia stepped from the trellis back into the white tower and ran to one of the open arches looking over the desert. A fiery crescent appeared, thin at first but brightening by the second, though the sky still had a queer cast.

When she looked back, the liminal gate to the Garden had vanished.

And strangest of all, the sword of the Morning Star was gone, too, leaving only the shaft of a single glossy black feather jutting from Balaur's chest.

Chapter Thirty-Seven

"Borosus!"

No answer came except for the rapid drumming of her heartbeat. Nikola tugged off her scarf and wiped the sweat from her brow. Then she crept up to the next landing and pressed against the curved stone wall.

"I'm sorry!" she shouted.

Flames shot down the staircase, scorching the stone. She swore under her breath. This was bad. Very bad.

"I want to talk!"

A long pause. "About what, Nikola Thorn?" came the furious reply. "You have come to kill the Mother!"

"No! I'm trying to save her. We're on the same side!"

"Then why did you attack me?"

"I was chasing after Balaur. I thought you were him!"

Another lengthy pause. "How do I know this is true?"

"Let us speak face to face. I'll come up. With my hands empty and palms raised."

No reply. She climbed the tight spiral steps, hoping he wouldn't roast her. Borosus stood where she'd left him, looking fierce and annoyed. He wore leather breeches and a golden breastplate etched with elaborate designs. His face was not human, not even close, but his eyes were very expressive.

Nikola stopped below the landing, showing him her open hands. If he wanted to kill her, she was well within range now. One blink and she'd be a greasy black smear. The Tooth of God regarded her stonily.

"Where did you come from?" she asked. "I didn't see you enter the tower."

"Through one of the platforms."

His tone indicated that this was a stupid question.

"How much do you know of what's happened?"

A forked tongue flicked out, tasting the air. "Only that the gates were finally unsealed," he replied. "The other Sinn é Maz are on their way."

"Well, Balaur has stolen another body. He drank the Mother's venom. I don't know if he *can* be killed now. She fled, wounded, and he pursued her." Nikola's gaze lifted to the tower's apex. "Up there, I think."

Slitted nostrils flared. "Why did you not say this first?!"

He spread his wings and leapt off the edge of the step, flying in a tight spiral up the hollow shaft of the tower. Nikola followed, leaping up the stairs two at a time. Around and around she went, following the curving wall. Here and there, tall, narrow doorways opened to half-moon platforms—the landing spaces Borosus mentioned, each only about a meter square and without railings. The soles of her feet prickled when she passed them. It was a long way down.

At last she burst into a round chamber with ornate archways all around and a domed cupola for a roof. Borosus knelt next to Valmitra.

"She lives," he said grimly. "Though as you said, she has been injured."

The hard lump of fear in Nikola's chest loosened. But then she spotted Kasia crouched over the body of an old man. Some new trick?

She fisted a projective stone but didn't dare use it. She wouldn't soon forget what had befallen Heshima.

"There he is!" Nikola pointed. "That's Balaur!"

Borosus flexed his talons. "Should I throw him over the edge?"

"Wait!" Kasia cried, backing away. "He's dead, truly this time. *That's* him!"

Nikola studied the body. She'd only seen the old Balaur once—just before she fried him to a crisp in Nantwich. This corpse *could* have been that man.

But she'd been lied to too many times, by too many people.

"Horseshit," she said angrily. "Balaur drank the venom. I saw it. Heshima tried to kill him and failed."

Borosus strode forward with a growl, steam drifting from his lips. The stone bubbled beneath his feet. Kasia pressed against one of the archways, eyes wide.

"Please," she whispered urgently. "I know what it looks like, but you must believe me . . ."

Nikola sensed white-hot flames gathering within the Sinn é Maz. Borosus opened his mouth. It was like an oven door swinging wide. Kasia flung an arm across her face. With a low curse, Nikola stepped between them.

"Get out of the way!" Borosus snapped.

"Now just hold on a minute," she said reasonably, though her heart still raced. "Balaur had the sword, but I don't see it now. And if it *was* him, why would he bother pretending?" She glanced at the Great Serpent. "Why would he have let Valmitra live? It's possible she's telling the truth, Borosus."

Kasia—if it *was* her—sank down next to the old man's body.

"Just look!" she urged. "The sword wasn't a sword at all. Cathrynne Rowan spelled it to look like one." She held Nikola's gaze. "You remember the prophecy. It was the final condition. Not with a weapon or by bare hands."

Nikola stepped forward for a closer look. She'd assumed the object buried in the man's chest was an ebony-hilted knife, but it was actually . . .

"A feather," Kasia said, pulling it out with a grimace and holding it up for them both to see. "One of Gavriel's, I imagine."

She flicked it and the blood rolled off like pond water from a mallard. Then she turned the feather this way and that, revealing the faint iridescence in its barbs. It was about the length of her forearm. An exquisite thing, like starlight on a still pool. Nikola could only imagine what the sweep of the full wing would look like.

"That is truth," Borosus said grudgingly. "The Morning Star was created from one of the Mother's scales. Every part of him held a spark of divinity. It is how he made a weapon against her."

Nikola regarded the body again. The muscles of the face had slackened, but there was no peace; just bitterness and disappointment, which didn't surprise her. Overall, Balaur looked pretty damned dead, yet part of her expected him to sit up and start laughing at them.

Or it was all a ruse.

"Go sit over there," she said to Kasia, pointing to an out of the way spot. "And be quiet. If you do anything at all, we'll have trouble."

Kasia nodded meekly. "There is one more thing. I don't have the power to break the last Ward. A witch made it. I think only a witch can unmake it."

Borosus inclined his head. "That is also truth."

Nikola plopped down on the ground and emptied her pockets of the gems she'd gathered, including Heshima's namestone, arranging them in groups. Then she closed her eyes, cradled a chunk of receptive green jasper, and set about tracing the complex weavings of the Rowan's Ward. It was like a tangled ball of yarn—one the size of a hill. She tugged here and there, hoping to find a loose thread, but her efforts only tightened the knots of power.

"This thing is diabolical," she muttered. "Beyond anything I was ever taught. Beyond anything I ever *imagined*."

"Keep trying," Borosus said.

There was an edge to his voice. Nikola felt it, too. A turbulence in the ley. She eyed Valmitra, then yelped as the serpent constricted her coils with a sibilant hiss. But the golden eyes were as blank and empty as ever. After a moment, her two heads lowered to the ground again.

"She is having a nightmare," Kasia said.

"I told you to be quiet!"

A defiant glare. "I am not Balaur. But I warn you, the injury he dealt her disrupted her slumber and sent her mind to dark realms. If she is not woken soon, she could unmake everything. Tear apart the very fabric of the universe—"

"Enough," Borosus snapped.

Kasia drew her knees up, staring out at the desert.

Yet Borosus did not deny that such a thing was possible.

Worrisome.

Nikola burned through the stones one after the other. She tried projective magic, receptive magic, combinations of the two. She used the last spark of ley from Heshima's bloodstone, which was supposed to open doors and break bonds.

Nothing.

The spell was impenetrable. She finally opened her eyes with a grunt of frustration, staring up at the Wards running in a circle around the cupola. All but this one were already dead, just etchings in the stone. Could they be letters? Or even words?

"What language is that?" she asked Borosus.

"Seraphic. The tongue of the angels."

"Can you read it?"

"Of course."

Nikola banged a fist on her thigh. "I'm a fool for not asking sooner. What does it say?"

"It says, *Follow the labyrinth to its heart.*"

She frowned. "That what's Malach told me. He said Cathrynne Rowan left a sweven in the sword. That she seemed to speak to him directly. I wonder if she wanted this spell to be broken someday?"

Borosus stalked over, his leathers creaking. "Cathrynne was always mercurial. Anything is possible." He glanced at Kasia. "But that person is right. You must break it soon. There is also trouble at Mount Meru. The place you call Sinjali's Lance." He waved a taloned hand. The air shimmered. For a moment, Nikola saw her own face reflected in a smoky mirror. Then the view changed. The Pontifex Lezarius appeared, along with Dmitry Falke and a dark-skinned young woman with a cap of short curls. Clavis?

And a group of pale children.

"That's Will Danziger," Kasia exclaimed. "And the other Reborn!"

Will looked straight at Nikola. His lips moved soundlessly. *Help us!*

A dozen knights in the Wolf tabards of Kvengard were desperately trying to hold a door. It splintered as Nikola watched. A sword cut through, slicing away a chunk of wood. One yellow eye with a vertical slit for a pupil peered through.

"Is that real?" she asked, fearing the answer.

"Yes," Borosus said grimly. "They've been pushed back to the top of the Lance. I can aid them if you break the last Ward. Mount Meru was the seat of Valmitra's palace. It has portals that open directly to all the towers of the Seraphim, including this one."

The door was buckling in its frame now. The knights backed up and drew their blades, giving themselves room to defend.

Nikola gripped her serpent's eye namestone. It radiated

heat and life. If she had to use up the last drop of power in it to wake the Mother, she would. It would cost her life, but that is what being a *laoch* meant. A guardian witch.

She gathered her courage. It must be why Valmitra had given her the rarest of all gemstones. The serpent's eye would be strong enough to break the Ward.

Tears stung her eyes as she thought of Malach and Rachel.

"I'm sorry," she whispered, then stilled her mind to open the floodgates of power—

A hand fell on her shoulder. Nikola startled. She hadn't heard anyone approach and when she saw who it was, she took a quick step back.

"Bicycle," Kasia said, her pupils large and dark.

"What?"

"There's another way. Don't you remember?"

Bicycle? What the fog—

Then it hit her.

The accident. Nikola used to ride a rusty old six-speed to work at the Arx, careening through the rain-soaked alleys of Novostopol without a helmet because she couldn't afford one (or, more accurately, because she spent all her extra wages at bars). Then one day a delivery driver opened his door right into her face. She braked hard and went over the handlebars. She'd lost a tooth, but at least she hadn't cracked her skull open.

The replacement was silver. Water element, associated with the moon and dreams. With the goddess of night. With healing and protection.

She thought she heard the Rowan's wicked laughter.

This was not a spell to be unravelled. There was no path through the maze. No way to outwit it.

How simple the answer was in the end. One had to cut to the heart of the matter.

Her upper lip went cold around the silver incisor. The

tower began to revolve—very slowly. She heard other sounds now. Guttural, wordless shouts.

Nikola held the glyph in her mind's eye. She shaped the tiny bit of ley inside her tooth into the illusion of a pair of silver scissors and snapped them straight through the spell.

The last Ward pulsed once and went out.

For a moment, nothing happened.

Then the Great Serpent uncoiled. The golden cupola exploded as she smashed through the top of the tower. Thick, scaled legs sprang from her body. She leapt into the air, which turned thick as jelly.

Nikola's feet left the ground. She floated up into the debris, heart thumping. The deck of cards she'd taken from Heshima fanned out in a bright spiral.

The Empress. The Fool. The Star. The High Priestess. The Knight.

All seventy-two cards, drifting like bits of pollen. Kasia was weightless, too, her body tracing a lazy upside-down arc, long hair fanning out as though she swam in an invisible current.

"Borosus!" Nikola cried in a choked voice. "Help!"

He ignored her, launching himself into the white sky. Up and up he soared, until he was just a speck.

The cards spun like dry leaves in a whirlwind, faster and faster.

So did the two women.

Nikola reached out and managed to clasp Kasia's fingers as they passed. They clung to each other like children on a merry-go-round.

"Is it really you?" Nikola screamed over the gale.

"Yes! It's me!"

An icy wind laden with fat, wet snowflakes poured through the broken archways of the cupola. The vortex of power built and built. Kasia shouted something, but the howling storm snatched it away.

"What?" Nikola mouthed.

Kasia gripped Nikola's cloak and hauled herself closer. She snatched something from the air and held it up. Nikola stared, her gut cinching tight.

The last card of the game was about to be played.

A STINGING in his jaw hauled Malach back to consciousness. He was lying on his back in the shadow of the white tower. Far greater agony in his leg swiftly followed. Alexei peered down at him, blue eyes dark with worry.

Malach caught his wrist mid-swing. "I'm awake," he growled. "You can stop slapping the shit out of me."

"Did you find her? Tell me she's alive!"

Rachel stood nearby, regarding them both with a solemn expression.

"I already told him Kasia was all right now," she said, brow notching as she gazed up at the tower. "I also told him he had to bring you back. He was afraid to, in case she still needed you, but I felt grandpapa die."

The sudden hope in Alexei's face was painful to see. "Is it true?"

Malach remembered the look in Balaur's eye as the sword ran him through. As he sat bleeding out in the rain, half in the world and half in Kasia's Garden, caught in the cage of his own body with no escape this time. How she'd managed to divide them, he had no idea.

But he'd recognized the creature behind the mask, Malach knew him now, and the old man who had fallen at his feet was the same who had taken his daughter, who had taken his sister—

"Malach!" Alexei was shaking him now. "Is it true?"

He smiled. "Kasia is alive. Balaur is dead. We won, priest."

Alexei briefly closed his eyes, face flooding with relief. "Where is she?"

Malach craned his neck, following the stark lines of the white tower to its apex. "I think she's up there. I could see a little through the gateway she made. The other side was high up, desert and sky."

By the time Malach said "up there," Alexei was already on his feet and running. "I'm going after her," he called over his shoulder.

He was nearly at the yawning black gap of the doors when Rachel caught up and seized his hand, forcing him to stop.

"We have to leave," she said. "Right now."

The first tremors started an instant later. Malach had been through an earthquake in the Morho once. The ground shook hard enough to uproot century-old trees. This was more like a steady humming vibration through the soles of his feet. The sands around the tower shivered, as if some great wyrm delved beneath them.

"What's happening, Rachel?" he called.

She seemed to know more than anyone.

She chewed her lower lip and dragged Alexei away from the door. The priest walked backward, head tilted up, a worried look on his face.

"I'm not sure, Malach." She sank down at his side. "But do you see it?"

Grubby fingers took hold of his chin, turning his head. The tower was splitting into two—one white, one black. The images wavered like river stones viewed through a swift current.

"Yes," he said softly. "I see it."

Then it got even weirder. One instant, the towers seemed near. The next, they receded into the distance, as if you'd flipped a pair of field glasses around and looked through them the wrong way. Malach swallowed queasily.

Flip.

The towers sped close again.

That's when he saw things swarming up the black one. They were using fingers and toes to find cracks in the stone. Marks covered their pale, naked flesh.

Perditae.

"Papa." Rachel's voice was barely audible. "I'm scared."

"Alexei!"

The priest turned.

"You need to take my daughter away from here. Now!"

"We're not leaving you," he replied stubbornly. He got an arm around Malach's waist and hoisted him to standing. The pain that shot through his leg was so bad he almost fainted. Everything dimmed. He bit the inside of his cheek until he tasted blood. Tried to focus on what was happening.

"That's Sinjali's Lance," Alexei said, eyeing the black tower. "I've seen it a hundred times. Though I can't say how the hell it just traveled a thousand kilometers."

"Maybe it's an illusion," Malach mumbled, hoping the words were true. "The magic finally tearing itself apart."

"Either way, she's right. We can't stay."

Alexei supported him as he hopped along with gritted teeth. They were nearly to the trembling mule when the sky tore open. A bolt of lightning speared down, forking to strike both towers. The Perditae had no time to scream. If they did, it was drowned out by the simultaneous thunderclaps.

Malach squinted. There was only one tower now. A fine ash swirled around it—the remains of the Perditae. The golden dome was gone. Lightning stabbed down again. The crack of thunder was so loud this time, he thought his ears might be bleeding. A second later, two figures were forcibly ejected from the top. They plummeted down headfirst, arms and legs flailing wildly.

Even half-blind, he knew them.

Time slowed. Rachel struggled to take his weight as Alexei

dropped him and ran back. Malach sagged against her. The pain gave him clarity, a sudden horrified recognition.

He'd seen this before—this exact same image—in Kasia's cards.

The godstruck Tower.

Chapter Thirty-Eight

The twittering of birds pulled Morvana from a fitful sleep. She sat up in the gray light of morning, stiff, chilled—and alone.

They'd hiked through the woods until Mikhail stopped at a vale buried in deep drifts. He dug a cave into a snowbank and lined it with pine boughs that he sawed off with his belt knife. By that point, she could no longer feel her hands or feet. Jalghuth was frigid during the day, but by the wee hours of the night, the air took on a dense, liquid quality that seeped through every layer of clothing.

Without a word, he'd unbuckled his armor, tossing it aside. Then he pulled her into his lap and wrapped his cloak around them both. Her shivering had abated at once. Some distant part of her knew that the ferocious heat of his body, like a bed of banked coals, signaled something amiss. But she was past caring. She snuggled into the warm embrace and drifted off with her head on his shoulder, the rough tickle of his beard against her forehead.

Now she was freezing again. She forced her stiffened limbs to move and crawled out, hands sticky with sap. Lizzie Brown greeted her with a snort, nosing at the snow where a few scattered grain pellets remained. He must have found some in the saddlebag and fed her breakfast before he left.

The skies were overcast, but it hadn't snowed again. A clear line of hoof prints led away from the makeshift camp. She relieved herself next to a tree, gooseflesh prickling her thighs. Did he go off to scout? Somehow that didn't feel right. His armor still sat there. And the man she knew wouldn't leave her alone—not with the chance of Perditae close by. Morvana felt a stab of apprehension as she saddled Lizzie and rode into the woods, following his trail.

Misha had taken a winding path up the shoulder of the mountain. As she climbed higher, dense fog enveloped the terrain, dampening her cloak. What was he looking for? A vantage point? It seemed unlikely. The whole mountain was socked in by clouds. The tree line fell away, replaced by ice-clad crags. At last the trail ended on a wide ledge. A dark silhouette stood at the far end. Lizzie greeted his charger with a soft nicker, trotting to its side. Morvana dismounted.

"Go back," he said, without turning. "I'm not safe."

His voice sounded strange. Harsh and rough.

"I don't believe that."

She approached him slowly. Was he changing, like the others? Is that what Will had foreseen? The thought was too awful to contemplate.

"Just go!" he repeated.

Misha turned to face her and a knot loosened in her chest. His eyes were as she remembered. A crystalline blue, though full of anguish.

"You are not this Mark," she said calmly. "It is a part of you but not all. Not even most."

He wearily shook his head. "You know nothing about me."

"I think I do." She took another step. "Why is he blind-folded? What is it that he cannot bear to look at?"

Again, Misha shook his head, a desperate denial.

"Just tell me," she said firmly.

In one swift, fluid motion, Mikhail yanked a knife from his belt. He closed the distance between them in four long strides. She fought the urge to run. He would never hurt her.

Mikhail thrust the knife into her hand, forcing her fingers closed around the hilt.

"Kill me," he growled. "Please, I'm begging you. I . . . I don't have the courage."

She looked down at the blade. "No."

He made a low sound, like a wounded animal. "I'm a murderer," he spat.

She remembered the coin she'd taken from Alexei when he turned up at Kvengard. His brother's name on one side, a motto on the other.

Foras admonitio. Without warning.

Morvana had despised the Beatus Laqueo. Despised Falke for creating them. A paramilitary force answerable only to itself, the order's very existence was an affront to the values of the *Meliora.* But she knew now that most of them were just boys, convinced they were all that stood between civilization and chaos. Had Misha committed some atrocity in the name of the Via Sancta?

Whatever he'd done, his mind was scarred and the Night-mark made it immeasurably worse. She knew he wouldn't listen to reason. He was beyond that point now. At the brink, Will had said. But there might be a way to reach him.

"Give me the sweven," she said. "Whatever it is. Let me judge you myself. Then, if I believe you deserve to die, I will help you do it." She touched the Wolf on her neck. "I swear by the ley."

He looked surprised—and afraid. "The Chariot of Justice," he whispered.

It was one of her Marks. "You remember," she said with a crooked smile.

"Of course I remember." He raked a hand through his

hair, somewhat calmer now. "I was a bastard to make you strip like that."

"You thought I had something to do with your brother's disappearance," she said evenly. "I have already forgiven it."

"Kasia Novak saw this," he admitted. "Before we left, she gave me a reading. I drew four cards. The Tower and the Pole Star. That meant north. The Wheel. She said it meant destiny." He drew a shallow breath. "And the Chariot of Justice. *You*."

Morvana swallowed. "That is . . . interesting."

"I tried to stay away from you." His voice was hollow. "But you're very persistent."

"It is one of my traits," she agreed.

The darkness crept back into his eyes. "If I agree, will you keep your word, Morvana?"

"I always do," she replied gravely. "Now, will you show me this wound you carry?"

He hesitated, then held out his hand. She twined their fingers together. His skin blazed like a furnace, sending waves of heat straight up her arm to the shoulder.

"Ready?" he whispered.

An eerie serenity came over his features. A surrender to the final reckoning.

She steeled herself. "Yes."

"BE a love and hand me my lighter, Mickey."

She's the only one who calls you that. You like the way she says it, in her crisp Nantwich accent.

"Sure, Mum." Your brother calls her *mama*, but he's practically a baby. You're ten, three years older, and growing like a weed. Sometimes she jokes that she won't buy you any more shoes or pants until you stop because you're bankrupting her.

That she'll make you run around barefoot in underwear until you're sixteen.

You fetch her lighter from the pocket of her beige raincoat and flick the wheel, feeling like a gentleman as you light the cigarette for her. Snap it shut and set it on her desk, which is deep in papers, like drifts of autumn leaves.

"How's the case going?"

"I have a court appearance in the morning." She exhales smoke and pushes her glasses up. "A motion to dismiss. We'll see."

She knows you're only asking to be polite. Alyosha is the one who's bent on being an attorney. He's always reading her law books, which are boring beyond belief. You like books, too, but the ones on philosophy. Faith and morality. Big ideas you can sink your teeth into.

"Do you like the new tutor?" she asks.

You shrug. "He's okay. I like learning the Old Tongue. It's logical. More than Osterlish."

She coughs. It usually stops after a moment, but this time she keeps going. An awful hacking sound. She covers her mouth with a hand, shoulders hunched forward, and when she takes it away, there's a crimson smear. You stare at it, mind going blank. She blots it on a handkerchief and smiles.

"It's fine, Mickey. Just . . ." She trails off and smiles. "Don't worry."

You wonder how she can say that. "What's wrong, Mum?"

"Nothing." She clears her throat and casts a wry look at the overflowing ashtray on her desk. "I should quit, is what."

She says that all the time, but she never does.

"Maybe you should see a doctor," you venture.

Mum frowns. "You're right," she replies absently, turning back to the papers. "I'll do that."

But she doesn't. You hear her arguing with your father about it, muffled voices in the bedroom. It's nine more months before she gets around to it, and by then her face looks very thin and she's coughing all the time. Getting headaches so bad she can't go to court.

You watch through the window as she gets out of the car, searching for some sign of what the doctor said, but she looks the same, not crying or anything, so you're sure it's a problem they can fix. She's young, only thirty-three. It can't be too bad.

You're hopeful when she comes inside and sits you down. Not your brother, just you. Which, in hindsight, should have given it away right there.

Because it is bad. As bad as it gets.

"Don't tell Alex," she says.

"I won't," you promise.

Because you'll do anything she wants you to do. Of course you will.

You don't know when she tells your father, not the exact moment, but after that he's hardly ever home. He wasn't around much before, but he practically moves into his big corner office at the bank. He knows you know so he doesn't bother with the talk. Your brother is the only clueless one, though Alex isn't stupid, not by a long shot, so you have to tell him something.

What you tell him is that she's sick, but she's going to get better.

When you ask Mum why your father is absent, she sighs and says he's in something called denial. That he loves her too much so it's very hard for him, and try to give him a break.

You don't find this answer to be acceptable. Not at all. If you love someone, you don't just abandon them.

So you do your Old Tongue lessons, and your maths, and you run the path around the wooded estate in Arbot Hills that's been in the Bryce family for generations. You run it ten times every morning, even when it's pouring, which it usually is. You get your first Mark and you beg the ley to save her.

But she only gets sicker. The worst part isn't even looking

at her, it's the pain. Burrowing into her bones like a sharp-toothed little animal that never sleeps.

In defiance of your father, you convince her to dismiss the nurse and take all that over. The pill regimen. Changing bloody sheets. Reading books and playing cards. Coaxing her to eat. Just keeping her company. You even sneak off and buy her favorite brand of cigarettes at the kiosk by the tram stop and light them for her. Because what difference does it make now? None.

You want to punish him. Make him feel guilty. If this strategy works, he shows no sign of it.

The pills are the only thing that help. Once, you steal one and swallow it, just to see what it does. It makes you nauseous and you don't do it again.

She's allowed two in the morning, two at night. Twelve hours apart. You set your new birthday watch for it.

And then the day comes, almost exactly two years after the diagnosis, when she looks at you and asks for more pills.

"But you had some . . ." A glance at the time. "Twenty minutes ago. The doctor said—"

"The doctor isn't here." Grayish sweat slicks her forehead. "He'll never know, Mickey."

So you give her two more. An hour later, more again. It seems to help. She's high as a cloud now, her pupils tiny pinpricks. When she asks you to please just hand her the bottle, you know what she's doing, no denying it now, but a recklessness takes hold of you and you say okay, Mum. You give her the bottle, and you refill her water glass, and you watch as she takes them all, one after the other.

What happens next isn't pretty, but you can't leave her alone, not for this, so you hold her and do what you can. Then it gets better. She's not in pain anymore.

You sit there, knowing you should feel something more than relief that it's finally over, that you should feel grief, but you don't. All you feel is an exhaustion so deep you can't even go fetch anyone.

Which is why you're still sitting there when your father comes home. It must be late. You hear his car outside, and then you hear the front door slam. His footsteps coming up the stairs. You realize you should cover your tracks. Hide in your room and pretend to be sleeping. Pretend you weren't there. Had nothing to do with it.

But you don't. You want him to find you. To know what he left you to do, all alone, just like you did everything else. You want him to hate you as much as you hate him.

The door opens. He sees her and he sees the empty bottle of pills, which you set next to the water glass. Sees the dried vomit on the pillow.

He makes a terrible sound. Then he's shaking you so hard your head whips back and forth and your brain rolls around in your skull like a loose marble.

"What have you done to her, boy? What have you done?"

Well, it's obvious what you've done. You don't say a single word, which makes him even angrier. He sends you away, to your bedroom, and you hear his hoarse, wracking sobs, the first time he's wept since the whole thing. But you still don't cry. Not until the funeral a week later, when everyone is talking about how great she was and it's impossible not to.

Neither of you speak of it again. Your father makes the situation go away. He's good at that. Cleaning up messes. He tells everyone that she died peacefully in her sleep, of natural causes, but you both know better.

You killed your own mother.

And no matter what you do, he will never, ever forgive you for that.

THE SWEVEN FADED. Morvana stared into space, her own cheeks wet with tears. Two years compressed into . . . how much time? The sea of mist over the valley had thinned enough to make out the tops of the tallest firs poking out, but it was still early morning.

She'd watched the first scraggly hairs sprout on his chin, felt the boyish crush he had on one of the maids, watched him race his brother through the woods, open Caristia presents.

And, like a black fog hanging over each day, she'd watched a beautiful, brilliant, funny young woman slowly waste away.

Misha had pulled his hand back. He watched her face, utterly still.

"Does Alexei know?" she managed.

He shook his head. "No one else. Just us two. Three, now."

She nodded, unsurprised, and took a moment to gather her thoughts. "I've always believed that there was a virtue missing from the five we vow to uphold. Can you guess what it is?"

He mutely shook his head.

"Name them for me."

A sigh. "Compassion. Courage, fidelity, and honesty." His voice roughened. "Forgiveness."

"You've honored them all, except for the last. But you forgot one other virtue. *Mercy*. So here is my judgment. If it had been me, I would have done the same." She clasped his hand again. "You did *not* kill her. The cancer did that. You set her free."

The wind rose, tugging at his black hair. For a moment, his expression softened and she thought she might have reached him, but then he gave a convulsive shiver and listed to one side. She caught his weight, barely managing to keep them both from falling. Lizzie neighed in alarm. Morvana knees buckled, but she managed to heave them both away from the edge and into a snowbank.

Shudders wracked his frame. "C-cold," he stammered.

She pulled him close, hugging his wide back. He murmured something too low to hear. She cast about for some kind of shelter, but they were too high up. It was only his feverish heat that had kept them both alive through the night. Whatever was happening to him now, he was in no state to walk.

Not that they had anywhere to go.

The real possibility that they would both die on this mountain hit her then. The Lance was besieged. No one knew where they had gone. She had no fuel for a fire, no matches to light it. No food or water.

Perhaps it was the lack of oxygen, but none of that dismayed her as it should have. Her mind felt clear. She had no regrets at following him into the heights of the Sundar Kush. Kasia had seen it in the ley. This was meant to be.

"They say freezing to death is peaceful," she said, her own teeth chattering now. "I just f-f-feel sorry for the horses."

Misha didn't respond. He'd lapsed into unconsciousness. Yet his heart beat against her chest, still strong.

Time passed. The mist burned away and the valley spread out below. From her vantage in the snowbank, she could see a slice of Lake Khotang, stippled with bergs and already dull with a new sheen of ice. The green sweep of the Morho beyond and, off to the right, a haze of woodsmoke over Jalghuth. Even the very top of Sinjali's Lance.

How strange, she thought. *It looks almost like ...*

Morvana blinked, expecting the optical illusion to vanish. It didn't.

Like a serpent is coiled about the tower.

The sun came out. It gave no real warmth, but she relished it on her face nonetheless. When she saw something launch itself into the air from one of the tower's ramparts, she knew for certain that her mind was starting to slip. Golden wings gleamed in the sunlight as it swept in circles over the peaks.

"Misha," she whispered, when it didn't vanish. Her body no longer bothered to shiver and his name came out clear as a bell.

To her surprise, he roused enough to turn his head.

"I see something."

He licked cracked lips. "What?"

"I don't know."

His head sank to her breast again. She watched the slow, steady sweep of wings and realized it was larger than she thought. She had the idea that they should hide, for the thing was clearly hunting.

She looked at the horses. They were stamping their hooves, but they hadn't bolted. Each pass brought it closer. Then it spiraled into a dive, a streak of burnished gold, straight for the rocky ledge, landing in a flurry of snow. The wings folded against its back. It stalked forward.

She stared into a set of alien eyes, doing her best to shield Misha.

A waking nightmare. That's all.

"If you're going to eat me," she heard herself say, "go ahead. But I warn you, I'll make a cold meal."

It stooped. The thing smelled like burnt metal.

"I am Borosus." Its gaze flicked to Misha. "This is the one I was sent to find."

Borosus? The name rang a distant bell.

"Sent by whom?" Morvana asked.

"The Kal Naz. The Heart of God." The creature's thin lips parted in a smile. "You call them the Reborn."

Chapter Thirty-Nine

The cell was six paces long and two wide—roughly the same proportions as a coffin. Beads of damp bled from the age-darkened stone.

"We have to get out of here before Hanne Danziger comes back," Natalya muttered. She paused to brace a hand against the wall, fighting a bout of nausea. It wasn't as bad as when she first woke up. That was like the worst hangover she'd ever had—times ten.

Faint torchlight played across Patryk's weary face. He leaned back against the bars, thick arms crossed. "No argument from me. Any ideas? 'Cause I'm all out."

They'd already tried using the ley to escape, but it was muffled down here, just a ghostly glow that faded the instant they tried to touch it. Something to do with whatever nasty drug Hanne had given them all.

"Cairness?" Natalya whispered.

A shadow shifted closer in the opposite cell, revealing the ginger-haired witch.

"Aye," she replied.

"No luck with a spell, I suppose?"

"They stripped me of everythin'," she replied grimly. "I

tried usin' the iron bars. They ought to have some projective power, and healin' magic, as well. It might've helped a bit. I'm not as bad as I was. But the ley is still slippery as a buttered eel when I try to catch hold o' it."

"Valdrian?"

The mage's cell was further down the row, out of view. "I can barely see it at all," he said thickly. "But I'll try again . . ." A few seconds passed. Natalya heard a vile retching sound.

"Hanne," she muttered. Then, louder: "It's okay, Val. Don't keep at it, there's no bloody point."

"At least we're all alive," Patryk said. "That's something."

"Poor Tashtemir."

"Do you think he—"

"Don't even say it. Maybe Merat can find a way to help him." She sighed. "What do you think happened to Kasia and Paarjini?"

"Maybe they got the keys."

"I don't think so. Those bastards knew what we were up to—"

"Someone's coming," Valdrian hissed.

Light footsteps approached along the corridor. At least it wasn't Fat Yagbu—the man moved like a landslide. She shared a glance with Patryk. Of course, the Imperator's torturer was probably busy with Tashtemir right now.

Natalya immediately regretted the thought.

It must be Hanne Danziger, come to take them away to her private laboratory so she could pump them full of poisons and potions and steal their bodies—or just the parts she fancied.

All in all, Natalya preferred Fat Yagbu.

The footsteps stopped. Caralexa stepped into the torchlight. The ley-forsaken bitch who had betrayed them.

Cairness started to curse loudly in Athaaran. Caralexa ignored her, stopping in front of Valdrian's cell.

Natalya heard whispering. She glared at the witch, motioning for her to shut up. Cairness curled her fingers around the bars, gripping them white-knuckled as though they were the mage's throat. She finally took the hint and quieted down. Natalya listened intently, but Caralexa had stopped talking.

Then she heard the click of a key in a lock.

Valdrian's cell swung open. His blond beard was dark with dried blood. They'd all fought hard when they were taken by the khedive's guards, but Valdrian got the worst of it. His clothes were torn and stained. The spring-blade he wore strapped to his forearm had been seized, along with the leather cap he wore over the puckered stump of his right wrist. His face was bruised and swollen.

But the worst part was his eyes. They were cold as a widow's bed on a winter night.

"You were in on it, too?" Patryk demanded, voice cracking with rage.

Valdrian crossed his arms and stared back. Caralexa finally answered.

"The three of you'll be dead soon enough so I suppose it hardly matters. No, he didn't know that I was reporting to Balaur." She slipped the keys to the cell back into her cloak. "But he's my cousin. I had to give him a chance to choose the right side."

She smiled. "And he did. Balaur has everything he needs to become a god. The others—Malach, Nikola, Kasia, that dumb priest—they're all finished." She shook her head in wonder. "Did you really think I'd betray my own? You and me —we're enemies and we always will be."

The purple-haired mage turned to Cairness. "Hanne plans to take you apart piece by piece, bitch. Dig into that pea-sized brain with a fucking fork. I doubt she'll find anything much, but it should be entertaining. And I'll be standing there, watching."

Behind her, Valdrian caught Natalya's eye and gave the barest nod.

"So you communicated with Balaur in dreams?" Natalya asked quickly, trying to hold Caralexa's attention.

"That's right. I threw away the stone you gave me to keep him out. I was reporting to him the whole time." A dry chuckle. Valdrian took a step closer, moving on the balls of his feet. "Balaur could have had you all arrested the moment we arrived, but he's smart. He saw a way to use you——"

She spun just as Valdrian lunged. He tried to grab her in a headlock. They slammed against the bars, grunting and struggling. He clawed through the folds of her cloak for the dagger sheathed at her belt. She twisted away, kneeing him between the legs. Valdrian collapsed. Caralexa dropped to a straddle on top of him, the dagger in one hand, her other hand pinning his good arm.

She looked off to the left, down the corridor. "Help me!" she yelled. "Get your asses over here!"

Both Natalya and Patryk mushed their faces against the bars, trying to see. Shadows shifted . . . and two smaller, hooded figures emerged from the gloom. The kids.

"Shoot him!" Caralexa screamed, as Valdrian bucked beneath her. "Do as I say, *now*! You'll be fucking royalty. You'll own the world!"

The children looked from her to Valdrian. "Don't," he choked out.

Caralexa's knee pinned one of his arms. His good hand gripped her wrist, trying to keep the dagger from his face, but it trembled, slowly weakening.

"Shoot!" Caralexa shrieked. "Or I'll beat the living shit out of you both!"

Sydonie unshouldered her bow. She nocked an arrow to the string, eyes dark and unreadable as she glanced at Tristhus.

"Yes, cousin," she said.

The arrow released with a soft *thwump*. It flew true . . . hissing past the cells and piercing Caralexa's throat. She flew back with a wet, crackling noise. Sydonie strode up and crouched over her, face set in a scowl. A moment later, Alice bounded down the tunnel and stood over the dying mage, barking fiercely.

"You shouldn't have tried to hurt Malach and Nikola," Sydonie said tightly. "You shouldn't have tried to hurt any of them! They're our friends." Her mouth twisted in anger and grief. "Why couldn't you see that?"

Caralexa's fingers spasmed. They closed around the dagger, which had fallen next to her. Natalya opened her mouth to shout a warning when Valdrian knocked the knife away.

"You're the one who chose the wrong side, Lexa," he growled, yanking the arrow from her throat.

Blood pumped in spurts from the unstoppered wound. Caralexa was gone within seconds, half-open eyes glazing.

"She's got the keys," Natalya said, grasping the bars. "In her pocket."

Tristhus quickly found them and unlocked the cells, while his sister helped Valdrian to his feet. They clung together for a moment and though he was fair-haired and Sydonie dark, the two resembled each other. *Comely angel bloodlines*, Natalya thought, wishing she could paint them someday.

"How did you find us?" Patryk asked, clapping a broad hand on Trist's shoulder.

"Alice caught your scent," he replied, standing up a little straighter. "We knew something was wrong because Lexa came back to the inn by herself and told us to wait some more because the plan had changed. She wouldn't say anything else." A quick shared glance with his sister. "But we decided we'd better come see for ourselves."

"How did you get across the lake?"

"We swam."

It was then that Natalya realized the kids were both soaking wet. She bent down and pulled Syd into a hug, which was awkward with the bow, but the girl hugged her back. She was skinny, but strong and tough. They both were.

"Thank you for saving us," Natalya whispered.

Syd's cheeks pinked. "Sure." She pressed a cloth-wrapped bundle into Natalya's hand. "Your second-best set of knives." The girl tossed a small leather pouch to Cairness. "And we thought you might want some gemstones."

The witch tugged it open, then gave her a beaming smile. "Ye bairns ken me all too well."

Sydonie's gaze lifted to the ceiling. "They're all up there for the ceremony. The Golden Imperator. Jamila ..." A scowl. "I mean, whatever her stupid name is. Like hundreds of people."

"What about Balaur?" Cairness asked.

She was standing with Valdrian—rather close, Natalya noticed.

"We didn't see Rachel," Syd replied sadly. "I hope Kasia got her back."

"They're going to make Jamila the next Imperator," Tristhus put in. "But we'd better hurry." Worry creased his brow. "I think they're going to kill Tashtemir first."

THE INAUGURATION of the next Golden Imperator was supposed to begin two hours after sunrise when the morning air was still cool, but the appointed hour came and went with no news—and now the richly-dressed crowds gathered before the palace on the Isle of Dreams were getting restless.

Tashtemir waited in chains amidst a contingent of the royal bodyguard. They stood with stiff backs and incurious expressions, but he'd heard the whispers. First, a solar eclipse just after dawn had caused great consternation. The astrologers claimed it wasn't on any calendars, finally declaring it a sign from the Alsakhan—though of what, no one dared say.

The second problem was that the khedive of Luba couldn't be found. It was the first time an Imperator-in-waiting had run late to her own ceremony. She finally appeared at the bridge, dusty and windblown and claiming she had gone into the desert to pray for a successful reign. Tashtemir wondered what had really happened, though it was not what preoccupied him at the moment.

No, his own imminent death was foremost in Tash's mind.

"You're up," a guard said, prodding his back with a cudgel.

A passage was cleared through the press of bodies. Tashtemir trotted, chains jangling, up a flight of steps to a wide stone terrace overlooking the multitudes gathered before the palace. It rose three tiers high and gave a view of the lake beyond. Sunlight sparkled on the crystalline waters. They shifted color in the light breeze, now aquamarine, now the azure of ocean waves. The sky was clear save for a few pinkish clouds that mounded on the western horizon.

A fine thing to see at the end, he thought, his throat tightening. *I am a lucky man.*

The top tier was occupied by the old Imperator, the Imperator-in-waiting, and a handful of close advisors that included Hanne Danziger. She caught his eye and smiled.

The second tier held rank upon rank of the Breath of God, looking like a murder of sinister crows.

The third was packed with the highest nobles of the land and their retinues. Tashtemir spotted his father, the khedive of Paravai. His black eyes held no sign of recognition. Tashtemir assumed his father had already disowned him. He wished he could apologize, claim it was all a mistake, but that would be another lie.

An empty space had been left in front of the balustrade.

As he was hauled forward, a tall woman broke from the crowd.

"Wait!" she screamed, raising a hand.

"Merat!" he cried, chest tightening.

She shoved her way through the mobbed lawns below, but before she could reach him a dozen guards rushed forward and dragged her off down one of the pathways. The Imperator pretended she hadn't noticed the disruption, but her mouth was clamped into a tight line. She muttered something to her successor, the woman who'd called herself Jamila al-Jabban. Tashtemir had taught himself to lip-read during his time at court and managed to catch a few words.

Embarrassment . . . stain on my legacy . . . get this business over with . . .

Now the Imperator rose, looking resplendent in purple robes embroidered with golden-maned dragons. "There is an order I mean to carry out before my reign comes to an end," she called in a loud voice. "My final act in office before I retire to my gardens in Marath."

The crowd shuffled impatiently. They'd been waiting for hours now to see the new Imperator ascend to the throne. The day was getting hot. A feast awaited, with iced wine and tables in the shade. If she would just lay the dragon mantle across the khedive of Luba's shoulders and be done with it . . .

The Imperator stabbed an accusing finger at Tashtemir. A hush fell over the assembled dignitaries.

"This man, by his own admission, stole two young dragonets from my bestiary to sell for his own profit," she said. "He committed this foul deed knowing full well that the punishment for such an offense is death."

A murmuring rippled through the crowd. Most of the nobles and courtiers knew him. He'd been one of them for years—before his downfall. A few of the younger ones whom he'd counted as friends eyed him with pity. The rest were palpably hostile.

"Tashtemir Kelevan fled to the Via Sancta. He thought himself beyond the long arm of the Imperator's justice. But his was a crime against the great Alsakhan himself and now Kelevan has been delivered back into our hands to face punishment."

Of course, she didn't mention that he came back of his own accord.

"The law calls for the Forty-Nine Agonies."

More foot-shuffling at this, and whispers of dismay.

"But as we do not have hours to spare"—a sharp glance at the khedive, who looked abashed—"the Kiss of Death will have to suffice."

One of the priests stepped forward and lowered his veil. The guards gripped Tash by the arms, dragging him to the center of the terrace. The khedive of Luba watched with an expression of satisfaction. Hanne Danziger was actually grinning.

Tash swallowed hard. He could smell the priest now, an acrid, chemical smell. The whites of his eyes were greenish, his skin the gray of a week-old corpse. Tash imagined the feel of those papery, dry lips against his. The soft exhalation of poison into his lungs.

At the last, he thought of Merat, and was grateful that she had been dragged off and didn't have to witness what happened next. For he'd seen this done before—not often, but on a few occasions when the crimes were judged severe. The Kiss of Death was neither swift nor painless. He remembered drumming heels, a back bowed in agony, yellow froth on the tongue.

He was within arm's reach of the priest when a black-fletched arrow took the man in the chest. More buzzed past, striking guards and one unlucky noble who'd elbowed her way forward for a better view. The guards surrounding him were knocked aside by an invisible hand. It swept them into the next rank of soldiers, who in turn stumbled backwards. The khedive leapt to her feet, yelling for her bodyguard to do something.

Tash's heart sang as Natalya and Patryk, Cairness and Valdrian fought their way forward. The two young archers were with them, nocking and firing as the Markhound snarled and snapped at anyone who approached. He'd feared they were all dead—or worse.

Tashtemir shambled forward as fast as the chains around his legs allowed. Spells erupted from Cairness's splayed fingers —some booming like fireworks, others knocking the guards about like dolls. Valdrian grabbed a passing soldier by the wrist. When he let go, the man's eyes were empty. He drew his blade and ran at the Imperator.

Tashtemir paused to watch. In the chaos, no one noticed him at first. She stood frozen in shock, staring at the melee. The soldier got within six paces of her before one of his fellows realized what was about to happen and cut him down.

Meanwhile, the Breath of God had regrouped. They surged down the stairs in a rush, veils lifted. The poisons they drank seemed to provide some protection from the ley because Cairness's magic didn't affect them. Patryk Spassov laid about with his mighty fists, and Natalya's knives flashed, but it wasn't enough. The children had run out of arrows. They were struggling to hold the dog, who tried to lunge at the priests.

A hand seized Tashtemir's robe. He turned and looked up into the ravaged face of a Nazaré Maz. The Breath of God.

"Sinner," it rasped. "Criminal."

A whiff of foul breath hit his face, like burning metal. It unhinged his knees. The priest pulled him into the final embrace, known as the Kiss of Death.

Then the light suddenly darkened, though the morning was cloudless. The priest looked up, squinting. A shadow had fallen across the palace. Things were descending from the sky. They came out of the east, out of the rising sun. Tashtemir could hardly make them out. Only that they were big.

The people who were left screamed even louder and scattered in all directions. The priest looked down in surprise. A knife jutted from his chest.

"Tashtemir!"

Natalya beckoned from the foot of the stairs. Tash yanked his arm free and lurched away, half falling down the steps. She met him halfway with a fierce grin. Cairness used a copper coin to open the manacles. He felt so grateful to see his friends, he hardly knew what to say. Then he got a better look at what had come to the Isle of Dreams and his jaw slowly hinged open.

Surely, they must be the Teeth of God.

Each was the size of a merchant vessel—longer if you counted the whiplike barbed tail. Four circled above the palace, two with gleaming scales, two with skin that glowed like forges. Wings tucked as they dove.

"Run!" someone yelled.

The group took off across the trampled lawn. Halfway to the trees, Tashtemir glanced over one shoulder. Jamila had torn the dragon mantle from the Imperator's shoulders and wrapped it around herself. Now they were tussling over the garment while Hanne Danziger screeched in a cracked, crazed, high-pitched voice at the creatures swooping from the sky. Marks twined around her bare arms. They might have been vines or flowers. The flesh looked pale and shriveled like a dried mushroom.

"You serve *me*, now! *Me!*" A sweep of her bony hand. "Kill the rest of them! Kill them all—"

The Teeth of God alit on the terrace's lowest level. Lashing, whiplike tails shattered the balustrade. Mighty jaws cracked wide and jetted streams of silver-white flame. In an instant, every soul on the top two tiers was burned to cinders. Hanne's charred skeleton remained erect for a moment, then toppled over.

Natalya had stopped next to him. "Fog me, that was

awesome," she whispered hoarsely, tugging at Tash's sleeve. "But we'd better get to the bridge."

He nodded, throat dry as dust. They pelted down the main road to the single bridge that led from the Isle of Dreams to mainland Qeddah. A column of black smoke billowed into the sky from the direction of the palace. Everyone on the island seemed to have the same idea, and they followed the general stampede. Items lay abandoned everywhere. Slippers, veils, small painted fans.

Tashtemir leapt over a fallen shawl and saw a familiar face beating her way against the tide. "Merat!" He waved and she broke into a smile of relief. The soothsayer ran up and embraced him.

"Thank the Alsakhan," she murmured into his shoulder.

"Thank *them*, actually," he said, nodding at his companions, who waited for the pair.

Enraged roars and more spouts of flame sent them all moving again. But when they reached the wooden bridge, they found it in ruins. Charred timbers floated in the water below. Only one gatehouse remained, and it looked abandoned.

The nobles were pushing and shoving each other. One slid into the gap, arms wheeling as he hit the water. A moment later, he bobbed to the surface and started swimming for the nearby Isle of Cats. It was separated from the Isle of Dreams by a narrow channel that was already churned to a white froth by hundreds of flailing bodies.

Left with no other choice, Tashtemir and the others ran straight into the lake. He found Merat's hand as she sank into the deep water.

"I can't ... swim!" she spluttered, her eyes wide and panicked.

She tried to wade back to shore, but the Sinn é Maz were venting their fiery rage on the entire imperial compound. The steel and glass dome enclosing the Imperator's menagerie shattered and her pets emerged, flapping madly to escape.

They looked tiny next to their larger cousins. Tashtemir's breath caught as one of the Sinn é Maz swooped down. But the Teeth of God only herded the dragonelles into a group. Two of them flapped off with the little ones, like geese trailing goslings.

The rest returned to their methodical destruction of the palace.

"You can't go back," Tash said gently. "Hold onto me, Mer."

She fought him for a minute more, but finally gave up and clung to his shoulder. Patryk Spassov paddled over and asked if they needed help, but Tashtemir shook his head.

"The Sinn é Maz don't want us," he said. "They want *them*."

The only other isle in flames belonged to the priests who had held the keys to Valmitra's prison.

"The knights have a boat," Patryk said, treading water. "We'll find them and come back for you, yeah?"

Tashtemir nodded. The lake was tepid as bathwater. After a while, Merat relaxed against him. The shouts and screams from the isle faded and grew distant. Tashtemir floated on his back, eyes closed, the sun warm on his face.

His father was dead. As the khedive of Paravai, he'd been standing on the upper dais. Tashtemir knew he should feel something about it, but the man had been a distant figure his whole life, spending most of his time maneuvering for power at the Imperator's court. They were practically strangers. He'd hated the fact that his oldest son went to veterinary school instead of studying law or how to make loads of money. Even when Tash was at court himself, working in the bestiary, his father hardly ever called for him.

A shame it ended that way, but he'd been willing to watch his own son be executed without speaking up—

Mer's hand squeezed his. Hard.

Tash opened his eyes.

A dragonelle hovered before his face, peering at him with a bright green eye. He recognized the markings, pomegranate red at the tips of wings and tail with a saffron orange band around the sinuous neck.

The one he had stolen.

The one he had then returned to its fellows and gotten caught for it.

The dragonelle emitted a tiny puff of flame and snapped its beak at him in a friendly, inquisitive manner.

Merat laughed in wonderment. "I have never seen . . . They are . . . "

"I know." He raised his hand from the water. The dragonelle alit on his knuckles. "Go, little brother," he said. "Go and be free."

It cocked its head. Tiny nails dug into his skin as it launched into the sky. He watched it wing across the lake, flapping hard to catch up with the rest.

"You feel it, too, don't you?" Merat asked softly.

"Yes." He looked at her. "Valmitra is awake."

Chapter Forty

❧❦❧

Kasia opened her eyes to sunlight streaming through gauzy white curtains. Alexei dozed in a chair, an indistinct dog-shaped figure at his feet. One of them was snoring.

"Alice?" she whispered.

The snoring cut off. The shadow knitted itself into a black-and-tan Markhound, which barreled onto the bed and licked her face. She threw her arms around Alice's neck.

"Your breath smells like old fish!" she exclaimed. "What have you been into?"

Alice looked away with a guilty eye-roll. Her master roused himself a moment later. He broke into a smile and crawled into the bed, gently nudging the hound to the other side.

"I was wondering when you'd wake," he murmured, kissing her.

"Where are we?"

She had a sudden fear that it was all a dream. Would she know the difference? But no, her fingernails were dirty and she had scratches on her arms. As stupid as it sounded, Kasia knew she wouldn't have dirty nails in a dream unless she'd been digging in the Garden flowerbeds.

"The Isle of the Blessed," Alexei replied. "You're safe here."

She stared out the window, which looked over the lake. She remembered killing Balaur. Nikola arriving with Borosus. The white tower going topsy-turvy and hurling them from the top, red sands rushing up to meet her—

"The Sinn é Maz caught you both," Alexei said, guessing her train of thought. "They brought us all back to Qeddah." He gave a funny-sounding laugh. "Even my mule, though I don't think he was too happy about it."

She raised a brow.

"We flew." He shuddered. "I hope never to do it again."

Kasia sat up against the pillows. "Is the dawn city gone?"

"The tower still stands, but no one is permitted to enter." He studied her face. "You were right about all of it. The readings were true, weren't they? Every one?"

"Yes."

"So if the Serpent was sleeping, who sent the messages from the ley?"

She drew her knees up and folded her arms around them. "I wish I knew."

He was quiet for a moment. "Both the Danzigers are dead. I didn't see it myself, but Malach told me. Jule drank the elixir. At first it restored him. But then something went wrong. He died screaming, in flames, with Balaur laughing at him."

Kasia nodded slowly. She'd vowed to kill Jule herself, but after the last few days, she'd had enough of death.

"And Hanne?"

"Burned to ash by the Sinn é Maz at the inauguration. Along with the new Imperator, the old Imperator, and all the priests."

Her mouth went dry, though surely Alexei wouldn't seem so relaxed if he had terrible news to impart. "Natalya and Patryk?"

"Both well." He smiled. "I'll let them tell the story. But we all got through it." His face darkened. "Except for the mage called Caralexa. She's the one who betrayed you."

"Tell me she's dead," Kasia said grimly.

"She is."

"Good. You know, I never trusted her. I thought it was just because she was a mage and I didn't trust any of them. But there was something slippery about her." She accepted the glass of water he offered and drank deeply. "What about the Great Serpent? Is she … here?"

Alexei shook his head. "I've seen her servants around, but not the goddess herself."

"Okay." Water slopped over the edge of the glass. "Whoops."

She set it on the bedside table.

"Your hands are shaking." He held them in his own. No gloves, just warm skin.

"I'll be okay." Kasia gave a weak laugh. "It's just that it felt like the end of the world. Literally. I thought maybe we'd screwed it all up."

"We saw it from below, Malach and Rachel and me. I dropped him and ran to catch you."

"I would have squished you like a bug."

"I know. But I couldn't help myself."

"And then the dragon-men caught us."

"That's right."

"I can't wait to see Nashka."

"And she can't wait to see you. There's a big dinner planned. Are you up to it?"

"Definitely. I'm starved." She sniffed herself. "And I want a bath."

"You shall have all those things, my love."

Smiling servants brought hot water and a clean abaya. She washed and dressed and went downstairs to the main hall. A space had been cleared for two long, low tables surrounded by colorful silken cushions. The doors to the terrace were open

KAT ROSS

and a cool breeze guttered the dozens of candles set about the room.

A cheer of greeting went up as she entered. In an instant, she was surrounded by friends: Natalya and Patryk. Cairness and Paarjini. Valdrian, Sydonie and Tristhus, who looked overjoyed to have Rachel back. Kasia waved at the three knights, Klaus, Ashe and Naresha. She embraced Tashtemir, who had brought the soothsayer Merat and her caracal Lupa. The cat prowled the balcony with lashing tail, hissing occasionally at Alice, who licked her own crotch with single-minded devotion and pretended not to notice.

All in all, they had gotten off light, though not entirely unscathed. Paarjini's arm hung in a sling. Malach was on crutches. Nikola's hair had been singed, though she covered it with a scarf. She gave Kasia a fierce hug, looking exhausted and a bit sad.

Hassan's troupe was there as well, full of jests and song and laughter, which made for merry tables. They dined on fresh perch grilled in garlic butter; a cold salad of spicy yellow beans sauced with sheep's milk yoghurt; eggplant stewed in cinnamon and rosewater; olive rice; and a dozen other savory dishes. For dessert, date and honey pastries with strong, bitter coffee.

Kasia sat next to Nikola, who told her that she'd spoken at length with Borosus.

"He admitted that it was him who attacked the *Wayfarer* in dragon form," Nikola explained. "But he never intended to hurt anyone. He'd just awoken and was flying along the coastline to get his bearings. Then he sensed someone working ley and went to investigate."

Kasia nodded slowly. "We were questioning Jamila al-Jabban."

"Not just questioning," Nikola said dryly. "*Compelling.* When Borosus tried to land on the deck, he didn't see Danna on watch. His wing clipped her harness and toppled her overboard." She sighed. "You remember how rough the seas were that night. He said he searched but couldn't find her. I believed him when he said he was sorry."

"But he attacked the ship again after that," Kasia pointed out.

"He smelled the bloodline of Gavriel. *You*. He said it made him lose his head." Nikola studied her. "I have a question. Why did you say the word *bicycle* to me?"

Kasia frowned. "When?"

"Back at the tower. Just before I broke the last Ward. You walked over and said one word. *Bicycle*. It was the solution to Cathrynne's spell—or part of the solution." She tapped her silver tooth. "I ended up using this. The original was knocked out in a bike accident. But how did you know? I never told you that story."

Kasia shook her head, baffled. "I . . . I honestly don't know. I don't even recall saying it."

"I thought you remember everything."

"I do. Usually."

"Well, that's weird." Nikola rubbed her arms, though the room was warm. "I'm sure I didn't imagine it."

Kasia thought back. There was an odd blurry point between the time when Malach killed Balaur, and when she and Nikola were hurled from the tower.

"At least it worked," she said.

They shared an unsettled look.

"Yeah." Nikola gripped the multicolored stone around her neck, twisting it on the chain. "Still weird."

Malach came over on his crutches then and stole her away. Kasia watched them on the balcony in heated conversation and thought she knew why Nikola had looked sad.

Then Natalya hit her with a pistachio shell from across the table to get her attention, and she had another glass of wine, and Rachel came and sat on her knee while Kasia tried to read her fortune with Merat's Lenormand deck.

After a while, she stopped constantly glancing through the windows overlooking the lake. It seemed Valmitra and her servants would not trouble them this night.

Later, she drifted off in Alexei's arms and for the first time in memory, she didn't find herself in the Garden.

She was in the dawn city walking among the phantoms, except that she was one of them now and she wore a fine dress and danced all the night with a handsome black-winged angel.

MALACH SIPPED a glass of iced wine and watched the sun set over the lake. Not a single boat plied the clear aquamarine waters. A week had passed since the destruction of the Isle of Dreams, but everyone was still lying low.

It sat across the channel, a blackened ruin. The Citadel of the Breath of God was in a similar state, though no other buildings in Qeddah had been touched.

"How is your leg?" Hassan asked, sinking into the lounge chair next to him.

"It itches." Malach dug his nails, which Koko had just painted electric blue, into the pale, tender skin at the edge of the cast. His crutches leaned against the marble balustrade of the terrace. Rachel was curled up in Koko's lap, listening raptly to a story.

"You'll ruin them," Koko scolded him. "You must wait for the polish to dry."

"But I need to scratch."

"So blow, like this." She took Rachel's hand and demonstrated, eliciting giggles of protest.

"It tickles!" Rachel cried.

"Makes them dry faster," Koko said with a grin.

Malach blew on his nails.

"Valmitra is gone," Hassan announced. "She left last night."

He frowned, lowering his hands. "But I never got to meet her."

"I thought you didn't want to."

"I didn't," he said firmly. "I don't. But . . ."

"You feel overlooked."

"Don't give me that amused smile."

Hassan bit his lip, clearly struggling not to laugh. "I'm sorry. I do understand. After all the drama over the Morning Star and the sword and you helping to save her in the end, you wonder how she could snub you."

Malach sank down against the cushions, staring into his wine. "Maybe."

"I am thinking the reason is because you so closely resemble her errant son. She does not wish to look upon your face."

"Then I ought to count myself lucky," he muttered, oddly disgruntled.

Koko shot him a look. "Do not blaspheme. Hassan and I were both brought into Valmitra's presence and she was perfectly charming."

"Perfectly!" Rachel echoed, playing with the sash of Koko's gorgeous brocade robe.

"She wasn't mad at you?" he ventured.

"Not at all. We are the Blessed, Malach. Always we have remained loyal and devoted." A small, secret smile touched her full lips. "I understand now where our title comes from." Koko stabbed her fan at him. "But you should guard your tongue. She sleeps no longer."

"You're right," he said sourly. "But it seems she has met everyone except me."

He did not mention Nikola by name; it was too painful. She'd already left for Dur-Athaara, along with Paarjini, Cairness, and, surprisingly, Valdrian, who said he wanted to see the "tropical paradise" Malach had described. He'd begged to be appointed the mages' emissary from Bal Kirith and Malach had finally relented, though he'd felt abandoned.

At least Rachel was still with him. Syd and Trist. And his sister. The priest, of course, who stuck to Kasia like a burr. They were all taking a ship back to the continent the next morning.

"Did Valmitra tell you what she intended?" he asked.

"A little," Hassan replied. "There will be no more Imperators. The Sinn é Maz are acting as regents of the Masdar League for now. I met their leader, Borosus. I have no objection to this change. There was too much corruption anyway."

"Borosus." Malach swallowed the dregs of his wine. "The one who tried to kill me—twice."

"He regrets the error," Hassan replied serenely.

"Are all the priests dead?"

"Most. I asked the Mother to spare any novices who escaped the fire and she did. They are being found new occupations." He twirled the wine stem with long, elegant fingers. "For twenty years, I have had nightmares about the Breath of God. I think it is all finally over."

Koko reached out and patted his hand.

"What about the continent?" Malach wondered. "Will Valmitra be collecting debts over there, too? The Via Sancta is the remnants of Gavriel's empire. That won't be good."

"I'm sorry, Malach, but I do not have the answer," Hassan replied. "It wasn't our place to ask."

Malach started to chew his thumbnail, then remembered the manicure and stopped. "I don't blame you, but that's what I would have asked, if she'd given me an audience. Because the mages just got Bal Kirith back—I mean, I think we have it —and I would like to know if we get to keep it."

Hassan held up the wine jug, but Malach shook his head. No more getting drunk, as tempting as it was.

"You will find out soon enough." Hassan produced an

ivory comb, unbraided his silky mane, and began to comb out the waves. "I can tell you where Valmitra went, though. To Dur-Athaara. She means to visit with her daughters and pay respects to the Mahadeva Sahevis."

"The sixty-day mourning period," Malach muttered.

That was why Nikola had left so quickly. First, because the bodies of the old queen lay in the hold of the *Wayfarer* and had to be brought home. Second, because Paarjini had cast some spell allowing her to communicate with the witches back home. They issued a formal summons for the *laoch* Nikola Thorn to return immediately and stand before the council.

He knew what that meant. Everybody did.

Once the mourning period was over, the Deir Fiuracha, the Sisterhood, would elect a new queen.

Malach made no attempt to stop her. He'd learned that lesson the hard way. Nikola Thorn was not a woman to be bent from her destiny. What he did do was offer to go with her.

She seemed to grasp how much it cost him to even suggest it. He had no trust for any witch except her. To be surrounded by hundreds of them again . . . the prospect made him feel like he still had the kaldurite inside him, a cold, ominous lump embedded deep in his gut.

Nikola gently refused and told him to take Rachel back to Bal Kirith. That she would send word when she could.

She made no promises and he didn't ask for any.

"Cheer up," said Koko, who had a knack for seeing straight through him. "If you frown like that it will give you wrinkles. Then I must send you home with jars of my special night cream made from rose-pearls and the tears of orphans." She shook her head. "Not cheap."

Malach laughed. "Koko, you can't do this to me. I will die without you. Why won't you come along? I will make you a princess!"

"And leave all this?" She waved a hand. "Look at that sunset."

It was pretty spectacular.

"Will you come visit me?" he pressed.

Hassan smiled. "Of course. I will drag her to a ship if I must."

"No need for dragging," Koko said. She frowned slightly. "You make a pun?"

Malach had told them the word for it in Osterlish.

"If you break your word," he warned, "Lucy will be very upset."

"So Lucy is not retired?" she teased.

"Never."

"I want to meet Lucy, too!" Rachel declared. "May I?"

"I promise," he said solemnly. "Koko, you must teach her to do makeup."

The wind shifted then, lifting Hassan's hair and riffling the pages of a poetry book next to Koko's chair. It carried the scent of the wild grapevines that grew down by the lakeshore and for a moment he was back in the liminal archway with his sister and his father and the black sun shining above.

He remembered the feel of the hilt against his palm, the way the quillions caught the half-light. The rain beading the edge of the blade. The contempt on Balaur's face turning to shock as he realized the truth.

Anathema wasn't a weapon after all.

Gavriel's inscription made perfect sense now.

My heart is as light as a feather and as heavy as an iron gate.

Perhaps—and he could never prove this, though maybe Valmitra suspected—perhaps Gavriel's vengeance was never meant for his mother.

"Come back to us, wool-gatherer!" Koko sang in her sweet, husky voice.

Malach came back. They talked late into the night. The rest of the troupe stopped by to toast him and say goodbye, and so did Tashtemir Kelevan, although he refused to call it that.

"We will meet again, Cardinal." Tashtemir kissed each cheek in the Masdari fashion.

"I'm giving up the title," Malach replied. "No more clergy. We'll do something different."

He thought of the city Gavriel had built, the beauty and splendor, and wondered if perhaps the dream could be revived.

And what Valmitra would do if she saw it.

"Behave yourself, southerner," Malach said, wiping a tear from his eye with his pretty new fingers.

Tash winked. "When have I not?"

Chapter Forty-One

Kasia stood at the stern rail of a Masdari merchant vessel as Port Sayyad dwindled in the distance. It carried a cargo of bokang wood, along with a contingent of passengers bound for the continent—Malach, Rachel, Sydonie and Tristhus; Natalya, Alexei and Patryk; and the three knights.

She wondered if someone else would be living in her flat. The day they fled—which seemed a lifetime ago, though it was less than a year—Tessaria said she'd paid the rent for months in advance. She could remember her benefactor without crying now. There would always be scars, but Tess would want her to move on.

Kasia resolved to buy a new outfit and get her nails done and go visit all of their favorite haunts. The ballet and theaters, the art galleries and coffee houses with dark polished wood and pressed-tin ceilings. She thought Tess would like that, and that she would also be pleased with how things had turned out.

I chose to be myself, Kasia thought. *I hope that's what you meant.*

In truth, she was eager to go home again. She missed hearing her native tongue. She even missed the traffic.

"What are you smiling about?" Alexei asked, joining her at the rail.

His hair was shaggy, down past his ears, but she liked it that way. He looked younger and less severe.

"I was thinking about my car. Do you remember when you found me changing the flat tire?"

He laughed. "How could I forget? I grilled you about Dr. Massot, with little success. Then you realized that you didn't have your car keys so I offered you a lift to Tessaria's."

She gave him a fond look. "You fell asleep at the wheel while we were crossing the river. I thought you were a mess."

"I was."

She curled her arm around his, resting her cheek against his shoulder. "I never did change that tire. I wonder how many parking tickets are on the windshield now?"

"It'll be at the impound lot most likely."

"You're very literal-minded, you know that?"

He smiled and rubbed the back of his neck. "Yes, I do."

"I should just buy a new car. I'll have to save for that." She gazed up at him. "I think I have twenty fides in my bank account. Not even that, since they would have taken it for fees."

His blue eyes twinkled. "My father is the president of the bank. I could beg for a favor."

"Ah, you see, Tess would approve of you after all."

He smelled nice. The sun warmed her face. Kasia decided she didn't care how broke she was, or who was living in her flat, if she could keep this man.

"We can save up together," Alexei said after a while. "I need a car, too."

"No big black Curia sedan with tinted windows and lots of chrome?" she teased.

He eyed her seriously and took a stone from his pocket. The lump of kaldurite that had belonged first to Nikola Thorn, then to Captain Aemlyn, then to Malach, then to the

461

witch Darya, and lastly to Balaur, who had thrown it away upon the occasion of his godhood.

"I'm done with all that," Alexei said, closing his fist around the stone.

And she said, "Good."

THE CROSSING WAS swift and uneventful. They sailed into Novoport on a warm, rainy afternoon at the end of Avostus month. The mocking cries of gulls trailed the three-masted schooner as it cruised through the busy harbor. Kasia stepped from the gangplank to the pier, breathing in the harbor's distinct stew of mackerel, diesel and waterlogged wooden pilings.

Home. She hadn't realized how much she'd missed it until now, with the familiar skyline spread out before her. Natalya and Patryk seemed equally happy, joking and arguing over where to have dinner—and whose turn it would be to pay.

Natalya took the fat purse of Masdari silver they'd been given by Hassan and paid the captain, who immediately set sail for Kvengard. He was a superstitious sort and held to the ban on any commerce with the other Curia cities.

The three knights bade them a friendly goodbye and headed off in search of a taxi to the Arx.

And so it was that they all stood on the pier with their luggage. Malach leaned on his crutches. The three children ran up and down, thrilled to be free of their small cabin. Alice sniffed at a piling with great interest, then peed on it. Patryk lit a cigarette. Natalya took the handle of her wheeled suitcase and marched for the taxi stand, the purse in her other hand.

After a few steps, her feet tangled up. She pitched forward with a loud curse, barely managing not to fall on her face. Kasia heard a faint splash. She hurried over. Natalya was staring through a gap in the warped boards of the pier. The sea sloshed below.

"Was that our money?" Kasia asked.

A nod.

"All of it?"

Natalya looked up, eyes wide. "Yeah."

"What did you trip over?"

"I don't know." She looked bewildered. "There isn't even anything there."

"Where are we going next, Malach?" Sydonie asked, bouncing on her toes. "I'm hungry."

"Me, too," her brother echoed.

"Me three!" Rachel hollered.

Malach gave a cheerful smile. "We'll figure something out, kids, don't you worry."

It was at least an hour's walk to Kasia's flat—more like three on crutches. The Arx was closer, but Kasia knew her brother would never accept Falke's charity, and it would probably traumatize Rachel all over again to go back there.

"Shit," Natalya said. "I'm so sorry."

"Lan-guage!" Sydonie sang, making it two long syllables.

"Anyone have any money?" Kasia asked.

No one did.

"This is ridiculous," Natalya muttered. "We still have friends. I'll make a collect call. What's Olga's number? She'll bail us out."

Kasia was trying to remember it when she noticed a girl waving from the end of the pier. She wore a pink slicker with the hood up. Strands of lime green hair poked out, sticking wetly to her pale cheeks.

"Hey, Father!" she called to Alexei. "Been looking for you!"

He stared at her for a long moment.

"Who's that?" Kasia asked.

"I requisitioned her car." He glanced at Malach, then

lowered his voice. "I was with your brother, and uh, we'd just had an accident. It was the night the ley surged and Lezarius escaped."

"Ah." Kasia lifted her brows.

"By the time I came to, Malach had run off. I needed to get to the Batavia Institute. So I flagged her down and took hers."

The three children were already flying down the pier, Malach hobbling after them. Patryk picked up his suitcase. "Well, she tracked you down, Alyosha. You better tell her where her car is."

"Saints," he muttered. "I think . . . yes, I left it in an alley when Tessaria showed up later with agents from the General Directorate. They took me to the Arx to meet Falke. He'd just been made Pontifex."

By now, they were almost up to the girl, who waited with her arms crossed. "What are you doing here?" he asked in a cautious tone.

"I was sent to pick you up. All of you." She cracked her gum and slid open the side panel of a nondescript white van. "Hop in!"

The interior was fitted out with four rows of seats like the car pool shuttles the Curia was always trying to get people to use in the crowded downtown district.

"Sent by whom?" Alexei asked.

"Some kid. He gave me two hundred *fides*."

"What was his name?"

She shrugged. "I forgot to ask. But he said he's your friend, Father, and you'd need a ride."

"A ride to where?"

The girl jerked a thumb at Kasia. "Her flat. The fare's already covered, plus tip."

Kasia looked around. There wasn't another taxi in sight— not that she could pay for one anyway.

"Do you trust this girl?" she asked in a low voice.

"I do remember her." Alexei hesitated. "I mean, the Order of the Black Sun is finished, right? She doesn't look the type anyway."

Kasia smiled at the girl. The girl smiled back. She wore a miniskirt and ripped fishnets over steel-toed pink platform boots.

"May I see your license, please?" Kasia asked.

The girl snapped her gum again. "Sure, Domina." She dragged a huge knockoff purse through the driver's side window, rummaged in its depths, and handed over the laminated card. Her name was Aura Orlova. She had a commercial taxi license and it looked legit.

"You're twenty?" Kasia looked at the photo, then back at the young woman, who eyed her with a touch of weariness.

"Uh-huh." She folded the chewed gum into a foil wrapper and tucked it in her skirt pocket. "You want the ride or not? 'Cause it's pissing out here."

Right on cue, the rain thickened to a steady, drenching downpour that Kasia knew from experience wouldn't relent for hours, if not days. The three children huddled around Malach, all of them soaked through.

"I'm cold," Rachel muttered, shivering.

"Fuck it," Natalya said, throwing her suitcase into the back. "Do you take dogs?"

They all got in the van. The upholstery reeked of keef, but it was clean. The kids shared a middle seat and started to fight over who got to sit by the window. Natalya and Patryk crammed into the back, while Kasia and Alexei sat with Malach behind the driver. Alice jumped into Alexei's lap, panting with excitement to be back home, and immediately started drooling on Kasia's shoulder.

The girl flipped the wipers to high, signaled even though there wasn't another car in sight, and pulled out to the main road that led down to the piers. She drove carefully in the rain, slowing for the deep puddles, stopping for the yellow lights, and keeping a light foot on the brake.

A true professional.

They cut along the waterfront, passing warehouses and fish markets and the trendy-seedy neighborhood on the southern fringe of Ash Court. At last, the girl turned onto Malaya Sadovaya Ulitsa. Number 44 looked the same as ever. The row of buzzers with handwritten names on peeling tape, the two worn steps up to the front door, the perennial smell of coriander and cumin.

A pale figure lurked under the sign for Kebab House, which occupied the building's ground floor.

"Isn't that . . . ?" Kasia asked, squinting.

"The kid who paid me," the driver affirmed. She lugged their suitcases from the back and dumped the luggage on the curb. Will Danziger walked over. He handed Kasia a set of keys with a smile, like they'd just talked on the phone and arranged to meet for brunch.

"How was your trip?"

She glanced down at the keys, recognizing the shape. Definitely the ones to her flat. "Er, fine."

Will turned to Alexei. It was impossible to read his expression because he wore a pair of Natalya's huge sunglasses. "It's good to see you, Fra Bryce. We need a few minutes with Kasia and Malach." He pointed to the restaurant. "In there. She wants to talk with them."

"She?" Malach said.

Kasia handed Natalya the keys. Somehow, she'd expected this. "Go on, we'll be fine." She smiled, hoping she didn't look as nervous as she felt. "I think there's even a couple of cold beers in the fridge."

"Praise the loving Saints," Spassov muttered, flicking his butt to the gutter.

"Come on, kids," Nat said, after a long look at the ghost-white boy. "I'll show you the flat."

Kasia watched Alexei, Patryk, Natalya and the three children head into the building and up the narrow stairs. Then she followed Malach into Kebab House. As usual, the place was packed. They squeezed past the line for takeout.

"Over there," Will said, unnecessarily.

Three people waited at a table by the front window, under a menu crookedly taped to the glass.

The first had a dark cinnamon complexion that contrasted with her silver witch's eyes. She wore a headscarf sewn all over with tiny colored beads and shimmering sequins. Or were they scales? A strong, careworn hand spun a copper coin on the tabletop; each finger sported chunky rings set with precious stones. When she turned her head, Kasia saw a faint scar in the shape of a fishhook running from the corner of her mouth to one cheekbone.

The second individual had a delicate oval face, almond-shaped eyes of deepest onyx, and pleasing androgynous features. An instrument resembling a lute rested on one knee. A river of shining red hair fell across their bare shoulders. They smiled and strummed the strings, producing a harmonious chord of greeting.

"Sit," the witch said.

Kasia eyed the third party at the table. She looked around at the other diners, who were eating and chattering away.

Why wasn't everybody staring?

Malach tugged her sleeve and she sank into a chair. He cleared his throat, admirably calm. "How do we address you?"

"I am Minerva," the witch replied. She glanced at the androgyne. "They are Travian."

Travian nodded, turning to the third. "And *he* is Valoriel."

The last was an honest-to-goddess angel. Impossibly gorgeous and dreadfully stern. He wore a midnight blue cloak that fell in rich folds to his sandaled feet. A pair of huge golden wings sprouted from between his shoulders, the feathers half-crushed against the dingy wall. He stared at Kasia like a schoolteacher about to hand down a detention.

"Val-Mi-Tra," Malach said slowly. He gave a strangled laugh. "So there are three of you? Like the Mahadeva Sahevis?"

"We have various incarnations," the witch replied. "You saw the Serpent. That form is regal and awe-inspiring but not always convenient. As for your next question, we share one mind" —a quick glance at Valoriel— "though we have our differences of opinion."

"I thought Gavriel . . ." Kasia trailed off under the angel's unblinking glare.

"Chopped his head off?" Minerva finished. "Yes, he did. This is a prosthetic. Think of it as a wooden head."

Kasia realized then that the angel did nothing but sit there and look fearsome and judgmental. "Is that what he was like before?" she asked.

"More or less," Travian said, baring a set of sharp white teeth.

"Well," Minerva said briskly. "We have other meetings lined up so let's get to the point." Her silver eyes settled on Malach. "You do look like our seventh son. It's uncanny." They drifted to Kasia. "You both have more of him than Cathrynne. *She* was mine. We each have our own children. Valoriel was Gavriel's father."

She paused as a skinny, mop-haired waiter hustled up, pushing a trolley that teetered with steaming dishes. Kasia knew the menu by heart, having ordered up to the flat countless times. It was the party platter, advertised as "A most joyous celebration in your mouth!" Natalya's favorite.

The waiter set out cutlery wrapped in paper napkins and arranged the dishes on the tiny table. Then he smiled all around and crammed in a variety of chutneys, oblivious to the imperious, scowling angel.

Kasia was starving. She filled a plate with a bit of everything.

"We should save some for the kids," Malach said, spooning a small amount of rice onto his own plate.

"Will already sent a delivery upstairs," Minerva said. "You can eat. I'll talk."

Kasia dug into a portion of flamingly hot kolyani. Travian shook out their napkin and also set to with gusto. Valoriel didn't seem to notice the food.

Minerva gazed out the rain-blurred window at the Saturday evening traffic. "Will told us everything that's happened since we fell asleep. The Dark Ages. The wars. I'll admit, when we first came to our senses, we considered wiping the slate clean." She waved a beringed hand. "Starting fresh."

The rice turned to ashes in Kasia's mouth. She swallowed and put her fork down. "Why didn't you?"

"Will said you'd been punished enough." A sardonic laugh. "You did it all on your own. But look, we're not angry at you. What do *you* know? Nothing. Nothing about anything."

"We did save you from Balaur," Kasia pointed out, as Malach shot her a warning look. "He was going to kill you and we stopped him."

"Balaur. He was nightmare made flesh." Minerva shook her head. "Why do you think he could walk in dreams?"

"But he's dead?" Kasia pressed.

Travian played a mournful dirge. "Dead as dead can be," he sang softly.

"And the dawn city?" Malach asked. "I keep wondering . . . about the illusions . . ."

"Yes?" Minerva prompted.

"*Why?* Why go to all that trouble when there was no one to see it?"

Minerva sighed. "Gavriel always loved pretty things. It was his weakness." She tapped the copper coin on the table. "Look, we never asked to be worshipped and we don't want it

now. Keep your free will. Keep your Marks. We don't care."
She leaned forward, gray eyes flashing. "We're too busy to
care. We've been gone a thousand years. You think the continent is the only place we built?"

She waited for an answer. Kasia and Malach mutely shook
their heads.

"That's right. We've got other offspring to worry about,
you know." Minerva crossed her arms, bracelets clinking.
"We're planning a little surprise tour."

Travian gave a droll smile and strummed a discordant riff
on the lute. "We'll see how that goes."

At that moment, a baby started to wail at the next table,
which, given the cramped confines of the restaurant, was less
than an arm's length away.

Valoriel slowly turned his head. The infant was red and
wrinkled and incandescent with rage. Unlike its parents, who
wore the blank expressions of knights fresh from the front
lines, it seemed to see the gleaming golden pinions, the tousled
dark hair and annoyed green eyes. Drool ran down its chin. It
smiled and gave a happy gurgle.

"But here's the thing," Minerva said. "You drank our
venom."

"It wasn't me!" Kasia protested.

"Maybe not. But that whole part about switching bodies . .
. Honestly, we don't even understand what you did. It's too
weird."

She chewed her lip. "I don't feel different."

"And you never will. You're immortal."

Her stomach dropped to the sticky linoleum floor. "But I
don't want to live forever," she whispered in horror.

"No?"

"No. No! It's the last thing on earth I want. It sounds
horrible!"

Travian arched a brow.

"Not for you," Kasia added hastily. "You're used to it. But you have to help me. Take it back!"

Travian and Minerva shook their heads in unison. "We cannot."

"But you're a . . . an omnipotent deity!"

There was a dry silence.

"If that were true," Travian said, "do you think Cathrynne Rowan could have——"

They cut off at a pointed look from Minerva. "The venom cannot be extracted," Minerva clarified. "Only given away."

Kasia brightened. "Then that's what I shall do. But give it to whom?"

"Not me," Malach said immediately. "Sorry, Kasia."

"It's all right." She patted his knee. "Believe me, I understand."

"I have an idea," Travian said casually. "Give it to Valoriel."

The angel's emerald gaze swept the room, oblivious to the conversation.

Think of it as a wooden head.

"How do I do it?" Kasia wondered.

Travian smiled. It didn't touch their black eyes. "Do you know the tale of *The Poisoned Prince*?"

She shook her head.

"It is long so I will relate only the end. A hedge witch finds him in the cave where he has lain senseless for a hundred years. He is so proud and beautiful that she falls in love with him at once. She brews a potion, but he cannot swallow it. The hedge witch feeds it to him with her own mouth."

"Did the prince revive?"

"Yes."

Kasia studied Valoriel. Perhaps the prince had deserved to be poisoned. Perhaps he wasn't very nice at all, which the witch later discovered to her regret.

But she saw no other way to rid herself of the venom. And

she suspected that Cathrynne Rowan had meant for this to happen, as well. An end to Valoriel's penance.

She rose from her seat. None of the other diners paid any attention. Their table might as well have been empty.

Kasia bent down and cupped Valoriel's face, resting her thumbs in the soft hollows of his cheeks. He was beautiful and haughty, just like the prince. He did not resist and she was mesmerized by the clarity of his irises, like new grass.

"The Summerlord," she said softly.

"Who told you that name?" Minerva demanded, gaze sharp.

"No one."

Valoriel's silken hair brushed her cheek as she kissed the angel's mouth. It was as if she kissed a statue. Stiff and cold and unwelcoming. Then his lips parted slightly and she filled him with her breath. It fizzed along her tongue like tiny champagne bubbles.

Kasia heard distant music, a sweet song full of hope and longing. The notes soared higher and higher, twining together in swoops and whorls like starlings in flight. Travian's lute.

Valoriel gave a sharp inhalation. Her hand slipped down to the juncture of his throat. A steady pulse beat against her fingertips now.

He gripped her wrists. She felt the strength in his hands, but he was gentle as he disengaged her grip. He glanced at her through his lashes and turned away, skin whiter than ever. There was no mistaking the hot look in his eye.

He wasn't grateful. He was *furious*.

Kasia stepped back so fast she bumped the table and almost knocked over a water glass before Malach righted it.

"We have to leave now." Minerva stood and shook out her bracelets.

Travian popped the last samosa in their mouth. "Nice talking to you."

"Where are you going?" Malach asked.

"I told you, we have other realms to visit," Minerva replied.

"Will you be coming back?"

"Someday," Travian answered. "You'll likely be dead by then."

"So . . . " Malach looked amazed at his luck. "You're not changing anything at all?"

"And what would happen if we did?" Minerva asked wearily. "Let's say we toppled the Via Sancta. Cast down the pontifices and announced that we were back."

"Civil war," he replied immediately.

Minerva leaned forward, pewter eyes intent. "Some of you would be for us, some against. Our name would be used to divide and punish. And you have already been punished enough."

Valoriel looked like he disagreed. He stared at Kasia, then Malach, gaze lingering on the man who looked so much like Gavriel.

"No one knows what really happened except you two," Minerva said. "And those who were at the tower with you, of course."

"We intend to keep it that way," Travian added. "Understand?"

They both nodded solemnly.

Valoriel spoke for the first time. "We made you free," he said, and his voice was as fair as his face, "so free you will remain."

The unspoken *"for now, assuming you don't piss me off again"* couldn't have been clearer.

Malach cleared his throat. "May I ask one other—"

"No, you may not," Travian interrupted tartly. "We will not discuss Cathrynne and Gavriel. Not now nor ever."

To Kasia's relief, her brother didn't argue. She was curious, too, but they'd already gotten away with a great deal.

"And if we need you?" she asked. "What shall we do?"

Valoriel folded his luminous wings. Elegant fingers brushed a bit of lint from his midnight-blue cloak.

"Pray," he advised in a mordant tone.

Travian plucked a dissonant cackle of amusement from the lute's strings.

"You made a hell of paradise once," Minerva said. "Try not to repeat that mistake." She paused at the door. "I almost forgot. This is yours."

She tossed Kasia the purse of silver that had fallen through the rotten, warped boards of the pier at Novoport. The three of them walked to the curb, where the young woman in the pink slicker was waiting with Will Danziger. The van doors slid open and shut. Aura Orlova signaled and carefully merged into the evening rush-hour traffic.

And that was the last Kasia saw of the Great Serpent.

Chapter Forty-Two

Morvana rode up to the gates of the Arx. Knights in Blue Flame tabards took her horse, then escorted her inside the Pontifex's Palace.

She was expected and they led her straight to Lezarius's study. He rose from his desk with a smile, coming forward to kiss her cheeks.

"How was the journey?"

"Long," she replied wryly. "But they've repaired the main roads through the Morho."

His shaggy white brows lowered. "No trouble?"

"None at all." She hesitated, unable to contain her impatience. "Where is he, Reverend Father?"

"Inspecting the new recruits. I'll send for him."

"You didn't tell him I was coming?"

He looked troubled. "No, I kept my word. Though I think it would have eased him to know."

She nodded absently and started chewing on a thumbnail before stopping herself. "Was he angry?"

"No." A rather severe look. "Just heartbroken, I think, that you left without telling him."

Her brow furrowed. "He was unconscious for days. I couldn't wait any longer. And I always meant to return."

"As you say, Morvana." He walked to the door. "I'll send for him. I imagine you'll want privacy."

The dire tone made her even more nervous. She paced to the window, peered into the courtyard, paced back. Tried to ignore the ticking of the clock. It was a cozy chamber, with a fire roaring in the hearth. She chose a book from the tall shelves and leafed through it, not seeing a word.

Her back was to the door when she heard it quietly open. Morvana turned. She was usually a sensible person, but the sight of him made her carefully prepared speech fly straight out of her head like a flock of startled pigeons. His black hair was twisted into a topknot, Kindu-fashion. The forest green cloak made his eyes appear even lighter, impossibly blue beneath his dark brows. They skewered her from across the room.

"Your Grace," he said in a formal tone, bowing at the waist.

She got a grip on herself. Saints, but the man could be irritating.

"I thought we were done with that," she said.

"So did I," he shot back.

"Well, you can't call me that anymore because I formally resigned my post as bishop."

His brow twitched. "I thought they'd make you pontifex."

She laughed. "Not likely. The new one's some stodgy old cardinal named Albrecht. Don't you hear the news up in the hinterlands?"

"Rarely," he conceded.

She took a step forward. "I could hardly resign by letter."

"Well, one *could*." His reserve cracked a bit. "But *you* wouldn't."

"I had to see my family. Settle my affairs." She drew a

breath. "Lezarius offered me the post of nuncio and I accepted."

Misha absorbed this in silence for a moment. "He knew? All this time?"

"I made him promise not to tell you. I wanted to do it myself."

He opened his mouth, then closed it again, looking out of sorts. "You're . . . staying?"

"I told you once that I always felt I was born in the wrong city. *Lux et Lex* is my favorite motto." She smiled. "Light and law. It has a ring to it." Her heart beat faster. "But that's not the only reason I came back."

"No?"

"I miss our chess matches."

"Because you usually win," he said dryly.

She eyed the board in the corner. "Care for a game?"

He cast her an appraising glance. "You're not too tired?"

"I stayed in one of the new hostels last night. They even had hot water."

Misha sat down at the table. She sat down opposite.

"Borosus is still here," he said. "With others of the Sinn é Maz."

"I saw them from the road, flying in and out of the Lance."

"I'm still not used to it," he admitted. "I went inside, all the way to the top. One side looks out over the valley. But the other . . . " He shook his head in wonder. "There's nothing but desert beyond, Morvana. Burning sands as far as the eye can see."

"Did you meet Valmitra?"

"No. Will told me she's gone."

"Will she return?" The thought was unsettling.

"I've no idea." He smiled. "But she didn't fry us to a crisp, so I suppose we'll just carry on as usual."

He started to arrange the board. She watched his hands, remembering how they'd circled her waist when he lifted her to her horse. Large hands, with calloused palms. Well-made though, the nails clean and neatly trimmed. The backs were dusted with fine golden hairs, which was odd since his beard was so dark . . .

"Morvana?"

Her gaze lifted. "*Ja?*"

He seemed to be suppressing a smile. "Choose."

He held his fists out. She tapped the left. It uncurled. "Black."

She reached for the piece, but ended up twining her fingers with his. The knight pressed between their palms.

"Do you really want to play?" she asked, pulse skipping.

He stared at her with a dazed expression. "No."

Later, she couldn't recall the precise order of events. But the chessboard was flung rather violently away, the pieces scattering across the carpet, and she found herself perched on the pontifex's fancy pearl-inlaid table with her legs around his hips and his lips on hers.

She loosened the bindings of his cloak. It slipped to the floor. Her breath caught as he tugged the Blue Flame tabard over his head. The Mark on his chest was still there. But it had changed.

She laid a palm against his skin. He felt warm, but it wasn't the ferocious, consuming heat she remembered. Just the temperature of a healthy man.

The blindfold was gone. So was the knife at his throat. The man's eyes were open and clear. His smile had lost its sinister edge.

"It was like that when I woke up," he said, bending his neck to kiss her again. "Odd, eh?"

"Well, I think you must show me the rest," she whispered against his lips, a bit breathless. "It's only fair since you've seen mine."

White teeth flashed in a grin. "As you command."

Lezarius was good enough to stay away from his study for the entire afternoon. When he finally appeared—knocking first, although it was his own chamber—they were back at the table, battling out the tail end of a bloody game.

"I thought you might be interested in supper," he said innocently.

Her stomach growled. "Now that you mention it, I'm starved."

"Call it a draw?" Misha suggested.

She met his gaze. "We'll finish it later."

He swallowed a laugh and they all ate a pleasant, if exceedingly spicy, meal in the large dark-beamed hall where the clergy gathered.

A month passed. She settled into the routine of life at Jalghuth. It was not so different from Kvengard. Few modern amenities, but she was used to that. She did rather miss the salt scent of the sea, but the view of the smoky, blue-gray Sundar Kush range through her bedchamber window more than made up for it—as did Mikhail Bryce, whom she loved with a passionate ferocity Morvana had never expected to find.

Summer came, blanketing the lower slopes of Mount Ogo in wildflowers. She set herself to learning the Kindu language and corresponded with the Reverend Mother Clavis, who was slowly recovering from her injuries.

One morning, she was sitting in her new office when Misha walked in. His expression made her rise to her feet, reports forgotten. "What's happened?"

He held a letter in his hands. "It's from Alexei. My father had a heart attack."

"Is he . . .?"

"He's back home from the hospital. But he's asking for me."

She came out from her desk. "Do you want to go?"

He nodded with the grimmest expression she'd ever seen. Worse than when they were being chased by a horde of Perditae across the lake.

"I have to," he said.

She hugged him. "Then I will go with you."

Chapter Forty-Three

※☆※

Rain washed the long windows of the conservatory. It had been Alexei's mother's favorite room and his father hadn't changed a thing since she died. Everything was comfortable and lived-in. It smelled of plants and damp earth now, but he could still detect a trace of tobacco. If her ghost did roam these halls, it would be smoking a cigarette—of that he had no doubt.

"I hear your law practice is doing well," Morvana said with a smile. "So well you decided to sue the Curia."

"He works too much," Kasia said. "I hardly see him anymore."

Alexei sipped his coffee and set the cup on a wicker table. "We're nearing a settlement. Once that's over, things will quiet down."

"What's the number?" Morvana asked.

"Big," he replied. "Very big."

After restoring his license, he had volunteered to assist in a class action lawsuit against the Curia by thousands of Unmarked citizens. Falke wasn't thrilled about it, but the Church had deep pockets. A judge found that the plaintiffs had legal standing to claim civil rights violations and sent it to arbitration.

"How is Lezarius?" Alexei asked.

"I think he's lost interest in governing. He spends most of his time poring over old maps." Morvana reached down to pet Alice, who stretched across the carpet belly-up with eyes half-closed. "This is a lovely house. You both live here?"

"Until my father recovers. Then we'll see."

He watched Kasia, who was gazing through the rain-blurred glass doors. The conservatory was nestled in a south-facing corner of the manor house. One side overlooked emerald lawns that flanked a long tree-lined drive. The other opened to a stone patio with heavy planters. Rolling hills of mixed forest and pasture lay beyond.

"I like it here," she said softly. "It's peaceful."

He had a sudden vivid recollection of his mother curled on the settee, the ember of her cigarette burning in the darkness. When she could still walk on her own, she would often wake in the night and come down here. She never turned on the lamps; why, he had no idea.

"I'm sure your father is grateful to have you both," Morvana said in a neutral tone that made him wonder what Misha had told her. "What about your friends? Patryk and Natalya?"

"She has a new gallery show," Kasia said. "You should come with us tonight. Natalya's doing abstract portraits now. You wouldn't believe the money she's making. Patryk will be there. He's back at the Interfectorem." Her voice lowered. "I suppose you know Archbishop Kireyev died in the starfall."

"I did." Morvana looked serious. "Not to speak ill of the dead, but he was a dangerous man."

Kireyev had headed the Office of the General Directorate —the Arx's spymaster under the Pontifex Feizah.

"He tried to have me killed," Alexei said flatly. "I'm not

mourning him. But Patryk says his replacement is cleaning house. Dismantling the network Kireyev built."

"I'm glad to hear it," Morvana said. "Paying people to inform on each other? That sounds too close to Bal Agnar for my taste."

Somewhere in the depths of the house, a clock chimed four. Glaine Days, the Bryces' longtime housekeeper, entered with a tray bearing a linen-covered plate. She whisked the cloth away and the heavenly aroma of cardamom *keksi* filled the conservatory.

"I love you," Kasia said, pouncing on the muffins. "Have I told you that today?"

Glaine winked. "You need plumping," she said. "All of you."

Kasia patted her belly. "Not me," she chortled. "But you know my weaknesses."

The two women had instantly gotten along. Glaine was in her sixties now, but when she was Kasia's age she'd been forced into servitude under Balaur. She didn't know most of what had happened in the Masdar League—there were secrets Alexei would take to the grave—but he'd told her that Balaur was dead because of Kasia and her brother.

Kasia said Glaine reminded her of Tessaria Foy. Big heart, small tolerance for foolishness. When he came home from his law office each evening, Kasia could usually be found in the kitchen, sitting on a stool with her cards spread across the counter while Glaine kneaded dough or chopped vegetables for supper.

"More coffee?" Glaine asked Alexei.

He shook his head. "Thanks, but I think I'll just . . ." He trailed off and stood. "Look in on them."

He searched the housekeeper's face for any sign of how the meeting might be going. She gave a slight shake of her head. He wasn't sure how to interpret that.

Morvana folded her hands in her lap and gave him a too-bright smile. "We'll be here!"

He followed Glaine from the conservatory, climbing the grand staircase to the second floor. When his father suffered a minor heart attack, Alexei had dreaded the prospect of coming home to care for him. Then Kasia had offered to come stay, too, for as long as he needed her.

He'd been hesitant, but like Glaine, Conrad Bryce had taken to her immediately. His father could be a charmer when he wanted to, and the two of them had slipped into an easy familiarity that Alexei hadn't seen him share with anyone for years.

After a few weeks, he was surprised to discover that he was glad to be back in Arbot Hills. The house held memories, but many were happy ones.

His steps slowed as he approached the master suite at the end of the hall. After Misha went inside an hour ago, raised voices had come through the door. Then a long silence, followed by someone crying. Alexei wasn't sure who, though he thought it was his father.

Glaine had come along at that point with fresh linens for the guest room piled in her arms. She hadn't remarked on his eavesdropping, but Alexei could hardly remain with an ear pressed to the wood so he'd left them to it.

His father wasn't dying. In fact, the doctors expected him to make a full recovery. But Mikhail and Morvana planned to go back to Jalghuth the next day. It was a long journey. Who knew when they would come again?

Well, all that mattered was that his brother was finally free of his demons. It had never even occurred to Alexei that the Nightmark might *change*. Kasia told him privately that Morvana had something to do with it. She'd seen it in the cards the afternoon she gave Misha a reading.

But his brother was cagey when Alexei pressed for details.

He said only that it happened around the same time that Valmitra had been freed.

Whatever the reason, it was the final piece in Alexei's own happiness. The weight of dread that had crushed him for the last four years was gone. He was glad to return to his true calling—arguing in court—and Kasia's cartomancy business was thriving. Natalya made her new business cards, silver lettering on black. *Katarzynka, the Soothsayer Mage.*

Alexei tensed outside the door to his father's bedroom. It was too quiet in there. Maybe they'd murdered each other.

He gripped the knob, expecting the worst, but then he heard voices and muffled laughter. They were actually talking.

He considered knocking and witnessing this miracle for himself but decided to leave them alone for a while. When he got back to the conservatory, the women were discussing Markhounds and the new kennels Morvana had built at Jalghuth. They would not be war dogs anymore, she explained, but companions.

The rest of the afternoon passed swiftly. His father insisted on dressing himself and coming downstairs. The five of them had a pleasant dinner. Afterwards, Alexei and Kasia took their customary evening stroll through the grounds. The skies had cleared and the lights of Novostopol twinkled below.

They walked side by side into the warm evening. Kasia wore a strappy white dress and no shoes. She never wore shoes anymore unless she was going down into the city. Their fingers brushed and the brief contact sent a jolt of desire straight through him. He suspected it always would, even when they were old and gray.

If she did grow old. He couldn't put his finger on it, but something was different about her now. She insisted that the serpent's venom was gone; that she was just a woman again.

As if Kasia Novak had ever been just a woman.

He fingered the lump of kaldurite in his pocket like he'd once fingered the talisman of his brother's corax. He still had twenty Marks, but the stone effectively erased them all. At night, he slept long and deeply—and dreamed. Strange dreams he scarcely remembered the next day except in flashes.

Armies meeting on a grassy plain. Men and women in beautiful clothes, eating and drinking in great halls.

Some of them had wings.

Those dreams came most often when she slept at his side.

When he told her about them, she'd looked thoughtful.

The dead are not always quiet, she said.

They wandered into the orchard, which was still dripping with rain. Three does and a speckled fawn were eating the windfalls. Their heads turned in unison and then they bounded away, white tails waving like flags. Kasia paused to pluck an apple from a low branch. A shaft of sunlight caught the gold in her eyes.

Volkishna, he thought. My little wolf.

She took a bite and held out the apple. It was a deep red, the skin perfect except for the white flesh she'd gouged out with her teeth.

"Want some?" Kasia swallowed, an inviting smile on her lips. "It's delicious."

Yes, he thought. She was different. Even more beautiful.

More *bewitching*.

Alexei reached for the fruit.

Chapter Forty-Four

"No, for fuck's sake!" Malach braced a hand on the dashboard as the car lurched forward. "I said *brake*."

Sydonie stomped her foot on the pedal. He jerked against the seatbelt hard enough to leave a bruise.

"Language, uncle," she said with a severe look.

He squinted through the windscreen. They'd screeched to a stop less than a meter from the lip of a stone fountain.

"You always bring out the best in me, Syd." He raked a hand through his hair and drew a steadying breath. "Try a lighter touch on the brake. And if you weren't going so fast, you wouldn't have to—"

She threw the car into reverse, slamming him against the varnished walnut dash again.

The deep, waterlogged ruts cratering the ring road around the Arx had been filled with fresh macadam, the blacktop resurfaced and painted with bright white lines—all the better for speeding.

"Watch out," he growled as she overtook a slow-moving truck filled with lumber, swerving to pass on the right.

"There's no one coming." Syd adjusted her perch on the

cushion that she required to see over the steering wheel. At least her scabby legs had no trouble reaching the pedals.

It was early morning—the only time he allowed her to practice—and the side mirrors were wet with dew. She drove six more circuits. Malach settled into the plush leather, relaxing enough to roll down the window and take in the scenery. It still amazed him how much he'd accomplished in such a short time.

The overgrown thickets in the Arx's central plaza had been cut back and replaced with a civilized lawn, though he'd kept a stand of blackberry bushes for the kids to forage in. Syd passed another truck—remembering to signal this time—that was ferrying solar panels for the roof of the Pontifical Palace, except it wasn't called that anymore. Now it was called the Populi Domus, which meant People's House in the Old Tongue.

"We're almost out of charge." He pointed to the instrument panel. "See the red needle?"

Syd rolled her eyes. "I know what it means, Malach."

"Good. Do you know how to recharge the battery?"

"Plug it in."

"That's right. Pull over by the swings and I'll show you how to do it later."

"Can I get a cherry soda pop, too? They sell them at the charging station."

"I'll think about it."

"Thank you, Malach," she said primly.

Syd drove like a ninety-year-old woman the rest of the way, obviously hoping to earn goodwill. She parked on the grass next to the new playground where her brother had Felix and Rachel crammed onto one swing. Their bare feet tangled together, filthy from dragging through the dirt. Both were giggling. Tristhus twisted the chain as tight as it would go, cinching the swing up and up and up, then released it so they unwound in a dizzying spiral. Rachel and Felix screamed as it jerked about, and promptly fell off.

Neither one cried; apparently, they'd been playing this game for a while.

"Now it's my turn," Trist said.

"Wanna go again," Felix protested, climbing to his feet.

"You already had your turn. You had like, seven turns."

"Don't be a baby," Rachel put in, blowing a lock of curly hair from her face.

They were half-siblings, almost exactly the same age, but Rachel fancied herself the older one. Malach had never seen her bossy streak until Felix arrived.

"Wanna go again!" he howled, turning red.

Malach eyed Sydonie. "Would you go push him on the swing? Please?"

She eyed him back with a speculative gleam. "What do I get?"

This was the standard response.

"More driving lessons."

"But you already give me those. How about my own car?"

Malach laughed. "Dream on. However, if you practice enough that I think you're safe, I'll let you have a set of keys."

She considered this, then nodded. "Deal."

Syd's front teeth had finally grown in, and her dark hair hung in a shining ribbon down her slender back. She no longer talked to the creepy doll Mark she'd named Mirabelle —or at least, not where he could hear it.

Thirteen. The thought of the next few years provoked an inward shudder.

Syd ran over to the fenced playground and let herself in through the wooden gate. With the city transformed into a giant construction site for the foreseeable future, Malach had needed somewhere safe for the kids to play outside. Besides the swingset, it had picnic tables, a sandbox, a domed playhouse built to resemble the basilica, and sprinklers for hot summer days.

He watched them for a minute, his unruly little brood. Felix and Rachel were both in awe of Syd, so when she showed up, they moved on to something else. A new game that involved running and freezing on one leg when she shouted a code word.

Malach loosened his collar. It was already getting steamy, the din of carpenters and stonemasons and heavy equipment kicking in as traffic thickened on the ring road.

As evidenced by the playground sprinkler, running water had been restored and about half the buildings were wired for electricity. They'd drained and cleaned the fountains, relocating the resident crocodilians to a marshland several kilometers distant. So far, the city's population was about six hundred, most of them nomads who'd been living in the Morho. Not just mages, but former citizens of Bal Kirith who had been displaced by the fighting decades before.

It started when Malach paid a visit to the village where he'd stopped on his way to find Nikola; the same place where Tashtemir helped a girl with a broken leg and the villagers loaned them a raft in exchange. It took some convincing, but the leaders finally agreed to come have a look.

He sat them down and explained his vision. Everyone would get a vote in how the city was run as long as they pitched in and did their share. All citizens would have the same rights and decisions would be made by an elected council, one that any sane adult was eligible to serve on.

The oldest were skeptical at first—they remembered the state of anarchy that had reigned in Bal Kirith before it fell to Curia knights—but Malach showed them all the progress that had been made and didn't try to hide how few mages there were. On the contrary, it was the main selling point.

"Look," he'd said. "There's barely a hundred of us. We

need people or this city will never get off the ground. Doesn't matter how many pretty buildings we build if no one lives there." He leaned forward. "I have children, too. I just want what's best for them."

The six men and women exchanged a look. The Morho was still a dangerous place. They'd done their best, but they were living in leaky huts with no medical care and subsisting on whatever they could kill or gather.

Within a fortnight, the whole village had relocated to new-built housing blocks—and sent their own emissaries to other villages hidden in the jungle's leafy depths. There were more than he'd suspected. And they feared the ley-crazy Perditae just as much as everyone else.

His own kin had preyed on them, selling unlucky strays to the witches. It was a way of making amends.

Brick by brick, stone by stone, Bal Kirith was rising from the rubble. All four Curia cities had sent artisans and crafts-men, architects and plumbers and engineers. Despite his initial reluctance, Dmitry Falke had personally overseen the return of art, statuary, and other priceless relics.

It was everything Malach had dreamt of. Yet it felt hollow, like one of his own bargains. There was only one thing he really wanted and it was out of his reach forever.

The kids helped fill the emptiness in his heart. He made mistakes often, lost his temper on a daily basis, and fell into bed exhausted every night. But somehow they loved him back and he thought that, in balance, he wasn't doing too horribly.

He got out of the car and leaned on the hood. It was the sporty, low-slung silver automobile Nikola had driven to Bal Kirith while he drowsed in the passenger seat, gut-stabbed and high on pills. Sydonie was too young for a license, but when he caught her stealing his keys and taking it for joyrides, he decided he'd better teach her how to drive before she killed someone.

Malach closed his eyes, the sun warm on his face. Like every day, he had a million things to do. Plans to review, workers to pay, letters to read and answer, problems to solve. He'd been up since dawn because that's when Felix and Rachel woke up and he liked to have breakfast with them before the day took over.

When he opened his eyes, something was coming over the tops of the trees. It moved fast and gleamed in the afternoon sunlight. The old skittish part of his brain screamed at him to grab the kids and run, but it couldn't be an incoming shell. It made no sound and the trajectory was wrong.

Besides which, in the time it had taken him to think that, the shell would have landed and blown them all to hell.

He shaded his eyes with one hand. Now he could make out flapping iridescent wings and a person on its back. The children had stopped playing to watch with open mouths.

Malach limped through the gate. He'd graduated from a cane three weeks before, though he still had occasional twinges in his knee. The kids gathered around him as a small dragon alit in the sand pit.

"Whoooah," Rachel whispered. "Is that my mom?"

"Nikola!" Syd shrieked.

She pelted up and hurled herself at the grinning creature in a slinky witch-dress and headscarf.

"Get over here, Trist," Nikola called.

The boy shook a lock of greasy hair from his eye. Since he turned ten, he'd taken to wearing all black and letting his hair and fingernails grow unchecked. Malach had traded him eyeliner and mascara for his knives, so that worked out well.

Now, the surly sneer that was permanently stapled to Trist's face melted into boyish excitement. He ran to Nikola and threw his arms around her. Rachel followed shyly, but in a minute Nikola was introducing them all to the red-scaled dragon she'd rode in on. Only Felix still clung to Malach's leg, staring with huge eyes. Malach stuck him on one hip and walked over. He wondered if the child could feel his heart banging away in his chest.

"Hey," he said casually, looking around. "So . . . where are the rest of you?"

Nikola cocked a brow like she didn't know what he meant.

"You were summoned back to Dur-Athaara to stand before the full sisterhood," he said. "I guess the mourning period for the Mahadeva Sahevis is over?"

In fact, he had been counting the days. A hundred times, he almost jumped on a ship and went to plead his case. To beg her to reconsider. To come back to him and Rachel. But Nikola Thorn had her own destiny. If he truly loved her, he wouldn't interfere with it.

So he had stayed and tried to put her from his mind, which was easier said than done.

"It's over," she said. "The Deir Fiuracha elected a new trinity."

His throat was nearly too dry to speak. "And?"

"They chose me."

No surprise there. Of course they did. She'd woken their goddess from a thousand-year coma. Nikola Thorn was the strongest witch in generations. And the thing was—she could actually be trusted with all that power. She didn't covet anything except her own freedom.

Stop feeling bloody sorry for yourself. She earned it. She deserves it. Be happy for her, for fuck's sake.

Malach molded his lips into a stiff smile. "That's great, Nikola."

She held his gaze. "But I turned them down."

"Are you . . . are you messing with me?"

"No."

The false calm shattered. "They let you say no?"

"Let me?" She considered this, frowning like it was an entirely new concept. "Well, I did it. I might have been the first. The sisters weren't happy, but there wasn't much they could do."

He wanted to laugh aloud. To dance a jig. "Who is it then?"

"Take a guess."

"Paarjini?"

Her silver tooth winked. "The Crone is terrifying. Even worse than the last one. But the Maid's a scamp. We should go visit sometime."

"We?" His heart gave another painful thump. "Does that mean you're sticking around?"

"I might. You'll just have to convince me that I can't live without you."

He nodded slowly, lightheaded with joy. "I'll get right on that. But are you sure you want me? I've got four kids and none of them are well-behaved."

She grinned, then grew serious. "What about Dantarion?"

He ruffled Felix's hair and set him on his feet. "Go play with your sister."

The boy ran off to examine the dragon, which already looked weary.

"Buried up north," Malach said.

Lezarius had brought Felix to Bal Kirith himself. He'd told Malach that Dantarion had fallen after helping to liberate Clavis and her knights. She could have escaped but stayed behind to search for Beleth. Her last wish was that their son be given to Malach.

"I'm very sorry to hear that," Nikola said. She glanced at Felix and lowered her voice. "That's her boy?"

Malach nodded. "Mine, too. He's had a rough time, but he's adjusting. It's good for him to be around the other children. Rachel secretly adores him. They're best friends and worst enemies. Syd and Trist have been remarkably kind—"

He cut off as a fight erupted over . . . who knew? Some bullshit. Malach couldn't tell what started it, but Syd settled them all down with a stern word, then shot him a *You owe me* look. Still angling for the cherry pop.

"Paarjini said she'd remove Rachel's Raven Mark, if you still want that," Nikola said.

Malach watched the kids run back to the swings. "I know I'll have to deal with it eventually. But right now my memories of the last time we tried are a little too fresh."

"Understandable. Oh, hey . . . " She reached into her cloak and pulled out a folded batch of papers. "I have a report from Valdrian."

Malach shook off the darkness. "How's he faring in Dur-Athaara?"

"I last saw him with Cairness. They were walking together by the sea. I think you'll find that relations between the mages and the witches are steadily warming."

Malach smiled.

"In fact, they've given me permission to test anyone who wants to for lithomantic ability."

"Anyone? Men, too?"

Nikola laughed. "You're funny. No, I meant women. Things haven't changed *that* much. But since I had the talent, the witches figure there's more on the continent. Find enough candidates and I might set up my own school."

"That's a great idea. I want you to be happy, Nikola. To do something that matters to you."

She studied him. "I think you actually mean that."

"You know I do." Malach tore his gaze from the smooth brown shoulder exposed by her dress. "What else?"

"Some of the people you sold to the witches want to come back," she added with an accusing look. "If they're promised good jobs and decent places to live. No tenements like Ash Court."

"I liked your flat."

"It was a pisshole."

"Only because you never cleaned."

"I'm serious, Malach."

He gave her a level look. "Do you see any slums?"

She glanced around. "No."

"Because there aren't any. I've been recruiting other refugees from the Morho. Our doors are open to all and sundry. Are the witches okay with people leaving?"

"Just read Valdrian's report."

"I will." He pretended to flip through the papers, studying her through his lashes. She looked even more gorgeous than he remembered. A little thin, but he'd fatten her up. There was something about Nikola Thorn, an aura of fragility combined with unshakable confidence, that had intrigued him from the moment he first saw her. Then he discovered how funny and ornery she was and he was done for.

"Want to see my rooms? They were just renovated." He cleared his throat. "New sheets and everything."

It was the worst, saddest line he'd ever used, but Nikola just smiled.

"And everything? How can I say no to that?"

He looked around, rather desperately, and noticed his cousin Jessiel, who tried to hide behind a mop of wild dark hair when he caught her eye. Jess was one of the few he trusted for babysitting duty.

Lately, he had the distinct feeling she'd been avoiding him.

"Jess!" he bellowed.

She winced—he could tell, even from behind—and turned around. "Oh hey, Malach."

"This is Nikola Thorn. Rachel's mom."

Nikola raised a hand. Jess smiled. "I remember you from Nantwich. Welcome."

"She just got here so I was going to show her around. Could you watch the kids for a bit?"

A regretful sigh. "Wow, I'd love to, but I have this thing——"

"I'll pay you."

"Loan me your car."

"Everyone wants that car," he muttered. "For how long?"

"A weekend. I want to go clubbing in Novo."

"Fine. But you'll watch them all day. And you'll feed them, too."

"Yeah, yeah." She sauntered into the playground and was greeted with screams of delight. They loved their cousin Jessiel because she let them do whatever they wanted.

"I missed you," he said to Nikola.

"I missed you, too."

"Bad."

"Real bad," she agreed.

They linked hands and ran into the People's House. Nikola admired the freshly painted walls and plasterwork in the antechamber. Malach tugged back a corner of the drop cloth covering the floor to show her the new tiles.

"Falke kept his word," he said. "You wouldn't believe how much stuff they brought back. It's being warehoused in the basement until construction is finished and we decide where to put it."

"Kiss me, Malach."

Blood rushed to various appendages. "Yes," he said hoarsely.

They made out like teenagers in one of the alcoves until a group of workers came along to collect the drop cloth. They were from Novostopol and had just finished repainting new wings at the Arx there. Falke put out the story that Balaur had caused the skyfall, sparing Rachel from blame. Malach would never like the man, but at least he paid his debts.

He chatted for a minute with the workers, then led Nikola up a broad staircase to the living quarters on the upper levels.

"I'll convert some of this to offices," he said, as they walked down a long empty corridor. "But you know, I grew up here. I wanted to keep my old chambers."

"I think you're entitled." She looked around. "Saints, this place is unrecognizable. In a good way."

"We've only just started. I'm restoring the original coffered ceilings and wood paneling, too—"

"Malach! Is that you?"

The thin, peevish voice drifted through a half-open door down an adjacent corridor.

"Shit," he whispered. "She usually sleeps late."

Nikola stared at him. "*Beleth* is here?"

He nodded.

"Is she still pontifex?"

"God's Teeth, no. We got rid of all that. But she thinks she is. It's just easier."

Nikola's jaw set. "I'm not curtsying."

"Malach!" the voice shouted again. "I need you!"

"Lezarius found her wandering the streets of Jalghuth," he explained. "He didn't want to keep her—no shocker there. What can I do? She had a stroke. Dante died for her."

Nikola looked somber. "I know."

"And she's a bit . . . " He twirled a finger.

"Batshit crazy? Yes, I remember that part."

"Malach! I hear you, boy! Who are you whispering with? Is it that cocksucker Falke?"

He gave an apologetic shrug. "Will you come say hello?"

She sighed. "Yeah, okay. Does she still wear the white wig and all that?"

"I hid it in the basement. The powder, too. Scared the kids."

"Scared everybody," Nikola said. "Lead on."

Beleth hunched at her overlarge desk, scratching away with a quill. He'd offered her a ballpoint but she seemed offended by the mere suggestion. She wore trousers and a man's plaid work shirt with the sleeves rolled up, revealing wiry forearms and the scarred stump of her severing. Cool blue eyes swept Nikola up and down.

"I remember you. You made me a fine granddaughter."

Nikola nodded warily.

Beleth turned to Malach. "What do you think?" She handed him a sheaf of parchment, looking a little anxious.

He scanned the pages. "You misspelled fellatio. Two L's, one T."

"Did I? Dammit."

"But I like where you're going with this one." Beleth looked away and he winked at Nikola. "Pray continue, Reverend Mother."

Beleth grunted and returned to her scribbling, face curtained by her long gray hair. Tottering heaps of parchment surrounded her. The latest manifesto that he would ensure was never, ever published.

"Is she safe?" Nikola asked as they walked down the hall.

"Well, she's only got one hand and she needs help to go to the bathroom. But, you know, it's Beleth. I'm not sure I'd ever call her *safe*."

Nikola considered this.

"We can move," he said quickly. "Wherever you want. There are new buildings going up all over the place."

"I'll give it a trial run," she said. "At least it won't get boring around here."

He showed her the kids' rooms. For Felix and Rachel, a sunny window seat with built-in bookshelves and miniature sleigh beds imported from Nantwich. For Tristhus, everything black and dismal. For Syd, a hat-rack and posters of sporty racing cars.

Then he opened the door to his own chambers and proudly flipped on the lamps, trying to imagine it all through Nikola's eyes. Warm yellow light burnished the fresco of smoky herons in flight from an approaching storm. Thick carpets covered the marble floor. He'd dragged a red velvet fainting couch into the corner, where Syd would sometimes recline in one of her floppy hats, reading picture books aloud.

"This is definitely swankier than my grotto," Nikola remarked. "Ah, the old lair does have its charms."

She gazed fondly at the enormous gothic bed with its needle-sharp finials and sea creature carvings, which she had once pronounced "grotesque."

Malach walked to the window and laid a hand on the drapes.

"Leave them open," she said. "I like the view."

It *was* lovely. From the third floor, you could see straight across the park to the mighty regnum trees that stood watch at the boundary of the Morho Sarpanitum, their leafy canopies unfurling like golden umbrellas a hundred meters high. Currents of ley flowed around their roots, though he rarely felt tempted to wield it.

Ah, the rich irony! He'd spent half his life scheming to destroy the Void. Now it was gone, his birthright restored, and he didn't want the ley anymore. Not since he'd learned who it came from. With luck, Valoriel would forget he even existed.

When Malach turned back, Nikola was staring at his ass.

"You're incorrigible," he said.

"Almost forgot. I brought you a present."

She tossed him a little egg-shaped bundle. He shook out a pair of fishnet stockings. *Could I love this woman any more?*

"Just my size," he said.

She sat on the edge of the bed and crossed her legs. "Try them on."

He did. Then *she* tried them on. Then they were put to other creative uses and the day passed in a happy blur. He must have fallen asleep, for when he woke it was getting dark out. Nikola lay nestled in his arms, her wiry hair tickling his chin.

Malach could not recall ever feeling as he did then.

In want of absolutely nothing.

"Don't we have to give the little darlings baths or something?" she murmured. "It must be their bedtime."

It was. And Jess would keep them up way too late, and

curse in front of them, and buy them cherry soda pops for dinner.

But sometimes you just had to cut your losses and soldier on.

"To quote my aunt," Malach whispered, rolling Nikola on top of him, "what hath night to do with sleep?"

Afterword

Dear Reader,

I hope you enjoyed the Nightmarked series. If so, you'll be glad to hear I'm not done with this world. There's still a tale to tell about Cathrynne Rowan and Lord Gavriel Morningstar and the events that led up to the founding of the Via Sancta. A prequel series is in the works, so be sure to join my newsletter at www.katrossbooks.com and never miss a new release. I also run regular giveaways and sales on all my books, so it's well worth it.

You can also check out my other epic fantasy series, the Fourth Element and Fourth Talisman. The first books of both are free to download. You can find them at all retailers.

The Midnight Sea (Fourth Element #1)

Nocturne (Fourth Talisman #1)

As always, thank you for coming with me on this journey. And please drop a line anytime with questions or comments, I love to hear from readers! Warmest, Kat

Glossary of People, Places & Things

Alexei Vladimir Bryce. A priest with the Interfectorem and former knight of Saint Jule. Suffers from severe insomnia. Marks include the Two Towers, the Maiden and the Armored Wasp. Enjoyed a successful law career before joining the Beatus Laqueo.

Alice. A Markhound and loyal friend to Alexei. Has a scar on her haunch from Beleth and harbors a special hatred for nihilim.

Alsakhan. The dragon god worshipped in the Masdar League. Said to be the brother of Valmitra.

Arx. The inner citadels of the Via Sancta, they're akin to small cities and sit atop deep, churning pools of ley power. The Arxes in the two rebel cities were largely spared by the Curia's bombing campaigns, but they've fallen into ruin.

Bal Agnar. Situated in the northern reaches of the Morho Sarpanitum, amid the foothills of the Torquemite Range, called the Sundar Kush in Jalghuth, the city was abandoned after Balaur's defeat. Emblem is the Black Sun, a circle with twelve jagged rays. Before the war, the city was controlled by a small, vicious oligarchy with the blessing of the Church.

Bal Kirith. Twin city to Bal Agnar, located in the central Morho Sarpanitum on the Ascalon River. Once considered the most beautiful of all the Arxes, its emblem is a Broken Chain symbolizing free will.

Beatus Laqueo. A specialized Order of the Knights of Saint Jule whose name means *Holy Noose* in the old tongue. Notorious for using extreme tactics against the mages. Motto is Foras admonitio. *Without warning.*

Beleth. Malach's aunt and the former pontifex of Bal Kirith. Fond of wigs, powder and decadent parties, she's spent the last three decades writing books of poetry and philosophy that are banned throughout the Curia, as well as a manifesto on the *Via Libertas*, a counter ideology to the Via Sancta that embraces the Shadow Side as inevitable and argues for the rule of the strongest. Despite Beleth's eccentricities, she's cunning and formidable with a sword. Dotes on Malach, whom she raised as her own.

Balaur. The former pontifex of Bal Agnar. His symbol is the Black Sun. Believed dead since the war, he still has secret followers in every city. His Tarot card is The Emperor.

Borosus. One of the Teeth of God and a chief servant of Valmitra. Can assume both draconic and humanoid forms.

Cairness. A witch of Dur-Athaara, very hostile to the mages.

Cartomancy. Divination using cards. Kasia uses it to foretell the future with oracle decks made by her best friend, Natalya Anderle. In Novostopol, it's fairly lighthearted entertainment, often done at parties, but also for certain wealthy men and women who are devotees of the occult.

Casimir Kireyev. The archbishop of Novostopol, head of the Office of the General Directorate. Widely believed to be the Pontifex's spymaster. Gnomelike and bespectacled, he is one of the most feared men in the Church.

Cathrynne Rowan. The soothsayer witch who aided Gavriel in his rebellion.

Clavis. The Pontifex of the Eastern Curia in Nantwich. The youngest ever to wear the ring, Clavis's special powers encompass doors, boundaries, and crossroads. A keeper of knowledge and technology from the past.

Corax. The word for *raven* in the old tongue. Symbolizes Fate's Messenger, a bridge between the material and spiritual realms. In common parlance, coraxes are copper coins given to knights in the field and used to identify bodies burned or mutilated beyond recognition. One side is engraved with the owner's name, while the other side indicates the Order within the Curia.

Dantarion. A bishop of Bal Kirith, she is Malach's cousin and daughter of Beleth. Also the mother of Malach's second child.

Dark Age (second). A cataclysmic period a thousand years before in which the world devolved into violent anarchy. Led to the founding of the Via Sancta and the abolition of most technology.

Dmitry Falke. The Pontifex of Novostopol, his card is The Hierophant. A keeper of dogma and tradition, but also ruthless in his quest to save the Via Sancta. He led the Curia to victory against the Nightmages and defeated Balaur in single combat, severing three of his fingers. Balaur's signet ring is now encased in a glass paperweight on Falke's desk.

Dur-Athaara. Capital city of the island of Tenethe, part of the witches' realm across the sea in the far east.

Feizah. The former Pontifex of the Eastern Curia in Novostopol, she was killed by Mikhail Bryce when he was Invertido.

Ferran Massot. The chief doctor at the Batavia Institute. Marked by Malach. Conducted illicit experiments on his patients, in the course of which he discovered Patient 9's true identity as Lezarius.

Forcing. Magic that violates the laws of nature. Dangerous and unstable, its use is banned in Dur-Athaara.

Gavriel. Valmitra's seventh son, also called *The Morning Star*. A Seraphim who betrayed his mother and brought on the Dark Ages.

Golden Imperator. The divine ruler of the Masdar League, chosen to serve for a term of seven years, during which time they wield absolute power.

Heshima. A guardian witch of Dur-Athaara who trained Nikola Thorn. Wears a bloodstone choker and is strong in projective magic.

Interfectorem. The Order tasked with hunting and detaining Invertido. Emblem is an inverted trident. The name means *murder* in the old tongue.

Invertido. Unfortunates whose Marks suddenly reverse, causing insanity. Symptoms include narcissism, paranoia, lack of remorse and severely impaired empathy. A genetic component is suspected as it often runs in families, although the condition can be deliberately inflicted using abyssal ley. Generally believed to be incurable.

Jalghuth. The capital of the Northern Curia, it's located in the far north. Surrounded by glacial fields with hundreds of stelae to repel nihilim. Its emblem is the Blue Flame. Motto is Lux et lex, *Light and law*.

Jamila al-Jabban. A Masdari advisor of Balaur, claims to be a servant of the khedive of Luba.

Kaldurite. A rare gemstone that blocks the ley.

Kasia Novak. A cartomancer with a rare ability to work the ley through her tarot deck. Classified as a sociopath by the Curia, although she adheres to her own moral code and doesn't always act selfishly. Her cards are both The Mage and The High Priestess.

Kvengard. The capital of the Southern Curia, it sits on a rocky, windswept peninsula between the Northern and Southern Oceans. Emblem is the Wolf, often depicted running in profile.

Ley. Psychoactive power that upwells from the core of the planet. Neither good nor evil, it's altered by interaction with the mind. Divided into three currents that correspond with the layers of consciousness: surface (blue), liminal (violet) and abyssal (red). These opposing currents flow in counterpoint to each other. The ley itself can become corrupted when thousands of people behave in selfish, wicked ways.

Lezarius. The Pontifex of the Northern Curia in Jalghuth. Also called Lezarius the Righteous. Creator of the Void and the stelae. A geographer by training.

Liberation Day. A holiday commemorating the surrender of the mage cities and the end of the civil war, marked with parades and celebrations in the streets.

Light-bringers. Also, **lucifers** and **aingeal dian.** What nihilim were called before Beleth and Balaur led their fellow clergy to disgrace and excommunication from the Via Sancta, they are a species distinct from humans, although the differences all involve the structures of the brain. Light-bringers learned to use the ley and offered refuge to those fleeing the Second Dark Age.

Lithomancy. Divination/magic using gems and minerals. Practiced by the witches in Dur-Athaara.

Lucas Gray. Chief aide to Clavis and a cardinal of Nantwich.

Luk. The Pontifex of the Southern Curia in Kvengard. His unique talent is wielding the ley as an evolutionary force. Luk created the Markhounds and the shadow mounts used by Kven knights.

Mage trap. Four interconnected Wards that form a box with no ley power inside the boundary. Can only be activated by someone with Holy Marks. During the war, it was one of the few effective defenses against the nihilim.

Mahadeva Sahevis. The witch-queen of Dur-Athaara. Has a triple aspect of Mother, Maid and Crone.

Malach. A mage of Bal Kirith. His card is The Fool, the most powerful of the Major Arcana.

Maria Karolo. A bishop at the Arx in Novostopol and head of the Order of Saint Marcius, which enforces the *Meliora*.

Markhounds. Creatures of the ley, bred to detect specific Marks. Invaluable during the war to hunt nihilim in the ruins. Now the hounds are mainly used by the Interfectorem because they sense it when someone's Marks invert and start to howl.

Marks. Intricate pictures on the skin bestowed by someone with mage blood. Civil Marks suppress anger, greed and aggression and enhance creative talents. They primarily use surface ley. Holy Marks are only given to the clergy. They can use the deeper liminal ley and twist chance. However, if the person who bestowed the Mark dies, it causes a sickness that begins with hallucinations and is invariably fatal.

Masdar League. A federation of kingdoms to the south of the continent, it is composed of seven Emiratis and ruled by the Golden Imperator, who serves a seven-year term. The name means the League of the Source.

Meliora. The foundational text of the Via Sancta. Written by the Praefators, it has forty-four sutras dealing with the human condition. Its title means "for the pursuit of the better." The

Meliora argues that form of government is irrelevant and the root of all evil is violence against Nature and ourselves. Technology is a false panacea that creates social disharmony. According to the *Meliora*, the Church itself will eventually become obsolete when society reaches a state of utopia.

Mikhail Semyon Bryce. Alexei's older brother. A former captain of the Beatus Laqueo, he spent four years at the Batavia Institute. Marked by Malach. His card is the Knight of Storms.

Morho Sarpanitum. The primeval jungle at the heart of the continent.

Morvana Ziegler. A Kven bishop who takes on Alexei's Marks. Luk's Nuncio in Novostopol. Her card is The Chariot of Justice.

Nantwich. The capital of the Western Curia, it sits on the shore of the Mare Borealis. Emblem is Crossed Keys.

Nazaré Maz. Also called *The Breath of God*. Priests who ingest poison over many years to develop immunity, their very touch can be lethal.

Natalya Anderle. A free-spirited artist and unrepentant rake. Kasia's best friend, she teaches herself to throw Tessaria's knives.

Nightmage. Also called **Nihilim**. A somewhat derogatory term to describe light-bringers after their fall from grace. They wear blood-red robes and maintain a church in exile called the *Via Libertas* that espouses a version of extreme free will. In Bal Kirith, they have human servants who've been promised wealth and status when the mages regain power. Motto is Mox nox: *Soon, nightfall.*

Nightmark. A Mark bestowed by a mage, distinguished from the Civil and Holy Marks given by the Curia in both form and function. First practiced by Beleth and Balaur, it allows the Marked to tap abyssal ley and to twist chance in their favor more directly and violently. In return, they are beholden to the mage. Nightmarks morally corrupt over time and the images are much darker in tone than regular Marks.

Novostopol. Capital of the Eastern Curia. Humid, warm and rainy. A port city, it sits amid two branches of the Montmoray where the river empties into the Southern Ocean. Despite the dreary climate, Novostopol is a lively place, with bustling cafes and nightlife. Thanks to the system of Civil Marks, crime is virtually nonexistent.

Office of the General Directorate. The most powerful organ of the Curia, headed in Novostopol by Archbishop Kireyev. Ostensibly, it oversees the other offices and reports directly to the Pontifex. Has a vast intelligence network and used to run covert operations in the mage cities. Emblem is the Golden Bough.

Oprichniki. A regular force of civilian gendarmes in Novostopol. Uniform is a yellow rain jacket and stylish cap. They carry only batons.

Order of the Black Sun. Human followers of Balaur who have awaited his return. Most bear an alchemical Mark of a small circle inside a triangle, inside a square, inside a larger circle.

Order of Saint Marcius. Tasked with enforcing adherence to the philosophy laid out in the *Meliora*, in particular, the tight restrictions on technology. Emblem is a sheaf of wheat.

Oto Valek. An orderly at the Batavia Institute. On the payroll of Archbishop Kireyev and the OGD, Oto is a shady mercenary—and a bad penny who just keeps turning up.

Paarjini. A witch of the *laoch*, the Guardians who protect Dur-Athaara. She captured Malach.

Patryk Spassov. A priest of Novostopol, Alexei's former partner at the Interfectorem and good friend to Kasia and Natalya.

Perditum (pl., perditae). Feral humans who live in the Void. Once residents of Bal Agnar and Bal Kirith, they were warped by the psychic degradation of the ley before Lezarius created the grid. Some are more intelligent than others, but all succumb to bloodlust when the ley floods. Smart enough to fear and avoid Nightmages (whom they recognize by scent), but anyone else is fair game. Also called leeches.

Praefators. Founders of the Via Sancta, they were visionaries who discovered how to use the ley through Marks. The name means *wizard* in the old tongue. Most now comprise the canon of Saints, but due to the tumultuous upheavals of the Second Dark Age, little is known about the first Praefators beyond their names. It is assumed they were all light-bringers.

Praesidia ex Divina Sanguis. Protectors of the Divine Blood, in the old tongue. Founded by Cardinal Falke, this secret Order strives to ensure the continuation of lucifer bloodlines in service to the Via Sancta. Motto is Hoc ego defendam. *This I will protect.*

Probatio. The office of the Curia that administers morality tests. Emblem is a trident, indicating all three layers of mind.

Rachel. Malach and Nikola's daughter, she has the ability to work celestial magic. Her card is The Star.

Reborn. Also called *The Wandering Cherubim*. The children from Kvengard who survived Balaur's alchemical Magnum Opus. They live at Sinjali's Lance and have a deep connection to the ley. The Reborn are immortal and have the ability to read minds, although they are incapable of doing harm to any living creature.

Saviors' Eve. The night before Den Spasitelya (Saviors' Day), a holiday commemorating the building of the Arxes. It has a grimmer theme, with young people donning masks and costumes evoking the evils of the Second Dark Age.

Sinjali's Lance. A focal point of the ley in Jalghuth.

Sinn é Maz. Also called *The Teeth of God*. Servants of Valmitra who can take the form of dragons and other reptiles.

Sweven. A memory, vision or fantasy shared directly with another person through the ley, as if they're experiencing it firsthand.

Stelae. Also called **wardstones**. Pillars engraved with Wards to repel nihilim. Found in the Void at the junctures of the ley lines. Most stelae are emblazoned with an emblem of the Curia (Raven, Crossed Keys, Flame, or Wolf, depending on the location) and a pithy maxim such as *Ad altiora tendo* (I strive toward higher things), *Fiat iustitia et pereat mundus* (Let justice be done though the world shall perish) and Vincit qui se vincit (He conquers who conquers himself).

Sublimin. A psychotropic drug used to bestow or transfer Marks, it temporarily dissolves the barrier between the conscious and unconscious.

Sydonie. A young Nightmage at Bal Kirith, sister to Tristhus.

Tabularium. A vast archive, it's one of the few buildings in the Arx to have electricity. The Tabularium holds files on every citizen of Novostopol, as well as a separate register for members of the clergy. An even larger Tabularium exists in Nantwich, with records dating back to the Second Dark Age.

Tashtemir Kelavan. A veterinarian who serves as the only doctor at Bal Kirith. Tashtemir was forced to flee the Masdar League when he offended the Golden Imperator, who put a bounty on his head.

Tessaria Foy. A retired Vestal and godmother of Kasia Novak. Close to Cardinal Falke and Archbishop Kireyev. In her mid-seventies, Tess was an elegant and enigmatic figure. Murdered by Jule Danziger.

Tristhus. A young Nightmage, brother to Sydonie, whose lead he follows without question.

Unmarked. Individuals who fail the morality tests administered by the Probatio and are denied Marks. The lowest caste of society, they live by the charity of the Curia since few will employ them. All the chars at the Arx are Unmarked, as proclaimed by their gray uniforms. Unmarked comprise about one percent of the population. In Novostopol, they're relegated to a slum district called Ash Court.

Valdrian. A mage of Bal Kirith, he wears a spring-loaded blade on the stump of his hand (which was severed by knights when he was just a teenager). Cousin to **Jessiel** and **Caralexa**.

Valmitra. The three-headed serpent goddess worshipped by the witches. They believe she coils around the core of the planet and her breath is the ley. Called the *Alsakhan* in the Masdar League.

Via Sancta. The Blessed Way. A social, scientific and spiritual experiment to improve humanity. Teaches non-violence and beauty in all things.

The Void. Also called the **Black Zone**. The region where the ley has been banished. Encompasses the cities of Bal Agnar and Bal Kirith and most of the Morho Sarpanitum.

Wards. Symbols imbued with emotional power that concentrate the ley for a specific purpose. Some repel nihilim, others force the ley from a particular area (see mage trap). A surge can cause them to short for minutes to days, but they self-repair. Most use surface ley and thus glow bright blue. Activated by touch.

Acknowledgments

Heartfelt thanks to Carol Edholm, for her eagle eye; Leonie Henderson and Laura Pilli for their early reads and insights; and Mom and Nick, as always.

About the Author

Kat Ross worked as a journalist at the United Nations for ten years before happily falling back into what she likes best: making stuff up. She's the author of the Nightmarked series, the Lingua Magika trilogy, the Fourth Element, Fourth Talisman, and Fourth Empire fantasy series, the Gaslamp Gothic mysteries, and the dystopian thriller *Some Fine Day*. She loves myths, monsters and doomsday scenarios.

www.katrossbooks.com
kat@katrossbooks.com

facebook.com/KatRossAuthor

instagram.com/katross2014

bookbub.com/authors/kat-ross

pinterest.com/katrosswriter

Also by Kat Ross

The Nightmarked Series

City of Storms

City of Wolves

City of Keys

City of Dawn

The Fourth Element Trilogy

The Midnight Sea

Blood of the Prophet

Queen of Chaos

The Fourth Talisman Series

Nocturne

Solis

Monstrum

Nemesis

Inferno

The Fourth Empire series

Savage Skies

Treacherous Tides (forthcoming)

A Wicked Wind (forthcoming)

The Lingua Magika Trilogy

A Feast of Phantoms

All Down But Nine

Devil of the North

Gaslamp Gothic Collection

The Daemoniac

The Thirteenth Gate

A Bad Breed

The Necromancer's Bride

Dead Ringer

Balthazar's Bane

The Scarlet Thread

The Beast of Loch Ness

Made in the USA
Monee, IL
16 January 2024

51882484R00310